IT WAS A CHALLENGE HE COULDN'T RESIST

"I wa... ... ... he differe... ... ic wante... ... under any pretext he could find!

There was just enough of a hint of challenge in Eric's words to make Andrea rise to the bait. "I do too know the difference. I've been kissed before!"

Eric stepped closer. "Have you?"

His voice had slipped an octave lower. His rough baritone sent a little shiver of delicious anticipation through Andrea. She was acutely conscious of his muscular body pressed against her softer form. "Why, of course I've been kissed!" she answered, a little breathlessly.

"But not by me," Eric answered, slipping his arms about her. "I think I need to show you the difference."

His lips met hers, and the world seemed to spin. Her legs trembled; her bones seemed to melt; her fingertips tingled. A low, strangled moan rose in her throat.

It was absolutely wonderful . . .

* * *

PRAISE FOR LAUREN WILDE'S *PASSION'S SPRINGTIME*:

"This story, so steeped in the history of the fortunes made off the profits of the Gold Rush, still maintains its identity as an arousing, romantic adventure. Filled with tension, this well-plotted romance is a joy to read!"

—*Rendezvous*

TODAY'S HOTTEST READS
ARE TOMORROW'S SUPERSTARS

VICTORY'S WOMAN (4484, $4.50)
by Gretchen Genet
Andrew — the carefree soldier who sought glory on the battlefield, and returned a shattered man . . . Niall — the legandary frontiersman and a former Shawnee captive, tormented by his past . . . Roger — the troubled youth, who would rise up to claim a shocking legacy . . . and Clarice — the passionate beauty bound by one man, and hopelessly in love with another. Set against the backdrop of the American revolution, three men fight for their heritage — and one woman is destined to change all their lives forever!

FORBIDDEN (4488, $4.99)
by Jo Beverley
While fleeing from her brothers, who are attempting to sell her into a loveless marriage, Serena Riverton accepts a carriage ride from a stranger — who is the handsomest man she has ever seen. Lord Middlethorpe, himself, is actually contemplating marriage to a dull daughter of the aristocracy, when he encounters the breathtaking Serena. She arouses him as no woman ever has. And after a night of thrilling intimacy — a forbidden liaison — Serena must choose between a lady's place and a woman's passion!

WINDS OF DESTINY (4489, $4.99)
by Victoria Thompson
Becky Tate is a half-breed outcast — branded by her Comanche heritage. Then she meets a rugged stranger who awakens her heart to the magic and mystery of passion. Hiding a desperate past, Texas Ranger Clint Masterson has ridden into cattle country to bring peace to a divided land. But a greater battle rages inside him when he dares to desire the beautiful Becky!

WILDEST HEART (4456, $4.99)
by Virginia Brown
Maggie Malone had come to cattle country to forge her future as a healer. Now she was faced by Devon Conrad, an outlaw wounded body and soul by his shadowy past . . . whose eyes blazed with fury even as his burning caress sent her spiraling with desire. They came together in a Texas town about to explode in sin and scandal. Danger was their destiny — and there was nothing they wouldn't dare for love!

Available wherever paperbacks are sold, or order direct from the Publisher. Send cover price plus 50¢ per copy for mailing and handling to Penguin USA, P.O. Box 999, c/o Dept. 17109, Bergenfield, NJ 07621. Residents of New York and Tennessee must include sales tax. DO NOT SEND CASH.

SOMEONE TO HOLD
LAUREN WILDE

ZEBRA BOOKS
KENSINGTON PUBLISHING CORP.

*For Annette, Betty, Lena,
Margaret, and Winnie,
my golden circle of friends,
with love.*

ZEBRA BOOKS are published by

Kensington Publishing Corp.
850 Third Avenue
New York, NY 10022

Copyright © 1995 by Joanne Redd

All rights reserved. No part of this book may be reproduced in any form or by any means without the prior written consent of the Publisher, excepting brief quotes used in reviews.

If you purchased this book without a cover you should be aware that this book is stolen property. It was reported as "unsold and destroyed" to the Publisher and neither the Author nor the Publisher has received any payment for this "stripped book."

Zebra and the Z logo Reg. U.S. Pat. & TM Off.

First Printing: May, 1995

Printed in the United States of America

Chapter 1

Eric Flemming sat on a park bench that overlooked Havana harbor. He spread his arms out on the back of the bench, and stretched his long legs out before him. In his spotless white linen suit and Panama hat, he looked like a businessman briefly resting from his hectic schedule to enjoy a moment in the warm winter sun, a respite that wouldn't seem at all unusual in a country where two-hour siestas were an everyday occurrence. But Eric was neither relaxed, nor engrossed with the view before him. Instead, his full concentration was on the small church across the street from the park. He watched the building anxiously from the corner of his eye. That was where his contact would come from if he came. The man would amble from the church, then cross the street and sit on the bench behind him.

Eric fervently hoped Diego would come. Eric had been sitting on this bench every day for the past week, and the Cuban had not made his appearance. Eric brooded over several disturbing possibilities. Had Diego's identity been discovered? Was the patriot at that moment in prison? Worse, was he perhaps dead? Or had he simply had trouble getting past the sentries into the city? Eric had never had to wait this long for General Gómez's messenger. He feared that if Diego didn't show up soon, the Spanish would begin to get suspicious. They were accustomed to seeing Eric in the city on "business trips," but his stay had never lasted this long. It wouldn't do to arouse the Spaniards' suspicion. Then his real purpose for being in the city might be revealed. He much preferred dying in battle to being slowly tortured to death for information—particularly at the hands of the Spaniards, who had been experts at extracting information and confessions, both valid and invalid, since the infamous Inquisition.

A movement at the water's edge caught Eric's attention. A woman stood at the guardrail there and looked out at the harbor. Even with her back to him, Eric knew she had to be American, but not because she was blond and pale. Here in Cuba, skin tones and hair coloring ranged from the darkest of dark to the lightest of light. Rather, he knew the woman's nationality by her attire. Although wealthy Spanish women were dressed as well as their European or American counterparts, they had not yet adopted the fashions so popular among working women in the United States. The woman's slim, dark skirt and white shirtwaist were too mannish for a woman from Havana. Eric noted that the woman at the guardrail was even sporting one of those stiff-brimmed sailor hats, and given the fact that she was as tall and willowy as one of Charles Dana Gibson's models, he imagined she could well have posed for one of the artist's famous sketches.

Why, he'd even bet she had blue eyes. Every Gibson girl he had seen thus far had. Besides, blue eyes would be a fitting match for that glorious mane of golden hair she wore piled on the top of her head in a thick pompadour. He had never seen such breathtaking hair.

As the woman continued to stare out over the water, Eric wondered what held her attention. She hadn't moved a muscle. She wasn't looking at Morro Castle—the ancient fortress that guarded the narrow entrance to the harbor. She was looking at something in the harbor itself. Eric finally realized that she was gazing at the ship anchored to a buoy in the middle of the port. The *Maine,* with her freshly painted, gleaming white hull, and her two black smokestacks and tall masts, was the largest and most impressive vessel in the harbor. The American ship made the Spanish warship anchored nearby, the *Alfonso XI,* look shabby in comparison. But of course that was the reason for the *Maine*'s presence. The ship was supposed to impress upon everyone in Havana, particularly the Spanish military authorities, that the United States had a naval force of considerable power. The Maine was also there to protect Americans in the capital of the war-torn country. However, neither of those reasons had been given to the Spanish. The official explanation offered for the *Maine*'s presence had been that she was here on a "friendly visit," a thinly veiled excuse that was believed by no one. The Spanish highly resented the American battleship, just as they resented any American interference in their confrontation with the Cuban rebels, but they had tolerated the *Maine,* much to Eric's relief. He had feared that the battleship's unannounced and unexpected arrival would provoke more bloody riots in the city. These days, hard feelings against Americans ran high.

At that moment, the woman turned. Eric caught sight of a sprig of *mariposa* pinned to her blouse and, sharply sucked in his breath. Nearby, on the boardwalk she stood on, he spied three Spanish soldiers making their way towards the young woman. Eric didn't stop to consider his actions. He jumped to his feet and closed the distance between him and the woman, then placed himself directly between her and the oncoming soldiers. He caught the sprig in one hand and ripped it from her blouse. "What are you trying to do? Get yourself killed?" he asked sharply.

Andrea Williams was so surprised by the tall, dark stranger's sudden appearance that she was speechless for a moment. Then she realized that he had actually had the audacity to touch her person—her bosom, no less—and take her possession. She was outraged. "Who the devil do you think you are, accosting me in such a manner?" she asked. "And give me back my jasmine!"

As Andrea made a grab for the sprig, Eric jerked it farther away, saying, "You crazy little fool! I'm not accosting you! I'm probably saving your life." He opened his fist where the crushed sprig lay. "Do you know what this is?"

"Don't call me a little fool!" Andrea retorted, drawing up to her full height.

Her action, more than her words, made Eric pause. He hadn't realized how tall the young woman was. The top of her head came to his chin. Most women barely stood as high as his chest. No, she wasn't little, he was forced to admit—slim, but far from dainty. But not too slim, he observed. The curves were in all the right places. And her eyes weren't blue, he noted with surprise. They were as black as coal, and flashing with fury.

When Eric didn't respond to her retort, Andrea asked, "Did you hear me? I'm *not* a fool!"

"Oh? So you *do* know the significance of this?"

He hadn't called her a fool again, but the tone of his voice clearly told Andrea he thought her one, which angered her all the more. "Of course I know the significance! The rebels wear butterfly jasmine as a symbol of their patriotism. That's why I wore it, to show my support of their cause."

"Which was incredibly foolish." Seeing Andrea stiffen, Eric continued. "Do you realize that just a few weeks ago those supporting the Spanish cause rioted in this city? That anyone even suspected of having rebel sympathies was beaten, many were killed, their businesses and homes were put to the torch? The army managed to put down the riots, even though many of their officers were the leaders, but this city is a tinderbox. The slightest incident could precipitate more violence. No one, not even an American, dares to display sympathetic feelings. No, I take that back," Eric corrected himself. "Particularly not an American. At the present time, we're even higher on the Spaniards' hate list than the rebels."

Andrea had realized the stranger was an American before he even identified himself. He spoke without an accent, although with his deep suntan and black hair he could have passed for a native. Even his blue eyes wouldn't have been all that unusual, though she had never seen such a vibrant shade of blue. But the last thing she was thinking of at that particular moment was the stranger's good looks. She was still angry with him, despite the fact that he had given her very good reasons not to wear jasmine. After all, he could have just pointed out her error. That would have been the gentlemanly thing to do. "That doesn't give you any right to accost me the way you did," she answered in a haughty, raised voice. "Besides, what I do is my business."

Eric glanced over his shoulder and saw the soldiers were almost on top of them. *"Sssh,* keep your voice down!" he cautioned.

"How dare you *sssh* me! I'm not a child. Just who do you think you—"

Eric had gone to great lengths to keep from drawing attention to himself. Fearing that the soldiers—who acted in a police capacity—would stop and ask questions, he silenced Andrea in the only manner he thought the soldiers might not question. Without preamble, he swept her into his arms and locked his mouth over hers.

Andrea was caught by surprise, and it took her a moment to react. By the time she'd recovered enough to resist, the trio of sneering men had passed; Eric effectively hid her struggles to escape his embrace from the sight of the men who glanced over their shoulders. Eric pivoted so that his body shielded her from view.

Andrea considered herself unusually strong for a woman. When wrestling with her older brothers she had always held her own. She was shocked at how strong the stranger was. His arms were like a steel vise closed around her, and his lips seemed glued to hers, no matter how much she tried to twist her head away. Struggling only made her more breathless and lightheaded, so she finally ceased to resist. Then something happened that really shocked her. She found herself enjoying the feel of her body pressed against this man's muscular length and the gentle glide of her lips against his warm ones. Her fingertips began to tingle as an insidious warmth crept up her body.

Abruptly, she was released. Everything seemed to be spinning. Then she heard the stranger saying, "Make another scene and you'll get more of the same."

Had the stranger realized she enjoyed it? Andrea wondered in horror. How humiliating that would be, particularly since he had only done it to keep her from making a scene. And what on earth had gotten into her? Belatedly remembering to react, she sputtered weakly, "How . . . how dare you!"

"Don't give me that outraged stuff," Eric answered in exasperation, wishing he had never gotten involved with the woman. "I warned you to be quiet. You may not care about your life, but I'm very attached to mine."

"What are you talking about? What does my being quiet have to do with your life?"

Eric motioned to the soldiers in the distance, and answered, "I'm talking about that trio that just passed us. What were you going to tell them when they asked why you were so irate? That I attacked you out of the clear blue? Or the truth? Either way, I'd have landed in Morro Castle. Prisoners have an alarming way of disappearing into its dungeons and never being seen again."

Andrea hadn't known there was anyone nearby or

that she was in any immediate danger. The stranger had blocked her view with his body. She knew that an apology of sorts was in order, but she couldn't bring herself to give the man one. Her pride was one of her biggest faults. "Surely you exaggerate the situation."

"No, I'm not exaggerating, and if you'd spent any time in this country, you'd know that." Eric paused, cocked his head, then asked, "Just how long have you been in Cuba?"

Andrea bristled. "Not that it's any of your business, but I arrived this morning."

Eric looked around, a quick search that included the church and park benches, then asked, "Where is your escort?"

"I don't have one."

"This is a Latin country. Respectable women don't wander about by themselves. Surely someone could have come with you. Your father, a brother, your mother, someone?"

"I don't have anyone here, or know anyone yet. I came alone."

A shocked look came over Eric's face. He recovered and blurted, "Why in the hell are you here? Don't you know there's a revolution going on in this country?"

"Of course I know that! That's why I'm here." Andrea drew herself up to her full height and announced, "I'm a journalist."

Eric's brow furrowed. "You mean a reporter? I've never heard of a female reporter, particularly one covering a war."

Andrea's eyes flashed. "Well, you have now!"

"What crazy, irresponsible newspaper sent you here? The *Journal?*"

"No! I wouldn't work for William Randolph Hearst if he was the last publisher on earth!"

"The *World,* then?"

"No. Pulitzer is no better," Andrea said with equal fervor. "They both publish yellow journalism. All they care about is selling newspapers. I deplore their irresponsible, inflammatory methods, their sensationalism. They're besmirching the good name of journalism, making a circus out of reporting, telling the public out-and-out lies, deliberately trying to goad the American people into war. A true journalist seeks out the truth. That's why I'm here. To tell the true story."

Eric was in total agreement with Andrea, but he didn't think a woman should be sent to do such dangerous reporting. "Then what paper do you represent?"

"Right now, none. I'm doing freelance. However, I have talked with Edwin Godkin, the editor of the *Nation.* He hates yellow journalism as much as I do. He told me if I could come up with some good stories, he'd consider publishing them."

Eric drew back and asked in disbelief, "Consider?" Then he frowned. "Are you saying you're here of your own accord, that you don't even know for sure if he'll buy anything? That's insane!"

"Why?" Andrea answered defensively.

"Because it's dangerous here. Why risk your life for nothing?"

"There are other freelance journalists here. Do you think they're insane too?"

"That's different."

Andrea's voice turned icy. "Why? Because they're male, and I'm female?"

"Frankly, yes."

"And if reporting on a war is too dangerous, I suppose you think it's also too rigorous?" Andrea asked in a deceptively calm tone of voice.

"If you're going to do the job right, yes."

At that moment the stranger seemed the epitome of everything Andrea hated about men. They all had this superior attitude, she thought, this misconception that women were beneath them in everything, this insane idea that men were stronger, smarter, braver, had more endurance, more stamina, more vigor than women. They assumed that it was a God-given right to be the leader, and that the female should be the follower. For the better part, the women of her day and age accepted the second-class role that men had placed them in eons ago, but the day of reckoning for the male egotists was coming, and for Andrea it couldn't come soon enough. A women's rights movement had been born, and every day, more and more women were joining its ranks as women went out into the world to hold down jobs. A few, like Andrea, even dared to take up professions that by tradition were exclusively male. But she knew it was going to be a long, uphill battle. But if that's what it took—a battle—she'd give it to them. She'd been battling since she took her first step, and she wasn't going to stop now.

She stepped forward, stuck her face in his, and said in a hard voice, "Let me tell you something, mister! I grew up on a ranch in Wyoming and faced danger every day of my life. And I'm as tough as any man. I've shot mountain lions and outlaws. I survived diphtheria, getting lost in the badlands without water for three days, being picked up and dumped by a tornado, getting stranded in a blizzard, and being trampled by a bull. I can outrun anyone on a horse and outrace anyone on foot. I can throw a two-hundred-pound yearling and toss a bale of hay with the best of them. In fact, I can do anything any cowhand on our ranch can do, only better, and I'm not scared of anything. So the only difference between me and those other reporters is that I'm stuck in a female body. I can probably take better care of myself, and I'm a much better journalist."

Eric had thought the young woman attractive, but not particularly beautiful. Her mouth was a little too wide and her nose a little too short for classic beauty, and there was a little scar on her chin that flawed her otherwise smooth complexion. But when she was angry—really angry like she was then—everything about her took on new dimensions. Her black eyes flashed, her entire body quivered, and Eric could have sworn there were sparks flying from her golden mane. She seemed so alive, so vital. He had never been so aware of another's inner force as he was at that moment. He had never dreamed a female could possess so much intensity. Then her words penetrated. He found himself not only impressed, but believing her claims. She was bolder than any woman he had ever met. She was magnificent, and although he didn't know it, Eric was already a little in love with her.

When the stranger just stood there and stared at her, Andrea asked, "Well? Aren't you going to say anything?"

Eric heard the challenging tone in her voice and

knew she expected some rebuff. She was the picture of someone aching for a fight. But Eric wasn't interested in sparring with the young woman. Instead, he commented, "You don't mind tooting your own horn, do you?"

Andrea had the grace to blush a little. Then she replied candidly, "No, I don't. No one else is going to toot it for me, and I've got a hard fight ahead of me to prove what I said. But I can do it!"

If she meant to challenge him, Eric ignored it. "What's your name?"

"Andrea Williams."

"Andrea," Eric repeated thoughtfully. "I've never met anyone by that name before."

Andrea's anger was slipping away. It took two to fight, and the stranger didn't seem to be willing to oblige. "It is rather unusual," Andrea admitted. "You see, it was originally Andrew. After five boys, my parents expected another. When I showed up, they just changed it to the female form. But all my family and friends call me Andy. You can too."

"No, I think I'll stick to the female form." Eric's eyes swept over her body. "It fits you better."

The look seemed too intimate to Andrea and, much to her discomfiture, made her feel peculiar. She drew herself up to her full height of five-foot-nine, a protective device she used to keep men away, and said, "I'd prefer Andy."

Eric suspected that Andrea didn't want to be female, but not just because she was pursuing a profession that was considered male. He remembered her saying that she was "stuck" in a female body. But like it or not, she was female, and that's the way Eric wanted her, although he didn't have the slightest idea why that was important to him. He smiled blandly and said, "No, I'll stick to Andrea." Then he quickly changed the subject, saying, "My name is Eric Flemming."

Andrea felt a keen disappointment when her ploy didn't work. But then, the stranger was taller than any man she had ever met. Even if he hadn't had the advantage of height, she suspected that he wouldn't have been intimidated. She had a distinct feeling he was a man who stood his ground no matter who or what his adversary. Also, he seemed like a man who would choose his own battleground. She remembered how he had refused to rise to her bait. She nodded in acknowledgment, then asked, "How long have you been in Cuba?"

"Since '94."

"Then you were here before the revolution began?"

At the mention of the revolution, Eric quickly scanned the church and park. Seeing no sign of Diego, he knew the messenger wouldn't come that day. He answered absently, "Yes, I was."

"What do you do?"

Presently, between fighting, I'm a courier, Eric thought. Then he answered, "I'm a mining engineer."

"Mining what?" Realizing how bold she sounded, Andrea laughed softly and said, "I'm sorry. I guess you can tell I'm a reporter by how inquisitive I am."

Knowing that he had time to kill, Eric shrugged and answered, "That's okay. It's no big secret. I work for a steel company."

"The Carnegie Corporation of Pittsburgh? I understand they have a lot of mining interests down here."

"That's true. Cuba has some of the highest-grade iron ore in the world. But the company I work for is much smaller. You've probably never heard of it. Lawson Steel?"

"No, I haven't," Andrea admitted. "Is your mine nearby?"

Eric caught Andrea's arm and turned her away from the harbor, answering, "Why don't I tell you about it while I walk you back to your hotel?"

Andrea jerked back her arm and said, "I don't need an escort back to my hotel."

Eric had fully expected Andrea to resist. Trying to remain patient, he said, "I realize you're a very independent woman, but I wasn't joking when I said that respectable women don't wander the streets of Havana without an escort. Maybe you can do that in Wyoming, or New York, but here, only street women do that. It's an open invitation to trouble, and may I remind you, this is a port. It's swarming with sailors from all over the world who are very well aware of the Latin custom—who is off limits and who isn't."

"Then I'll just carry a gun."

"That could still cause problems. If you shot someone, even in self-defense, then you'd have to explain what you were doing wandering the streets by yourself. You surely wouldn't want to tell them you're a reporter. Right now, the Spanish hate American reporters with a passion. They know what a hornets' nest they've stirred up against Spain with their inflammatory reporting, not only in our country, but all over the world. Public opinion influenced the new government in Spain to recall General Weyler—the very thing the loyalists here were objecting to when they recently rioted. They saw it as a show of weakness. If there's one thing I've learned about the Spanish since I've been here, it's that they're a very proud people. You don't trample on their national honor, or their customs. They are quick to take offense."

"But what was printed about General Weyler wasn't inflammatory," Andrea objected fervently. "It was true! He needed to be recalled. What he'd done was inhumane, unforgivable."

"That's irrelevant to what I'm trying to tell you. What matters is how the Spanish here feel about it, and right now, Cuba is dangerous for any American, particularly a journalist."

This time, when Eric took Andrea's arm, she didn't resist. He had convinced her to exercise caution. As he led her through the park, she asked, "But how am I going to get material for my stories, if I can't move about freely?"

Eric shrugged his shoulders, inadvertently drawing her attention to how broad they were. "Do as the rest of the reporters do. Sit at a bar and make up wild tales."

"I'm serious!" Andrea snapped.

"I'm serious, too. The majority of the reporters in Havana rarely leave their hotels, and then only to walk to the telegraph station. As for getting out of the city and reporting on the war, the officials won't let them into the countryside. Every road is blocked. You can't get through without a pass, either way. Only a few reporters who lived here before the revolution and who know their way around Cuba have actually had any contact with the rebels."

"I've heard the rebels are hidden in the mountains."

"When they aren't raiding, yes."

"God, I'd love to get to them, to interview one of their generals."

Eric sliced Andrea an alarmed look, then said, "Forget that! Like I said, the only journalists that have gotten to them are men who know their way around the country. There are jungles out there so thick you can't see three feet in front of you."

Andrea was practical enough to know she was dreaming. She'd only been saying what she'd like to do. "Then I'll do an eyewitness account of how things are in one of the concentration camps. No one has ever written about one from a woman's standpoint before."

"You can forget that, too. They're not letting anyone into those camps, not after all the newspaper stories about how horrible they are." Eric stopped and asked, "Where are you staying? At the Hotel Inglaterra?"

"No."

"I thought that's where American reporters stayed," Eric commented.

"That might be true, but I told you, I'm not like the other journalists. I'm staying at a little out-of-way hotel that was recommended by the captain of the ship I traveled on. The hotel La Habana. He said it had a good reputation."

"It does," Eric answered after he had gotten over his surprise. "As a matter of fact, that's where I'm staying."

As they resumed their walk, Andrea asked, "How is the food there?"

"Excellent."

"Good. I'm starving. I haven't had any lunch."

Yes, she was different, Eric thought in mute appreciation. Direct and to the point. No pretense. "Neither have I. Perhaps we could dine together."

As soon as the words were out of his mouth, Eric wondered why he had said them. He didn't have any business getting even remotely involved with a woman. He should have taken her back to the hotel and let her fend for herself from there on. He'd warned her about how the land lay. If she got into trouble, she'd have no one but herself to blame.

Maybe she would refuse to dine with him, he thought. After all, they were strangers. But that hope died when he realized that Andrea wouldn't be here if she was the sort to obey social conventions. And that was the crux of the problem. Andrea wasn't an ordinary woman. She was a journalist. She was nosy by nature and she didn't know the meaning of keeping a secret. No, undoubtedly she considered it her business to tell the world everything she could learn in Cuba, particularly if it had anything to do with the war. He'd have to be awfully careful that she didn't find out what he was doing in Havana. He couldn't trust her with the truth.

Chapter 2

Sitting in the hotel dining room a little later, Andrea opened her menu. She frowned.

"Are you having difficulty reading it?" Eric asked.

"No, I can read Spanish," Andrea answered a little sharply. She wondered if he thought that she was unprepared for the job of reporting in a foreign country. But Andrea had done her homework. She had learned how to speak and write Spanish. Her journey to Cuba hadn't been any spur-of-the-moment undertaking. She had been preparing for it for a good ten months. "I'm thinking this must be a misprint. *Moros y cristianos.* Moors and Christians?"

"No, it's not a misprint. It's black beans and rice, and goes back to the days when the Moors invaded, then occupied the southern part of Spain."

"But isn't it a rather strange thing to be serving at a hotel restaurant?"

"No. It's pretty much the backbone of the Cuban diet, particularly the rice, which I find strange."

"Why do you say that?"

"Because the rice is imported. You'd think people in

such a highly agricultural country as this would grow their own daily staple, but they don't. They grow everything else: sugar, tobacco, cocoa, a little coffee, every imaginable kind of tropical fruit, and a multitude of vegetables. But they import their rice, and almost every Cuban main dish has it in it, and if not, the rice is served as a side dish."

"Maybe rice won't grow here," Andrea suggested.

"I don't know why not. I understand they're growing rice in Louisiana, right next to fields of sugar cane. If it works there, it ought to work here."

"But the cane here is native to this country."

"No, it's not," Eric informed her. "It was introduced in the middle of the sixteenth century, but it really didn't come to the fore as a major crop here until after the Haitian revolution, when so many of the French fled Haiti and brought their skilled laborers and advanced sugar technology to Cuba. Before that, tobacco and cattle were Cuba's major products."

"You certainly know a lot about Cuban agriculture," Andrea commented.

Eric took a sip from his water glass before he answered, "I have a friend who runs a sugar plantation down here. He's been here for years, and he is quite knowledgeable about anything that has to do with Cuba. He's one of those men who seem to feel it's his duty to educate you. Whether I wanted to or not, I've learned a lot from him."

"Then his plantation hasn't been destroyed by the rebels?"

"No, not the last I heard. It's about fifty kilometers southwest of Havana, just a little too close to the

Spaniards' stronghold for the rebels to risk attacking it."

"Has the destruction to the plantations really been as devastating as the newspapers have reported?"

"Probably more so. Unless you've actually seen the interior, you can't begin to imagine how extensive the damage is. First the rebels burned every Spanish plantation they could get to, and a few American-owned ones, too, if the owners didn't come up with the protection money the rebels demanded. Then—"

"Protection money?" Andrea interjected. "But that's extortion!"

"A form of it, yes. How else are the rebels going to get money for guns and ammunition, except for the smattering of contributions their exiles in the U.S. have collected? Despite the fact that they have their own government—officials chosen in a nationwide election—no foreign government will extend them credit to finance their war. The powers in Europe wouldn't think of angering Spain, particularly over possession of a colony, no less. Most of them have been in Spain's position. They sympathize with the Spaniards. Our government won't recognize them—not even the rebels' belligerency, which would at least allow American arms merchants openly to sell war materials to the Cubans, instead of doing it undercover and then having our cutter service confiscate the cargo before it reaches Cuba. Yet we claim to be freedom's champion, and our people cry out in horror at the inhuman methods Spain is using to put down the insurrection. And the Latin countries in America, which support the Cuban rebels fully, are too poor to help. So the Cuban rebels finance their war in the only way they can. Think of it as collecting taxes, not extortion, if it makes you feel better. But believe me, it is necessary, and the American sugar companies haven't made much of a fuss about it. I suppose they think it's a small price to pay for the enormous profits they're making from this country."

Andrea frowned. In the papers or journals back home, there had been almost nothing about recognizing the Cuban government, not even their belligerency. Spain, England, and other European countries had recognized the Confederacy during the Civil War. The Cuban rebels had the American public's full sympathies, but their elected government was being ignored. The point had never been brought to her attention. "In that context, I can understand," she admitted, "and I'm sorry I interrupted you. You were talking about the condition of the interior of the country. Please go on."

"It's very simple. What the rebels didn't destroy, the Spanish did. Every little farm—crops, buildings, everything—was razed when they moved the entire rural population to designated towns on the coast and put them in concentration camps. It's a wasteland out there. Everything that was once farmland is now scorched earth."

Andrea absorbed the information Eric gave her. Then she remarked in puzzlement, "I'm afraid I don't understand either the Spaniards' or the insurrectionists' logic. They both claim to want the country, with its valuable farmland, yet they're destroying it economically. What will sustain them after the war is over?"

Eric had also wondered if there would be anything

left of the country after the war. Before he had come to Cuba and seen the situation first-hand, he'd had no idea how destructive the war was. "The rebels think if they destroy the valuable crop that keeps the Spanish here, their enemies will leave. They used the same methods in their revolt back in '68. When the war ended ten years later, the sugar industry had been pretty much destroyed. It's taken all this time to build it back up. American investment made that possible. But the rebels are desperate. Off and on, for well over fifty years, they've been struggling for independence. They're determined to get it this time. They will accept nothing less. Not even if it means the total destruction of their economy. After all, the *peninsulares*—members of the select Spanish ruling class—have always looked down on the *pobre cubano,* the poor Cuban, even if he was one of the wealthy *criollos* born in this country. The *mambis* feel they might as well play the part to the hilt."

"*Mambis?* I'm afraid I'm not familiar with that word."

"It's not Spanish. It's African. It's what the rebels call themselves, particularly those doing the actual fighting."

For a moment Andrea pondered what Eric had told her. Then she said, "I suppose I can understand the rebels' desperation, and they are concentrating on destroying select industries, but why are the Spanish taking such drastic steps to put down the revolution? Their destruction seems so wanton. Surely, they're not desperate too."

"Oh, but they are. All along, they've been beating the insurrections back. And it's not a new battle to them. One by one, they've lost their colonies in the new world. In this hemisphere Cuba is their last holding of any value to them. Puerto Rico has never held the importance Cuba has. This island was their first foothold in the new world, the central base from which they launched their ventures of conquest in the Americas. Their stiff-necked pride won't let them lose it, particularly not now, when imperialism is running high and many of the European powers are gaining new colonies in Africa. The Spanish have to win this confrontation, or admit to the world that they have slipped into the position of a second-class nation. And in the effort to win it, they have had to resort to drastic measures. They've had to separate the rebels from the *pacíficos,* the peasant farmers who fed and sheltered them. So they moved the rural population to the coast and destroyed anything the rebels might use. They thought to starve the enemy out, but it hasn't worked. They hadn't counted on the rebels' determination. Despite everything, Spain is losing this fight. It's just a matter of time."

Andrea was stunned when Eric said that the Spanish were losing the confrontation with the rebels. She had thought it was the other way around. As she opened her mouth to comment, Eric cut across her words, saying, "I think we'd better order now. The waiter is getting a bit impatient."

Andrea glanced to the side and, to her surprise, saw the waiter standing there. She wondered how long he had been there. Then she wondered if that was why Eric had put such an abrupt end to their discussion. Could the man possibly understand English and have Spanish loyalties? She turned her attention back to the menu and noted that most of the entrees did have rice in them, just as Eric had said. *Arroz* was all over the menu. "I never did develop a taste for rice," she commented. "I come from meat and potatoes country."

"I didn't care for it, either, until I tasted Cuban rice. There's nothing drab about it. It's highly seasoned. Not hot, but spicy. The *arroz con pollo* is very good. That's yellow rice mixed with chicken, red pimento, and peas."

"I'm not all that crazy about chicken either," Andrea admitted. "I grew up on a cattle ranch, remember? I like beef."

"Then why don't you try the *picadillo?* It's made with chopped beef, onions, green peppers, olives, raisins, tomatoes and spices, served with white rice and fried ripe plantains."

Andrea wrinkled her nose. She had never heard of such a God-awful conglomeration of ingredients. Particularly the raisins and tomatoes. Ugh! "I can't believe that's a Spanish dish."

"It isn't It's pure Cuban. Their cooking is different from that of the other Latin countries. It's a mixture of Spanish and African. Cuban cooking bears no more resemblance to pure Spanish cuisine than the Creoles' cooking in New Orleans does to classical French cuisine."

"How do you know that?"

Eric gave a little self-derisive smile and answered, "My friend, Paul, told me. He's from New Orleans."

Andrea found the crooked smile appealing. *He's really very attractive,* she thought, with his dark good looks and those striking eyes. "The one who runs the plantation?"

"Yes," Eric answered, then seeing the waiter shuffle his feet in what seemed to be a reminder of his presence, asked, "Have you decided yet?"

"Yes, I think I'll have the *ropa vieja.*"

"The shredded flank steak? I'm disappointed in you."

"Why?" Andrea asked in astonishment.

"I thought you were adventuresome."

"I am!"

"Then why not try something new? Order the *picadillo*. It seems ridiculous to go to a foreign country and not even sample their unique cuisine."

"I'm not a tourist!" Andrea replied in disgust. "I didn't come here to try the food or see the country. I came for writing material."

"I'm here on business, too, but that hasn't stopped me from appreciating what the country has to offer. But then I'm not a journalist. Maybe you've been to so many foreign countries, you don't find newness exciting any more."

This was the first and only foreign country Andrea had been to. She was so intent on proving herself that she had forgotten her dream of seeing the world. Eric was right, she realized. There was more to Cuba than the revolution. The tropical island had a unique culture. Why, she'd look downright silly if she went back and her friends asked her what the country was like and she could tell them only about the war. "All right, then," she conceded grudgingly. "I'll try the *picadillo.*"

After the waiter had taken their order and left, Andrea said, "I forgot you were here on business, too. Is your mine near here?"

"No, there are no mines on this end of Cuba.

They're all in the east end of the island, and actually, my company doesn't have a mine yet. Things are still in the exploratory stage. We're still looking for the right site, a place where the ore is rich enough and in enough quantity to justify investing in a mine."

"Isn't four years a little long to be just looking? I got the impression the country was rich in iron ore."

She was sharper than he thought, Eric realized. An ordinary person wouldn't have picked up on that. "We're not looking for iron ore. We're looking high-grade ore called ferromanganese. It's used to produce a hard grade of steel which is needed to make rock-crushers and mining machinery."

"Then it will be worth your time and effort if you find it?"

"Yes, and it's here. We just haven't found a large enough vein to go after yet. But we will. It just takes time."

That was the story Eric had fed the Spanish authorities to explain his extended presence in the country. He and his crew hadn't yet located the big vein of ferromanganese they were seeking in the Sierra Maestra, the mountains in eastern Cuba. What the authorities didn't know was that the company had suspended their explorations when the war got too hot and they had pulled their employees out of the country. Had they been a bigger firm, like the Carnegie Corporation, the Spanish would have noticed the withdrawal, but a small mining expedition far off in the rugged mountains was too inconsequential for them to keep track of. That was why Eric made such a good courier for the rebels. His visits to Havana supposedly to pick up supplies for the expedition weren't suspect. As far as anyone here in Cuba knew, including Eric's American friends, the expedition was still going on.

The food arrived, and Eric and Andrea ate in silence. Andrea found the *picadillo* different, but tasty. But she didn't particularly like the fried plantains. Having never eaten a banana of any kind, she found their taste a little too foreign. But when dessert came, she thought the *flan,* with its rich caramelized sauce, absolutely delicious.

As they were drinking their after-dinner coffee, Andrea said, "I've been thinking about something you said before the waiter appeared. You said the Spanish were losing the war. I've never heard that."

"Of course not. If the American public knew that, it would be hard to convince them to go to war on the rebels' behalf, wouldn't it? What would happen to all those people who planned on profiting on that war, including the newspapers?" Eric answered with biting cynicism. "But the truth is, the Spanish can't hold out much longer. They outsmarted themselves when they destroyed the Cuban farms. Spain hasn't been able to keep their forces adequately supplied with food, and except for a few of the bigger coastal cities, the Spanish army is starving, too, along with everyone else on this island. Nor do they have the arms and ammunition they should have. That's why if the United States would just recognize the independence of this country and give them a little financial aid, the rebels could end this war."

"Then that's all the rebels want? Financial aid? Not military?"

"If you mean sending soldiers, emphatically no! In fact, they were warned not to solicit that kind of aid by one of their most respected leaders. José Martí. Have you ever heard of him?"

"Yes. I went to a lecture he gave at one of the universities while he was in New York. Of course he was invited there because of his success as a poet, but he did answer questions afterwards concerning the Cuban quest for independence. I was impressed by him. He seemed so intense, so zealous in the cause of freedom."

"Yes, he was, so zealous he insisted upon joining in the invasion and fighting, even though he wasn't a soldier. He should have stuck to organizing the revolution and collecting contributions. He was killed in the first battle he took part in, six weeks after the landing. Cuba lost a great patriot and leader, but more important, they lost one of the few men who knew Americans well enough to see us as a threat to Cuban freedom. He warned the other leaders to ask only for recognition, perhaps economic aid given in good faith with no strings attached, but not troops. He feared that if the American government ever got a foothold in the country, the Cubans would still be denied their freedom. It would be pointless for the Cubans to exchange a Spanish yoke for an American one."

"Why, our country would never do that!" Andrea objected hotly. "Trample on another country's freedom?"

"Then you don't think our country has any imperialistic ideas at all? That's the trend, you know. All of the big powers on earth are looking around to see what territory they can grab before everything is gone. And you can't deny that the United States wants Cuba. They've tried to buy it from Spain off and on since the War of 1812, when Spain allowed the British to use Cuba as a naval base."

"You make it sound like we might want Cuba for security reasons," Andrea responded in surprise.

"I think that's a very good possibility. In any other country's hands, it's a threat to us."

"I've never heard of anything so ridiculous. If anything, we want Cuba for its economic value, and even then, we'd never hold the Cuban people against their will. That would be totally against the very principles our country is built on. What kind of an American are you, to believe such terrible things about your own country?"

"A realist. I believe what I see, not what I'm told. But if you believe differently, that's your privilege. I only ask that you keep an open mind in your reporting."

"Of course, I'll keep an open mind! I told you, I came to seek the truth." Andrea sat back and sipped her coffee. She was silently steaming over what she considered Eric's unpatriotic attitude. Then she realized that, with his knowledge of the country, he could be very helpful. It would be best not to alienate him. Pretending there had never been any disagreement between them, Andrea smiled and said, "I've been thinking. If I can't interview any of the rebel leaders or get into one of the *reconcentración* camps, maybe I could interview your friend. You know, there haven't been any stories published about sugar plantations. Oh, everyone knows that the sugar business is being drastically affected by the war, but people don't know what a plantation is really like. It might be a good start for me."

Eric made no comment. He just stared at her.

Andrea added, "That is, if you don't mind introducing me to him."

"No, that's not it at all," Eric lied smoothly, again wishing he hadn't gotten himself involved with the woman. Not only had he almost given himself away with his strong pro-Cuban feelings, but now she was expecting favors he could ill afford. "It's just that I can't leave the city right now. I'm expecting ... expecting an important shipment to arrive any day now."

"Then maybe you could give me a letter of introduction," Andrea replied, not in the least discouraged.

Eric frowned. "Have you forgotten what I said about going around without an escort?"

"No, but surely, I can hire someone to escort me—a Cuban who can also act as my guide, someone who can be trusted. Perhaps you even know someone?"

"Offhand, no, but I'll think about it," Eric hedged.

Eric turned in his seat to signal the waiter for the check. Then he froze when he saw a Spanish officer walking towards him. Damn, he thought, why did he have to run into that bastard? Colonel Reyes headed the department assigned to ferreting out spies and those who actively aided the enemy. If there was anyone in Cuba whom Eric had to dance around it was this man, and the colonel was a worthy adversary, sharper that most Spaniards.

Eric turned back to Andrea, leaned across the table, and asked in a lowered, urgent voice, "Does anyone here in Havana know why you're here?"

"No. Why do you ask?"

"I'll explain later. Just go along with what I say."

By that time, the colonel had reached their table. He

bowed slightly to Andrea, then said to Eric, *"Buenos días, Señor* Flemming. I'm surprised to see you're still in Havana. Your business trips don't usually last this long."

He's suspicious, Eric thought. Even if the slimy Spaniard hadn't practically said so, one would know by the sneer on his face. Eric smiled blandly and answered, "Good day, Colonel Reyes. And yes, you're correct. My business doesn't generally delay me this long. However, I'm not in Havana for business this time. I'm here for pleasure."

The Spaniard's dark eyebrows rose. "For pleasure, *señor?"*

Eric reached across the table, possessively took one of Andrea's hands in his, smiled warmly at her, and answered, "Yes, for pleasure. May I introduce my fiancée, Andrea Williams, who's come to Havana for a visit."

Chapter 3

Andrea was as shocked at Eric's announcement as the colonel, but she hid her surprise. Looking much more composed than she felt, she smiled and said to the startled officer, "I'm pleased to meet you, Colonel."

Recovering, Colonel Reyes bowed stiffly and responded, "My pleasure, *señorita*." Then arrogantly dismissing her, he turned directly to Eric and said, "Don't you think it a dangerous time for a visit, particularly for a loved one? There's a rebellion going on in this country."

Eric smiled and answered, "I couldn't agree with you more, but I'm afraid my fiancée is a woman with a mind of her own. I couldn't dissuade her any longer."

Andrea couldn't imagine why Eric was lying, but she did know she didn't like the Spaniard, and not just because he had insulted her. There was something about him that made her skin crawl. She took her cue from Eric and said brightly, "That's right. Eric tried to talk me out of it, but I've been putting off this visit for years, since he's been too busy with his work here to come visit me, and that's entirely too long for a woman to go without seeing her betrothed. Why, I was beginning to forget what he even looked like. Rebellion or not, I decided to come, even though he forbade me to do so."

Colonel Reyes was tempted to believe Eric's story. The *señorita* was clearly one of the pushy American women whom he found so objectionable. He could see her deliberately disobeying. Not only did she act the part, but she dressed it. However, there was something curious about their story. "I have not seen you around the city," he remarked to Andrea. "When did you arrive?"

Andrea had no idea what to answer, and thankfully, Eric did for her. "She just arrived this morning." Eric assumed a sheepish look, then said, "I'm afraid I was so anxious to see her I came a little earlier than necessary to meet the boat."

"Oh, did you, darling?" Andrea asked in mock surprise. She affected a coy pose and said, "You didn't tell me that, you devil. See, you're glad I came, after all."

"You're right, dear. It wasn't particularly wise, but I am glad."

Eric's last words sounded so sincere that Andrea felt a warmth stealing over her. Her eyes met Eric's across the table, and held.

The performance convinced Reyes. Gazing across the table at each other, they were the picture of silly lovers who didn't seem to know that the world around them existed. Fools! Reyes thought. And to think that he had always credited Flemming with having unusual intelligence. Now he had nothing but contempt for the American. Not only was he unable to control his woman, he was letting his emotions rule his senses. The officer excused himself with frigid politeness, clearly telling the couple he did not approve of Andrea, or her visit.

As soon as the colonel was out of hearing, Andrea realized she was playing her role too well. She wondered what Eric must think. She jerked her hand back and asked him a little too sharply, "What the devil was that all about? Why did you tell him I'm your fiancée?"

Eric wasn't about to admit that he had made the story up to protect himself. "Well, you wouldn't want him to know you're a journalist. Then he would have had your every movement watched and probably thwart your efforts to seek out information. Colonel Reyes is in charge of counter-intelligence here in the city, and he views every journalist as a spy."

"He didn't seem all that interested in me. Just you. He never asked what I'm doing here."

"Oh, no, he would have made inquiries," Eric assured her. "He watches every American like a hawk."

"Are you trying to tell me you lied to him for my benefit?" Andrea asked, clearly skeptical.

"Why, yes," Eric answered, trying hard to look innocent. "Then when he sees us about, he won't think it at all unusual."

"And why would he be seeing us about?"

"You need an escort around town, don't you? Well, I'm him. Until my business is concluded here, that is," Eric added quickly.

"Just like that, you're going to be my escort? You

must think I'm stupid!" Andrea retorted, feeling highly insulted. "I don't for one minute believe you lied for my benefit."

Damn, he had to keep on his toes just to stay a jump ahead of her, Eric thought, partly in vexation and partly in admiration. "All right, it wasn't solely for your benefit," he admitted. "I don't want him to know why my business here has been delayed. I'm waiting for an important shipment. He might investigate, and confiscate it when it arrives."

Andrea's dark eyes danced with excitement. She leaned across the table and whispered, "I know! You're running guns, aren't you?"

"Guns?" Eric asked in surprise, then responded, "Hell no!"

"Then what are you waiting for that you're afraid he'll confiscate?"

"A generator," Eric fabricated.

"Why would he confiscate a generator?"

"Because the Spanish army needs them along the *trocha* between Mariel and Majana to generate electricity at night. Just like weapons and ammunition, the government in Spain hasn't kept them adequately supplied."

Andrea's brow furrowed. *"Trocha?* Yes, it seems like I remember reading something about the Spanish army digging ditches."

"Two of them, and they aren't ordinary ditches. They cut across the country through steaming jungles, fifty miles long and fifty yards wide. A railroad runs down the middle to keep them supplied. Behind barbed wire on each side, there is a solid line of forts, bristling with artillery. In some areas, where the jungle isn't so thick, they've even laid out land mines."

"And they're actually lit at night?" Andrea asked in astonishment, for electricity was still rather new. It was found only in the larger cities back home, and the U.S. was one of the most progressive nations in the world.

"The one I mentioned is. It's the newer one, on the western end of the island. The older one, the Morón-Jucaro *trocha,* was built in the Ten Year War and restored. The ditches were General Weyler's idea, to bar the passage of the rebels from one section of the country to the other. They've been very effective. It's virtually impossible for the rebels to get across those *trochas,* particularly the western *trocha.* It completely isolated General Maceo and his calvary, who had been raiding freely in all of the western provinces and doing tremendous damage. It pretty much brought the rebellion to an end in that part of the country. Right now, most of the fighting is going on in the eastern end of the island, which was where the revolution began."

Andrea felt a tingle of alarm. "Isn't that where you're conducting your business?"

"If you're thinking about my crew and me being in any immediate danger, we aren't. Oh, there's fighting going on all around us, but we're up in the mountains, where it's safe. However, there are some problems about going back and forth from here. Once the railroad that transverses the island passes over the Morón-Jucaro *trocha,* there's no telling who is going to be in possession of the territory in the eastern part of the country. It changes hands, back and forth, and the going is terribly slow. Sometimes the train is detained for days at a time, while a battle ahead is fought."

"But you can freely travel from one section of the nation to another?"

"As a businessman of a neutral country, yes, which is something a Cuban can't do. Almost without exception, they're all under suspicion. The Spanish gave me a pass. And because I'm American, the rebels consider me a friend."

Eric glanced around and saw the waiter glaring at him. "I think we'd better leave. The dining room is getting crowded, and we've held this table far too long."

As Eric signaled the waiter and the man walked towards them, Andrea said, "I'll pay for my meal."

Eric wasn't surprised. He realized that Andrea was independent. Thankfully, he didn't have to come right out and admit that he objected. Instead he said, "I think that might seem very strange, since we're supposed to be engaged."

Andrea looked around, then asked, "You don't think we're being watched, do you?"

"You never know," he answered evasively.

When the waiter was almost upon them, she whispered, "Then I'll pay you back later."

"I'd rather you wouldn't," Eric answered.

Andrea sat bolt upright and replied icily, "I'd rather I would!"

Eric sighed in exasperation and turned to the waiter.

"Would you like to pay now, *señor,* or have it added to your hotel bill, as usual?" the Cuban asked.

"Added to my bill," Eric answered, rising from his chair and slipping the Cuban a generous tip.

"Gracias, Señor Flemming." The waiter turned to Andrea and bowed, then just as Eric was pulling out her chair, said, *"Buenas noches, señorita."*

"Buenas noches," Andrea answered, coming to her feet. Eric watched the Cuban's face as she stood up. She grew taller and taller, until she towered over the shorter man. The poor waiter was so astonished that Eric had to bite back a laugh. But if Andrea felt any awkwardness at the situation, she didn't reveal it. If anything, she looked regal as she turned to Eric and offered him her arm.

As they walked from the dining room, Andrea whispered, "By the way. I have a bone to pick with you."

"Oh? What about?"

Andrea didn't answer until they reached the hotel lobby. She stepped aside, where a potted palm would partially shield them, and said, "I don't like to be used by anyone, for any reason, and you used me when you made up that story about our being engaged. Do you realize what a difficult position you've put me in?"

When Eric had contrived the story, he *had* been using Andrea. His only concern had been to present a likely excuse for his presence, but he hated to admit as much to her. "I don't look at it that way. It seems to me it could be of mutual benefit to us. It's a cover for our reasons for being in the city."

"Then you will act as my escort?" Andrea asked in surprise.

He was in too deep to get out now, Eric thought. Besides, until Diego showed up, he had time on his hands. As long as he could get away every day at siesta time, why not? So far, he had enjoyed Andrea's company. "I said I would, didn't I?"

"That was when you were still trying to convince me you had lied for my benefit," Andrea pointed out.

"I *will* escort you about the city," Eric promised. Then he hastily added, "within reason, of course. I have things I need to do, besides waiting for my generator to arrive."

"Of course," Andrea agreed, hardly believing her good luck. Not only would she have a knowledgeable American to escort her, relieving her of the chore of having to struggle with conversing in a foreign language, but she had a guide, a very handsome one. Then, realizing that she was actually becoming attracted to the tall, broad-shouldered engineer, she was horrified. She had sworn to put her journalism career before everything. There was no place for romance in her life. Reaffirming her vow, she stuck out her hand and said in a very businesslike manner, "Well, good evening, Eric. I'll see you tomorrow. Where shall we meet? Here in the lobby?"

Eric looked at the hand in a mixture of surprise and disbelief, then took Andrea's arm and drew her close to his side. "Have you forgotten you have a role to play? Do you really think your fiancé would say goodnight by shaking hands in the lobby? Hardly! I'll walk you to your room."

Andrea was a little more than disconcerted at the turn of events as Eric walked her across the lobby. With her arm locked tightly against his chest, she could feel the hard muscles there, as well as the heat that radiated from his body. Both gave her a peculiar feeling in the pit of her stomach. She didn't like it. "Why did you have to tell that colonel I was your fiancée?" she asked irritably. "Why not your sister, or cousin?"

Eric had no idea why he had said fiancée. The word had slipped out. "I guess because I thought it would be more believable. A sister or cousin didn't seem as likely to ignore my warnings and throw caution to the wind as a fiancée might."

Unfortunately, Andrea had to agree. A woman being ruled by her heart, particularly one who might be beginning to feel a little neglected by her future husband, would be much more likely to do something rash than one who wasn't as emotionally involved. She wouldn't risk her life to see a brother or cousin, either, but a lover, particularly if he was this man? No sooner had the thought crossed Andrea's mind than she regretted it. She was finding it awfully hard to deny how appealing she found Eric. Not only was he handsome and interesting, but he seemed to exude masculinity, strangely even more than the rugged Western men she had grown up with. He wore his maleness like a mantle, as proudly as any king wore his rich robes, and he was much more polished. And then there was that air of mystery about him, that aura of danger. That's why Andrea had suspected he might be a gunrunner.

"What floor are you on?" Eric asked.

"The third." As they approached the elevator, Andrea asked, "Do you mind if we take the stairs?"

"No, but why?"

There was still a lot of country in Andrea, despite the fact that she had attended an Eastern college and had worked in New York City for several years. She didn't trust newfangled machinery. "That wire cage makes me feel like a trapped animal."

"Oh? Not because the cable might snap and the elevator fall?"

Andrea hated to admit she was afraid of anything after she had brazenly told Eric just the opposite. "Well, I never thought of that. I suppose there is that possibility."

Eric saw right through Andrea and he thought her dissembling amusing. It was also nice to know that she wasn't the Amazon she pretended to be. Although he was coming to admire her intelligence and gutsy manner, Eric was male to the bone. Like all men, he felt he had to be bigger and braver than his female counterpart. After all, that was the male's designated purpose in life—to protect—wasn't it?

As Eric and Andrea walked down the dim hallway on the second floor, Eric became aware of Andrea's scent. He seriously doubted that it came from a bottle. The faint natural smell did strange things to him. His heart beat a little faster; his breath came a bit shorter. From the corner of his eye, his gaze swept the length of her, pausing just a fraction of a moment at her bosom, then again at the curve of her neck. Then he noticed her ear, nestled in the soft puff of her golden hair. He had never seen such a dainty, sweet-shaped ear. The longer he looked at it, the more enticing it seemed. Suddenly, he had the urge to kiss it, to slip his tongue inside. His unbidden desire made an entirely different part of his anatomy respond, catching him totally off guard and making him miss a step.

When Eric tripped slightly, Andrea said, "Oh, I should have warned you. Be careful on this rug. This morning I noticed it was loose."

Eric was glad for the excuse for his clumsiness. He

tried to will the arousal away, but his body refused to obey his brain, to his utter frustration. When they reached the door to Andrea's room, she reached into her reticule and pulled out the key. He took it from her over her objections and unlocked the door, needing to be in control at least of that.

As the door swung open, Andrea said sharply, "I'm perfectly capable of opening my own door!" Then spying a piece of paper on the floor, she asked, "What's that?"

Eric bent and picked the paper up, then held it towards one of the dim hall lights so he could read it. "It's a flyer advertising the bullfights this Sunday. Mazzantini, the famous gentleman bullfighter from Spain, is in town."

"I've never seen a bullfight," Andrea said excitedly, stepping back into the hallway and looking down at the flyer in Eric's hand. "Do you think we could go?"

"I wouldn't advise it. It's rather brutal. The bulls are killed, you know, after being more or less tortured. Besides, I doubly advise against it right now. The spectacle seems to stir up the crowds. It arouses their blood lust. There are more riots and fights following a bullfight than at any other time, and considering the high level of bad feelings against us, I think it would be sheer folly for two Americans to show up at an event that will draw practically every Spaniard in the city."

"But I read just before I left the States that Commodore Sigsbee, from the *Maine,* went to the bullfights last Sunday."

"He did. He asked General Parrado, who's been left in charge here since Weyler was recalled, if he could go. The general wasn't too happy about it, for the same reason I told you, but he agreed. Luckily nothing happened. The Americans were tolerated, probably only because of the armed guards Parrado ordered. But the Americans were clearly unwelcome. In view of how tense things are here, I think it was stupid of Sigsbee to even ask."

"Well, he's probably like me," Andrea answered defensively. "He probably doesn't realize how touchy the Spanish are right now." She paused, then said, "I'd love to be able to interview Sigsbee. When you accosted me and kissed me, I was wondering if there was any way I could get to the *Maine* and interview the commodore."

"Kissed you?" Eric asked in surprise. Then he shook his dark head and said, "I wasn't kissing you. I was trying to silence you. A kiss is an entirely different matter."

Why had she said kiss, Andrea thought. Why not just accost? But she knew why. All the way down the hall, she had been wondering if Eric would kiss her good-night. If he did, would it be because he liked her? Or was he keeping up the pretense of being her future husband? Now, she felt guilty, like a child caught with her hand in the cookie jar. Flustered, she answered, "Well, I know that! I just didn't know what else to call it."

Now that Andrea had brought it up, Eric found himself very much wanting to kiss her, under any pretext he could find. "No, I don't think you do know the difference between a kiss and what I was doing."

There was just enough of a hint of challenge in Eric's words to make Andrea rise to the bait. "I do too know the difference! I've been kissed before!"

Eric stepped closer, lightly pinning Andrea to the wall behind her. "Have you?"

Eric's voice had slipped an octave lower. His rough baritone sent a little shiver of delicious anticipation through Andrea. She was acutely aware of his muscular body pressed against hers. "Why, of course I have!" she answered, a little breathlessly.

"But not by me," Eric answered, slipping his arms about her. "I think I need to show you the difference."

It seemed an eternity to Andrea before his lips touched hers. Belatedly, she thought to object, or at least make some pretense to, but the feel of his mouth against hers, his lips brushing, nipping, softly testing was incredibly thrilling. Shivers ran through her, and her knees were so weak she wondered if they could support her. Then when his tongue glazed her bottom lip, her legs didn't support her. They buckled, and she made a wild grab for his broad shoulders.

Eric pulled Andrea into a tighter embrace, molding their long bodies together. His lips were still coaxing, teasing, his tongue still flicking, tormenting her, making her want something more. Then Eric gave her what she unknowingly desired as he slipped his tongue inside her mouth, sliding along the length of hers, tasting her sweetness. The world seemed to spin, and somewhere in a haze, Andrea realized she had never been kissed this way before, so totally, so masterfully, not by any man. Now she knew what it meant to be kissed until she was breathless, until her lungs felt as if they were on fire and would burst. She didn't want him to stop. It was absolutely wonderful! She pressed even closer, thrilling to feel his hard chest against her soft breasts and to feel the bulging muscles beneath his clothing where her hands lay on his shoulders. Her legs trembled; her bones seemed to melt; her fingertips tingled. A low, strangled moan rose in her throat.

Her moan brought Eric to his senses. What in hell was he doing? he thought. He hadn't meant to kiss her so passionately, but once she was in his arms, he hadn't been able to help himself. Where was his usual iron control tonight? He had to stop. Now! Before it was too late. Andrea was independent and gutsy, but he knew instinctively that she was a lady to the bone. Why, they hardly knew each other, and he was taking liberties reserved for a lover or, worse yet, a tramp.

Eric released Andrea so abruptly that she would have fallen if she hadn't reached out and supported herself on the wall. His breath was uneven and his voice husky as he asked, "What time should I pick you up tomorrow morning?"

Eric knew that the question sounded stupid after such a passionate kiss. But he couldn't begin to explain or understand his powerful attraction. He was determined he wasn't going to apologize, because deep down it had seemed so natural, so right.

Eric needn't have worried. The transition from hot passion to cold reality was too sudden for Andrea. She was still dazed. "What?"

"I asked what time I should pick you up in the morning. I promised to escort you around the city, remember?"

"Oh, yes," Andrea muttered, vaguely remembering something to that effect. "Is nine too early for you?"

"Not at all. I'll see you tomorrow, then. Good night."

As Andrea watched Eric walk away, she wondered

what had happened. Had he really kissed her, or had she just imagined it? He certainly didn't act as if anything had happened. Had she been temporarily lost in romantic fantasies? But if that was the case, why were her lips still tingling?

Chapter 4

When Eric and Andrea were seated at breakfast the next morning, Andrea alluded to the evening before. She asked, "Was there anything in that after-dinner coffee we had yesterday? A liqueur perhaps?"

"No. Why do you ask?"

Andrea was still trying to figure out if the kiss had been a figment of her imagination. If Eric had seemed too casual last night for it to be true, he was downright aloof this morning. "I just thought there might be," she answered. "I slept sounder than I ever have."

Andrea's fabrication didn't help Eric's disposition. He had hardly slept at all. In retrospect, he had realized that he might have dug a hole for himself in promising to escort Andrea about the city. His unwanted attraction to her could make things difficult. Above all, he had to keep his mind on his business. A romantic interlude of any kind was out of the question. In truth, he was a little puzzled at her appeal. She wasn't the most beautiful woman he had ever seen, nor the most amicable, with her annoying independence and sharp tongue. But he was drawn to her. He could hardly wait to see her this morning. His eagerness irritated him and added to his ill-humor. If he could have reneged on his promise, he would have done so, but he knew Andrea wouldn't stand for it. Besides, he never broke his word. However, if she should change her mind—"I hope you have your plans for the day figured out. There's no need to waste my time any more than necessary."

If there had been any doubt in Andrea's mind that Eric might be less than enchanted at being with her, his rude words would have wiped them out. She was both hurt and angry. Her anger came rapidly to the fore, and she answered sharply, "Yes, I have, and there's no need for you to act so testy! You came up with that ridiculous story, not I. I'd be quite willing to find another guide, if you want to explain to Colonel Reyes why another man is escorting me about town after you were so anxious to see me."

He really *had* dug a hole for himself, Eric thought glumly. "I said I would do it, but I never said I would like it."

"No, you didn't!" Andrea retorted, "and for your information, I don't care for it either. I'd much rather spend my time with a guide who at least has the decency to be civil. But I wasn't given a choice in the matter, if you'd be so kind as to remember."

God, she was beautiful with her color up and her black eyes flashing, Eric thought. Then he answered, "Fine. Now that we've established how we both feel about the matter, could you be so kind as to tell me where you plan to go?"

Andrea forced her anger down with great difficulty and answered, "I thought we could go back to the harbor. I'd like to see if I can board the *Maine* and get an interview with Commodore Sigsbee."

And how would he explain that little lovely to Reyes, who undoubtedly had men doing surveillance on the ship? Eric thought. But then, why not tell her the truth? "You can forget that. The *Maine* is under tight security. No one has been allowed on her, except for the Spanish officials who toured her, and naturally Sigsbee couldn't refuse them. After all, it is their harbor. But there were armed guards stationed at their side every inch of the way."

"Oh, that's just great!" Andrea grumbled. "I can't get to the rebels; I can't get into one of the *reconcentración* camps, and I can't get to Sigsbee. What else could I possibly write about?" She paused for a second, then said, "Just show me around the city. Maybe I'll see something that will give me another idea for a story."

Eric hired a small open carriage and drove Andrea about La Habana—the Grand City—as it was called by Spanish and Cubans alike. There were many broad plazas, into which narrow, cobbled streets emptied. The plaza almost invariably had either a statue of some famous Spaniard, or a fountain at its center. Many of the houses in the city came right up to the street. Typically, they were two-storied structures, painted in pastel colors, with small iron-grilled balconies on the upper stories, some so close Andrea imagined their owners could lean over and shake hands. In the wealthier sections, the houses were set back from the streets among lush tropical gardens. All of the homes had arched windows, massive, intricately carved doors, red-tiled roofs, and decorative balconies. The style was typically Spanish, but many houses also had towering marble columns and sweeping flights of stairs leading to broad verandas, reminiscent of Greek architecture.

They drove past the governor's palace and several other government buildings. The red-and-yellow Spanish flags were snapping in the brisk breeze above them. Then the couple stopped and went into the nearby cathedral. Andrea had never been in a place of worship anything like it. The church she had attended as a child had been a small wooden structure, stuck in the middle of the prairie. The building served as a school during the middle of the week. In Havana, the cathedral, built along with the palace over a hundred years before, was richly appointed and massive. Everything seemed to be gilded, the rows of columns on each side, the statues, the altar, the towering dome. But the trappings did not impress Andrea so much as the spiritual aura that filled the building—its hush, its flickering candles, its spears of colored lights coming through the stained glass windows, its scent of incense mixed with must, its smattering of worshipers kneeling with heads bowed in supplication, although there was no service taking place. She left feeling subdued and filled with a strange peacefulness.

At Eric's insistence, they retired to the hotel and their separate rooms during siesta. Andrea assumed it was in respect of the Cuban custom. She couldn't imagine anyone as vital and robust as the engineer feeling in need of a midday rest. Since they had reached a silent agreement of cool civility, she didn't object too strenuously, for fear of ruining their fragile relationship.

That afternoon, Eric drove her to the business district. Two- and three-story buildings housed restaurants and elegant small shops as well as other businesses. Then he drove her to San Rafeal Street and took her through Fin de Seglo, a magnificent store that had been built almost a decade before. Not only was the establishment comparable to the best department stores in New York, but the customers were stylishly dressed, right down to the young girls in their ruffled skirts and wide sashes. The only difference seemed to be the language that was being spoken.

As she and Eric drove back to the hotel, Andrea remarked, "It's hard to believe there's a war going on in this country. Everything seems so quiet, so normal."

"That's what Fredrick Remington wired Hearst after he had been here a few days. He said he couldn't illustrate the atrocities he'd been sent to cover, because there wasn't anything going on. Hearst wired him to stay put. He'd provide the war."

"That sounds just like that warmonger!" Andrea responded angrily, then asked in puzzlement, "But where did you hear that tale?"

"I was in the bar at the Inglaterra and overheard some of the reporters talking about it. The hotel is a gathering-place for all Americans, businessmen as well as journalists."

"That must have been before that disgusting story Hearst ran on the woman the Spaniards suspected of being a spy. I'm sure you saw it."

"No, I didn't. I spend the better part of my time off in the mountains, remember?"

"Well, it was another of Hearst's typical shockers. Remington sketched a young naked girl being searched by Spanish authorities on the open deck of the ship she was taking to the United States. The pose was from the rear, but the sketch had its desired effect. The American public, particularly the women, were outraged. When the woman the story was written about arrived in New York and saw how it was portrayed in the newspaper, she was mortified. It was true she was searched, but in one of the cabins by a matron, and she had never been stripped naked. Naturally, Hearst never bothered to print a correction."

A moment later, Eric turned the carriage and drove down the wide street beside the harbor. Andrea had to keep her hand on her hat to prevent it from flying off. "Goodness, it's much windier today, isn't it?"

"We get a lot of these brisk north winds in the winter. *El Norte,* the Cubans call the wind."

"And it never gets any colder than this?" Andrea asked in amazement. It had been snowing when she had left New York.

"Very rarely."

Andrea looked out at the harbor. The wind was kicking up whitecaps on the entire bay. She spotted a lighter coming from the *Maine.* She watched as it crossed the water, then put in at a small dock beside the street they were traveling on. Seeing a white-clad sailor helping a passenger from the boat, her eyes widened. Then she turned to Eric and said in an accusing tone of voice, "I thought you said they didn't allow visitors on the *Maine.*"

"They don't."

"Then who is that woman? She sure isn't a member of the crew."

Eric turned his gaze from the street to the lighter, then responded, "I have no idea who she is, or why an exception was made in her case, but I do know one thing. At her age, it couldn't have been for immoral reasons."

Andrea didn't ask for an explanation. She knew sailors were notorious for trying to slip prostitutes aboard ship, particularly in foreign ports. As Andrea passed the lighter, she took a closer look at the woman, then exclaimed, "I recognize her! That's Clara Barton. I completely forgot she was down here distributing the food and supplies that the American Red Cross had collected for the *reconcentrados.*"

Eric scoffed. "Yes, the biggest waste of American effort and money I've ever seen. As soon as the Red Cross pulls out, the Spanish army will confiscate everything."

"They wouldn't dare!" Andrea objected.

"Who's going to stop them? Have you forgotten that their soldiers are starving too?"

"I still say they wouldn't dare. That food was sent to starving civilians. To do such a dastardly thing would bring the wrath of the whole world down on them."

Andrea turned in her seat and saw Clara Barton climb in a carriage. "Turn around!" she ordered Eric.

"What for?"

"I want you to follow Miss Barton's carriage, so I can find out where she's staying. Maybe I can get an interview with her."

"I can't turn around in this busy street."

Andrea ignored his objection and said, "Hurry, before the carriage disappears!"

"I told you, I can't turn right now. Besides, I think it's rude to follow someone."

Andrea righted herself on the seat, reached across, and yanked the reins from Eric, then turned the carriage so sharply that it teetered on one wheel for a moment. With an expertise that amazed Eric, she maneuvered the vehicle into the traffic going the opposite way—but not without throwing a few of the drivers and their teams into a panic.

When everything had settled down and they were moving at a steady clip, Eric took the reins back, saying between clenched teeth, "Don't ever try a fool trick like that again. You could have gotten us killed, to say nothing of the people in those other carriages."

"They weren't in any danger. No one was. They just thought they were. Why, I can drive circles around all of them."

Eric didn't dispute it. He'd seen the way she had handled the carriage, after he had gotten over his initial fright, that is. "Where did you learn to drive like that?"

"Back in Wyoming, except it was a buckboard, and not a carriage. This thing handles easier."

"No wonder. You can pull a reckless stunt like that out in the wide-open spaces."

"I wasn't talking about the wide-open spaces. I was talking about driving through town on Saturday night, when everyone was liquored up. You had to make a quick run for it, because there were bullets flying around. It took a little skill at that speed, weaving around men fighting in the streets, or drunks passed out, as well as cowhands racing their horses. All the while I was trying to dodge wild bullets, wagons trying to get to the other end of town, and bog holes so deep you could bury a calf in them."

"Why were you driving? Wasn't there anyone with you?"

"Sure there was. I always tagged along with my brothers on Saturday to buy supplies, but by that time of the day they were in no condition to drive. Why, we would have had a wreck for sure."

Eric found himself a little irritated at Andrea's brothers. He thought they should have taken their responsibilities a little more seriously. At least one of them should have made a point of staying sober. What if she had been accosted by a drunken cowhand? Who would have protected her? Then Eric realized that Andrea probably didn't need protecting. She was so independent and self-sufficient. It was her wild brothers' fault, Eric thought sourly. If they had treated more like a female, maybe she'd act like one. "I guess your family approves of your being a journalist."

"Certainly not!" Andrea paused, then shrugged her shoulders and said, "But then, it was always that way. They had their own ideas of what I should be, particularly my mom and dad. I was their only little girl, and they wanted me to do all those silly little girl things, but I couldn't. I hated dolls, and embroidering, and practicing on the piano."

"Piano?" Eric interjected in surprise.

"Yes, the piano. They had one shipped from back East just for me, at considerable cost. Then they hired the piano player from one of the saloons in town to come out and teach me the rudiments and how to read music. I hated it. I wanted to be out doing all those exciting things my big brothers were doing, and I did, too. I snuck off every chance I got. My parents and I were always butting heads over me being such a tomboy. Even my brothers didn't completely approve, particularly when I got older. They thought I should act more ladylike. When I decided to go East to study to be a schoolteacher, they were all tickled pink that I'd finally come to my senses. But I didn't really want to be a schoolmarm. That was too dull for me. Then, just for the heck of it, I took a course in journalism. The professor said I had a real knack for it. I always did have an inquisitive mind. I was hooked from then on." Andrea craned her neck, then said, "They're turning up there."

"Yes, I see," Eric answered, irritably. God, didn't she give him credit for anything?

They followed Clara Barton and her party a relatively short distance to where the vehicle came to a halt beside a house. "Pull over and stop," Andrea directed Eric.

"Why?"

"Because I want to catch her before she gets inside."

"You're going to pounce on her, right here in the street? That's invading her privacy."

"It is not! She's a public figure working for a public cause. Now pull over!"

"No, I won't! If it isn't invading her privacy, it's rude. You can come back tomorrow and do it properly."

"And just how is that?" Andrea asked tartly.

"Ask her secretary for an appointment. I'm sure she has one."

"You're darn-tootin' she does! And what do you think that secretary's job is? To keep journalists away, that's what!"

Andrea made a grab for the reins, but Eric was

expecting it. He jerked them away, saying angrily, "I told you not to try that again. Dammit, I'm driving this vehicle!"

Andrea glanced over her shoulder and saw Clara walking to the door. She decided to try another approach. "Please?"

"No!"

Andrea considered jumping, but Eric must have suspected as much, because he deliberately sped up. Seeing the pavement flying by, Andrea knew she would be risking breaking something if she took the plunge. Deciding against it, she jerked around and sat rigid, staring straight ahead.

Eric could feel the fury radiating from her. "There's no need to pout. I'll bring you back the first thing in the morning."

But Andrea wasn't mollified. She maintained an icy silence for the rest of the ride back to the hotel. She curtly informed Eric that she'd eat in her room that night—alone. Then she excused herself.

As she walked across the marble floor of the hotel lobby, Eric watched, wondering if she was spoiled or just naturally willful. Either way, she was a handful.

Over the breakfast table the next morning, Eric found Andrea just as frigid as she had been when he had left her the previous day. She could freeze hell if she put her mind to it, he thought in exasperation. Then he decided the best approach would be to act as if he hadn't even noticed.

After breakfast, he drove her to the house Clara Barton was residing in while she was in Cuba. He parked the carriage, and waited in the vehicle while Andrea went inside. A scant ten minutes later, Andrea emerged, and Eric knew by one glance that she was furious. Her color was up and her dark eyes were flashing. Her hips were swinging provocatively as she flounced up to him. As usual, Eric thought her both magnificent and sexually exciting.

Eric jumped from the carriage and made an effort to help Andrea alight, but she jerked her arm away from him and scampered up. Eric climbed in and sat beside her, then asked, "What happened?"

Andrea turned to him and spat, "Just what I feared would happen! Her secretary turned me down. Damn you! I hope you're satisfied! Because of your stubbornness yesterday, I've lost the only possible story left for me here."

Eric ignored her cursing him. His full attention was on the tears he saw swimming in her eyes. Was she so disappointed, he wondered, that she was on the verge of crying? Or was she just so angry? Either way, her tears had a profound effect on him. He wanted to take her into his arms and comfort her, yet he knew he didn't dare. Upset as she was with him, she was liable to slug him. "I'm sorry. I really thought all one had to do was ask for an appointment, that if she was going refuse an interview, she would have done so personally."

Andrea could tell by the expression on Eric's face that he was sincere. Grudgingly, she said with a sigh, "No, I never got past her secretary. He said she's much too busy to be bothered with interviews."

"To tell you the truth, that surprises me. I should think the more publicity she gets for her organization, the better, since the Red Cross is funded by public donations."

"She has her own journalist who travels with her and handles all that. He's right there beside her at every disaster and gets the stories first hand. I understand he's a charter member of the Red Cross. Lucky stiff! Charter member or not, I'd give my right arm for that job."

"You might do better freelancing," Eric pointed out, "financially, that is. I don't imagine the Red Cross pays its employees very high salaries."

"Anything would be better than what I'm making right now, which is nothing so far," Andrea answered bleakly. She paused for a moment, then said, "Damn that secretary!"

"It's probably not his fault. He's probably following Miss Barton's instructions. And if she is too busy for interviews, she would have probably turned you down, too, even if you had gotten to talk to her yesterday," Eric pointed out, relieved to remove some the guilt he was feeling.

Andrea didn't agree. Clara Barton had a reputation for helping people who were down on their luck. Her organization was full of people she'd taken in and given jobs. Andrea had hoped that if she explained that she was a journalist in need of a break, Miss Barton would accommodate her. She still thought she had a chance if she could just get past that secretary.

When Andrea didn't answer, Eric asked, "Do you want to continue your tour of the city?"

"Why not? I don't have anything else to do," Andrea answered distractedly. Her busy mind was already delving into new possibilities for obtaining the interview.

Eric drove them to a part of the city he had not yet shown Andrea, and as they turned on one street, they were stopped by a crowd of people blocking their way and watching a disturbance taking place in a building to one side. Through the wide broken window of the establishment, Andrea could see furniture being viciously smashed with axes, and she saw papers from file cabinets being strewn everywhere. "Why doesn't someone stop those men?" she asked, outraged. "They're destroying that place!"

"Keep your voice down," Eric cautioned. "They aren't criminals. They're soldiers!" He looked over his shoulder, saw that traffic was piled up behind them. He muttered a curse.

Andrea glanced at the sign hanging over the building, then exclaimed in surprise, "Why, that's a newspaper!"

"Yes. Now, dammit, sit still and be quiet!"

Ordinarily, Andrea would have balked at such a brusque command, but the Eric she saw at that moment was someone she had only gotten only a brief glimpse of, on the day he had snatched the jasmine from her. With his blue eyes glittering like shards of broken glass, his chin set like granite, his lips compressed, he was a man in absolute control. He would obviously tolerate no disobedience. The power and fierce determination radiating from him were almost smothering and more than a little frightening. Andrea watched in frustrated silence while the office was made a shambles and the expensive printing machine was smashed beyond repair. Then, as three men, battered and bleeding, were led at gunpoint from the building, she couldn't hold back any longer. "Where are they taking them?" she asked. "What will happen to them?"

"Sssh!" Eric hissed.

It was almost as if Andrea's questions were a signal of some sort. The suppressed fury of the crowd suddenly erupted. An angry roar rose from their throats, and bricks and stones, as well as curses, were hurled at the soldiers. Gunshots pierced the air, followed by screams of pain. More soldiers appeared on the scene, seemingly from out of nowhere, their boots were drumming on the cobblestones as they ran. Cubans tore from the surrounding shops, wielding clubs, bottles, and machetes, yelling, *"Cuba Libre!"* and *"Grito de Baire!"*

"Dammit!" Eric muttered, and then, without ceremony, he shoved Andrea from the seat to the floorboard and said in a tense tone of voice, "Stay down there, until we get out of this mess."

Eric cracked the whip over the horse's head, but the animal didn't need any urging. The gunshots and shouting, combined with the smells of blood and gunpowder, had terrified it. It was as anxious to be away from the scene as Eric. The horse tore off through the crowd, sending more than one person diving to the side to keep from being bowled over. Then the horse just barely avoided a head-on collision with another carriage, and swerved. Spying a break in the mob, Eric sawed on the reins to the left, and the horse dashed through the clearing, but not before a bullet whizzed by Eric's ear.

From the moment Eric had pushed her down, Andrea had struggled to get up—to no avail, since he held her down with his foot on her back. After they had put several blocks between them and the scene, he released the pressure, and with one hand helped her regain her seating. Seeing how furious she was, he said, "Sorry I was so rough, but I figured the safest place for you was down there."

"I'm not mad about being treated so roughly, I'm mad about not being able to see it all!" Andrea responded hotly. "I *am* a reporter, remember?"

"I just wanted to protect you."

"I don't need protecting! I told you, I'm used to danger."

Eric was determined not to apologize. Protecting her came as naturally to him as kissing her. Thankfully, Andrea didn't demand an apology. She was too full of questions. She brushed the dirt from her skirt and asked, "Why did they destroy that newspaper? Was it publishing pro-independence material?"

"Not at all. It supported autonomy."

Andrea frowned. "But that's just asking for some say-so, some meaningful representation in how they're governed. Why, if that's granted, Spain wouldn't even have to give up the colony. As a matter of fact, I've heard rumors that Spain is considering doing just that, offering autonomy to Cuba."

"The rebels won't accept it. Five, ten years ago, they would have, but too much blood has been spilled for them to accept anything less than full independence."

"But that still doesn't explain the needless violence we just saw. Why did the Spaniards react so strongly to a policy that their own government may offer the Cubans?"

"The army and the *pensinsulares* feel that any concession, including autonomy, is selling them out. They feel strongly about keeping things as they are in Cuba—as strongly as the rebels feel about complete independence."

"What does *Grito de Baire* mean?"

"It was the rallying cry at the first battle of the revolution at Grito, a town in eastern Cuba. That's where Martí lost his life. Since then, it's pretty much become the battle cry for freedom."

"It all happened so suddenly," Andrea remarked, having had no idea of the crowd's temper until it erupted. The people watching had been so quiet, so still.

"Now you know what I mean about this country being a tinderbox. I only hope that incident doesn't touch off more riots. Just in case, we'll stay at the hotel for the rest of the day."

Andrea scowled. That didn't suit her at all.

Chapter 5

Eric took Andrea back to their lodgings. After they had agreed to meet in the dining room for an early dinner, he left the hotel and headed for the park by the harbor. Again, Diego didn't appear. Eric returned to the hotel and pondered whether to abort the mission or not. He would hate to. General Calaxio García had an extremely important message for him to relay to General Máximo Gómez, Cuba's *general en jefe:* an urgent plea for the chief commander to send him troops—if he could possibly get them through the Spanish eastern *trocha*—to help with the siege García had laid at Victoria de las Tunas, a heavily fortified town in eastern Cuba. After several hours of deliberating, Eric decided to wait a little longer. Deep down, he knew that Andrea played as much a part in that decision as his dedication to the Cuban cause.

At the agreed time, Eric went to the dining room. Andrea was not there. He waited for thirty minutes, then went to her room. When she didn't answer his knock, he became alarmed and forced open the door to the empty room. He rushed downstairs and asked the desk clerk if she had left any message for him. There was none, but the clerk did volunteer that he had seen the young lady leaving the hotel a few hours before.

Eric was furious. Obviously, Andrea had taken off on her own. He had no idea where in the big, sprawling city she had gone. He was also terrified, an emotion that was totally foreign to him. Oh, he had known fear before—he had fought in too many battles not to have—but not this kind. This powerful fear for another left him feeling helpless and impotent. He turned and headed for the door. Then he came to an abrupt halt as he spied her hurrying across the lobby to him.

Andrea knew that Eric was angry. He had a thunderous expression on his face. The look made him appear formidable and dangerous. She forced back the little tingle of fear she felt, and said brightly, "Good afternoon. I hope I didn't keep you waiting too long, but—"

"Where in hell have you been?" Eric ground out through clenched teeth, catching her arm with one hand and dragging her closer. He almost overturned a potted palm.

Despite his dangerous appearance, Andrea bristled at his tone of voice. She jerked her arm away and answered coldly, "I was going to tell you, before you so rudely interrupted me."

"Don't try to distract me by shifting the blame to me. I have a right to be angry. I warned you it was dangerous out there, particularly today. And you deliberately ignored my warning. You could have been killed!"

"I was never in any danger. I—"

Eric cut across her words, saying harshly, "You willfully disobeyed me!"

"Disobeyed you?" Andrea asked sharply, her own rage coming to the surface. "How dare you! Who do you think you are? I'm not answerable to you. You don't own me. No one does, or ever will!"

Andrea whirled around and walked angrily towards the stairs.

Watching her, Eric knew he was overreacting. He also knew why. He genuinely cared about her. Dammit, she was getting to him in too many ways. In a few quick strides he caught up with her and asked, "Have you forgotten our pose? Don't you think your fiancé would be a little angry if you endangered your life?"

Andrea jerked open the door to the stairs and started up them before she answered, "Oh, I'm sure he would, which is exactly why I'll never get myself into that foolish trap. I'll never marry. No man is ever going to tell me what to do. Ever! I control my life. Me and me alone."

Because the stairs were so narrow, Eric was forced to walk one step behind her. Her vow that she would never marry disturbed him, but before he could make any response, Andrea turned suddenly, bringing them eye to eye. "And don't try to use our pose as an engaged couple as an excuse for your behavior. I know you're not pretending just for the sake of anyone who might be watching. You're really angry. And I know why. Because you're arrogant and overbearing. You're simply not used to having anyone defy you in any way."

Dammit, why did she have to be so appealing when she was angry? Eric thought in frustration. It was all he could do to keep from taking her in his arms and kissing her. Then, deciding that it was better to have her think him an arrogant bastard than know the embarrassing truth—that he was falling for her despite himself—he answered, "Yes, I am accustomed to being in total control, but that doesn't discount the fact that for you to go out by yourself, particularly today, was dangerous. Where did you go, anyway?"

Considering how angry she was, Andrea ordinarily wouldn't have answered, but she was too excited about her success to hold back. Besides, he had admitted the truth about his anger and himself, which surprised her. "I went back to Miss Barton's residence and got my interview."

"How did that happen?"

Eric's obvious astonishment only increased Andrea's smug pleasure at her accomplishment. "I remembered seeing her appointment book open on the desk while I was talking to her secretary. I knew she was going to lunch with the American consul. I hired a hack, and had him drive me to her home. I waited until she returned, then approached her before she got inside. It was just as I thought it would be. She's notorious for taking in former prostitutes, drunks, and misfits, you know. I guess I fit into the latter category. As soon as she found out that I was a struggling journalist trying to compete against a bunch of arrogant men, she agreed. We have a lot in common. She's just as independent, and determined to succeed as I am. Why, she even started out like me. In fact, it's amazing how similar our backgrounds are. She was a tomboy, too, who hated dolls and loved horseback riding. And she studied to be a schoolteacher just like me, except she actually taught in a little country school. She said didn't regret it either. That's where she learned to handle difficult males, keeping those big, smart-alecky farm boys in line. We talked for quite a while, not only about her mission here, but other things. Did you realize she's seventy-six years old? You'd never guess it. Why, her servant, who served us tea, said she used to sit on the floor to organize her papers until a few years ago. And she's still agile and bursting with energy, a most amazing woman."

Andrea turned and walked up the stairs. Eric decided to ignore her attacks on men. It was useless to offer any defense. No matter what he said, it wouldn't change Andrea's poor opinion of men. He followed her, asking, "Then you knew when you returned to the hotel that you were going to go back, despite the violence you saw this morning?"

"Yes."

"Why didn't you ask me to take you?"

"Because I knew you wouldn't have agreed. You were convinced I couldn't get an interview with her."

Eric didn't bother to argue. She was right.

Andrea opened the door to the landing on her floor, and as she walked down the hall, Eric stepped up beside her and commented, "So now you've got your story on the *reconcentración* camps."

Andrea frowned and came to a stop. "I have the facts, yes. According to Clara, it's much worse than anyone in the States ever imagined."

"Clara?" Eric asked in surprise.

"Yes, she insisted that I call her by her first name. She said I reminded her so much of herself that she couldn't help but feel close to me. I admit it felt strange, particularly in view of her age, but I agreed."

It appeared that Andrea had not only been successful in obtaining an interview, but she had gained a powerful friend, whom Eric wasn't too sure he approved of. Andrea didn't need anyone encouraging her independence. She already took too many risks.

Unaware of Eric's thoughts, Andrea continued, "Clara said that over half a million people were put into the camps, and over 300,000 have died of disease and starvation. It seems unbelievable."

Eric believed it. Only, he'd put the death toll even higher. He had seen some of the camps in the eastern part of the country, where the plan had been initiated. They were places straight from hell, and Miss Barton hadn't even gotten a glimpse of them yet.

"Something else which she pointed out, that I hadn't been aware of, is the number of orphans that were left." Andrea continued, "Pitiful children were left to fend for themselves, sleeping in the open, starving, practically naked. She said that's the first thing she did, set up a string of orphanages. But she didn't bring enough food and supplies. She simply wasn't prepared for what she found. She has to go back to the States to collect more. She hopes my story gets published, and that it will be a big help in soliciting money, except . . ." Andrea's voice trailed off.

"Except what?" Eric prompted.

"Except I don't know if I've got enough to really give the story the justice it deserves. She gave me facts, plenty of them, and I know her heart goes out to the *reconcentrados,* but the interview lacked . . ."

"Lacked what?"

"Well, it's hard to explain. Passion, I guess. She's

seen so much pain and suffering over the years that I guess she's learned to keep herself at a distance. I guess she has to, to maintain her sanity. I just feel I could portray the situation better if I could see it myself, if I could get closer to experiencing it."

Eric still feared it was a waste of time and money. The Spaniards would confiscate the supplies as soon as the Red Cross left. Then he remembered that Andrea was talking about raising money for more supplies and food, to be delivered in the future. That could take months, and at the rate things were escalating, with the United States becoming more and more involved, the war could be over by then. He certainly couldn't deny that the *reconcentrados* needed every bit of help they could get, and the new Cuban government certainly wouldn't have the money to help them. Memories of the things he had seen in those camps flashed through his mind. Horrible memories would haunt him to his dying day. Suddenly he wanted to help.

Andrea was stunned when Eric abruptly announced, "I may be able to help you after all. I can't get you into one of the camps, but I can get you close to the experience of someone who's been there."

"Who?"

"An old woman who survived two years in one. I think she'll give you an interview, when she realizes it may help others. But you must promise me never to divulge the name of the woman who gave you the information or where she lives. She's an escapee, and if found, she'll be shot."

"I'd never divulge information of that nature," Andrea answered resentfully. "No respectable journalist would."

"Still, I'd like a promise," Eric persisted.

"All right, I promise!" Andrea snapped. She paused thoughtfully for a moment before asking, "Why are you offering to help me now? You've known all along I wanted information on the camps, but you've never mentioned that woman. Why now?"

Eric had more than one motive in offering to help. The *reconcentrados* were part of it. He had been feeling guilty about not trusting Andrea's judgment. He had also come to realize that her endangering herself that afternoon had been his fault. If he'd had more faith in her, she wouldn't have been forced to go against his wishes. Offering to take her to the old woman was his way of trying to make it up to her, but he didn't feel he could admit that to her. It hinted too strongly of feelings he had no damn business having. "I guess I didn't realize until this afternoon how serious you were about getting your story."

"I assume you're referring to my *endangering* myself?"

Eric was hesitant to answer, for fear it would start the argument all over again. She would be insisting she hadn't been in danger, and he would be insisting she had. But there wasn't any way he could avoid it. "Yes."

"Good! Now you know how determined I am to succeed. Nothing is ever going to stop me from getting the material I need for my stories, particularly not a little danger."

To Eric, the answer was far from comforting, and not in the least encouraging. It would take a remarkable man to stand aside while the woman he cared for placed herself in danger, repeatedly—for a newspaper story, no less. He seriously doubted he had it in him. Besides, she had vowed she would never marry, never give any man control over her life, and Eric was a firm believer in the institution of marriage as he knew it. The accepted practice in pretty much the entire world, was—for the man to have absolute authority over his household.

But then, Eric thought, he should be glad their beliefs were so radically different. That would help keep his strange attraction at bay, or at least keep it from going too far.

The next day, Eric drove Andrea into the slums of Havana where the paint on the walls of the buildings was peeling and the underlying adobe was crumbling in many places. Here, the twisted streets were so narrow that the carriage could hardly get through. The streets were dark and forbidding places. The stench of rotting garbage and raw sewage was overpowering.

Then, much to Andrea's relief, they rode into an open area lightly planted with coconut palms. She took in a deep breath of fresh air and looked about her, then asked in surprise, "Isn't that Morro Castle across the bay?"

"Yes."

"Where does this woman live?"

"In one of those little *bohios* up ahead."

Andrea saw a cluster of huts made of bamboo and palm fronds nestled on the rocky cliffs overlooking the entrance to the bay. "I don't remember *bohio* in my Spanish lessons. Is that an African word, too?"

"No, it's Caribbean—from the language of the original inhabitants of this island, the Tainos. It's what they called their huts, and the dwelling places haven't changed much over the years. They named this island Cuba—which means 'central place.' Of course, the Spanish tried to tag their own name on it, but it never stuck. The English and Americans also picked up a few words from the Indians of this area: *canoa,* 'canoe,' *hamaca,* 'hammock,' *huracán,* 'hurricane.'"

"I didn't know that Cuba had had any Indian tribes. I can't recall ever hearing them mentioned in anything I've read."

"Well, they certainly never gained the attention the Aztecs or Incas did, but they were here. Maybe you never heard of them because they weren't here long after the white man came. Unlike many of the other native tribes on this continent, they didn't accept the European interlopers with open arms. When the Spanish landed, the Tainos attacked them. They were swiftly shown the true character of the conquerors. Their chief was burned at the stake and the entire tribe enslaved. By the late 1500s they had been totally exterminated. That's why there is no *mestizo* class here in Cuba, like there is in the rest of Latin America. There was never any intermingling of the two races. Yes, in the case of the Tainos, the Spanish were particularly effective in their genocide," Eric ended caustically.

"Genocide?" Andrea asked in astonishment. "But surely, that's not what the Spanish intended."

"Didn't they? Isn't that what you call the systematic destruction of an entire nation? They wanted to get rid of the Tainos, wipe them off the face of the earth, and they did. Unless you're one of the people that don't consider Indians human beings."

Andrea winced. She was a Westerner to the bone and had no love for Indians, but she didn't go so far as to think them without souls, as some people did. "I consider them human, but the Spanish were at war with the Tainos. You said the Indians attacked them when they landed. That's not genocide."

"I'm sorry, but I happen to believe it is," Eric answered stubbornly, "just as I believe what our government is doing to our Indians is genocide, or damn near it."

"What do you know about Indians?" Andrea asked, her hackles raised. "Where are you from, anyway?"

"Pennsylvania."

"Ah! It's just like I thought! God, I hate you sanctimonious Easterners! Trying to tell us Westerners how to deal with the Indians. What do you know about it? Have you ever been shot at by an Indian, had them slaughter your cattle, burn your home?"

Eric brought the carriage to a halt and turned to Andrea. "No. Have you?"

The direct question took Andrea aback for a moment. Then she answered, "No, but my grandfather did, and they were always stealing our cattle, until they were finally put away on a reservation."

"Ah, yes, a reservation. Have you ever been on one?"

"No. Have you?" Andrea answered, throwing Eric's own words back at him.

"Yes, I have, an Apache reservation in Arizona, when I was working on building a mine nearby. It was a hellhole if I ever saw one, stuck in the middle of desert where nothing would grow except cactus. The place was infested with flies and fleas and scorpions. Disease ran rampant, and Indians who didn't succumb to cholera or smallpox or diphtheria or typhoid were slowly and methodically being starved to death."

"It may be true they're starving, but it's not deliberate on the part of the authorities," Andrea answered defensively. "I refuse to believe that!"

"Do you?" Eric asked sarcastically. "Well, just keep that in mind while you're doing your interview. The Spaniards claim what's happening to the Cubans in the *reconcentración* camps isn't deliberate either, that they had planned, on paper, to care for them."

"And just what is that supposed to mean?"

"That sometimes you can't recognize your own flaws until you see them in someone else."

With that candid observation, Eric turned his attention back to his driving and cracked the reins. As they drove off, Andrea wondered what had gotten into him. It was almost as if he had been deliberately trying to start a fight with her. He was bound to know they'd be at odds in their opinions about Indians. Damn him! He kept her off balance, one minute running hot, the next cold. When he had offered to help her with this story, she'd let her defenses slip, despite all of his arrogance and bossiness. All during breakfast and the trip out here, she had been acutely aware of how appealing he was, how handsome, how utterly masculine, how very exciting. Why, she had been even thinking he could have a charming side, when he put his mind to it. Then he had started all that controversy over the Indians. He was much more complex than she had ever dreamed, and much more exasperating. In fact, he was the most exasperating male she had ever met, and she'd met more than her share of bull-headed men in her lifetime.

Chapter 6

Andrea sat in the carriage and waited while Eric approached the old woman about the interview. Andrea occupied the time studying the *bohio* and wondering what held it together and if the palm-leaf roof actually kept out the rain. She knew hurricanes plagued the island and she marveled that the natives could face such devastating storms in such flimsy structures.

Eric stepped from the *bohio,* ducking his head to keep from hitting the low doorway. He walked up to the carriage and said to Andrea, "She's agreed. You can come in now."

As he helped Andrea alight, she asked, "What is that vine growing all over? Why, almost every hut is covered with it."

"Bougainvillea."

"Does it bloom?"

"Profusely, when everything else blooms, during the rainy season."

"Then that's why I haven't seen anything blooming. It isn't the right season. I wondered about that. The vegetation seemed so lush and green, but there weren't any flowers anywhere, and yet it was so warm."

"It's not the warmth that triggers the blooming, it's the moisture. Oh, a few things bloom at this time of the year, but when the rains come everything that blooms goes berserk, the bougainvillea, the oleander, the frangipani, the flamboyant tree, the *huisache,* even the cactus. Everything seems to be trying to outbloom the other."

"Cactus?" Andrea asked in surprise. "Here in Cuba?"

"Yes. There's quite a bit of it around the coast. You find it even growing out in the jungles sometimes."

Andrea was amazed. She had always thought that cactus grew in only arid climates.

The inside of the *bohío* was dark. The only light entering the structure, came through the cracks between the bamboo. Not until Andrea's eyes adjusted to low light was she able to make out two small rooms, which were bare except for reed mats strewn about the dirt floor and one small table made from bamboo. There was nothing more, except for a few pieces of clothing hanging on one wall. Andrea couldn't imagine living in such austerity.

"María is waiting for us in the kitchen," Eric informed Andrea, leading her through the hut to a roofless, enclosed area at the back of the house.

A dark-skinned woman crouched before an open fire in the enclosure, stirring something in a kettle there. Andrea was a little shocked when she realized that the Cuban was bare breasted. All of the native women she had seen in the city had been appropriately covered. Then, when the woman spied Andrea, she rose. She swept up a naked infant who was playing beside the fire, and she hurried from the enclosure.

Eric tugged gently on Andrea's arm, turning her attention to someone sitting on a mat to one side of the enclosure. He said, "María prefers to stay out here, where the sun can warm her. She says she is always cold now, no matter how hot it may be."

As Eric performed the introductions, Andrea tried to hide her horror, although she knew the bent, grey-haired woman was blind and couldn't see her reaction. The woman's eye sockets were just masses of puckered scar tissue. Andrea had never seen anyone so emaciated. María looked like a skeleton covered with dry, wrinkled skin. Even her color had been diminished to a dull grayishness. Her cheeks were sunken over her toothless mouth and her hands were horribly twisted.

Andrea thanked María for the interview. Then, when asked to have a seat, Andrea sat on a mat across from the old woman and asked her to tell her everything she could remember about her imprisonment, from the beginning to the very end.

María's voice was weak and reedy, but there was obviously nothing wrong with the woman's mind or her memory. She began her story with the day the soldiers came unexpectedly to their farm. Her family was told they would be moved to another place. They could take no clothing, no food with them. When they resisted, her husband was hacked to death with a machete and one son shot. Their farm animals were slaughtered and their home and fields, even the cart they used to carry their produce to the market, were put to the torch. She told how she, her seven children, five in-laws, and four grandchildren were marched to the coast along with other peasant farmers' families through the boiling heat of the summer. Fifteen were drowned in rampaging streams during torrential downpours, including a grandson of hers. People fell by the scores with fevers and were left to die. The entire trail was littered with skeletons, the bones having been picked clean by land crabs.

María continued her story. When the Cubans arrived at the little coastal town that had been evacuated to imprison them, they were put in abandoned warehouses which had no roofs to protect them from the daily downpours. Soon so many people were crowded in, that the buildings could no longer contain them. People spilled out into the courtyards and streets and slept in the open with no covering except the rags on their back. There was never enough food, not even in the beginning. People fought like animals over scraps of garbage that were covered with flies, ate rats if they could get them. There were no toilet facilities. The streets became the latrines. Their stench added to that of sickness and death. During the rainy season people were eaten alive by mosquitoes. Disease ran wild. The Cubans dropped like flies from smallpox, yellow fever, dysentery, cholera. Not a day went by without at least a score of deaths. A flock of black buzzards continuously hovered over the camp. Some were bold enough to swoop down and feed, before they could be chased away by an outraged relative. Every day, the dead were collected, piled on carts and driven into the countryside, to be buried—without benefit of a priest—in shallow common graves.

María hesitated, as if reluctant to continue. Then she told of the horror of having to stand by and watch her twelve-year-old daughter being raped by the guards; then of her shame when the same daughter, who had been so good, so religious, sold her body for scraps of food. She related how one by one all of her relatives died, from either starvation or disease, until only she and her grandson were left. She recalled holding the swollen-bellied boy in her arms while he cried pitifully for food. He couldn't weep because he was so dehydrated and weak, and she prayed for his death, for the release from his suffering. But it took so long, so terribly long.

Again María paused, and Andrea watched as a single tear squeezed through the puckered tissue and trickled down her wrinkled cheek. Tears glistened in Andrea's own eyes as compassion for the woman who had suffered so terribly welled up in her like a tidal wave. She reached over, covered the old woman's cold, gnarled hands with hers, and said in Spanish, "I'm sorry. Please forgive me. I should have never asked you to do this. It's too painful for you. You don't have to continue."

The old woman's head came up like a shot, and Andrea could feel the fierceness in her as she said, "No! I will tell it, and then you will tell the world. That is how it was meant to be. Until today, I did not know why I was spared."

Before Andrea could make any response, María continued her story. She told how she'd had no desire to live. She attempted to escape, thinking being shot would be an easy death, compared to the one that was surely awaiting her. But she wasn't shot. The soldiers who caught her took perverse glee in putting out her eyes with a hot poker instead. For the rest of her miserable life she would grope in darkness. Then a more merciful commandant came to the camp. Once a week, he allowed the *reconcentrados* to go into the countryside to forage for food under armed guard. Occasionally some of María's friends would take her with them, even though, since she couldn't see, she could be of no help. María relished those trips, simply because of the fresh air she could breathe. On one of those excursions, her friends escaped and took María with them on their bid for freedom, despite her pleas to leave her behind for fear she would slow them down and jeopardize everything. They made their way to the jungle, where they were found by Cuban rebels. One of them later slipped her into Havana, where she could live with her distant cousins.

For a moment after María had finished her story, Andrea remained silent. María's mention of foraging in the surrounding countryside had made Andrea wonder why the Spaniards had not allowed the Cubans to grow their own food, if not in the town, then on little plots of land in the countryside. After all, the Cubans were farmers. Surely, the authorities had enough soldiers that they could have put guards around the plots of farmland, if they could guard fifty-mile-long trenches. It was totally unnecessary for the Cubans to have been starved to death.

Almost as if she sensed what Andrea was thinking, María said, "Sometimes, in the camp, we sat and talked about what was being done to us and why. The authorities said we had been brought there to keep us from feeding and sheltering the rebels, to keep our young men from joining them. But we knew there had to be more to it than just keeping us away from the others. A wise one among us finally pointed out the reason. We were hostages. Every one of us had relatives fighting with the rebels, husbands, sons, brothers, cousins, and they knew how terribly we were being treated. The Spaniards were sending them a clear message: give up the fight, and we will give back your people. Continue, and they will die, one by one. But our freedom fighters would not bow to the Spanish pigs," María said proudly, "despite terrible personal sacrifices, they fight on, until we all are either free, or there is no Cuban left."

María's last words rang in Andrea's ears over and over. "No Cuban left." She remembered what Eric had told her about genocide. She feared that what Eric had said was true. What the Spanish had done to the *reconcentrados* had been calculated. It was a horrifying way to win a war. And for what? National pride? She felt sick to her stomach.

Eric stepped forward. He bent and cupped Andrea's elbow in one hand. Lifting her to her feet, he said, "We'd better leave. María is exhausted."

Andrea saw that it was true. The old woman seemed to have crumbled. Her shoulders were sagging and her grey head was resting on her chest. Andrea thanked her profusely, then stood back and watched while Eric pulled the tattered shawl closer around María's frail shoulders, then kissed her forehead, muttering, *"Que Dios te bendiga!"*

Andrea found Eric's gentleness and his blessing the old woman both surprising and touching, for at that moment he didn't seem at all the arrogant, cynical, exasperating man she had come to know.

It wasn't until they were seated in the carriage and

driving away that Andrea asked, "How did you come to know María?"

Eric had warned María not to reveal to Andrea that he was the man who had slipped her into Havana. It had been an arduous trip from the jungle for the weakened, blind woman. He greatly admired her courage. For that reason, he gave her the respect he thought a grandson might bestow. But he hadn't anticipated Andrea's question and he cursed himself for not realizing that she would ask. He made a quick fabrication. "Through the cousin she lives with. He owns a small boat which I occasionally rent for fishing. I saw her outside the hut one day and knew she wasn't one of the regular family, so I asked about her."

Eric's answer didn't ring true to Andrea. If María was in danger of being discovered, Andrea couldn't imagine the Cuban telling Eric, unless she really trusted the American. And even if that were true, it still didn't explain Eric's behavior at their parting. His kissing and blessing María had been too familiar. She decided, however, not to challenge his answer and asked, "You said family—are there other members beside her cousin and his wife and child?"

"Yes, eleven people live there."

"Eleven? In that little shack?" Andrea asked in disbelief.

"Yes."

"Then where were they?"

"The men were out fishing, and the others left to give María more privacy for her interview."

They must have gone out the back door, through the kitchen, Andrea realized, then asked, "How old is María?"

"How old do you think she is?"

"I don't know. Eighty. Ninety. She looks ancient."

"She's thirty-six."

"That's impossible!" Andrea gasped.

"No, it isn't. She had her first child when she was fifteen and she was a grandmother at thirty. The horrors she survived, aged her far beyond her years."

"Are they so poor they can't feed her decently?" Andrea asked, thinking if María gained some weight maybe she wouldn't look so terribly old.

"No, being fishermen, they eat better than most Cubans these days, but María can't hold much food down. After years of starvation, her stomach rebels."

Andrea fell silent, mulling over everything María had told her. Eric drove for a short distance, then asked, "Well, do you think you can do justice to the story on the *reconcentrados* now?"

It dawned on Andrea that she not only had a story, she had a great, powerful story that would knock the socks off anyone who read it, including the most skeptical editor. Her spirits soared like a rocket. She turned to Eric and, caught up in the excitement of the moment, threw her arms around him and hugged him, saying, "Yes, oh, yes, I can do the story now! Thank you! Thank you so much!"

With Andrea's dark eyes dancing with excitement and her cheeks flushed with pleasure, Eric found her just as appealing as when she was angry, if not more so. Then feeling her soft breasts pressing against his arm, her thigh against his, the rigid control he had held over his desire broke. He drew sharply back on the reins, then dropped them as he turned in the seat and slipped his arms around her.

Andrea was stunned by the suddenness of it all. One minute she was hugging Eric, and the next, she was in his arms, and he was kissing her, first achingly sweet, then with increasing passion and urgency, until all thought fled as she gave herself up to the wonderful sensations his lips and tongue were provoking. She melted in him, wrapping her arms tightly around his broad shoulders, fearing she would float away if she didn't hang on for dear life.

Andrea's womanly scent filled Eric's nostrils as he savored the sweetness of her mouth. Leaving her dizzily whirling, he dropped a trail of feathery kisses over her temple, forehead, and eyes—as his hands roamed urgently over her back and the gentle curve of her hips. He nibbled at the long column of her throat. Then, spying her seemingly erotic ear, he felt a stab of fire that seemed to go straight to his groin, and make his already aroused manhood strain even harder at the confines of his trousers. He traced the outline of her ear with his tongue, then gently probed it. A wave of intense pleasure washed over Andrea. She trembled and moaned. Encouraged by her response, his mouth returned to capture hers in a demanding, possessive kiss while his hand rose to cup one breast. As he was caressing it, his long fingers teased the hardening bud through the material of her shirtwaist.

It wasn't Andrea who stopped Eric's passionate advances. Even if she had had the strength to resist, she had no desire to. Under Eric's searing kisses and sensuous caresses, she was drowning in a sea of feverish heat. Unlike Eric, she didn't hear the lurid calls coming from the fishermen on a passing boat, calls that brought him suddenly to his senses.

When Eric tore his mouth from her and suddenly released her, Andrea almost fell from the seat. She stared at him in utter confusion, then muttered, "What happened?"

"I kissed you, but I shouldn't have gotten so carried away."

Andrea realized that he'd gotten a little too familiar, kissing her intimately and touching her breast, but she couldn't bring herself to take him to task for it. It had been absolutely wonderful. So wonderful, she'd like to continue. She leaned forward. Her mouth was parting in silent invitation, as she was muttering, "That's all right."

Eric knew that Andrea was still aroused. Her eyes looked like liquid ebony, and her breath was coming in little gasps that made her breasts rise and fall temptingly. He swallowed hard and pushed her back gently, saying in a voice hoarse with desire, "No, I'm afraid it isn't. We have an audience."

It was then that Andrea saw the fishing boat, with its leering occupants. Eric picked up the reins and drove away. Andrea finally had the presence of mind to blush, but not because she was ashamed of herself for having allowed Eric to take liberties and for enjoying it. Rather, she blushed at having been seen. And just as perversely, she gloried in the knowledge that Eric desired her—that what had happened had not been a figment of her imagination, but real. Her vow to keep all men at arms' length was completely forgotten.

At least, temporarily forgotten.

Chapter 7

Andrea spent the rest of that day and the entire next one in her room working on her story about the *reconcentrados*. Eric was surprised at how much he missed her company. He tried to tell himself that he was simply bored here in the city with nothing to do, and that Andrea had relieved that tedium. But it didn't ring true. Havana was a busy, exciting city that had never bored him before.

On the evening of the second day, despite his vow not to pursue her, Eric went to Andrea's room and knocked on her door. He felt a surge of joy when she opened it and he saw her. It irritated him to no end, but he couldn't help himself. His feelings for her appeared to be ungovernable, as well as irrational. His only consolation was that she seemed just as happy to see him.

"Why, hello there!" Andrea exclaimed, her dark eyes sparkling with pleasure.

"Hello," Eric responded, his eyes going to her hair. With the light coming from the window behind her, it looked like a glorious, shining halo around her face.

Then, remembering why he had come, he said, "I was wondering if you had finished your story yet."

"Yes. I just finished proofreading it."

"In that case, why don't we do a little celebrating?"

"That sounds wonderful," Andrea answered, her heart racing at the prospect of being in his company. "What did you have in mind?"

"I'll let you choose. We could either go to one of the *zarzuelas* in town, or to a restaurant I know that features a Cuban band."

Andrea didn't think she'd be all that crazy about a Spanish operetta. She had enough trouble following Spanish when it was spoken, much less being sung at a key high enough and loud enough to make a hound howl. "I think I'd prefer the band. If you'll just give me a few minutes to change clothes, I'll be right with you."

"If we're going to the restaurant, that won't be necessary. It's not that formal. What you have on will be fine."

"Not with these stains all over my shirtwaist," Andrea answered, holding out the bottom of her blouse so he could see what she was referring to. "I look like I've been playing in a pigpen."

Eric noticed that there was a smudge on her cheek, too. "Are those ink stains?"

"Yes. I never could change a typewriter ribbon without getting ink all over me. You should have seen my hands before I washed them."

"You have your own typewriter?" Eric asked in surprise.

"Yes, I do. Once you learn how to use one, it spoils

you. Writing something out by hand seems so tedious and time-consuming now."

"Where did you learn?"

Andrea laughed, the first time he had heard her do so, and Eric discovered he very much liked the clear, joyous sound. "That's how I made my living after I graduated," Andrea informed him. "No one would hire me as a journalist, so I became a typist."

"I've heard about typewriters, but I've never seen one. Do you mind?"

"No, of course not. Come on in. It's over there on the desk."

Eric had an engineer's curiosity about machines. He examined the typewriter minutely, even removing the cover to see how it worked inside, while Andrea told him the names of the different parts. He commented, "It looks awfully awkward and heavy to carry around with you."

"I don't carry it. I had it shipped in a small trunk, and it was all I could do to lift it from the floor to the table. That's an old Sholes machine. He's the man who really perfected it. They had some new Remingtons where I worked, but I couldn't afford one of them."

"Remington? Is that the same people that make guns?"

"Yes."

"Do all journalists use typewriters?"

"Are you serious? Typewriters are machines for females, like sewing machines. The reporters I know wouldn't be caught dead sitting at one. Besides, they're probably too stupid to learn," Andrea added contemptuously. "And that's all the better for me. It should give me an edge. I'm sure an editor would much rather read my typed article than one of their messy handwritten ones."

Eric smiled. He remembered being fascinated with his mother's new treadle sewing machine when he was a small boy, and not just its mechanism. If no one was watching, he fiddled with operating it every chance he got. Achieving just the right rhythm in pumping the treadle had taken a little skill. He had been proud of himself until his older brothers walked in and caught him at it. They'd laughed at him and called him a sissy. He never got anywhere near the machine after that. Yes, it was true. People did associate certain machines with women and others with men. But he'd never realized how silly that was until Andrea pointed it out. "Is it a difficult machine to work?"

"Not really. It just takes practice. If you have many reports to make, you might consider learning to type."

He just might do that, Eric thought, when, and if, he got back to engineering. Eric had learned not to make plans for the future. He knew how quickly death could come in battle.

Eric waited in the hall while Andrea changed. Then they walked to a quaint nearby restaurant where they dined on the patio close to a tinkling fountain. Andrea allowed Eric to order for her and found the *lechón*—roast suckling pig served with a sauce made from garlic, olive oil and orange juice—followed by *pan con timbra*—a bread roll with a guava jelly and cheese filling—absolutely delicious.

The entertainment was as exotic as the food. Like Cuban cuisine, Cuban music was a mixture of African and Spanish, unique in its own right. The instruments consisted of several guitars, a pair of matching drums tied together, rhythm sticks which Eric called *claves,* a notched gourd that produced a rasping sound he identified as a *guero,* and a strange instrument called a *guijada de burro*—bones of a donkey's jaw—that produced an eerie noise. The resulting music was like none Andrea had ever heard. It was both strange and exciting, its rhythm reaching out to some primitive part of her that made her want to get up and pound her feet on the ground, gyrate her hips, throw her head back, and dance with wild abandon.

When they left the restaurant, Andrea's heart was still pounding, and she didn't know if it was the effect of the music or of Eric's presence. Just being around him made her feel lightheaded and quivering all over. She wanted him to kiss her—so badly she ached for it—but to her utter disappointment, he was the perfect gentleman. By the time they were walking down the hallway to her room, she had given up any hope that anything romantic would happen.

It wasn't that Eric didn't want to kiss Andrea. He'd been wanting that since she had opened the door to him. His desire had grown during the evening. Watching her across the table, with her dark eyes dancing with excitement and the pulse beating in her throat seeming to throb in unison with the drums, had been an agony for him. But he didn't dare yield to his desire, for fear he wouldn't be able to stop at just a kiss. His hunger for her had surpassed the preliminaries of lovemaking. He wanted it all, so much so that his need was almost overpowering.

When they reached the door to Andrea's room, Eric rigidly stood back and said, "Thank you for joining me this evening."

"Thank you for inviting me," Andrea answered politely, feeling keenly disappointed. She turned to slip the key in her door.

Eric cursed himself. He didn't want to leave, particularly not without knowing when he would see her again. "Will I see you tomorrow?"

Andrea pushed the door open. The light from the lamp she had left on, spilled into the hallway. Then she turned and answered, "Yes, if you wouldn't mind escorting me to the telegraph office."

Eric frowned. "Is that how you plan on sending your article to the States?"

"Yes. Isn't that how the other reporters do it? I want it to get there as quickly as possible, although it's going to cost me a small fortune."

"Are you aware that everything that goes through that office is censored by the Spanish authorities?"

"No I wasn't. Why is that?"

"They don't want anything being relayed out which might be of any military value to the rebels. Once your story has gone through there, your identity as a journalist will be known. Then your activities will be curtailed, just like those of the other reporters." Eric shrugged his shoulders, adding, "Unless you weren't planning on doing any other articles, and that isn't important to you."

"No, it *is* important. I do plan on doing more. Just what, I don't know yet, but something. This is just the beginning. But I hate to send it by regular mail. It takes so long, and it's so unreliable."

"I may have a solution," Eric offered. "I have a friend who's first mate on a ship which sails between here and Tampa three times a week. He could take the article back to the States for you and mail it by special delivery. It would take a few days longer, but it wouldn't cost you near as much."

It sounded like a perfect solution to Andrea. "Do you think he would mind?"

"Well, his ship docks tomorrow. I'll take it down there and find out."

"Oh, thank you. I'll write a quick cover letter, slip it into an envelope, and give it to you right now." Andrea walked a few steps into the room, then suddenly turned and asked, "But would you mind doing me one more favor?"

"What's that?"

Andrea didn't know why she suddenly felt so unsure of herself, but she did. "Read it for me first, and see what you think."

Andrea's wanting his opinion pleased Eric. He wanted her trust. "I'd be happy to."

Closing the door behind him, Eric followed Andrea into the room. She picked up a small stack of papers from the table where the typewriter sat. Then she looked around her before saying, "Sit there, in that easy chair."

Eric sat in the chair across from the bed, as she had directed him, and took the papers she handed him. As he sat back, crossing his long legs before beginning to read, Andrea nervously paced. She had never allowed anyone to read anything she had written, other than her professors and editors. And even that wasn't the same. They weren't right there in the same room with her. It left her feeling very vulnerable, almost as if Eric were peering into her soul. Eric gave her absolutely no hint of what he thought as he read, which only increased her apprehension. By the time he had gotten to the last page, she had stopped pacing and sat perched anxiously on the side of the bed, facing him.

When Eric finished the article, he lifted his head and stared at Andrea. He had once again underestimated her. He had never dreamed she had such talent. She had fulfilled every obligation of a good journalist, giving every cold-blooded fact, telling the how, when, where, why, and who. Then she had taken it a step farther. She had breathed life into her story, so much so that Eric could feel María's confusion, her fear, her anger, her shame, her terrible pain. Andrea had communicated her passion to her readers. Whether or not that was considered good journalism, it had certainly been effective. She had created a story that would inflame them, and bring forth a profound compassion as well. It was the most heart-wrenching, gut-twisting, soul-stirring article he had ever read.

When Andrea couldn't stand the suspense any longer, she asked, "What's the matter? Why are you staring at me like that? Isn't it any good? Did it sound silly? Too dramatic, maybe?"

"To the contrary. It's excellent!"

Andrea rose from the bed, asking apprehensively, "You're sure?"

Eric placed the article on the table beside him and came to his feet. He stepped up to her and answered, "I'm positive." He smiled. "I think that article is going to launch a very successful career for you."

"You do?" Andrea asked, suddenly beaming.

"Yes. I have only one thing about it to discuss with you."

Eric's remark wiped the broad smile from Andrea's face. "What's that?"

"Your by-line. I believe that's what it's called."

"Yes, it is, but what's wrong with my name?"

"You used Andy, and not Andrea."

"Yes, of course. I told you everyone calls me Andy."

"Are you sure that's your reason, that you're not hiding behind it, like George Sand, hoping to be more acceptable as a writer if everyone thinks you're a man?"

Eric's observation hit a little too close to home. Before Andrea could respond, Eric caught her shoulders in his hands and said fervently, "Don't do it, Andrea. Don't sell yourself short. You're good. Damn good! Good enough that there's no reason for you not to let every reader out there know you're female. You have every reason to be proud of what you've done. You said you didn't mind tooting your own horn. Then do it on paper, too. Use your real name, not your nickname. Besides, didn't you say you had something to prove? How are you going to do that if you don't let them know your real sex?"

Andrea knew that Eric had a legitimate point—her reason told her that—but at that moment she was more concerned to have his praise, his unqualified support. Nothing he could have done or said could have pleased her more. Unknowingly, Eric had done something that no other man had ever been able to do before him. He had reached past her defenses and touched her heart, leaving her both bewildered and suffused with a strange warmth.

When Andrea made no comment, but just stared up

at him, Eric pressed his suit and asked, "Will you change your by-line?"

At that moment, Andrea would have jumped off the ends of the earth if Eric had asked her, if for only to please him as much as he had pleased her. "Yes," she answered, so softly it was almost a whisper.

Eric knew it was time to release her, but he couldn't. He could feel her heat, smell her sweet, intoxicating scent. Her generous mouth seemed to be beckoning to him. As he lowered his head, somewhere in the back of his mind a voice screamed for him to stop, but he didn't heed it. He followed his impulses just as surely as the bee seeks the nectar of a flower.

From the moment Eric's soft, questing mouth touched hers, Andrea thought she had died and gone to heaven. The kiss deepened, his strong tongue went darting into her mouth and ravishing it at will. The warmth she had been feeling burst into a fire and her bones seemed to dissolve. She embraced him back and arched her body into his, wishing that she could melt into him—that somehow she could become a part of him. Then she felt his rigid arousal through their clothing against her thigh. Andrea had grown up on a ranch and knew very well what it meant. She couldn't become a part of him, but he could become a part of her. A wave of excitement washed over her, then settled in the core of her womanhood, leaving her throbbing with need. Excited beyond anything she had ever felt, she started kissing him back. Her tongue at first was tentative, then more bold and urgent, until it flicked around his in an erotic dance. Through her dulled senses she barely heard Eric's sharp intake of breath, then his tortured groan as he jerked his mouth away.

She looked in a daze to see Eric gazing down at her, with an intense expression. "Do you know where this is leading?" he asked. His breath was coming in ragged gasps. "We've got to stop, before it's too late."

"No, I don't want to," Andrea breathed, leaning into him.

Eric caught her shoulders and pushed her away, saying firmly, "I'm serious, Andrea. It's different with men. Once they reach a certain point, there's no turning back."

"I don't want to turn back," Andrea persisted, feeling she had to have release from the fire he had ignited.

"You're aroused. You don't know what you're saying. You'll hate me when it's over."

"No, I won't. I *don't* want to stop!" Then, to prove her point, Andrea stepped up to him, wrapped her arms tightly around his neck, and pressed herself against his rock-hard erection.

Eric's thin thread of restraint broke. He brought her to him in a fierce embrace. His mouth crashed down on hers in a bruising, demanding kiss that might have frightened a meeker woman. Andrea, however gloried in his wanting her so badly, so urgently. She kissed him back with equal fervor, then sank onto the bed with him.

Eric placed a trail of torrid kisses over Andrea's face and neck, all the while unbuttoning her shirtwaist, then her chemise, silently thanking God she wasn't wearing one of the silly, awkward corsets that he would have to unlace. He could hardly wait to see her. When she was bare, he drew back and avidly took in the sight of the ivory mounds with their rose tips, noting with pleasure that her breasts were fuller than he had expected. Then, anxious to taste the creamy flesh, he lowered his head and began kissing them.

In the aftermath of Eric's kisses, Andrea had been floating on a warm hazy cloud, just barely aware of Eric's presence. Her breath caught at the feel of his lips kissing and nibbling on her breasts. She had never dreamed that might be a part of lovemaking. Touching, yes, but— Then as his mouth took one nipple, rolling it around his tongue, before he started suckling on it, Andrea felt a whole new realm of delicious sensations engulfing her, and all thought fled. She tangled her fingers in the dark hair at the nape of his neck and held him to her, moaning and trembling uncontrollably while Eric ministered to one soft mound, then soothed its jealous mate.

When Eric lifted his head, Andrea muttered, "No, don't stop."

"You like that?" Eric asked unnecessarily.

"Oh, yes," she answered with a sigh. "I never knew that went along with it. It's wonderful."

Eric smiled, her innocence and total honesty pleasing him. He nuzzled her neck, saying, "There'll be more. That's just a sampling. But right now, I want to see the rest of you."

It suddenly occurred to Andrea that Eric was still fully dressed. "And I want to see you," she answered boldly.

Eric rose, pulling her from the bed with him, and facing each other, they quickly undressed. Standing in a puddle of clothes, Andrea was acutely aware of Eric's eyes sweeping over her length, then dallying at the juncture of her legs, before his eyes rose to meet hers. She was stunned by the blazing need she saw in his blue eyes. "You're beautiful," he muttered thickly.

Andrea took in his broad shoulders, the muscular chest with its mat of dark hair, the taut belly. But she couldn't force her eyes to follow the thin line of dark hair that seemed to point like an arrow to his manhood. "You're beautiful, too," she answered, stepping up to him.

Eric smiled in amusement at Andrea calling him beautiful. It seemed a ridiculous compliment for a man. He knew she hadn't looked at him fully, and was glad for it, for fear she would find his blatant arousal frightening, or worse yet, repulsive. He turned and extinguished the lamp beside the bed. He'd gone too far to turn back.

Once again, Eric lowered Andrea to the bed. He bathed her face, neck, and breasts with kisses. His hands were stroking her hips and thighs, slowly stoking her fires. She jumped when his slender fingers slid up her thigh and touched the golden curls between her legs. Instinctively, her hand darted down to catch his.

"No, don't try to stop me," Eric objected, kissing her ear. "Remember what I said about there being more? This is part of it."

Then as Eric's fingers parted the soft folds, and he began sensuously stroking her there, Andrea's hand fell away. The waves of exquisite pleasure washing over her exceeded everything before. She arched her hips to get even closer to those warm tantalizing fingers. The waves turned to powerful spasms that left her weak and making strange mewing sounds.

Andrea's uninhibited response to his lovemaking

had pushed Eric to a red-hot edge of desire. His need for possession was urgent. He kissed her fiercely. His hands roamed at will, exploring, caressing, exciting until Andrea was writhing beneath him, begging incoherently for release. He rose over her, nudged her legs apart with his knee, and placed his hot sex against her portal.

"Andrea?"

Andrea heard Eric softly saying her name through a haze. She opened her eyes and saw him hovering over her, then she felt the tip of his erection against her.

"This is your first time, isn't it?"

Andrea felt a tingle of fear and hated herself for it. She nodded her head.

"I'll be as gentle as I can."

Andrea girded herself for pain as Eric pressed against her, slowly, insistently invading. She felt a quick, stabbing pain as the membrane broke and he slid inside. She lay perfectly still as he bathed her face in kisses. She was waiting for something more, as the pain was diminishing into a dull ache. After all the wonderful things she had felt before, she found the act itself very disappointing. Finally, she asked, "Is that it?"

Eric had been waiting for her to become accustomed to him before continuing, not wanting to cause her any more discomfort than necessary. He chuckled and answered, "Hardly. We haven't even begun yet."

Haven't even begun? Andrea thought. Did that mean it was going to get better, even better than before? Her heart raced at the tantalizing prospect, and her mouth turned dry with anticipation. "Then what are you waiting for? Let's get on with it!"

Eric could only shake his head, thinking how like his bold, brash Andrea, to make demands. Then he gave her what she wanted, exciting her wildly while he rode her superbly, fully awakening her passion and taking her to a world of shining, shimmering ecstasy and exploding stars.

Afterwards, as Eric held her in his arms, Andrea marveled at everything she had learned that night. She'd had no idea lovemaking could be so wonderful. "Is it always so good?" she finally asked.

Eric breathed a sigh of relief. He'd been afraid she'd condemn him for what he had done, despite her earlier assurance that she wouldn't. "I guess that depends upon the people who are doing it." He rose on his elbow and looked down at her. "Then there's no regret on your part?"

Andrea had sworn she didn't want to get involved with any man. Her career was first and foremost in her life. Now, having experienced the joys of lovemaking, she would have hated going through life without it. It had really been quite an eye-opener. She wondered why all the women she had known had downgraded it so. And she didn't really feel that her career was threatened. Eric had said nothing about marriage, or even love. She felt a little tingle of disappointment at the last, then firmly pushed it away. "No, I have no regrets," she answered. "Do you?"

Eric did. Since he had gotten a taste of Andrea's passion, he only wanted more. She had given of herself so completely, so totally, holding back nothing. "No," he lied smoothly.

Andrea laughed, then snuggled up to him and confided, "You know, I feel like a real woman of the world. Oh, I know I'll never be sophisticated. I'll always have too much country in me for that. But I just wrote the story that will launch my career, and now, I have a lover."

Is that what she wanted of him, a brief love affair during their remaining time together? Eric's body was more than willing to oblige, but there was another part of him that didn't welcome the prospect, a part that cared too much. He knew he would just be digging a deeper hole for himself.

Andrea noted Eric's silence. It suddenly occurred to her that maybe she was reading too much into what had just happened. Feeling terribly vulnerable, she asked in a hesitant tone of voice, "That is what we are, isn't it? Lovers?"

Andrea's uncertainty tore at Eric's heartstrings. He realized that there was very little he could deny her. Then as she ran her silken thigh up his muscular thigh, and his body reacted with an eagerness that stunned him, he knew he was a doomed man. Feeling utterly helpless, he turned to her, muttering, "Yes, lovers."

Chapter 8

The next day, Eric gave Andrea's article to his friend to mail. When Eric returned to the hotel, he met her in the dining room where she was dallying over a late cup of coffee.

Before he could even sit down, she asked him anxiously, "Did your friend agree?"

"Yes," Eric answered, taking a seat across from her, then added, "and he had some interesting news. It seems the *Journal* had a spy who intercepted a letter written by Deputy de Lôme to someone in Spain. The letter portrayed President McKinley in a very unflattering light. The *Journal* printed it, and everyone back home is in an uproar over it."

Andrea wasn't surprised at the Americans' reaction. They were already inflamed. "Isn't de Lôme the Spanish envoy to the United States?"

"Yes."

"What did he say about the president?"

"That he was a weakling who sought the crowd's admiration."

"Do you think the letter is legitimate?" Andrea

asked, knowing Hearst's reputation for printing false material. "It seems to me de Lôme would be a fool to put something like that down on paper."

"He sounds just like the typical arrogant Spaniard to me," Eric replied. "And he's not denying it. It's expected that our government will demand his resignation. Of course that won't do any good. Everyone is already stirred up."

"I've scanned the headlines on a couple of Cuban papers the past few days. I didn't see anything that even hinted at such a thing," Andrea remarked. Then she remembered the riot she had seen. She added, "But then I guess it's not being printed here. Not if it's putting a Spaniard in a bad light."

"I'm sure it's not," Eric agreed wryly. "Not even the most fearless Cuban paper would dare to print that story. If you want to know what's really going on back in the States, you have to hang out at the Inglaterra bar, and of course I haven't been there in the last few days. That's one place I haven't shown you yet. I imagine it's a beehive today, with everyone speculating on what will happen next. Would you like to see it?"

"Maybe some other time. Today, I want you to take me back to that exclusive department store we saw the other day. I'd like to shop for some new clothes."

Eric was surprised. It seemed like such an utterly feminine request, so unlike Andrea. Then, as they drove to the store, he became aware of a subtle change in her. She seemed softer, more radiant than before, and he realized that their lovemaking had brought about that change. His feelings were mixed about the discovery. The part of him that stemmed from his male ego was utterly pleased, thinking it a testimony to his sexual powers. But the part of him that was striving so hard to remain unaffected saw her new beauty as a threat.

That night, when Eric went to pick up Andrea for dinner, she opened the door to reveal the surprise she had bought that afternoon. She had left the lamp on, so that Eric could get a good look at her.

Eric felt as if he had been hit by a thunderbolt. Her shimmering golden hair hung about her shoulders. Wearing a wispy white nightgown that hid nothing, she looked both ethereal and incredibly desirable.

"Do you like it?" she asked. Her smile only provoked him further.

Eric didn't answer. He couldn't. His tongue seemed glued to the top of his mouth. He stepped into the room, absently shoved the door shut behind him with one hand, stripped the gown from her in a quickness that stunned her, and took Andrea straight to bed, where they stayed the rest of the night. Andrea had no objections to missing her evening meal. In fact, she had planned it that way. She was gorging on the new sensual feast she had just discovered.

Much later, when Eric was sleeping beside her in exhaustion, Andrea marveled at his endurance and his skill. She wondered where he had learned, what women had been his teachers, for surely that must have been how he'd gained his expertise. How else would he know what pleased a woman so much? Then she was filled with a jealousy so raw it stunned her, even though she knew it was irrational. She had no hold on Eric, and wanted none. Yet, she couldn't shake the unwanted emotion. It clung to her as persistently as a tick on a steer's ear.

When he was dressing the next morning, Eric spied another pile of papers on the desk. "Is that a new article?"

His question startled Andrea. She was lying among the twisted bed linens, and admiring him as he dressed. She was thinking that he was a magnificent specimen of masculinity. "What?"

"I asked if you've written another article."

"Yes, I did that yesterday morning, after you had left and before I went to the dining room. It had been rattling around in the back of my head for a while, so it was easier to write than my first one. It's about that riot we witnessed. You can read it if you like."

Eric picked up the article and read it while Andrea left the bed and slipped into a robe. Once again, in her article, she had done everything expected of a good journalist—then more, this time delving into the combustive anger of the crowd as well as depicting the smoldering hatred between the two factions all around her. He realized then that she had an unusual perceptiveness. "This is excellent, too," he remarked, placing it back on the desk. "What do you plan on writing next?"

Andrea came around the bed, saying, "I've been meaning to talk to you about that. I'd still like to do a story on sugar plantations. Won't you please reconsider taking me to your friend's plantation?"

"I told you I can't leave the city."

Andrea threw her hands up in exasperation. "For heaven's sake! We'd only be gone a day or two. Even if your generator came in while we were gone, it wouldn't delay you that long."

Eric didn't want Andrea to know the truth, but not

because he was afraid she would expose him, either on purpose or inadvertently. The less she knew about his real mission in the city, the less danger she would be in if his association with the rebels should be discovered. He decided to take another approach. "Have you forgotten what I told you? You have to have a pass to get in and out of this city. I have one, but you don't."

"Then I'll get one," Andrea said with her usual confidence. "Who issues them?"

When Eric was slow in answering, Andrea persisted, saying, "I asked who issues them."

"Colonel Reyes," Eric responded reluctantly.

"Why, that's perfect! He thinks we're engaged. He shouldn't find it at all unusual for you to want to take me to meet your best friend."

"There are other problems."

"Like what?"

"Transportation. One can't hire a carriage for a trip like that, and the public coaches stopped running a long time ago. The Spaniards are trying to keep everybody contained, remember? The only way you can get to my friend's plantation is by horseback."

Andrea laughed. "And you think that's a problem? Have you forgotten I was raised in the saddle?"

"I'm not talking about a little ride into town. I'm talking about a thirty-mile trip."

"Why, that's nothing! I've ridden as far as two hundred miles on horseback."

"Two hundred miles?" Eric asked in astonishment.

"Yes, when I thirteen, and snuck off to join a cattle drive my brothers were making to deliver some of our beeves to an army fort near the Canadian border. They didn't realize I was there until the third night out.

I'd hung back out of sight until then. Then it was too late to turn back."

Andrea's story of her past recklessness upset Eric because he knew she hadn't outgrown it, and that worried him. "Couldn't one of them have taken you back?"

"Oh, sure, but none of them wanted to do it and miss out on the adventure, so I went along. So, you see you don't have to worry about me. I can handle thirty miles easily."

Eric knew he had run out of excuses, and he supposed if Diego showed up in his absence, the Cuban would wait around for a couple of days until he returned. After all, Eric had been waiting for two weeks. "All right, I'll take you," he finally agreed. "I'll go to Reyes this morning and see if I can get you a pass. Then we'll leave the first thing in the morning."

"Oh, thank you!" Andrea cried, hugging him. Then she drew back, asking, "Are you going to make arrangements for our horses, too?"

"Yes, I guess so. Why?"

"I want a regular saddle. None of that silly sidesaddle stuff for me."

Eric wasn't in the least surprised. He turned and walked to the door, wondering why he hadn't simply said no, and stuck to it. The man he had been two weeks ago would have. Damn! If he didn't watch out, she'd bring him completely to his knees.

When Andrea appeared in front of the hotel the next morning, she was wearing a blouse, a leather split skirt that came to her calves, and Western boots. Eric wasn't particularly surprised at her attire. She had told him she intended to ride astride, and he had spent time in Arizona where such clothing was perfectly acceptable for women. But it was obvious by the shocked looks coming from everyone else that it wasn't acceptable in Havana.

"What the devil are they staring at?" Andrea asked, handing Eric her small valise, so he could tie it to the rear of the high-backed Spanish saddle.

"Your split skirt, I'm sure. Women don't wear pants of any sort here."

"What about those bicycling suits? You know, the ones with a fitted jacket and bloomers. I've seen women wear them back in New York, high-class women."

"I've never seen a woman here wear one."

"Well, they wear swimming suits, don't they?" Andrea persisted, becoming more and more irritated at the Spaniards' prudishness. "They have bloomers."

"Under their skirts."

"In other words, they think only skirts are respectable?"

"I'm afraid so."

"Well, they're dead wrong!" Andrea pronounced adamantly. "As long as no bare skin on my leg is showing, I'm respectable. What's good enough for that fancy beach at Coney Island should be good enough here."

With that, Andrea swung up into her saddle, bringing another round of shocked gasps from the crowd outside the hotel.

Thirty minutes later, Andrea and Eric showed their passes to the soldiers guarding the road they were traveling, then left the city behind. As they rode, Andrea looked around at the rolling countryside that was dotted with towering palm trees. She could see in the distance the lush, green mountains in the center of the island. But the grass beside the road looked a little dry to her. She remembered Eric's comments about the rainy season and remarked, "I guess the coconuts are like the flowers here. They don't appear until the rainy season, either."

Seeing her gazing at one of the palm trees, Eric answered, "These aren't coconut palms. They're royal palms. They do produce a fruit, but it's not edible."

Andrea felt stupid. She imagined a tenderfoot who had mistaken a steer for a bull might feel the same way. "Well, I know I read somewhere that there are coconut palms here," she answered defensively.

"Yes, there are, mostly on beaches around the shoreline. They were imported, you know."

"No, I didn't. I thought all tropical islands had coconut palms."

"Not necessarily. There are quite a few plants and trees around that you'd think were native here, but were imported. The teak and banyan tree, also the mango, from India, and the flamboyant tree, from Madagascar."

"Banyan? I've never heard of that."

"Well, if you ever saw one you never forget it. It's similar to a mangrove. It puts down roots from its branches, except it grows on land, while the mangrove thrives in tidal marshes around the coast. Each root it puts down becomes a new trunk, until it's just a thicket. In the case of the mangrove, I can see its purpose. The roots collect sand and expand the island.

But for the love of me I can't understand why anyone would deliberately plant a banyan tree."

"And the flamboyant tree? What does it look like?"

"Do you remember the umbrella-shaped tree that you saw all over Havana?" Andrea nodded. "Well, that's it."

Andrea wasn't at all impressed. It had very few leaves, and everything else seemed so lush. "Why in the world did they name it that?"

"Because when it blooms, that's the only way to describe it. Its branches are completely covered with brilliant orange or scarlet blossoms. If you're out in the countryside, you can spot one miles away. They're that spectacular."

They rode for a while in silence, following a narrow road that twisted and turned between a thick growth of palmetto, their horses leaving a trail of red dust in their wake from the iron-rich soil. As they traveled, Andrea admired the way Eric rode, and was glad for it. Like a typical Westerner, she thought a man who didn't sit a horse well was no man at all. Oh, she knew he didn't have the expertise her brothers had—undoubtedly, he could never turn a stampede—but neither did he have their bow legs. She would hate for anything to ruin Eric's long, muscular legs. They were as straight as a cottonwood trunk and well muscled, and she loved the feel of his rock-hard thighs against hers when he made love to her. She loved it almost as much as she loved the feel of him inside her. The thought brought about a spontaneous response in that part of Andrea's anatomy. Feeling a sudden wetness, she flushed at her own wanton musings. Trying to distract herself, she asked, "Where did you learn to ride?"

"In Arizona. That was the only way we could get back and forth from the mine."

"You didn't ride before that?"

"No, I grew up in a little farming community. The only horses around were work horses or carriage horses, and no one would have dreamed of throwing a saddle on one."

"Then you grew up on a farm?" Andrea asked in surprise. She had always thought farmers dull, unexciting people. Eric most definitely wasn't like that.

"No, my father owned a general store."

To Andrea, that didn't seem to fit either. She didn't know what background she'd expected. The only thing that popped into her head was that he might be the son of a buccaneer or a dashing highwayman, because of his dangerous, mysterious aura. "What made you decide to become a mining engineer?"

"Boredom, I guess. I wanted some excitement in my life, to see the world. Mining engineers get to travel all over."

Andrea understood perfectly and answered, "That's why I chose the kind of journalism I'm doing. I couldn't stand the thought of living my entire life in one place."

By that time they had cleared the palmetto thicket and were riding next to a small farm. The house on it looked almost identical to the *bohío* María lived in, except its sides were made of twisted palm leaves instead of bamboo. Andrea took in the small field of maize, before the sight of the Cuban farmer plowing another field in the distance caught her attention. "What will he be planting?" she asked Eric.

"I don't think he's getting ready to plant. I think he's digging up. If I'm not mistaken, those are cassava plants, they produce a type of potato."

Andrea studied the animals in the double yoke that were pulling the plow, then commented, "I've never seen cattle with humps on their backs like that."

"They're actually a type of ox called a zebu, imported from Asia because of their resistance to the tropical heat and ticks."

Was everything imported? Andrea wondered in exasperation, then asked, "Wouldn't that make them too expensive for the average farmer to own?"

"No, I'm afraid I misled you. They were imported centuries ago, and still are the only kind of cattle raised on this island, even on the biggest ranches."

Andrea couldn't imagine an entire herd of the strange-looking beasts.

They entered another area that was thick with palmetto and other tropical growth. They stopped beside the road and ate the lunch which Eric had asked the kitchen staff at the hotel to pack for them. When she had finished, Andrea excused herself and started into the thicket to relieve herself. "Wait a minute!" Eric called. "You may need this."

Andrea turned and saw Eric holding a fierce-looking machete. "Where did you have that?" she asked in surprise.

"Tied on the other side of my saddle."

"Why will I need it? Are there poisonous snakes in there?" Andrea asked with a tingle of fear. She could shoot a sidewinder through the head at ten paces, but she didn't know a thing about wielding a huge knife.

"There aren't any poisonous snakes on this island. In fact, the only dangerous creatures here are crocodiles, and they live in the swampy areas around the coast. You'll need it to chop vegetation out of the way."

Eric handed the machete to Andrea. It was much heavier than it looked, so that it dragged her down. "This thing weighs a ton, doesn't it?"

"Well, come to think of it, I guess it is a little heavy for a woman," Eric admitted. "Here, step aside," he said, moving her with one hand and taking the machete from her with the other. "I'll clear a path for you."

Before Andrea could object, Eric starting swinging the machete, sending the tough palmetto palms and twisted vines flying everywhere. She stared at the muscles on his back, muscles that strained against his shirt as he wielded the huge knife. She was amazed at his strength and his skill, and for a fleeting second, the image of a corsair swinging his cutlass passed through her mind. When he turned and walked back through the path he had made, she commented, "You handle that thing like an old pro."

Eric had gotten his expertise by hacking his way through the jungle with the rebels. He realized he had almost given himself away. "There's some pretty dense foliage in those mountains we're exploring," he answered glibly.

They continued their trip shortly thereafter, passing several other small farms, then a tobacco plantation. Andrea marveled at the size of the tobacco plants, six feet tall, with leaves twelve inches or more across.

Then she curiously studied the *casa de tabaco*—the shed where the bundles of leaves were dried. Noting that no one was around, she commented on it to Eric.

"I suppose raising tobacco is like raising sugar cane. There's a *tiempo muerto,* a dead season when there's no work in the fields . . ." he said.

"Then there won't be anything going at your friend's plantation?" Andrea asked in alarm.

"If you're talking about a harvest, no. Right now the cane is just putting on its last growth before ripening."

"What about at the mills?"

"Nothing there, either."

"But how am I going to write about the sugar industry, if I don't see anything happening?"

"You'll see plenty, believe me, and I'm sure Paul will explain everything in detail. That's as much or more than you had with your *reconcentración* story," Eric pointed out, then said, "By the way, that's the beginning of Paul's plantation up there."

Ahead of them, Andrea could see the twelve-foot cane towering over the tobacco field.

They left the main road and followed another road that twisted and turned through solid walls of cane that completely obliterated everything from view, other than the blue sky above them. To Andrea, it was almost as if the rest of the world had ceased to exist, and she and Eric were alone on this lonely road through an endless field of cane. The only sound was of the horses' hooves on the road and a soft rattling as the breeze rustled the tops of the cane. Andrea lost all sense of direction, and the cane seemed to be closing in her. It was an eerie, frightening feeling that she couldn't understand. She had ridden down narrow canyons before, and not felt this way, but the cane seemed so alive, almost voraciously so. "How much farther is it to the plantation house?" she asked apprehensively.

Eric noted her pale face and asked, "Are you feeling a little claustrophobic? Don't let it alarm you. The same thing happens sometimes in the jungle, where the vegetation is so dense you can't get your bearings. We're not lost. Keep that in mind. We should clear this field in another five minutes or so."

In an effort to get her mind off her strange apprehension, Andrea asked, "How much taller does the cane get?"

"Not much. Another foot or two perhaps. The heaviest growth is during the rainy season."

"And when is it harvested?"

"In late June, early July. Definitely before the wet season hits with its torrential rains. After that, people can't get into the fields to cut it. Everything becomes a quagmire."

Suddenly the cane field ended, as abruptly as it had begun, and they rode into an open area. Andrea saw a large building surrounded by clusters of open sheds in the distance. "That's the sugar mill, or factory, as Paul calls it," Eric informed her. "The plantation house is this way."

Andrea followed Eric down another dusty red road that led to another group of buildings in the distance. As they drew closer, Andrea saw the sprawling one-story plantation house sitting among lush tropical gardens, with its whitewashed walls gleaming in the bright afternoon sunlight. A wide veranda surrounded the home. Its roof was supported by white columns, and the green shutters on its many windows were thrown open, as were the double doors that opened out onto the porch. Then Andrea's eyes widened with surprise as she realized that the roof was thatched with palm leaves, just like the peasants' *bohíos*.

Eric spotted a man riding a horse tearing around the corner of the house and racing towards them. "I guess they must have seen us coming. Here's our welcoming committee."

Chapter 9

Andrea watched as the dark-haired man rode up to them, reined in sharply, then leaned across and slapped Eric on the back, saying, "By God, it *is* you! I couldn't believe my eyes when I saw you riding up. How long has it been since I've seen you? Two years?"

"About that," Eric answered, feeling a little twinge of guilt at not having visited his friend more often. But he hadn't had time since he'd joined the rebels. Up until now, his trips into Havana had been hurried—a matter of getting in, getting the information he came for, then getting out. "How are things going with you, Paul?"

"Fine, just fine," Paul answered absently, shooting a quizzical look in Andrea's direction.

Realizing that introductions were in order, Eric said, "Andrea, this is my friend, Paul Deboise. Paul, this is Andrea Williams. She's a journalist looking for material here in Cuba. She'd like to do a story on the sugar industry, what with all the attention being focused on Cuba these days. I thought you could give her a hand."

Paul looked at Andrea in amazement, then said, "A journalist? I've never had the pleasure of meeting a lady journalist before. I'd be happy to help in any way I can."

Andrea didn't particularly like being called a lady. In her opinion, ladies were weak, submissive creatures—to say nothing of their being disgustingly prissy and vain. But she decided to let it pass. She politely shook the hand Paul extended to her, and answered, "Thank you, Mr. Deboise. I'd appreciate any information you could give me."

"Oh, no," Paul objected with a big, friendly grin. "If we're going to work together, let's skip those silly formalities. Please call me Paul, and I hope I can call you Andrea."

"But of course," Andrea answered with relief, "but please call me Andy."

As the three rode towards the plantation house with Andrea between the two men, Paul asked her, "What journal or paper do you write for?"

"Right now, I'm freelancing."

"Holding out for the highest bidder, huh? Good for you!"

Andrea didn't want to tell Paul that so far she wasn't published, for fear he might think it a waste of his time. She held her breath for fear Eric might say something. She could have hugged him in gratitude when he said, "She can afford to hold out. I've read some of her work. She's good. Damn good!"

Paul noticed that Eric's praise seemed a little too enthusiastic for just casual acquaintances. Paul heard the pride in Eric's voice. Paul was curious about the relationship. As far as he knew, Eric had never been emotionally involved with any woman, and not because he hadn't had the opportunity. Many very attractive women here in Cuba had offered him encouragement, despite the stringent courting rules practiced by the Spaniards. "Where did you two meet? Back in the States?"

"No, in Havana, a few days ago," Eric answered.

There was a slight edge to Eric's tone of voice, and Paul sensed he was warning him away from any questions of a personal nature, yet his curt answer was making Paul all the more curious.

"Eric sort of took me under his wing when he found out I had just arrived in Cuba," Andrea informed Paul. "I was so naive that I didn't even know it was dangerous for a woman to move about without an escort. It's been my good fortune that the generator he's been waiting for hasn't arrived from the States yet, and he's had time on his hands to show me around."

"So that's what you're doing on this end of the island, waiting for a generator to arrive?" Paul asked Eric.

"Yes."

"Then you and your group are still exploring in the Sierra Maestra, despite the war?"

"Yes."

"That's amazing," Paul remarked. "I thought the fighting was going hot and heavy over there."

"We're deep in the mountains, where no one pays any attention to us."

Again, Paul heard a subtle warning tone in Eric's voice and wondered at it. Was his old friend hiding something, or was he being evasive because he didn't want Andrea unduly alarmed about his safety, which would again hint at a relationship which included much more than just lending a hand to a fellow American in a foreign land.

Andrea broke into Paul's musings by saying, "Eric tells me that you're quite an authority on Cuba. How long have you been in this country?"

"Seventeen years."

Andrea saw that Paul was a bit older than Eric, by the grey hair at his temples. She estimated his age to be around forty. She could see that he was an excellent horseman. Clearly he took his job as overseer seriously. She also knew by his last name that he was of French descent, which explained his dark eyes and rather swarthy complexion. In all, she decided, he was an attractive man, with his dark, good looks and sturdy body. But he didn't begin to compare with Eric with his exciting aura and raw masculinity. "Where are you from, Paul?"

"Louisiana. That's where I learned my expertise in growing sugar, on my grandfather's plantation. It was one of the few to survive the War between the States."

"What made you decide to come to Cuba?" Andrea asked, then realizing she might be getting too bold, said, "I'm sorry. If any of my questions are too personal, just tell me so."

"No, I don't mind answering. I was bitter about it at the time, but I've gotten over it. You see, of all his sons and grandsons, I was the only one interested in the plantation, and my grandfather taught me everything he knew. For years and years, I was his shadow. But he was Creole to the bone. When he died, he left the plantation to his oldest son, as was the Creole custom. My uncle offered the job as overseer to me, but I was so furious I turned him down. I told him I would rather work for a total stranger than break my back for him to get rich. But it wasn't really a matter of money. I loved that plantation, not just the buildings on it, but the land itself. I knew every little nook and cranny on it. Even though I knew it would never be mine, I had always thought of it that way. I just couldn't stand the thought of it belonging to someone else. So I got this job with the American Sugar Refining Company and came to Cuba. I've been at this same location all these years. This plantation doesn't belong to me either, but I've come to love it just as much as the one in Louisiana. It's my home now, and hopefully, I can live out the rest of my life here."

"Which explains why this plantation is the best-producing one in Cuba," Eric added. "It takes more than know-how to get the success this place has gained. It takes dedication, too, and Paul has more of that than any *colono* on the island."

Andrea saw the little flush of embarrassment on Paul's face at Eric's praising him at being even better than the Spanish planters and she liked him even better. "Where did you two meet?"

"At a reception the Spanish governor-general had in Havana for American businessmen, before the revolution," Paul answered. "Eric and I hit it right off. Since then, every time he'd come to Havana on business, he'd pay me a little visit, or, if he knew he was coming in the dead season, like now, he'd drop me a line and we'd meet in Havana for a few days." Paul looked directly at Eric and commented, "I guess you haven't been making many trips the past few years."

"No, because of the war intensifying, I've kept them to an absolute minimum. And then I try to get back to my men as soon as possible, for fear I might get cut off from them."

"I understand," Paul answered. "It's a shame the mail service is so disrupted. At least, we could still correspond."

Again, Eric felt a twinge of guilt and vowed to tell his friend the truth before they parted.

By that time, they had reached the plantation house, where a servant, dressed in a white, pajamalike garment, and sandals made from woven palm leaves, waited to take their horses. They dismounted, and while Eric removed his and Andrea's valises from their horses, she and Paul walked up the short flight of stairs to the veranda.

Seeing her glance at the thatch, Paul asked, "Does my roof surprise you?"

"Well, yes it does. I should think if this is the best-producing plantation in Cuba, the company could afford to give you a better roof," Andrea answered bluntly.

"This house did have a red tile roof at one time," Paul informed her. "On three occasions during my first two years here, hurricanes blew it away. This was my idea. It's cheaper to replace. Many of the country houses, even on the *latifundias*—the large tracts of land owned by one Spaniard—have these roofs."

"But does it really keep out the rain?"

"If the leaves are layered correctly, yes. In fact, this roof can take higher winds without blowing away. It gives, or breathes, as I call it. And since there's no shortage of palms," Paul continued, making a sweeping motion at the towering trees all around them, "I can have a new roof anytime I feel like it."

Andrea laughed and answered, "Well, I suppose that is an advantage."

Another servant rushed from the house and took the valises from Eric. After Paul had told the man which rooms to put them in, the three walked into the building. As she stepped into a broad hallway, Andrea was relieved to note that there were ceilings in the house. Now, she could stop worrying about a spider dropping down on her from the roof.

Paul led them into the *sala,* a spacious, sunny room with several double doors that opened onto the veranda for cross ventilation. Almost as soon as they were seated, a servant appeared with a tray holding several tall glasses and a pitcher. "I hope you don't disapprove of alcohol," Paul said to Andrea, "because I'd like you to try my punch. The rum in it was made from my very own molasses."

"No, I have no objection to alcohol," Andrea answered, taking a glass from the tray placed before her. While the servant was serving the two men, she took a sip, then said, "Why, this is delicious. What's in it, besides the rum?"

"Orange and lime juice, and a little ginger," Paul answered. "This is my basic punch, but I like to experiment. I mix my rum with juices from different fruits where they're in season. Mango juice with cinnamon makes an interesting punch. Also one made with papaya juice, which the Cubans call *fruta bomba.*"

"Fruit bomb?" Andrea responded. "What a strange name. I've never heard of it, or the mango, until recently."

"No, I imagine not. They're tropical trees and grow wild all over this island, although the mango was imported. I have several fruit trees growing in my gardens. If we have time, I'll show them to you, but neither has ripe fruit at this time of year."

Andrea took another swallow, then commented, "I can't get over how tasty this is." She laughed. "It certainly beats that 'white lightning' my brothers used to guzzle. One swallow of that would knock your socks off."

"White lightning?" Paul asked in puzzlement.

"Yes," Eric interjected. "Where I worked in Arizona, it was called 'red eye,' but it's the same thing, cheap, one-hundred percent alcohol guaranteed to burn a hole in your stomach. Andrea grew up on a ranch in Wyoming."

"Then you're talking from personal experience?" Paul asked Andrea, more fascinated than shocked.

"Yes, I tried it," Andrea answered candidly. "But it was too strong for me. Not at all like this."

As Andrea took another swallow, Eric frowned. She was such a strong supporter of female rights—he had assumed she was also a follower of Susan Anthony, who preached so adamantly against liquor. That's why he hadn't suggested some wine with their meals. He should have realized it wouldn't be that simple with Andrea. She wasn't going to fit into any neat niche. She was her own woman. She let her own personal beliefs guide her, instead of adopting those of others. She was a fierce individualist blazing her own trail and setting her own code of conduct. Eric had learned to accept many of her 'differences,' but he didn't like the way she was drinking so freely. Like her recklessness, it alarmed him. "You might want to take it a little easy on that," he said. "Because it tastes so good, it's deceiving. But that rum can be as potent as white lightning."

It was more the disapproving look on Eric's face than his words that made Andrea's hackles rise. Who did he think he was, she thought. Her keeper? Well, just because they were lovers didn't mean he could tell her what to do. If that's what he thought, he was sadly mistaken. She could do what she damn well pleased! And would! She shot him a murderous glance, then replied coldly, "Thank you for the warning." Then she turned to Paul and asked, "May I have a refill?"

Andrea's deliberate defiance didn't sit too well with Eric, and his expression showed it. As the two glared at one another, Paul was aware of the tension between them. He knew his suspicions were true. Their relationship was far from platonic. And although he agreed with Eric—the punch could be deceiving—good manners prevented him from siding with his old friend. He rose, took Andrea's glass, and refilled it from the pitcher.

As he handed the glass back to her, Paul asked, "What's the news in Havana? I'm so isolated here, I'm usually running weeks behind."

Eric hung back just a fraction of a moment to give Andrea the chance to speak first, a surprising courtesy that Paul noted as it slipped by Andrea. Then Eric told his friend the latest events. When he had finished, Paul asked, "How far do you think the United States will go with their involvement with this rebellion?"

"All the way, if things keep up."

"Yes, I agree," Paul answered firmly.

As Eric had talked, Andrea had come to realize that his warning about the punch had been valid. The room had started to whirl a little. Her resentment towards him continued, but she backed off from the rum. Feeling a little more in control of her senses, she asked Paul, "How do you feel about our government getting into an all-out war with Spain?"

"From the standpoint of the company I work for, or personally?"

"Both."

"The American Sugar Refining Company owns nineteen refineries here in Cuba, to say nothing of the thousands of miles of cane fields in their possession. With what is produced here in Cuba, they supply the United States with ninety percent of the sugar the public consumes. So, you see they have a major, legitimate interest in what is going on in this country, as do the other American investors down here—those with mining interests, or involved in cattle raising, fruit and tobacco plantations, public utility companies. I've heard that fifty million American dollars has been invested in this island. The revolution isn't helping business. The longer it drags out, the more those investors stand to lose. It isn't at all unreasonable to assume that the investors would be more than happy to see a quick, decisive end to the conflict. The United States could bring that about through war. To be perfectly honest, I don't think the investors would be averse if the United States took over the island completely."

"But what about the revolution?" Andrea objected. "That's what this conflict is about. Freedom for Cuba."

"Big business doesn't give a hoot for Cuba's freedom—but please don't print that. Right now, their concern is keeping their interests down here intact. Nothing else. The sooner they can get things back to normal, the better. And I have no doubts that they are using every bit of their political influence to do just that."

Andrea knew that what Paul had said was true. She had made a private investigation into which companies were lobbying Congress for American intervention. For the better part, they were companies with interests down here, or businesses that would profit from manufacturing war materials. She had wanted to confirm her suspicions. "And your personal feelings? Would you like to see the United States enter this conflict militarily?"

"No, I wouldn't. For one, I'd like to see the Cubans win their independence by themselves. They've certainly fought long enough and hard enough for it. But I'm afraid the main reason I'm against the U.S. entering the war is more personal. If that comes to pass, Havana will be the top military target, since it's the capital of the country and the most heavily manned and fortified city. The territory all around it, including this plantation, will become the battlefield, as the Spanish shift the war back to this end of the country. I've been very fortunate so far, in that my plantation hasn't been harmed. I don't think I could bear to see it destroyed. You see, in my own way, I'm as selfish as the investors."

Andrea didn't agree with Paul. This was Paul's home. He loved it. But for the investors, it was just a means for making a profit.

While Andrea was thinking those thoughts, Eric

frowned. He hadn't considered what might happen to Paul if the U.S. came into the war. "If it comes to war, don't you think your company will pull you out? You know, the first thing the authorities here are going to do is confiscate all American property."

"Yes, I'm sure they will, but I'm not leaving."

"They might imprison you," Eric pointed out. "You'll be the enemy."

"If it comes down to that, I'll join the rebels," Paul answered calmly, then asked, "What about you? Will you leave the country?"

"I don't know," Eric answered evasively.

Paul stared at Eric thoughtfully for a moment, then turned and said to Andrea, "You know, I'm surprised Eric hasn't already joined the rebels, in view of what happened to his uncle."

"What uncle?"

"Oh, he didn't tell you?" Paul asked in surprise.

Andrea shot Eric a sharp glance. "No, he didn't."

Paul looked at Eric and asked, "Do you mind if I do?"

Eric could have rung Paul's neck, for fear that knowing about his uncle might give Andrea ideas about him. But Eric hid his feelings beneath a bland expression and answered, "No, go ahead, although I don't see what it has to do with anything."

"To the contrary," Paul remarked. "You wouldn't have come to Cuba if it hadn't been for him. You said so yourself. You were curious to see the place where he died."

"Died?" Andrea asked, her curiosity thoroughly aroused.

"Yes, shot by the Spaniards," Paul informed her.

"He was a member of the ill-fated *Virginius*. Have you ever heard of that incident?"

"No, I don't believe I have."

"It happened during the Ten Years War," Paul continued. "The *Virginius* was an American ship with an American registry and an American crew that smuggled guns to the rebels down here. She was a paddle-wheeler that had served as a blockade runner during the War between the States, so she was fast, but not fast enough on that particular trip. She was intercepted at high seas by a Spanish warship, and boarded. Everything was confiscated and the 150 British and American *expedecionarios* on their way to join the rebels were arrested. Despite her captain's strong objections, they were taken to Santiago, where the Spanish governor sentenced them all to death, the captain, the crew, every single man on board."

"But they couldn't do that!" Andrea interjected angrily. "Board a ship and arrest everyone in international waters? Why, that could be considered an act of war!"

"True, but the Spanish said they didn't care, that they knew the *Virginius* had violated the neutrality laws in the past and had fully intended to do so again. I don't think anyone would have objected too strongly, despite the flagrant disregard for international law on their part, if the Spanish had just kept the ship and cargo and perhaps imprisoned the men for a few months to teach them a lesson. But they carried their vindictiveness too far when they began executing them. Both the United States and Great Britain objected strenuously, but it wasn't until a British warship sailed into the harbor that the executions stopped. By then, fifty-three men had been killed, including Eric's uncle."

Andrea looked at Eric and asked in outrage, "And nothing more was done about it?"

"The United States demanded compensation to the men's families. And the government requested that the Spanish governor be punished, since he didn't have the authority to sentence American citizens taken on the high seas to anything, much less death. Spain paid $80,000 in indemnity, a pitifully small sum when you split it among that many lives unjustly taken. In my estimation, that was insult enough, but nothing was ever done to the governor. He resigned his post and returned to Spain, where he was regarded as a hero," Eric ended bitterly.

"That's terrible!" Andrea responded. "Why didn't our country declare war on Spain then, if they've wanted an excuse to get Cuba all along?"

"The time wasn't right," Paul answered. "That was over twenty years ago, when Spain was regarded as one of the world's most powerful nations. We were afraid to face up to them. You notice, it was Great Britain who sent the warship as a threat, not us. Besides, Americans hadn't invested heavily down here yet. That didn't occur until after the Ten Years War."

Andrea didn't like the idea that her country might be afraid of another country, since there was very little she herself was afraid of. She turned to Eric and asked, "Were you close to your uncle?"

"To be perfectly honest, I didn't really know him that well," Eric answered. "I was just a kid when he died. Besides, he was an adventurer, a soldier of fortune, always chasing off to one part of the world or another in search of excitement and flirting with death. But I did envy him that, being able to move about so freely and see the world."

Andrea thought she had solved the puzzle concerning Eric's dangerous and exciting aura. Whether he realized it or not, he had the same adventurous spirit as his uncle.

Shortly thereafter, a servant announced that dinner was served and the three walked to the dining room. As soon as they were seated, Paul said, "I must apologize for the simplicity of the meal I'm offering you. Had I realized I had guests coming, I would have my cooks prepare something much more elaborate than *ajiaco.*"

But Andrea found the country dish made from *yucas, malangas, chayotes,* and *boniatos*—root vegetables—and chicken absolutely delicious, so much so that she asked for seconds, to Paul's delight. She didn't know if it was the fresh air or the rum that had stimulated her appetite, or if she was acquiring a taste for the unusual cuisine.

After dinner, they retired to the *sala.* But despite the strong after-dinner coffee Paul served, Andrea found she could hardly keep her eyes open. She finally rose, saying, "Please forgive me, but I'm afraid I'm going to have to retire. I guess the trip must have tired me more than I realized."

Eric knew otherwise. Andrea had weathered the trip as well as any cavalry trooper. It was the excess of rum and food she had consumed. But he made no comment.

"Besides, you two haven't seen each other for a long

time," she continued. "I'm sure you have some catching up to do."

Paul rose, saying, "I'll show you to your room."

"No, that's not necessary," Andrea objected. "Just give me directions."

She's accustomed to being self-sufficient, Paul thought with approval. "If you like," he agreed. "Just follow that hall to the end, then turn left. It's the third door down."

After Andrea had left, Eric and Paul spent another hour or so talking. Then Eric also excused himself and walked to his room. As soon as he shut the door behind him, he realized that Paul had given him and Andrea the adjoining rooms reserved for visiting company officials and their wives. He wondered if Paul suspected something, or if he had only done it because they were his two largest and most private guest rooms, sitting on the opposite side of the house from his.

Eric, knowing how easily accessible Andrea was, had a sudden urge to see her. He walked to the door that joined their rooms, then knocked softly on it. When there was no answer, he opened it and looked in. As his eyes adjusted to the darkness, he saw her asleep on the bed.

He felt a keen disappointment. He hadn't realized until then that he had been hoping she would be awake so they could make love. The realization didn't set too easily with him, particularly in view of the fact that he had been angry about her defiance just a few hours before. Why in hell couldn't he stay mad at her, he asked himself in frustration. At least he could practice some control and stay away from her? But he couldn't.

She seemed to be drawing him deeper and deeper into a silken web of desire.

Feeling nothing but self-disgust, he stepped back and closed the door.

Chapter 10

The next day, Paul took Andrea on a tour of the plantation, and Eric tagged along.

Riding down a maze of narrow, twisting trails between the towering cane, Paul explained that the plant was grown from cuttings buried in long trenches. In the tropics, the cane would grow from its own stubble, if cut correctly, for as long as fifteen years, but he planted a new crop, rotating the fields, every five to seven years for better production. Paul related how the first chore, after the rainy season had passed, was to hack away the undergrowth that threatened to choke the cane, for these fields had once been jungles that were always trying to reclaim the land. He told how the tassels on the top of the plants took on a purplish tinge as they ripened, hence why many planters referred to it as 'blue grass.' It never fully ripened in Louisiana as it did here, due to having to be cut before winter. The more swollen the joints, the more juice it held and the better its yield.

"And it's not harvested until late June or July?" Andrea asked, remembering what Eric had told her.

"Yes," Paul answered, "and cutting is an art in itself. It can't simply be hacked down. The cut must be made at a certain height and a certain angle for it to achieve proper growth for the next season. That's why I use only skilled cutters." Paul paused and gazed out at the field, then said, "I wish you could see them in action. The stalk is cut with one powerful stroke of the machete, the second stroke removes the leaves on one side, the third, those on the other side, then the stalk is cut into pieces and thrown onto a pile. The men move as gracefully and rhythmically as ballet dancers. Scores of them are lined up and down the length of the field, slicing, stripping. Their dark skin is glistening with sweat and the blades of their knives flash in the sunlight."

Andrea tried to picture the scene. Even if she couldn't witness an actual harvest, she wanted to write as if she had seen one. "What do they wear?"

"Nothing, except a headband to keep the sweat from their eyes."

"They're stark naked?" Andrea asked in shock.

"Yes. I see no reason to require clothing. There's no one but men here, and to labor in that heat with clothes on would be courting death from heat prostration."

"You have no idea how hot it can get here in the summer," Eric commented, joining the conversation. "It's not just the high temperature; it's the humidity, too. There's no place for sweat to go with that much moisture already in the air. Clothing gets waterlogged, holding in the heat. Many of the *mambis* fight in the nude during the heat of the summer, wearing only their cartridge belts slung over their shoulders."

Andrea wondered if Eric worked in the nude in the mountains during the worst of the summer, too, since she had noticed he was tanned all over. Paul's thoughts, however, took a different vein. He wondered how his friend knew that interesting piece of information about the rebels.

The three rode to the brick sugar mill with its huge black smokestack. They dismounted and went inside. Paul explained that the mill was a *centrale*. Since the Americans had taken over so much of the sugar business, the industry had been restructured so that each plantation no longer had its own mill. Only those who were the best producing had one. Cane was brought here from less-productive plantations to be milled along with his. He showed her the huge machine where the cane, transported to the factory in carts pulled by oxen, was crushed between ponderous rollers, then where the juice, called *guarapo,* was boiled in a monstrous kettle before being strained through burlap into kettles nine feet in diameter and reboiled under open sheds, using the *bagazo*—the fiber left from the crushed cane—as fuel. Going back into the mill, he explained how the *melado,* the molasses, was taken from the kettles and passed through enormous centrifuges where it was precipitated into raw sugar, which was dark brown, thick, and moist, then transported by private rail to the refineries where it became the white sugar Andrea was familiar with.

As they walked from the mill, Andrea was amazed. She had always taken sugar for granted. She'd had no idea how much work went into producing the final product. She was sure the average American didn't know the process. She could hardly wait to start on her new article.

As they mounted their horses, Eric remarked to Andrea, "I came for a visit once when everything here was going in full swing. With the smoke coming from that smokestack and the fires under those sheds, a thick, black cloud hung over everything, blotting out the sun and making it look like it was dusk, and the smell of boiling sugar was so heavy in the air, it was sickening."

"Yes, it does has a very distinctive smell," Paul agreed, "particularly when it's burnt. On several occasions during the last eighteen months, I've seen black smoke billowing into the sky in the distance. I always knew it was a sugar plantation being torched by the rebels on account of the faint smell of burnt sugar in the air."

"There's no way burnt cane can be harvested and milled, and at least that crop salvaged?" Andrea asked.

"It would have to be done very quickly, or else it would produce a poor syrup, and that's next to impossible if a great deal of cane was burned. That's why the sugar planter's greatest natural enemy is lightning."

As they rode back to the plantation house, Andrea asked, "Where do all of the workers go during the dead season?"

Paul shrugged his shoulders and answered, "Some move on to plantations harvesting other crops, others head to the coastal cities and find odd jobs, still others go back to family farms, until recently. Now, I think most of them probably join the rebels during the off season. I really feel sorry for the laborers. I wish I could keep more of them on, year-round, but the company won't stand for it. Unnecessary and too costly, they say. To be perfectly honest, I think all this restructuring is causing a lot of Cuba's problems. It's putting more people out of work, and unemployment always lends to discontent. It's hard to tell a hungry man to be patient, because reforms in government are coming. Progress can often be very cruel to the working man."

That someone other than the Spanish government might be at least partially responsible for Cuba's woes was a point Andrea had never considered.

Instead of riding directly back to the house, Paul took them to a remote corner of the gardens surrounding it, so that he could show Andrea his tropical garden. He pointed to a tree with shiny leaves and covered with large, dark, pear-shaped fruits. "That fruit is known as an alligator pear here in Cuba because of its dark skin. Actually it's an avocado. It has a creamy, rather bland tasting yellowish-green pulp."

"Avocado?" Andrea responded. "That's a strange sounding word. Is it African or something?"

"It's derived from the Central American Indian word, *ahuacatl.*"

"What does the word mean?"

"I don't really know," Paul answered, knowing full well it meant testicle, so named because of the fruit's shape.

Andrea saw the flush on Paul's face and wondered at it, particularly since Eric seemed to find his answer amusing. She turned her attention to a tree that was a good forty feet tall with a dense crown of lustrous tapering leaves, six to eight inches long. She noted that it was covered with green fruit, each the size of a small melon.

"That's my mango tree," Paul informed her. "When the fruit is ripe, its skin turns yellow or yellow with a rose blush. Its pulp is also yellow and it has a rather spicy odor. It has a strong, peachlike flavor, and a large beanlike seed that can be roasted. Those trees to the side of it are my papayas. The fruit on them gets much larger than the mango. Many get as large as watermelons, and when they're ripe, they often fall from the trees, hopefully not while you're walking beneath them."

Andrea could imagine one splattering on someone's head. She laughed and said, "That's why they're called fruit bombs."

"Exactly." Paul motioned to the banana trees growing to the other side of the mango, saying, "I have four varieties of bananas here, the large plantain, for cooking, two types of eating bananas, and the *platano datel,* which produces date-sized fruit. Actually, the banana is an herb, not a tree. It has a false stalk, not a trunk, formed by the curled bases of the leaves, which wrap themselves about the flower stem."

"They actually flower?" Andrea asked in amazement.

"Yes, when the plant has reached its full growth, a huge flower bud appears on the stem, which opens and shows a bunch of tiny purple flowers, each of which produces a banana. The great flower cluster hangs towards the ground, but as the fruits grow, they turn upward, like that hand over there, which is what we call the bunches.

Andrea could understand why they were called

hands. The bananas did look rather like curled-up fingers. But she was surprised at how they actually grew. She had seen several bunches hanging in the open markets in Havana. They had always hung in the opposite direction, with the fruit pointing downward. Spying a hand on another tall plant, she asked, "Why is that hand wrapped in paper?"

"To speed up the ripening process, which under normal conditions is very slow. If I were exporting my bananas, I would pick them green and allow them to ripen in transit or in warm storage houses. Of course, all of my bananas are the cultivated varieties, in which the seeds have degenerated. The wild varieties are so full of seeds you can hardly eat them."

"And those trees?" Andrea asked, motioning to a line of shorter trees with shiny leaves.

"My citrus trees. I have two varieties of orange trees, a lime tree, and a lemon tree."

"And you should see those lemons," Eric commented. "They're as big as small melons. One lemon is enough for an entire pitcher of lemonade."

Andrea's eyes swept appreciatively over Paul's tropical orchard. She saw something in the thick junglelike growth to the rear of it, and asked, "What is that stone wall back there?"

"That is what's left of an old *barracón,* one of the pens the slaves were kept in at night."

"Pens?" Andrea asked in a shocked voice. "I thought they lived in cabins, or something."

"In our country, yes, but here, the *colonos* didn't feel it necessary to build them shelters, since it never gets that cold. They lived in the wide open, taking refuge from rain under the palmettos."

"That's horrible enough, but why were they penned?" Andrea asked, her shock turning to outrage.

"The Spaniards were afraid of uprisings. If you look closely, you can see the towers where the guards sat with their guns. Many slaves were kept in ankle chains."

"I'd like to see it more closely," Andrea said, then before Paul could respond, she rode off.

When Andrea reached the *barracón,* she dismounted, walked to an iron gate between the crumbling walls, and pushed it open. The squeaking of the rusty hinges made shivers run up her spine. She could only go a few feet into the pen, due to the thick tangle of growth. Then, spying a large, wide-mouthed, stone jar sitting to one side, asked Paul, who had followed her, "What's that?"

"A *tinajón.* It probably held their drinking water."

Andrea stood for a moment in the dead silence. She wondered if the place still held the stench of unwashed bodies, open latrines, and death—if she could faintly hear the clink of chains, a mournful wail, the throbbing beat of African drums—if she could feel the slaves' homesickness, their loneliness, their fear, their misery, their anger and hatred. Or maybe it all was just her imagination. She jumped when Eric touched her elbow. He was saying, "Come on. Let's go. This place is giving me the willies."

"Yes, I agree," Paul commented. "There is something about it that is terribly disturbing. That's why I'm letting the jungle reclaim it."

As they walked back to their horses, Andrea asked, "Where do your labororers sleep?"

"I have several large *bohíos* and a dozen or so open

sheds. The migrant workers seem to prefer the latter, since they're cooler."

They passed a small plot of ground where vegetables were being grown. Andrea looked in surprise at the two men tending the plot. Then she said to Paul, "What are those Orientals doing here?"

"After slavery was abolished, many Chinese were imported. They worked cheaper than the native laborers. However, those two are the only ones I hire. They work my gardens. They seem to have a natural talent for gardening, while no one can wield a machete like a Cuban."

When they returned to the house, Paul took them to a patio to one side that also housed an aviary. Andrea marveled at bright iridescent colors of the birds. Each breed seemed vying to outdo the other, but she enjoyed the *cotorras* the most. Paul had taught the small parrots to talk, and they were absolutely amazing.

"You can have one if you like," Paul offered Andrea. "They make wonderful pets and companions. Surprisingly, they all have their own personalities, just like people."

"No, thank you," Andrea answered. "That's very kind of you, but I plan on traveling around a lot with my career. I'd never be able to take care of it properly."

"That's the same thing Eric said when I offered him one," Paul remarked.

They lunched on the patio. They were serenaded by several of the *ruiseñors,* songbirds. Then they retired to Paul's office, where he gave Andrea more material for her story, telling her the complete history of the sugar industry in Cuba. Then he quoted so many business facts and figures that her mind was reeling. She was grateful for the late afternoon break. She took a leisurely bath both to relax and refresh her, before returning to dine that night.

After a magnificent dinner of Cuban dishes, in which Paul really outdid himself in showing off his cook's talents, the three returned to the *sala,* where Paul entertained Andrea with interesting and sometimes amusing stories about the island and the people he knew on it. Watching the rapt attention she gave to Paul, Eric wondered if Andrea was attracted to him. After all, Paul was handsome and charming, as well as a fascinating conversationalist. Eric felt the sharp sting of jealousy.

In a lull in the conversation, Paul noticed Eric glowering at him, and wondered at it. "Do you really have to leave tomorrow?" he asked him.

"Yes."

To Paul, it sounded more like a growl than an answer. "Well, I'm very sorry to see you leave. I've enjoyed the your company so much."

Not our company. Andrea's company. Eric thought sourly, then hated himself for it. He'd never been jealous before. It definitely brought out the worst in him.

Still having no idea why Eric was acting so strangely, Paul said in a congenial voice, "Well, I guess by the time you get back to Havana, the carnival will have begun."

"What carnival?" Andrea asked.

"The pre-Lenten carnival. Many countries have them, particularly the Latin countries. We even had one in New Orleans. Mardi Gras, we called it."

"But just what is it?" Andrea wanted to know.

"Celebrations. Almost a week of celebrations. Colorful parades through the streets, music, dancing, parties, everyone wearing masks and costumes so no one will know who they are."

"Why don't they want anyone to know who they are?"

"In the old days, the people were very class conscious. Every class had their own celebration, and the others couldn't attend. Then someone figured out they could get into the others' party by disguising themselves. Now everyone does it. The African slaves were so taken with these festivities that they demanded a carnival of their own, to celebrate the end of the cane harvest. They're called *parrandas*. So we have two carnivals here in Cuba, one in February and one in July."

"That sounds like great fun," Andrea answered enthusiastically. "I'd at least like to see one of the parades. Can we, when we get back?" she asked Eric.

With her dark eyes dancing with excitement, Andrea looked very beautiful, Eric thought. He felt the familiar stab of desire, and realized that he was falling under her spell once again. Fighting it tooth and nail, he answered gruffly, "It might be too dangerous."

"But I don't see why," Andrea countered. "It's not an event like the bullfight, where everyone's blood lust is stirred up. It's a happy occasion. Everyone's celebrating. And if we wore costumes, no one would even know we're Americans."

"We'll see how the land lies when we get back to the city," Eric answered, effectively ending the discussion.

Shortly thereafter, Andrea retired, using the excuse that she wanted to get a good night's sleep before the long trip the next day.

After she had left, Eric told Paul the truth about his involvement with the rebels. Paul admitted that he had suspected something. Then he asked several questions about Eric's activities. Finally, he asked, "And Andy? Does she know any of this?"

"No. At first I didn't think I could trust her. Now, I don't want to involve her."

Paul, pensive for a moment, then observed, "I always knew you'd pick an extraordinary woman, and Andy is certainly that. She's intelligent, spirited, and daring, as well as beautiful. And from what you tell me, extremely talented. An amazing woman. No wonder you've fallen in love with her."

Eric felt like he had been kicked by a mule. He shot up in his seat and asked sharply. "Who in the hell said I was in love with her?"

"Oh, come now, old friend, I'm no fool. I knew the day you arrived that you two didn't have a platonic relationship. And if I hadn't suspected as much from the very beginning, I would have known today. Why, the electricity between you fairly crackles, and neither of you can keep your eyes off each other."

"All right, so we're lovers," Eric admitted. "But that doesn't mean I'm in love with her. Nor do I intend for that to happen. There's no future in it."

"Why not?"

"First, I don't know what is going to happen to me before this war ends. Second, my work takes me all over the world, and I like it that way. I'll never settle down to one place. And third, Andrea has very definite plans for her life, and they don't include marriage. She told me so herself. So it would be pointless to get emotionally involved."

"I see," Paul answered, but secretly he had his doubts. He knew that the best-laid plans often went askew when destiny threw that special person in one's path. He sincerely hoped that both Eric and Andrea would have enough sense to recognize and accept that fact of life.

Eric bade Paul good-night. As soon as Eric shut the door behind him, his eyes moved to the door between his and Andrea's room, almost as if they had a will of their own. He wondered if she was still awake. He knew where that thought was leading him, and he cursed himself. Determined that for once he would control his desire, he turned away and started removing his clothing. He had stripped as far down as his pants and was undoing the top button on them when he heard the door opening behind him. He turned and saw Andrea standing in the doorway, wearing one of those flimsy gowns that hid nothing. He could clearly see her rosy nipples through the sheer material and the golden down between her long legs.

"I discovered this door this morning," she told him, as she came walking across the room to him. "I peeked in and saw your coat on the chair, so I knew it was your room. Did you know mine was next door?"

Eric thought to lie. He hated to acknowledge his hunger for her, but he couldn't deny it. Her sweet, womanly scent was like a powerful aphrodisiac. "Yes. I walked into your room last night, but you were asleep."

Andrea knew that what she was doing was terribly bold. Why, she was all but begging him to make love to her. But she couldn't seem to help herself. She had been acutely aware of him all afternoon and evening, so much so that she had had to force herself to pay attention to what Paul was saying. But Eric had always been there, on the periphery of her senses, exciting her with his powerful masculinity. Now, knowing that he had at least wanted her last night, she felt less insecure. She leaned into him, wrapped her arms around his neck, and said in a honeyed voice, "I'm sorry about last night, but . . ." She hesitated just long enough to put emphasis on her words, ". . . I'm awake now."

Eric knew only too well Andrea's level of consciousness. He could feel against his chest her nipples hardening and growing, just as his male flesh was. Her heat seemed to surround him, bringing an answering fire to his blood. His temples throbbed, his breath became more labored. But he refused to accept the invitation of her soft lips, already parted in anticipation of his tongue. Instead he slipped his arms around her, caught her delicious, rounded bottom and kneaded it, before cupping the soft mounds and bringing her hard against his erection. As her passion rose, he watched her dark eyes looking like liquid black velvet. He noted her breath quickening, then he felt her tremble all over. It gave him satisfaction to know that he held power over her desire, as much as she held power over his.

Andrea slipped her hands between them and finished unbuttoning Eric's pants, then his underwear. Feeling the brush of her fingers against his heated skin was exquisite, so Eric made no move to stop her. Then as the garments fell to the floor and she took him in her hands, caressing his feverish length with sensuous strokes, he felt a red-hot electrical jolt run through him, almost making him lose control and spill his seed. He sucked in his breath sharply, caught her hands, and stilled them. Shocked at how quick she could bring him to the brink, he kissed her hard, wanting to punish her for her power over him. But when Andrea started kissing him back just as furiously—her tongue dueling erotically with his, then swirling—all thoughts of retribution fled. Then there was only passion, wild, hot, mindless passion as a consuming fire spread through his entire body, searing his brain.

They fell to the bed, exchanging fierce kisses. Their hands went roaming at will. Eric quickly stripped Andrea's gown from her, then dropped a shower of hot kisses over her face and shoulders. Then despite his raging desire, he noticed her proud thrusting breasts with their rosy pert nipples. Even when she was on her back, they didn't flatten out. They're like Andrea, he thought, impertinent, refusing to behave like other women's. He bent his head and dropped tiny little love bites over the mounds. Then he laved them with his tongue before he took one straining nipple in his mouth.

Andrea reached for him. He, sensing her intent and remembering the last almost disastrous time she had caressed him, deflected her hand with his hip. Then as his hand slipped between her thighs while he still worked his magic at her breasts, Andrea was lost in a maelstrom of pure sensation. She wasn't even aware when he slipped lower and his mouth replaced his hand between her legs. When she realized what he was doing, there was a brief moment of shock, followed by a fleeting wonder at where he had learned to use his tongue so devilishly, then utter bliss as she was swept away on a tidal wave of ecstasy.

Eric gave her no respite. Before the powerful undulations of that climax could even die away, he buried his rigid heat in her sweet depths with one swift powerful thrust that made Andrea feel like she had been impaled on a lightning bolt. He filled her with his extraordinary strength, taking her to a world of shimmering colors, filling every inch of her body with exquisite sensation, then lifting her to a wild turbulence. At the end Eric meant to hold back, to show that he could control himself even in this most intimate of all embraces and thereby prove himself the stronger, the master of the situation. When Andrea threw her head back and cried out, he steeled himself to the feel of her hot, moist flesh contracting around him. But when Andrea tightened the long legs she had wrapped around his hips, as if to squeeze the very life from him, Eric was forced to surrender to his own rapture as a thousand stars burst within him and his life-giving essence filled her.

Later, after they had recovered and were drifting in a warm afterglow, Andrea roused herself from her drowsiness and asked, "Do women do that to men, too?"

"Do what?"

Andrea flushed, partly in memory and partly in embarrassment. "You know. Make love with their mouths—there."

Eric frowned. He had never made love to another woman like that, had never wanted to. It seemed too intimate. And yet, he had been driven by a burning desire to taste her there, and then to pleasure her until she was mindless. "Did you like it?"

Andrea laughed and answered candidly, "I think that was obvious. But you didn't answer my question. Do women do that to men?"

Why was she asking? Eric wondered. Was she toying with the idea of doing it to him. The tantalizing prospect brought about an immediate reaction to his body that filled him with self-disgust. "Not respectable women," he answered in a firm voice calculated to convince himself as much as Andrea. "No lady would ever dream of doing that."

But Eric's words did nothing to dissuade Andrea. She wasn't a lady, had never wanted to be one, and usually bristled at being called one. And the idea of making love to Eric in that manner, to have him writhing in passion beneath her, begging for release, totally at her mercy was very tantalizing. Then as her exhaustion once again took over and her eyelids drifted down, she promised herself that someday she was going to show Eric she was no lady. And he was going to love every minute of it.

Chapter 11

As soon as Eric and Andrea returned to Havana, she started badgering him to take her to one of the pre-Lenten parades. Things seemed quiet in the capital and Diego had still not shown up by the following day—and Eric knew full well she was liable to sneak out without him—so Eric finally agreed. The next day, they went to a shop that rented costumes, where Andrea insisted, to Eric's total bafflement, that he go disguised as a buccaneer. Deciding on a costume for herself, however, proved to take the majority of the afternoon as Andrea rummaged through the impressive, and often gaudy, array of outfits. Finally, she narrowed her selection down to three possibilities: a Queen Isabella gown with wide panniers and a stiff ruff; a *bata criolla*—long frilly, polka-dot dress, short in the front with a long train in back, worn by flamenco dancers—and a velvet cavalier's suit, with a flowing cape, knee-high, cuffed boots, and huge hat adorned with a sweeping feather.

Finally deciding, she said, "I'll take the cavalier's

suit. Then no one will know I'm a woman, much less an American."

"No!" Eric responded.

Eric's answer was much too forceful for Andrea. Her hackles rose. "What do you mean, no? I can wear whatever I damn please!"

"Not if you're going with me," Eric answered in a firm voice.

"Why? Because it's not respectable, or do you feel I'm infringing on your male rights by wearing pants?"

"Don't start that," Eric replied in exasperation, wondering why every time they butted horns, she tried to make it a male-female thing. "It has nothing to do with rights. It's just that I'll be damned if I'll dance with someone dressed like a man. And not just because you wouldn't see it done in this very *macho* country. I'd wouldn't do it anywhere."

"We're going to a dance?" Andrea asked in surprise.

"There's street dancing with every parade. It's a part of the festivities. You don't just stand there and watch. Not down here. The spectators join in."

Andrea realized that his objection had nothing to do with her personally. She relented and picked the flamenco dancer's costume instead. As they walked from the shop, she wondered what Eric would think if she told him that it was common for the cowhands back home to dance together when there was a shortage of women partners. One wore a scarf tied to his arm to signify who was taking the female part, without feeling in the least that his manliness was being questioned. Then she had to admit that they did look ridiculous, stepping on each other's feet and stumbling all over each other, cursing all the while. In a few cases, it had even ended in out-and-out fist fights. She was glad Eric had taken his stance. Looking foolish would never fit his image.

That evening, the two left the hotel and walked to where the parade was to take place, since the streets would be too crowded for carriages. Andrea thought Eric looked very dashing in his buccaneer costume. She was glad he had chosen to wear a simple black mask over his eyes, instead of one of the more elaborate ones with sequins and feathers. Many men and women wore them. He looked very manly, a fact made more and more evident by the looks cast in his direction by many of the women.

It was a beautiful balmy night. The sky was a black canopy above them, filled with millions of glittering stars. Gazing above her as they walked, Andrea remarked, "I used to think the stars were beautiful back in Wyoming, but they look even bigger and brighter down here."

"That's always true in the tropics. The closer to the equator, the larger and brighter they seem. You can even see the Southern Cross at this latitude."

"Where?" Andrea asked, having never had the constellation pointed out to her.

"The buildings are blocking it from view. Sometime, when we're in the wide open, remind me to show it to you."

As they drew nearer to the location of the parade, the streets became more and more congested with costumed revelers. Then, when the parade took place, the crowd was so thick Andrea could barely see the long lines of participants with their colorful and original costumes. Had it not been for her height, she wouldn't have been able to see even that much. But she really didn't have to see the parade itself. The excited people all around her were enough entertainment as they danced to the stirring Cuban music and threw paper flowers and strings of beads.

It was impossible not to get into the mood with all the laughing, singing, and dancing going on around them. Eric took Andrea into his arms and swung her around in a two-step that was every bit as boisterous as anything she had seen back home. Spinning around, they brushed shoulders with people dressed like birds, burrows, witch doctors, angels, court jesters, turbaned slave women, and at least a half-dozen other pirates, as well as two or three conquistadores. Someone had even dressed like a monk, and some costumes were just a conglomeration of wildly colored clothing. The rum flowed freely, and street vendors hawked their delicious wares, adding to the joyous din. Then, shortly after nine-thirty, there was a tremendous blast that shook the earth and knocked almost every person from their feet.

With the street lamps suddenly extinguished along with the lights in the surrounding buildings, the crowd panicked. Terrified screams filled the air, as well as muted prayers. Andrea heard someone yelling, *terremoto!*

"What happened?" she anxiously asked Eric as he helped her to her feet. "Was it an earthquake?"

"No, that was an explosion. Two, in rapid succession if I'm not mistaken."

Andrea heard someone speculating that the rebels had blown up the governor's palace. "Oh, my God! Do you think that's what happened?"

"I doubt it," Eric answered. "The blast came from the direction of the harbor. If the rebels blew up anything, it would be the arsenal at Reglo, across the bay."

By that time, the lights were coming back on, flickering on and off. The people were rushing here and there, shoving anyone that got in their way, seeking the safety of their homes.

"Come on," Eric said, taking Andrea's hand, "let's get back to the hotel."

Andrea jerked her hand away. "No! If that's what happened, I want to see it. I'm a journalist, remember?"

"You're crazy! If that's what happened, the Spanish in this city are going to go berserk. No one will be safe from their retribution, particularly not Americans."

"I'm *not* going to go and hide like a scared rabbit!" Andrea answered with fierce determination. "Besides, you don't even know if that's what happened. You're just guessing. At least take me to the harbor, so we can see."

"No, we're going back to the hotel," Eric answered, making a grab for her hand.

But Andrea was quicker. She turned and darted away. Eric ran after her and would have caught her if he had not been knocked off his feet by two men running in the opposite direction. After that, the best he could do was try to keep her in sight as she weaved her way through the frightened mass of people.

The harbor was a good mile away, and Andrea had to fight for every foot she gained. Once or twice, she looked over her shoulder to see if Eric was following, but she saw no sign of him in the crowd. By that time church bells were ringing and whistles were blowing, adding to the din and confusion. Finally, the crowd thinned out. Then, she was almost bowled over by a coach coming from behind her, racing towards the harbor. From the corner of her eye, she caught a fleeting glance at the Spanish royal crest on its door, and she knew its occupant had to be an official.

Finally, she cleared the buildings and came to dead halt as the waterfront came in view. The entire bay was covered with a great, blinding glare of light. Then she heard footsteps running towards her, and she turned and saw Eric.

"Damn you! I ought to throttle you!" Eric said angrily, grabbing her arm. But before Andrea could respond, he looked out at the bay and muttered, "Jesus Christ!"

"What?" Andrea asked anxiously.

"That fire isn't across the harbor. It's in it." Then seeing a great cloud of smoke, he exclaimed, "Oh, my God, no!"

"What? What do you see?" Andrea asked, straining her eyes to see against the glare.

"It's what I don't see," he answered in an ominous tone of voice. "The *Maine* was anchored where that great cloud of black smoke is floating."

"The *Maine?*" Andrea asked in a shocked voice. "Do you think those explosions had something to do with her?"

Eric greatly feared so, but didn't want to upset Andrea. "It's possible. Come on, let's go over over to that crowd by the waterfront and see if they know what happened."

They found a man who had been strolling beside the

harbor when the explosion occurred. He verified Eric's worst suspicions. The *Maine* had blown up. One minute it was there, and the next, the air had been filled with a blaze of intense light, with innumerable colored lights above it resembling rockets.

"How did it happen?" Andrea asked Eric, trying to come to terms with the shocking news.

"At this point, I don't think anyone knows."

In stunned silence, Eric and Andrea stood and watched as ships were launched from the customs house across the bay to join the rescue boats that had been put down by the ships closest to the disaster. Pieces of burning wreckage littered the entire harbor, lighting up the sky. The two could hear ammunition exploding from where they stood.

Finally Andrea said, "Where do you think they'll take the survivors, if they are any?"

"I don't know. There are several large hospitals here in the city. Why?"

"I thought I would offer my services."

"Do you know anything about nursing?" Eric asked in surprise.

"Technically, no, but neither does Clara Barton, and I'm sure she's there."

"Well, you're not going to be," Eric announced in a determined tone of voice.

"And why not?" Andrea challenged.

"Because no one would dare harm a hair on Clara Barton's head. She represents an international organization that's greatly respected the world over. She's safe, but we're an entirely different matter. We don't know how this is going to affect the people of Havana. Those who hate Americans may see it as a signal to act against the rest of us. Those who support the rebels may see it as an attack on their friends and they might rise up. Hell, we don't even know how our government is going to react. So, we're going back to the hotel and stay there, at least until daylight."

"Go back to the hotel?" Andrea asked, clearly taken aback by Eric's announcement. "Are you crazy? This is the biggest story I've ever had. I want to see more."

"There's nothing else to see tonight."

"Maybe we could find where they're bringing in the survivors," Andrea suggested.

"The Spanish are on top of this now. They're not going to let anyone but authorized personnel get anywhere near those survivors. You can bet your last dollar on that. No, we're going back to the hotel, now!"

Andrea drew herself up to her full height. "You can't force me to go back."

Eric already had a firm hold on Andrea's arm. "Do you want to put money on that?"

Andrea knew he meant it, by the fierce gleam in his blue eyes. From the last time they had stood beside the harbor, she realized that he had the strength to follow through. Why, she wouldn't put it past him to throw her over his shoulder and carry her back, she thought angrily. The brute! Seething with resentment, she allowed him to lead her back to the hotel, then through the lobby littered with fallen plaster and splintered glass from the broken windows. When he followed her into her room, she whirled around to face him and said, "I didn't invite you in!"

Eric knew she was absolutely furious. Her black

eyes were spitting sparks, and she was trembling with rage. "I know you didn't," he replied calmly, "but I'm staying. I don't trust you not to try and sneak out again."

"Well, if you have any ideas about sharing my bed, forget it!" Andrea answered. She was so frustrated she was dangerously close to tears. "You can sleep on the floor. You bastard!" she added for good measure.

"That's fine with me."

Eric closed the door behind him, locked it, then started to turn on the light.

"That's not necessary!" Andrea told him. "I'm going straight to bed."

"Whatever you say."

Eric's staying so calm while she was so furious upset Andrea all the more. She stripped to the muslin chemise she was wearing, tossed her clothes angrily across the room, then yanked back the covers and crawled in.

"May I have a pillow?" Eric asked, standing at the end of the bed.

Andrea grabbed a pillow and threw it at him, so hard he had to step back to retain his balance. "Thank you."

Hearing no response to his words, Eric tossed the pillow down on the floor, then lay down. A pregnant silence filled the room. Then Eric said, so softly Andrea had to strain her ears to hear: "Good night. And just to save you a lot of trouble, don't entertain any wild ideas about sneaking out on me while I'm asleep. When I put my mind to it, I can be a very light sleeper."

Andrea had been considering just that. Furious, she

pounded her pillow with her fist, wishing it was Eric's face.

When Andrea awoke the next morning, she saw Eric standing at the window, looking out. Her curiosity overcame her anger and she asked, "What's going on?"

Eric turned. "Nothing. All of the businesses have hung black wreaths on their doors and are closed. There's hardly a soul in the streets. I think I'll go down and pick up a few papers while you're dressing. It will be interesting to see what the official reaction to this is."

Andrea dressed swiftly, and when Eric returned, each took several of the papers and scanned them. They all contained pretty much the same information. The *Maine* had been sunk by two explosions occurring in rapid succession at 9:40 P.M. It was known that the second blast was caused by the ship's magazines exploding. The cause of the first, however, was unknown. Since the men's sleeping quarters were close to the magazine and most of the crew had retired for the night, the fatalities were high. How high, was not known, since recovery operations were still going on. The authorities had opened the telegraph offices so Commodore Sigsbee could send word to his superiors. Every article ended with the announcement that the Spanish authorities expressed profound regret at the tragedy.

"Well, those didn't tell us very much," Andrea remarked in disgust, tossing the last paper aside.

"It's probably all they knew at the time. If we want

to find out anything more, we'll have to wait for the afternoon papers. But remember, no matter how many papers come out, we're only going to hear what the authorities want us to hear. You saw yourself what happens when newspapers exercise any freedom of expression." Eric rose saying, "Let's go have breakfast. Then we'll go over to the Inglaterra and find out what our newsmen have ferreted out and what the reaction is back in the States. But I warn you, we'll have to walk. I think the livery is closed, too."

It was, but before they went to the hotel where most of the American correspondents hung out, they walked to the little park beside the harbor where they had first met. When they reached the place, it became obvious that they weren't the only ones curious to know how the recovery efforts were going. The entire waterfront was lined with spectators, and patrols of Spanish soldiers were everywhere.

Eric used his broad shoulders to their advantage. They managed to get close enough to the water's edge that they could see out into the harbor. The only thing to be seen of the *Maine* was a mass of twisted metal and her mainmast. Andrea was shocked. She had expected to see more of the vessel left intact. If the blast had done that to steel, what damage had it done to humans?

She looked about the harbor. Around the wreckage a circle of small ships stood, all flying Spanish flags, while other small vessels crisscrossed the bay, apparently searching for bodies. She spied several boats heading to a spot to one side of where they stood. She asked Eric, "Where are those ships going?"

"Apparently the dead are washing up on the seawall."

"Can they see from that far out?"

"The body, no. But they can see that." Eric motioned upward with his head.

Andrea looked up and saw the flock of black buzzards circling overhead. "What ugly creatures they are," she commented with a shudder of revulsion.

"Yes, but necessary, I'm afraid. Lately, there's been so much death here on the island that they'll even follow columns of soldiers, hoping for a battle, I guess. Many times, that's how the *mambis* in the jungles know the enemy is coming, by the *tinosas* circling overhead."

Eric glanced over at the park and, to his surprise, saw Diego sitting on one of the benches. Glancing at Andrea, he saw she was engrossed with watching the boats. "Are you ready to leave?" he asked her, knowing full well she wasn't.

"No. I want to see if they're going to find more bodies."

"Well, in that case I think I'll go over and sit down on one of those benches."

Her eyes never left the scene. Andrea shook her head in acknowledgement, and Eric swiftly walked away, noting that the soldiers were just as engrossed with what was going on out in the harbor as the spectators. When he reached the rows of benches, he sat on one behind the Cuban, who was pretending to be dozing. Eric said in a low voice, "I'm glad to see you, old friend. I've been worried about you."

"One of the sentries on the road I've been using to gain access to the city became suspicious of me. I had to make a run for it and took a bullet in my leg. It got badly infected before I could get help. It's taken awhile for it to heal. Do you have a message for me to relay to General Gómez?"

"Yes, but I don't know how much attention he's going to give to it, after the shocking events of last night. García is in dire need of men to help him with his siege of Victoria de las Tunas."

The well-educated *criollo* remained thoughtful for a moment, then answered, "I'm afraid I agree with you. If the United States goes to war over the sinking of the *Maine,* it will probably change our entire strategy. Do you think the Spanish did it?"

"Is that what our people are thinking?" Eric asked in surprise.

"Yes, particularly among our leaders here in the city. What else can they think? They know we didn't do it."

"Maybe it was an accident," Eric suggested.

"I understand that is what the Spanish admiralty claims. Something about the type of coal the *Maine* burned being very explosive in tight confines."

Eric hadn't realized the *Maine* used bituminous coal for fuel. "How do you know that?"

"We have a spy in the telegraph office in the governor's palace. He telegraphed the news of the explosion to Key West before the office was even officially opened last night, then later took the message from the Spanish admiralty." Diego paused, then said thoughtfully, "Then there is the possibility that the Americans might have done it themselves, to have an excuse to go to war. I've heard that bandied about also."

"My God, no!" Eric responded with force, then fervently hoped not.

Diego was silent for a long moment, allowing a patrol of soldiers to pass before he whispered back, "I must go now. I will relay your message. But don't leave town until you hear from me. I strongly suspect the *general en jefe* will have his own message for you to relay to your superiors."

"How long should I wait?" Eric asked.

"Give me a month. It's getting harder and harder for me to get through the roadblocks. If I am not back by then, return to your commanding officer. And I'll contact you. You're still staying at the La Habana?"

"Yes, but what if my country declares war before that?"

"That's an entirely different situation. Get out of here as fast as you can, if not by your usual route, then by the emergency route given you." Diego rose, stretched his arms, then whispered over his shoulder, *"Adiós, amigo."*

"Vaya con Dios," Eric answered back. Andrea came walking towards him. Eric rose and hurried to meet her.

Chapter 12

When Andrea and Eric reached the Inglaterra, the place was such a beehive of activity that no one even noticed that a woman had entered the hotel bar and was seated at one of the back tables—which suited Andrea just fine. She could gather a wealth of information by just listening.

But shortly after they had arrived, Eric scowled and said, "I apologize for bringing you here. I guess I never realized how rough their language is. We'd better go."

"And miss out on what's going on?" Andrea objected. "No, not on your life."

"But—"

"I'm not shocked by profanities. I grew up with them. These men can't possibly say anything I haven't heard before. And where else are we going to find out what's going on back in the States?"

"Then, we'll at least let your presence be known."

Andrea knew men. As soon as they found out a woman was present, they'd either start whispering or fall silent—partly because it was impossible for them to converse without using profanities, as was the case with a surprising number of men, or else because they thought a woman wouldn't be intelligent enough to be interested in the subject. Then she'd have to be content with their resentment. "No, I like it this way, where everything is spontaneous."

"All right," Eric warned, "but remember, a lot of what you hear is going to be speculation or pure gossip."

Andrea could have pointed out that a good journalist knows how to separate the truth from conjecture, but she didn't bother. She just smiled and nodded her head.

Over the next hour Andrea learned that of the 354 men on the *Maine,* 230 sailors, 28 marines, and 2 officers had been killed. Most of the bodies were buried in the wreckage. A dozen or more were in critical condition at either San Ambrosio Hospital or Havana City Hospital, where the survivors had been taken. She learned that Commodore Sigsbee in his telegram to his superiors had been careful to place no blame, but several American naval officers had voiced opinions that the primary explosion had been external, probably from a submerged mine. The general consensus, both at the hotel bar and back in the States, was that the Spaniards had been responsible, although Spain was emphatically denying having anything to do with it and had suggested a joint investigation into the blast.

Overhearing what two men were discussing, Andrea finally broke her long silence. She leaned across the table, and asked Eric in outrage, "Did you hear that?"

"I'm afraid not," Eric answered. "I was listening to something someone behind me was saying."

"Well, you're not going to believe this," Andrea continued, but the *Journal* this morning had huge red headlines that read, This means war! They're claiming the submerged mine was detonated electrically from some position ashore. What mine are they talking about? That's just a supposition. The investigation hasn't even begun and they're blaming Spain. How totally irresponsible can you get? And how did they latch onto the story so fast? The *Journal* is a morning paper. Why, I wouldn't put it past Hearst to have had the *Maine* blown up, he wants war so damn bad!"

"Well, I at least I can understand Hearst's motives. He wants to sell newspapers. But I can't understand the Under Secretary of the Navy saying something so inflammatory, at least not publicly."

"Are you talking about Theodore Roosevelt?"

"Yes, if he's the Under Secretary."

"He is. What did he say?"

"According to those newsmen behind me he said, 'The *Maine* was sunk by an act of dirty treachery on the part of the Spaniards.' In view of what else we've heard—that both the Navy Department and President McKinley are trying to approach this calmly—that seems totally out of line. What do you know about this Roosevelt?"

"He's a jingo, and doesn't care who knows it. He's good friends with Senator Henry Cabot Lodge, another known jingo. In fact, it was the senator's influence that got him his present position."

Eric frowned. He thought that patriotism was a good thing so long as it wasn't carried to extremes. When patriotism favored an aggressive, warlike foreign policy, then it became dangerous to everyone—

especially if the believer was in a place of power within the government.

"Is it possible to detonate a mine from that distance?" Andrea asked Eric.

"Yes, through a previously laid underground wire."

"But that would have to mean that the mine was set before the *Maine* arrived."

"Yes, that's what those fellows over there were saying, that the *Maine* was anchored in an area in the bay never before used, and since the port authorities designate where every vessel is anchored, they think the authorities deliberately placed the battleship over a submerged mine."

Andrea gasped, then said, "My God! Maybe the Spaniards did blow her up."

"Not necessarily. They may have had a very good reason. Havana has an excellent harbor, but it's not deep, particularly towards the shoreline. That's why there are no piers or wharfs, and everything has to be taken back and forth by lighters. The *Maine* is one of the biggest battleships to visit this harbor. Spain doesn't have anything to compare with her. A ship that size needs considerable depth. That could very well explain why she was anchored where no other ship had been before."

Andrea felt ashamed of herself. She had been behaving just like the others, jumping to conclusions, something her favorite journalism instructor had always cautioned her about. However she was curious to know what was going on in Eric's mind. "Who do you think did it? Spain?"

"No. The last thing they want is a war with the United States. They've got their hands full with the insurrections both here and in the Philippines and I don't think their navy is in much better shape than their army. Most of their ships still have wooden decks. They're fire traps. And if they're as short on ammunition as the army is here, they haven't had enough to spare for gunnery practice, something I've been told is an absolute must in naval vessels."

"What about the Cubans? Maybe they did it."

"No. Remember what I told you about the Cubans' not wanting the United States to jump into this war? Besides, the rebels don't have that kind of expertise with mines. Oh, they use dynamite to blow up bridges and railroads, but they don't have the skills to wire a mine, particularly an underwater one. Besides, when would they have laid it?"

"Who then? It just didn't blow up on its own!"

"Maybe it did," Eric answered thoughtfully. "I understand the *Maine* burned bituminous coal. All coal, particularly that kind, puts out a gas which in confined spaces becomes very combustible. Coal mining is dangerous for that reason."

Andrea didn't stop to wonder how Eric knew what kind of fuel the *Maine* burned. She assumed he automatically knew such things because he was an engineer. "Are you suggesting it was an accident?"

"I think that's a good possibility."

"Then why hasn't the navy suggested that possibility?"

"If they investigate, I'm sure that's what they'll try to rule out."

But Andrea found that theory hard to believe. It seemed too coincidental for a natural disaster to occur at a critical moment, when it could change the course of history.

The next day, Eric and Andrea watched the funeral procession for the American dead who had been pulled from the bay and the burning wreckage. Nineteen horse-drawn hearses left the governor's palace with a Spanish military escort and wound their way through the city to the cemetery. The horses' hooves were beating a tattoo on the cobblestone streets while the church bells tolled mournfully. After the procession had passed, the two fell in with the crowd following the hearses, and Andrea was deeply touched with what she saw. Spaniards and Cubans trudged along side by side and murmured their prayers as they fingered their beads. They passed lines of spectators standing on the side of the road, many with tears streaming down their cheeks. Everyone was solemn, from the bent and wrinkled aged to the youngest baby in arms. And every house, even the poorest hovel, had some kind of wreath on the door, while every flag flew at half-mast. Havana was a city in deep sorrow, and Andrea doubted that the sailors who were buried that day could have been any more sincerely honored in their own country than they were in this city which harbored their supposed enemies.

Later, walking back from the funeral, Andrea remarked to Eric, "I can't believe that Commodore Sigsbee had to conduct the ceremony himself, because a protestant minister couldn't be found somewhere in this big city."

"Personally, I don't see why it would have mattered

if a Catholic priest had conducted it. I'm sure the Bishop of Havana would have, if he'd been asked. For all I know, he might have volunteered to. After all, both religions worship the same God."

Andrea scoffed and replied, "Oh, that really would have set everyone on their ear back home, and you know it. Many people hate the Spanish simply because they are Roman Catholics."

"Yet the Cubans, whom they claim to champion, are Catholic, for the most part," Eric pointed out.

"Well, the Americans probably think they can convert them as soon as the Spanish are thrown out of the country," Andrea pointed out. Then she asked, "But why did you say for the most part? If there aren't any protestants here, then what other religions are there?"

"Some of the Cubans with African origins practice *Lucumi*, a religion that's much like the voodoo of Haiti. They worship Yoruban gods called *orishas*."

"They're devil worshipers?" Andrea asked in horror.

"No, not as I understand it. They believe in magic and spell casting. Their ceremonies have a lot of drum beating, wild dancing, and animal sacrifices, but it's not so much evil as it is primitive."

"I'm surprised the Spanish allow it."

"They don't. It's a religion that's practiced in utter secrecy. The Spaniards know it's around, but outlawing it doesn't do a bit of good if they can't prove who's practicing it."

"If it's so secret, how do you know so much about it?"

Eric realized he had almost given himself away—again. He knew, because he had witnessed some of the ceremonies while fighting with a particular group of *mambis*. "I hired an ex-slave to help out around camp. He told me about it."

Eric frowned. He had become an adept liar as of late. Andrea brought out a lot of the worst of him.

During the next weeks, with Eric always at her side, Andrea scoured the city for stories concerning the *Maine* disaster. She found a man who had been a passenger on the *City of Washington,* a vessel anchored nearby the *Maine* the night of the tragedy. He told her he had seen the ship rise a little, then from the middle of the ship, a mass of fire burst out, before everything went up in black smoke, throwing bodies and fiery debris into the air. He related how he could hear the falling material and cries for help. He had watched in horror as some of the survivors had been brought aboard the ship, terribly burned, a few of them missing limbs or having sustained awful crushing injuries. Sigsbee had later made a tour of the injured, looking haggard and sick at heart.

She found another man who had taken part in the rescue. He told of the bravery of Spanish and Americans alike, who had risked their own lives among the exploding ammunition and burning debris to pull the dead and injured from the water.

She had the good fortune to gain an interview with one of the divers working for the Spanish commission investigating the explosion—the United States had demanded a separate investigation. He told her he knew the Americans had recovered forty bodies so far and that the wreckage under water was such a mass of twisted metal that he doubted any more bodies could be recovered, much less if positive proof could be obtained on whether the primary blast had been internal, as claimed by the Spanish, or external, as claimed by the Americans.

When Andrea was occupied in her room writing her articles, Eric spent his time at the Inglaterra bar, monitoring the news from the States. Within days of the disaster, the *Journal* had offered a $50,000 reward for information concerning the party or parties responsible for the explosion, and had given the country its battle slogan, "To hell with Spain. Remember the *Maine!*"

In the weeks that followed, it became obvious that the American public didn't much care what conclusion was arrived at by the Board of Inquiry investigating the disaster. Spurred on by angry jingoes and yellow journalism, the majority of the country wanted war, regardless. The pressure made the Spanish government more and more defensive. Soon they were so indignant at being blamed, that they in turn claimed that the Americans had caused the explosion themselves simply for an excuse to start a war. According to those newsmen who had diplomatic connections, Spain was searching Europe for allies in the event war did break out.

On March 9th, Eric was sitting at a table listening to the reporters talk when a newsman rushed in and announced that Congress had passed the $50,000,000 bill to provide money for the army and navy. While everyone else in the bar started to celebrate over the news, Eric rose, grim-lipped, and shouldered his way through the cheering crowd. Nothing in heaven or hell could stop his country from entering the war now, and he was sure the officials in Spain knew it too. Meaningless political maneuvering would follow, mostly for show before the rest of the world.

As soon as Eric walked into Andrea's room, he said, "Congress passed that bill. I guess you know what that means. Come hell or high water, they're going to get into this thing."

Andrea looked up from her typewriter and answered, "I'm not surprised. It's been coming for a long time."

"It's coming quicker now. War could be declared any day. It's time for you to go back to the States."

"Is that official? Are they telling American citizens in Cuba to leave?" Andrea asked in surprise.

"No," Eric admitted, then added ominously, "but it's just a matter of time."

"Then I'll wait until then."

"Did it ever occur to you that if you wait until the last moment it may be too late to get out? You might not be able to secure a place on a boat. If war seems imminent, Americans aren't going to be the only ones trying to leave this city, you know. There'll also be many Spaniards who don't want to get caught in the fighting."

"I still don't think things are going to move that fast. Surely, President McKinley will wait until he has the results of the inquiry. To act before that would appear overly aggressive to the other countries, and the Senate is still taking hearings on the matter."

"What if I have to leave?" Eric asked, taking another tack. "What if my company orders me out of the country? Will you leave then?"

"Certainly not!"

"Don't you think that will look strange to Colonel Reyes?"

"Colonel Reyes?" Andrea asked in surprise, then answered, "Why, he's probably completely forgotten about us."

"Not Reyes, and particularly not with our nations at each other's throats. He probably knows every move every American in the city is making."

"Then I'll just tell him the truth, that I wasn't ready to leave yet."

And Eric was sure that Andrea would do so in such an independent and cocky manner that the officer would believe her. "And how are you going to get about without an escort?"

Andrea laughed. "That won't be any problem. It came to me that day we were looking for costumes. I'll just disguise myself as a man. With my hair dyed and my skin darkened, no one will ever guess, particularly with my height. And I know my way around Havana now. No, I'm not leaving until the last possible minute."

"Didn't you hear what I said?" Eric asked in exasperation. "You may not be able to get out then."

"Then I'll just stay for the duration of the war," Andrea answered with maddening calmness. Then realizing what that could mean, her dark eyes lit up and she said in excitement, "God, can you imagine the stories I could get? Inside of the country itself, right here on the battlefield? Even if I don't get my articles published until after the war, they'll be blockbusters. Eye-witness details, never-before read. Why, I'd have the publishers fighting over me!"

Terrified for her life, Eric stepped forward, caught her shoulders and brought her to her feet. "Are you crazy?" he asked, shaking her lightly. "Have you forgotten you're a known American. You'd be thrown in prison, if not incarcerated in a camp, like the *reconcentrados.*"

Andrea jerked away and stepped back, saying angrily, "Don't manhandle me! I won't stand for it!"

"I'm sorry," Eric answered lamely, "but you upset me. I don't want to see anything bad happen to you."

Andrea knew that Eric cared about her. But just how deeply he cared, she didn't want to know. She was fighting getting too involved with the exciting engineer. This was the first time she had begun to make her dream become a reality, and she was finding the journalism she was writing exciting, heady stuff. She couldn't give it up now. But she knew she couldn't tell Eric that, without upsetting him further. "Perhaps you're right," she admitted with pretended reluctance. "That would be foolish. But I still don't have to leave quite yet."

A shiver ran up Eric's spine. He didn't believe a word Andrea said. He had seen the fanatical light in her eyes while she had been talking about staying. He had noticed that look often, during the past weeks. She reminded him of a drug addict. The more she got, the more she wanted, even if it meant endangering herself in the process. He knew it would be useless to attempt reason. Under ordinary circumstances she was stubborn and prone to take too many risks. But once she got that look in her eyes, she was unswerving.

And he couldn't let her put her life in jeopardy. He was going to have to figure out a way to get her out of the country. Somehow, some way, and, unfortunately, without her consent.

Chapter 13

Three days after the fifty-million-dollar bill was passed by Congress, Eric was walking back from the Inglaterra when he came face to face with Colonel Reyes.

"Ah, *Señor* Flemming," the colonel said in a silky voice that made Eric cringe, "how fortunate that I bumped into you. Now I won't have to send one of my men to inform you that your pass has been revoked."

Eric wasn't particularly surprised. He had known that the authorities here in Havana would react to the news of the bill. But he pretended innocence, saying, "I'm afraid I don't understand, Colonel. Our countries aren't at war. Why are my privileges as a neutral being taken away?"

The officer's dark eyes glittered angrily. "I have no intention of waiting until your country declares war and you are in the interior where I cannot find you. You would be in too good a position to observe and inform your government of our military movements."

Eric affected indignation. "I am a businessman, Colonel! Not a spy!"

The Spaniard's eyes narrowed. "I am not too sure of that. You have been in Havana overly long and have been all over the city. I find it hard to believe that you and your fiancée are doing that much sightseeing. Perhaps you are studying our fortifications."

Eric found it ironic that Reyes thought him an American spy after all the years he had been a courier for the Cubans, reporting not only everything he saw in the city and the port, but carrying vital information and orders. "That's ridiculous. You're seeing ghosts where they aren't any."

"No, *señor,* I don't believe I am. I would advise you to leave this country, before I get more suspicious and have to take further action."

"What about my men in the Sierra Maestra? They're depending on the supplies I bring them. What will happen to them if I don't show up?" Eric asked, playing his role to the hilt.

"If, there are any men, they will either die of starvation or learn how to live off the land."

"At least let me go and bring them out. They don't even know our countries are at odds with one another."

"Then you have been remiss at keeping them informed. Our countries have been at odds for some time now." A hard look came over the Spaniard's swarthy face. "You cannot go back. If you attempt to, you will be shot. Nor is it wise to extend your visit in Havana too much longer. I want you out of Cuba, *Señor* Flemming. The sooner, the better. I do not think I can make myself any clearer. *Adiós!"*

Colonel Reyes turned and walked stiffly away. Son-of-a-bitch, Eric thought, glaring at his back. Now, what was he going to do? he wondered. He couldn't leave until either Diego showed up or the designated time had passed. Would Reyes hold off for at least another couple of days? That's all he needed. Just a couple of days more. He had to risk it.

Eric anxiously waited out the next two days. He found trying to hide his apprehension from Andrea—while expecting a squad of soldiers to appear any minute to arrest him—more harrowing than any battle he had taken part in. His worry about how he was going to get Andrea out of the country only added to his apprehension. He was terrified that if Reyes moved before he could, the Spaniard would implicate Andrea and arrest her, too. Between Andrea's endangering herself by refusing to leave, and his endangering her, Eric's nerves were strung taut.

On the afternoon of the third day, Eric returned to the hotel from a visit to the port. As had become his habit, he stopped at the desk and asked if there was any message for him.

"Ah, *sí, señor,*" the clerk answered, "I believe this is what you have been waiting for. A gentleman left it a few hours ago."

"*Gracias,* Eric answered, accepting the envelope. Walking a few feet away, he tore it open and read the scrawled message that read, in Spanish, "your suit is ready." Since Eric had no suit being tailored, he knew the note was from Diego. He glanced around the lobby to see if he was being watched. Not spying anyone who looked suspicious, he hurried out into the street once more.

On his trip to the waterfront, Eric looked over his shoulder several times to make sure no one was following him. Then, deciding to play it safe, he ducked into an alley, and quickly stepped into the back door of a cigar factory. The fragrant smell of tobacco filled the air as Eric swiftly wove his way through the rows and rows of tables where the *torcedores* sat and rolled the huge tobacco leaves into foot-long cigars. So engrossed with the novel the *lector de tabaquería* at the front of the building was reading to them, hardly a one of the workers even glanced at Eric. And Eric wasn't surprised. If he wasn't mistaken the *lector* was reading one of the most exciting scenes from *The Count of Monte Cristo*.

Eric stepped from the cigar factory and hurried to the park beside the harbor. When he arrived he saw Diego waiting for him, sitting on one of the benches and pretending to be sunning himself. Deciding that meeting in the open might not be wise, since he knew Reyes suspected him of spying, Eric strolled by Diego and whispered, "Meet me in the church."

Eric walked across the street and into the small church that sat there. Once inside its dark, musty interior, he looked around and saw, with relief, that there was only one person there, an old woman kneeling before the burning candles at the side altar. Eric chose a pew in the middle of the church where no one else entering could hear without being seen. Eric genuflected, then sat in the pew. A moment later, Diego walked down the aisle, genuflected beside the pew behind Eric, then knelt on the kneeler.

"What is wrong, *compadre?*" Diego asked, his head bent over his folded hands as he pretended to be deeply engrossed in prayer.

"Reyes has revoked my pass," Eric whispered back.

"He told me—now get this—that he suspected me of being an American spy and wanted me out of Cuba. You didn't get here any too soon. I've been expecting to be arrested any day now."

Diego sucked in his breath at the news, then said, "I'm sorry you had to wait so long, but it was your government that caused the delay. General Gómez was waiting to see what your Congress would do with that big bill. And of course you know how long it takes news to travel by heliograph. I have an important message for you to take back to your superiors. They are to prepare to move as many of their men as they can possibly spare to the vicinity of Havana."

"Then the war is shifting back to the west?"

"*Sí*, as soon as your government declares war, the move will be made, and from the way things are escalating, I would guess that will not be much longer. How soon will you be leaving?"

"Early tomorrow morning, if those fishermen can get that boat ready for the trip down the coast by then."

"I will go when I leave here and see to it myself. If Reyes suspects you, I do not think you should wait any longer. Even better yet, you can go with me now."

"No, I have some personal business I have to attend to first."

"Whatever you say." Diego looked around, then dropped his arm over the pew, extending his hand and saying, "*Adiós amigo*. If you are under suspecion, I don't imagine we will meet again, at least not as couriers."

Eric half turned in his seat and shook Diego's hand,

answered, "No, but maybe I'll be back with those troops and we'll fight side by side."

"I would like that—a good, brave friend to see battle with," Diego answered with sincerity. "Until then, *Vaya con Dios.*"

Eric had an uncanny feeling that he would never see Diego again, despite what they had said. He didn't know which man would not make that meeting, or what circumstances might prevent it, but his intuition was so strong, a heaviness came to his heart. He squeezed the Cuban's hand, looked him directly in the eye, and answered, "And God go with you."

Andrea was busy typing an article when Eric walked into the room. She was so absorbed in her work that she didn't notice him standing in the doorway and staring at her as if he were trying to commit everything about her to memory. Then, sensing his presence, she said, "Oh, you're back. What's the news from the States?"

"I didn't go to the Inglaterra. When I went downstairs, there was a telegram awaiting me. My company has recalled me. I've been at the harbor, booking passage. My boat leaves tomorrow morning, at sunrise."

Andrea was stunned by the news, even though Eric had warned her it might happen. "You *have* to go?"

"I do."

"But what about your men? Aren't you going to go back and take them with you?"

"I can't," Eric answered, shutting the door behind him. "Colonel Reyes revoked my pass several days ago. That's what made my company pull me out. I had to notify them of the new development."

"Revoked your pass? You didn't tell me that!" she said in an accusing tone of voice.

"I decided to wait and see what they said. No need to upset you until I knew exactly where I stood. You are upset, aren't you?"

Andrea would have denied it, if she'd thought Eric would believe her. But she knew he had noticed her hands trembling. "Well, yes, I am, a little bit. It seems so sudden."

Eric swiftly crossed the room and pulled Andrea to her feet. He asked her, "Are you sure you won't reconsider and leave with me?"

The woman in Andrea wanted to, desperately, but the ambitious, driving journalist in her held back. "No, I don't think so. I want to wait a little longer." Then, as she saw a closed expression fall over Eric's face like a mask, a sudden fear that she might not see him again took hold of her. "This doesn't have to be good-bye, does it? We can get together back in the States, sometime, can't we? We are still . . . friends, aren't we?"

Eric smiled sadly at Andrea's calling them friends. For him, it had become much more than that long ago. "Yes, we're still friends." He turned away, saying, "Since tonight is our last night in Havana together, I thought we might do something special. Do you have any ideas?"

Despite her desire to stay, Andrea felt a sadness creeping over her. "Why, yes, I do. I'd like to go back to that little restaurant with the band."

"You'd prefer that to the theater?"

Andrea wondered why the night Eric had taken her to that restaurant was so dear to her heart. Then she realized—that was the night he first made love to her. She knew she was already getting sentimental, and he hadn't even left yet. But this time her tender female heart had its way. "Yes, I would."

That night, when they returned from the restaurant, Eric unlocked Andrea's door and said, "I'll be back in minute. I want to get something from my room."

"What?"

"If I tell you it won't be a surprise, will it?"

Andrea watched for a moment while Eric walked down the hall. She admired his confident, graceful walk, then his broad shoulders. She admitted that she was going to miss him, terribly. Then she realized that her thoughts were eroding her resolve, and she deliberately put his parting from her mind.

Andrea wasn't even fully undressed before Eric returned. As he sat the tray with a pitcher and glasses on the table beside her typewriter, she asked, "What's that?"

"My version of Paul's punch. You liked it so much, I decided we might have a little bon-voyage drink later on."

"I thought you didn't approve of my drinking."

Eric heard the challenging tone in Andrea's voice, but this was one night he wasn't going to risk getting into an argument with her. "I just didn't want your senses to be dulled when we made love later on, that's all."

"We didn't make love that night," Andrea pointed out.

Damn, Eric thought, what was it with her? He honestly believed she enjoyed arguing. She was as feisty as a fighting cock. "No, you were asleep, remember?"

"Oh, that's right," Andrea admitted lamely. Then she laughed and said, "I guess that's why you said *later*. You don't want me falling asleep on you."

"That would be a terrible blow to my ego any time, but particularly not tonight. I had other things in mind for our last night together."

If Andrea hadn't known before what things he had in mind, she would have certainly known then. Eric's eyes were that warm dusky blue that seemed to admire, possess, and ravish at the same time and always made her legs turn to rubber and her heart race in anticipation.

They undressed with a startling swiftness, then she was in his arms and they were on the bed. Their naked bodies molded together, their muscles were trembling with need. Eric's mouth claimed hers in a deep, hungry kiss as his hands roamed over her soft hips, her back, her thighs. He pulled the pins from her hair, then tangled his hands in the long, golden tresses and increased the intensity of the kiss, kissing her as if he were trying to crawl inside her, leaving her so weak she feared he had robbed her of her soul. Even then he gave her no respite. His lips and hands were everywhere—her face, her breasts, her stomach, her thighs, between her legs—fierce and demanding a response one moment, incredibly tender the next.

At first, Andrea was stunned by Eric's intense, almost violent lovemaking. But soon she was whirling

Wish You Were Here?

You can be, every month, with Zebra Historical Romance Novels.

AND TO GET YOU STARTED, ALLOW US TO SEND YOU

4 Historical Romances Free

A $19.96 VALUE!
With absolutely no obligation to buy anything.

YOU ARE CORDIALLY INVITED TO GET SWEPT AWAY INTO NEW WORLDS OF PASSION AND ADVENTURE.

AND IT WON'T COST YOU A PENNY!

Receive 4 Zebra Historical Romances, Absolutely <u>Free</u>!

(A $19.96 value)

Now you can have your pick of handsome, noble adventurers with romance in their hearts and you on their minds. Zebra publishes Historical Romances That Burn With The Fire Of History by the world's finest romance authors.

This very special FREE offer entitles you to 4 Zebra novels at absolutely no cost, with no obligation to buy anything, ever. It's an offer designed to excite your most vivid dreams and desires...and save you almost $20!

And that's not all you get...

Your Home Subscription Saves You Money Every Month.

After you've enjoyed your initial FREE package of 4 books, you'll begin to receive monthly shipments of new Zebra titles. These novels are delivered direct to your home as soon as they are published...sometimes even before the bookstores get them! Each monthly shipment of 4 books will be yours to examine for 10 days. Then if you decide to keep the books, you'll pay the preferred subscriber's price of just $4.00 per title. That's $16 for all 4 books...a savings of almost $4 off the publisher's price! (A nominal shipping and handling charge of $1.50 per shipment will be added.)

There Is No Minimum Purchase. And Your Continued Satisfaction Is Guaranteed.

We're so sure that you'll appreciate the money-saving convenience of home delivery that we guarantee your complete satisfaction. You may return any shipment...for any reason...within 10 days and pay nothing that month. And if you want us to stop sending books, just say the word. There is no minimum number of books you must buy.

It's a no-lose proposition, so send for your 4 FREE books today!

YOU'RE GOING TO LOVE GETTING

4 FREE BOOKS

These books worth almost $20, are yours without cost or obligation when you fill out and mail this certificate.

(If the certificate is missing below, write to: Zebra Home Subscription Service, Inc., 120 Brighton Road, P.O. Box 5214, Clifton, New Jersey 07015-5214

Complete and mail this card to receive 4 Free books!

Yes! Please send me 4 Zebra Historical Romances without cost or obligation. I understand that each month thereafter I will be able to preview 4 new Zebra Historical Romances FREE for 10 days. Then, if I should decide to keep them, I will pay the money-saving preferred publisher's price of just $4.00 each...a total of $16. That's almost $4 less than the publisher's price. (A nominal shipping and handling charge of $1.50 per shipment will be added.) I may return any shipment within 10 days and owe nothing, and I may cancel this subscription at any time. The 4 FREE books will be mine to keep in any case.

Name _____

Address _____ Apt. _____

City _____ State _____ Zip _____

Telephone ( ) _____

Signature _____
(If under 18, parent or guardian must sign.)

LP0595

Terms, offer and prices subject to change without notice. Subscription subject to acceptance by Zebra Books. Zebra Books reserves the right to reject any order or cancel any subscription.

A $19.96 value. FREE!

No obligation to buy anything, ever.

ZEBRA HOME SUBSCRIPTION SERVICE, INC.

120 BRIGHTON ROAD

P.O. BOX 5214

CLIFTON, NEW JERSEY 07015-5214

AFFIX STAMP HERE

and gasping. Her blood went coursing hotly through her veins. A fine sheen of perspiration was covering her trembling body.

"Oh, God, I need you!" Eric muttered thickly in her ear as he rose over her and covered her quivering body with his own.

He took her fiercely, with deep, bold, powerful strokes. His mouth claimed hers in a hot, devouring kiss. His tongue was moving in unison with his thrusts, bringing her over and over to the shuddering brink, then backing off, until Andrea was in a frenzy of need so exquisite she feared she would die. Then when he brought her up that thundering height, taking her in a sweet-savage storm to a mindless, searing burst of passion, she did die, a little.

Eric made love to Andrea over and over during the long night, sometimes with fierce urgency, sometimes with aching tenderness, driven by a desperation to satisfy his hunger for her completely, for he didn't know when, or if, he would ever see her again. And though Andrea couldn't understand why his lovemaking was so intense, the very fierceness of it was infectious, and she responded with equal fervor.

Andrea was dozing after their long marathon of lovemaking when Eric rose from the bed and dressed. Finally waking a little, Andrea saw him and muttered, "What are you doing?"

"Getting ready to leave. It will dawn in a little over an hour."

Suddenly Andrea was wide awake as the realization that the time for them to part was almost upon her. She was besieged with a bewildering mixture of fear, dread, and doubt. Eric sat on the bed and handed her a tall glass of rum punch, saying, "How about that bon-voyage drink now?" But she couldn't force a word from her mouth.

She accepted the glass. Eric raised his and said, "Here's to the next time we meet." The toast brought tears to Andrea's eyes. She took a swallow, forcing it past the big lump in her throat. Then she winced and exclaimed, "It's so bitter!"

Eric had hoped the sugar he had put in the punch would disguise the bitterness of the drug he had slipped into Andrea's glass, but apparently he hadn't used enough. "Is it?" he asked in mock surprise. He took a swallow and said, "Damn that Paul! I bet he uses sugar in it and wouldn't tell me, he's so proud of his secret concoction. But the toast has already been made. It's bad luck not to finish a bon-voyage toast, you know," he fabricated. "Do you think you can grit your teeth and force it down?"

Andrea would have jumped off the ends of the earth to keep Eric from having any kind of misfortune. She nodded her head, and following Eric's lead, tilted the glass and drained it with several large swallows, making a terrible face as she handed the empty glass back to him.

"That's my girl," Eric said, kissing her on the tip of her nose. "I knew you wouldn't let me down."

Strangely, his calling her "his girl" didn't irritate Andrea. On the contrary. It gave a her a little thrill. As Eric walked back to place the empty glasses on the tray, Andrea said, "I just realized, I don't know what your address is back in the States."

"Do you want my business address or my home address?"

"Both, I guess," Andrea answered, wondering why everything was looking so fuzzy.

Eric walked to her desk and asked, "Is it okay if I use one of these blank pieces of paper to write them down on?"

"Yes, of course," Andrea muttered, then she lay back down, seeing the ceiling going round and round over her.

Eric deliberately took his time as he wrote on the paper. He knew that Andrea was feeling the effects of the drug. When he saw her eyelids flutter down, he hurried back to the bed and tried to rouse her, without success. Then he looked down at her sadly and said softly, "I'm sorry, sweetheart. I know you're going to hate me for this, but I can live with that. What I can't live with is your death."

Knowing that time was his enemy, Eric quickly dressed Andrea, threw her clothing, purse, and manuscripts into her trunk, then carried the trunk down the back stairs to the alley, where the carriage he had rented much earlier was waiting. He returned to the room, glanced at Andrea's typewriter, then shook his head regretfully. Eric swooped her limp body up in his arms and walked across the room. He peeked through the crack of the door to make sure no one was about. Then he carried her to the carriage.

The ride to the harbor and the waiting lighter took less than fifteen minutes. The Cubans who ran it asked no questions when Eric carried an unconscious woman aboard, her long hair hanging about her like a golden cape. He'd paid them well, in advance, to turn a blind eye and perform a certain task. Within another fifteen minutes, the boat was beside an American steamer and Eric was calling to the officer of the watch to lower the gangplank.

"Who the devil are you?" the officer yelled back, straining to see in the dim predawn light.

"I'm Eric Flemming. I have a cabin reserved for me and my wife."

"Why in the hell didn't you come aboard with the other passengers last night? Do you realize we depart at sunrise?"

"A few of our friends gave us a bon-voyage party and we lost track of time."

The second mate shook his head in disgust and ordered the metal stairs lowered. When Eric stepped aboard with Andrea in his arms, the officer asked in alarm, "What in hell is going on here? What's wrong with her?"

Eric pasted a shamefaced look on his face and said, "Please lower your voice, sir. This is humiliating enough without having it broadcast to everyone on the deck. My wife had a little too much to drink at our party. She didn't realize how those fruit rum drinks can sneak up on you. I tried to sober her up, but I didn't have any luck. That's why we didn't get here until the last minute. I'd appreciate if you'd just show me to our cabin. As limp as she is, she's as heavy as a rock."

What in hell was a lady doing drinking in the first place, the officer thought sourly. And he imagined she was heavy. She wasn't exactly a dainty woman. With a grunt, he led Eric and the Cuban carrying Andrea's trunk to a cabin on the starboard side of the ship. As Eric placed Andrea on the narrow bed, he felt the sudden trembling and knew the ship was getting up a head of steam. "Oh my God!" he exclaimed. "I forgot something. I've got to go back!"

"You can't go back!" the officer objected. "It's too late. We're fixing to leave."

"Then you'll have to leave without me," Eric said. "I must go back."

A faint whirling sound was heard. The officer said, "Then you'd better get off this ship in a hell of a hurry. That's the capstan raising the anchor."

Eric bolted from the cabin and ran down the deck with the Cuban a few steps in front of him and the officer behind. When they reached the gangplank, Eric and the Cuban clambered down it, then leaped into the lighter, which was already drifting away from the steamer.

"What in hell shall I tell your wife?" the officer called down as the distance between the two boats widened.

"Tell her I'll catch the next boat!" Eric yelled back, then added silently, And tell her I love her.

The second mate watched from the deck of his ship as the lighter got up its own head of steam and moved away. Then, as the sun came up a bright red ball of flame, tinting the eastern sky in hues of rose and violet, he muttered to himself, "Why in hell are they going that direction? There ain't nothing in that part of the bay but a bunch of fishing villages."

Chapter 14

Andrea stood on the lawn of the Tampa Bay Hotel and stared at the resort the army had temporarily taken over. She found the immense, sprawling building, with its domes, Moorish arches and minarets, more than strange-looking, as it was so often described. She thought it ostentatious and totally out of place, particularly since there was ordinarily nothing else in Tampa except for a few saloons and a smattering of cigar factories. That was before the war, and before the army marked this as its point of debarkation, but still the new prosperity did nothing to enhance the resort. Shabby tent cities had sprung up everywhere. Shopkeepers were selling everything from lemonade and whiskey to red and blue bandannas to be worn around the neck, a fad started when the Rough Riders copied their commander's habit of wearing a blue and white polka-dotted scarf.

Andrea turned away from the hotel and strolled between dark-leaved oleander bushes, still blooming here and there in pinks, whites, and reds despite the terrible heat, which sometimes soared to one hundred and ten degrees. Then hearing the sound of Cuban music drifting from the Oriental Annex of the hotel, Andrea came to a dead halt as a powerful wave of nostalgia swept over her and memories of Eric came flooding back, bringing tears to her eyes, until she remembered his terrible deception. She deliberately hardened her heart.

Her mind drifted back to the day when she had awakened in a cabin on a steamer well on its way to Florida. At first she had been confused, waking in a strange place with a terrible pounding headache. Then she realized what had happened, and was furious at Eric's tricking her into leaving with him. When she discovered that he had not left the island, she was even more furious, and deeply hurt. She had thought he understood her, and respected her independence—that he was beyond trying to bully her. His arrogant taking control of her life seemed a betrayal, as well as a deception.

She had thought of going right back to Cuba to give Eric a piece of her mind, as well as to show him that she could control her life. But as it turned out, she couldn't afford the trip. She could barely afford to have her typewriter shipped to her, which the bastard had thoughtlessly left behind. She didn't receive word that her article on the *reconcentrados* had sold until the United States had declared a blockade of Cuba. So by the time she had the money, it was too late.

It seemed as if everything had happened so fast. Less than two weeks after she had returned to the States, the results of the navy's investigation into the sinking of the *Maine* had been released. According to the report, the primary explosion had been caused by a submerged mine. But the investigators were unable to find evidence fixing responsibility upon any person or persons. It didn't really matter. Spain was still being blamed. By Easter, Spain had been forced by the United States to agree to arbitrate the matter of compensation for the *Maine,* to revoke the *reconcentrado* policy, and to declare an armistice with the Cuban rebels. Spain was bowing to all the demands but one— independence for Cuba, and it seemed even that was on the way. But by then, the American people didn't want peace. They were experiencing a patriotic fervor such as they had never had. They were spoiling for a fight.

On April 11th, President McKinley had asked Congress for permission to declare war on Spain. Andrea hadn't been surprised, but she was outraged that he refused to recognize the Cuban Republic. Remembering what Eric had said on the matter, she had written a scathing article, in which she questioned how the government could ask for independence of a people without recognizing that people's government. How could we profess to love liberty, yet deny the Cubans liberty? Finally, she asked what our motives truly were in this war. Andrea had been surprised when a journal actually bought and published the controversial article. But unfortunately it was swamped by the patriotic features that flooded the newspapers and journals, particularly after Admiral Dewey and his command defeated the Spanish fleet in Manila Bay on May 1, 1898. Her only consolation was that she knew there were others in the country just as outraged as she, many in Congress.

Now, she was in southern Florida, compiling information for stories on the invasion force that was being gathered here. But she was looking ahead to the time to depart for Cuba again. A thrill ran through Andrea. She could hardly believe her good luck. Because her article on the *reconcentración* camps in Cuba had been so helpful in bringing in contributions to the Red Cross, Clara Barton had consented to let Andrea return to Cuba with her when she delivered the supplies to the victims in Santiago de Cuba. Andrea could do a follow-up story on the camps. She wouldn't be able to return to Havana and report on the war first-hand, as she would have been able to do if Eric hadn't interfered so highhandedly, but at least she would be getting back into the country. God, how she wished that bastard could know it. She would dearly love to see Eric's face when he realized that he had gone to all that trouble for nothing. His shoving her out of the country had been to no avail. He couldn't make her do anything she didn't damn well want to do! The trouble was, that she'd never have the satisfaction of throwing it in his face. She had no idea if Eric was still in Havana. Maybe he had left with the rest of the Americans right before war had been declared, and he was now somewhere in the States. He had simply walked out of her life, without even giving her the addresses she had requested. That, too, had hurt. It was as if he wanted her out of his life for good.

Remembering her earlier vow to put Eric and his painful deception behind her, Andrea turned her attention back to the business at hand. As she looked about the grounds, in the distance she saw Clara Barton talking with a huge officer. She knew that he could only be General William R. Shafter, the man who had been put in command of the Cuban offense. Andrea frowned. She wondered how the general, at three hundred pounds, was going to contend with the terrible heat in Cuba. And she had heard that he suffered from gout, sometimes so badly it crippled him. To his advantage, however, she had heard that he was an experienced Indian fighter and a doer, not a talker.

Catching a flash of light from the corner of her eye, Andrea turned her head and saw that it had been caused by the sun hitting Lieutenant-Colonel Theodore Roosevelt's eyepiece. She looked at the man who had wanted this war so badly, that he had resigned his position as Under Secretary of the Navy so that he could get a taste of the action. Roosevelt was stocky, well-muscled, with a toothy smile and fierce mustache. He had put together a volunteer group, The First U.S. Volunteer Calvary Regiment, better known as the Rough Riders. The regiment was made of up an unlikely assortment of cowboys, miners, gunfighters, bear hunters, gamblers, stagecoach drivers, lawmen, Indians, storekeepers, together with a smattering of Ivy League athletes, a few sons of tycoons and Wall street brokers, a couple of ex-policemen from New York, and a playboy or two thrown in for good measure. For some reason or other, perhaps because Roosevelt himself was so extroverted and amicable with newspapermen, his regiment had already been singled out by the press. More was written about them than about any other volunteer group, and more attention was paid to Roosevelt than to any other commander, volunteer or regular, including Colonel Leonard Wood, his immediate superior and the commander of the Rough Riders.

SOMEONE TO HOLD

Andrea turned her attention to Colonel Wood, standing next to Roosevelt. Wood was an army veteran who had won the Medal of Honor while fighting renegade Apaches in the Southwest. He was an athletic, blond-haired, blue-eyed ex-boxer with sledgehammer fists, and he had been an outdoor companion of Roosevelt. It was said that because of this friendship Roosevelt had appointed Wood commander of the volunteer group, instead of taking the position himself. There was apparently no jealousy between the two men, despite all of the attention given Roosevelt by the press. The men who served under Roosevelt adored him. Wood was the just the opposite of Roosevelt: reserved, cautious, a trained soldier who did not mix with rank and file. But it was said that he would go to any extremes for his men.

Andrea scowled as another officer walked up to Roosevelt and Wood, and interrupted their conversation. Of all the army officers, this was the man she liked the least. General Nelson Miles was the Army's commanding general at the time, a fifty-nine-year-old professional soldier who was athletically built, with a roman countenance and an iron grey mustache. He had a reputation for being a hard man to get along with and he was not particularly liked by his subordinates or anyone else. However, it wasn't only his lack of tact and diplomacy that Andrea found so abrasive. It was his firm belief that civilians had no business meddling in war or even expressing opinions about it—not Congress, not the Secretary of War, not newsmen, and most certainly not the average citizen. War was the army's business, and no one else's.

With a sigh of disgust, Andrea turned her attention

away from the man who was going to run the war. She looked about the crowd. She spied a spry older man with the twin stars of a major general on the shoulder straps of his blue uniform. Andrea thought, if the decision were left to her, he would be the commanding general, and not Miles. "Fightin' Joe" Wheeler, the spunky little cavalry officer who had bedeviled Sherman's supply lines all the way from Atlanta to Nashville, had been brought out of retirement by McKinley in the hope that commissioning an ex-Confederate officer to a position of importance in this war would help reunite the country. But from what Andrea had observed, Wheeler was much more than a figurehead. He was the liveliest, the quickest, the most observant, the most intelligent, the most gracious of all the officers present, and yet he made himself inconspicuous. Even his headquarters remained mostly unnoticed, marked by just a cavalry guidon floating from a low staff and a few A-tents. He appeared to be very much a man who shunned glory and attended business, yet his men both respected and liked him.

Andrea began strolling through the grounds, noting that there were others here besides the officers. Many had families visiting: wives, daughters, sweethearts, even a few in-laws. Military attachés from Great Britain, Germany, France, and Russia brushed shoulders with newsmen and photographers. There were also some wealthy Cubans and their families who had fled Cuba.

As Andrea made her way to the hotel, her path was blocked twice, once by a male peacock proudly parading for her admiration, and then by an artist who had set up his easel in the middle of the path. His total disregard for others irritated her to no end. Several unattached officers tipped their hats to her and made friendly overtures, but Andrea brushed them off coldly. Her painful experience with Eric made her all the more determined to keep men at bay. Finally she reached the wide veranda of the hotel. She passed a long line of rockers, before entering the building.

Andrea briefly stood and allowed her eyes to adjust to the dark interior, then she made her way to the rotunda. Along with almost every passerby, she anxiously scanned the bulletin board posted there, but saw no notices that were new. The war had come to a standstill while everyone waited for the navy to locate the fleet that had left Spain for parts unknown several weeks before. It was assumed that the fleet was on its way to Havana with reinforcements. Otherwise it might be headed for Cienfuegos, on the southern coast of the country, since it was linked by railroad to the capital, but not a sign had been seen of the fleet, and the army didn't dare to invade Cuba as long as there was a possibility that enemy warships were sneaking about. Nor could Clara Barton deliver her supplies until the area had been secured by the invasion force. The edict came from Admiral William T. Sampson, the naval officer in charge of the Cuban blockade. It seemed that Sampson feared the supplies might otherwise fall into the enemy's hands. Clara had been furious. She argued to no avail that she represented an international organization on a humane mission for a civilian population, and that thousands more might die because of the delay. Sampson countered that it was his job to keep food out of Cuba, and McKinley sided with his admiral, much to Clara's disgust. Thus, until the army did their job, Clara couldn't do hers, and Andrea couldn't get back into Cuba.

Disappointed, Andrea turned away and wandered aimlessly through the hotel, where she overheard many rumors. The most frequent was that the army planned to land on the southern coast of Cuba, and then to march across the island to Havana. Of all the rumors, this one frightened the men the most, for they were all terrified of contracting yellow fever, a tropical disease for which there was no known prevention or cure. Survival depended upon luck or God's grace, depending upon how one looked at it. But regardless of how the attack would come about, the rumors all agreed on one thing. The strike would be on Havana, the enemy's stronghold. Andrea wondered where Paul was, if he had fled to join the rebels or if he had been arrested. She fervently wished him safe.

Hearing women shrieking and men laughing, Andrea turned and walked to the casino, where the noise came from. Reaching it, she stopped and watched the men and women cavorting in the delightful pool there, thinking they looked ridiculous in their long, waterlogged suits that covered practically every inch of skin. As far as Andrea was concerned, there was only one way to swim—buck naked, as she had done so often in a nearby creek back home.

Again, she turned and strolled through the hotel, passing the ballroom where dances were held every night except Sunday. Then she stopped on the east veranda for a few moments to listen to a concert given by the 6th Infantry Band. Spurning the advances made towards her by several officers, she left the hotel and hired a rickety wagon to take her back to town, since the few hacks available were already in use.

The road was deeply rutted. The ride was bumpy, hot, and dusty. And boring, since the ancient Negro who owned the wagon and drove it, didn't think it proper to converse with a white woman. Andrea tried to occupy her time by watching the passing scenery. Through the pines and palmettos, she could see the tents of the various camps, even an occasional squad of men drilling, despite the fact that this was the Sabbath.

As they neared Tampa, the traffic became more congested. The narrow road was filled with wagons, each pulled by six mules. They were hauling provisions to the army. Each wagon was jostling for space on the road, while the teamsters were cracking their whips and cursing a blue streak. Beside them, train crews worked frantically, switching cars back and forth from the only two tracks entering the town. As the cars were shunted to freshly built spurs, the crash of cars coupling and the wail of engines blowing their whistles added to the general din. And as if there wasn't enough confusion, excursion trains carrying gawking sightseers disrupted the business at hand with disgusting regularity. Andrea wondered why the army didn't put a stop to it.

Activity at the port was frantic. Eight ships stood in the channel that had been dredged there, but only two could tie up at the pier, which was actually a long finger of land. Nearby, additional railroad tracks had been laid. Supplies were being unloaded and hauled across fifty feet of sand and up a steep ramp to the waiting ships. Sometimes, the vessel being loaded had to put back out into the bay, and another would be brought in, because there were insufficient invoices on the provisions and it was impossible to assemble complete cargoes. No one seemed to know what went where, nor what was in the crates and boxes. Everything was cramped and disorganized. Andrea didn't wonder that many of the foreign attachés had told their governments that the Army's Quartermaster Department had gone to pieces. It was true. It couldn't handle the job of readying an army of 25,000 men in such a short time, through a port as ill-equipped as Port Tampa.

Andrea finally tired of trying to weave her way through the madhouse of confusion on the road. She paid the harassed man, climbed down, and walked the rest of the way, passing through what there was of the town. Every little business, every residence, every cigar factory was sporting a limp American flag. Even then, her path was barred once by a train of wagons carrying field mortars, monstrous siege cannons, howitzers, and Gatling guns to a waiting ship.

Finally, Andrea left the better part of the disorder behind her and boarded a small lighter to take her out to the *State of Texas,* the Red Cross ship that had become her home since she had arrived in Tampa. But she couldn't get away from the cramped feeling, for the bay was crowded with ships: freighters, either loaded or waiting to be loaded; freighters being converted for use as troop-transport ships; scows; squatty tugboats; grim, metal-plated monitors; a smattering of warships; and a couple of small streamers that belonged to the Plant Steamship line. She couldn't get away from the noise, for she could hear the sawing and hammering as the bunks and stalls were constructed in the holds of the ships destined to carry men and animals to war.

By the time Andrea reached the deck of her ship, the sun was going down in a red and gold blaze of light. The electric lights along the pier were coming on, so that the frantic work could continue into the night. As she walked to her cabin, she saw a young woman standing at the rail, gazing off at the town. When Andrea came abreast with her, the woman turned and said, "Hello. I've seen you coming and going, but I haven't had a chance to meet you yet. I'm Susan Wilson, one of Clara's nurses."

Andrea was pleased. The young woman had a big, friendly smile, which transformed her rather plain features and made them almost pretty. But Andrea hadn't had a chance to meet any of Clara's staff yet. They always seemed to be in their cabins or on shore. "I'm happy to meet you. I'm Andy Williams."

"Andy? That wouldn't by any chance be a nickname for Andrea would it?"

"Well, yes, but I prefer Andy," Andrea answered firmly, not wanting to be called by the given name that only Eric had used. What before had been distasteful to her was now painful.

"I'll call you anything you like, but I must tell you how very pleased I am to see you use your real name on your byline. It makes me feel so proud every time I see it, a woman's name up in headlines, well almost headlines," Susan added with a little laugh. "But what's important is that it's there, telling everyone a woman did this fine job of journalism."

"Then you've read some of my articles?"

"Oh, my goodness, yes! Ever since Clara showed me that article you did on the *reconcentración* camps, I've been a big fan of yours. I've tried to get my hands on everything you've written. Not only do your articles have a depth others seem to lack, but you approach everything in an entirely different light."

It was Andrea's turn to laugh self-consciously. "Perhaps, a little *too* different. I'm afraid I'm getting a reputation as a rogue reporter. If all the others say aye, I say nay."

"If not following the crowd is being a rogue, then good for you! We're getting some fresh reporting for a change, some honest reporting. And I know that takes guts. I'm a little of a rogue myself," Susan admitted, "becoming a trained nurse. You know how the public feels about us. Not only have we chosen careers that are not acceptable for women, but we're generally considered to have the morals of an alley cat. It's always amazed me that it's perfectly all right to stay home and care for family sick—a chore delegated to women since the beginning of time. But if you make a career of it, your respectability is immediately suspect. For the love of me, I can't understand the logic."

Andrea agreed with Susan. And Andrea couldn't understand the logic either. All women who worked outside the home received some public disapproval, but for some reason or another, nurses were equated with actresses and barmaids—all were assumed to have loose morals regardless of what they did, or didn't do. That wasn't fair, but she thought it particularly unjust for nurses, since they were usually motivated by a desire to help people. "How long have you been with the Red Cross?"

"Since I graduated from nursing school five years ago. Since then, I've worked at the Red Cross Hospital in New York City. When Dr. Lesser asked for volunteers to go to Cuba, I jumped at the opportunity."

"Is that where you're from? New York?"

"No, I was born and raised in a little New England fishing village, then trained at Philadelphia Blocky Hospital. I always wanted to be a doctor, but my mother couldn't begin to afford that kind of education for me. She was a widow and ran a boarding house. My father died at sea when I was five years old. But now, I don't have any regrets. Working with the Red Cross has been so fulfilling and rewarding. I'm really needed. And how many women get to travel to a foreign country, like I'm going to be doing? That's really exciting." A flush rose on Susan's face. "Goodness, listen to me. My mother always said I talk too much, particularly about personal things.

"No, please don't feel that way. I like it when someone is open," Andrea replied. "I guess because I'm so used to pulling information out of people. That does get tedious."

Susan pushed back a wisp of brown hair that had come loose from her pompadour, then said, "Well, at any rate, that's enough about me. I'd like to know more about you."

The two young women, both slender, one tall and one much shorter, stood on the deck and talked far into the night. It turned out they had much in common: their fierce independence, their spunk, their beliefs, their dreams for their careers, their interests, their likes and dislikes, even their opinions concerning the events of the day were in perfect agreement. Andrea had never had a close female friend before, had never felt so relaxed around one of her own sex, and by the time she retired that night, she knew she had found more than a good friend. She had found a soul-mate.

Chapter 15

During the next week, Andrea spent her days in her small cabin on the *State of Texas* working on her articles, always with the door left open in hope of getting a breath of sea breeze in the terrible summer heat. Her evenings, she spent with Susan, who introduced her to the other four trained nurses—called sisters—and to the rest of Clara Barton's staff. Susan was even acquainted with the crew of the ship. She was one of those people who made friends with everyone.

Andrea found she liked everybody in Barton's group, particularly Dr. Lesser and his nurse-wife, Bettina. They were all friendly and supportive of each other. They were obviously accustomed to such activities as collecting supplies, learning Spanish, and feeding the starving Spanish prisoners of war taken from Spanish prizes. But these chores weren't enough for them. Unlike many of the volunteer soldiers, who looked upon the entire thing as an adventure and a lark, they longed to get down to the real business at hand. Tension among the staff increased every day.

During their long evenings on deck, where they

could take advantage of the cool breezes, Susan related stories that gave Andrea a glimpse into the private and political workings of the organization. It seemed there had been a little scandal, caused by a supposed love affair gone sour between two of Barton's employees. In another incident one of the top officials had been forced to resign because of his alcoholism. Susan also told Andrea that Clara had left Havana in a huff, because one of the members of a private group that collected funds for Cuban relief, a certain obnoxious know-it-all named Louis Klopsch, had tried to take charge and override Clara's authority. He'd annoyed everyone with his meddling, which hampered the work. He confused local officials until Clara had had enough and went back to the States, where she complained to the secretary of state that she would not go back to Cuba until Klopsch was gone and it was agreed that the Red Cross was solely responsible for distribution of all supplies and monies collected for Cuban relief.

Then Susan told Andrea of the battle Clara had with the military after war had been declared. The battle was still going on, in regard to the role of the Red Cross. According to the Treaty of Geneva, the Red Cross was to supply bandages, ambulances, volunteers, and personnel to eliminate needless wartime suffering. War was the organization's primary reason for being, yet most of the military officers didn't know of the treaty, or didn't care what it said. Surgeon General George M. Stenberg firmly refused all offers for assistance as well as all offers for volunteer service. Ambulance drivers, stretcher bearers, orderlies were turned down on the grounds that they were untrained and liable to lose their heads under fire. Admiral William Van Reypen had refused to allow the boxes of relief goods to be marked with with a red cross, which would have ensured their impartial use. The surgeon general was also adamantly against using nurses in military hospitals, both at home and abroad. He argued that females were likely to be flighty, demanding, or skittish. Thus, even though the *Olivette,* a hospital ship, was to accompany the invasion force, there wasn't a trained nurse on it.

Andrea was infuriated by the military's attitude—particularly by the surgeon general's biased, ungrounded insult to females. And she had never had any idea that Clara was having to weather so many storms, and fight so many senseless battles, on top of everything else she was trying to do. For if there was one thing Andrea knew for sure, no one could organize a project as well as Clara. The United States Quartermaster Department could learn a lot from from her.

The following Sunday afternoon, Andrea was sorting through some notes in her cabin, when Susan knocked on the open door, then stepped in and said in a rush of words, "I know you're busy, but I didn't think you'd mind being interrupted when you heard the news. The army has received orders from Washington to embark. Dr. Gardner and his wife just got back from the hotel, where they heard the news."

"When will they start loading the men?" Andrea asked, just as excited at the long-awaited news as Susan.

"Tomorrow, I imagine. But not everyone is going to get to go. There's not enough room on the transports. Of the 25,000 originally planned, only 17,000 can go. Dr. Gardner said Colonel Wood was sick about it. Four groups of his command are going to be left behind, and those that are going, can't take their horses with them. Can you imagine what a disappointment that must be for them, cavalry troops with no horses to ride?"

Knowing that the majority of the Rough Riders were cowboys, Andrea thought they would be more than just disappointed. They'd feel lost without their mounts. Nor did she think they'd make good infantry troops. She had never met a cowhand who didn't have tender feet. That wasn't where they'd grown their calluses.

The next day Andrea and Susan stood on the deck of their ship and watched as the troops were loaded on the transports. What had been confusion and disorder before was now total chaos. Troops were milling about on the small pier looking lost amid the last-minute loading of supplies.

Hawkers selling lemonade from buckets were doing a thriving business. Many whiskey stands had been thrown up on "Last Chance Street," a thoroughfare that had hardly existed until that day. Noting the long line before the only building on the street, a restaurant, Andrea remarked, "I've wondered how the food is there. It must be good. They always seem to have a pretty good business going."

As Susan broke into laughter, her grey eyes were dancing.

Andrea looked at her as if she had lost her mind. "What's so funny?"

"You are. Don't you know what that place is? It's a brothel."

Andrea felt foolish, particularly since she was a journalist. Supposedly she was adept at ferreting out information. But the building looked so innocent, so respectable. There was an edge of resentment in her voice as she asked Susan. "How do you know that?"

"Sister Bettina told us nurses. Her husband told her to ask us to keep an eye out for any of our crew visiting that place, so they could be treated. Dr. Lesser doesn't trust them to own up to it. You know what they say, the dalliance of Mars and Venus will be treated with a dose of mercury."

"Who says that?"

"According to Bettina, the army doctors."

"Is that how venereal disease is treated? With mercury?"

All signs of amusement left Susan's face. "Yes, and it can be toxic, if the treatment is done over and over. Yet, to neglect treatment is even more dangerous. It's unbelievable how many brilliant men have gone insane when syphilis reached their brain, to say nothing of how many men have lost their lives. And the statistics are extremely high among army men. I suppose that's why their doctors try to keep such a close watch." Susan turned and looked once more at the line of men standing outside the restaurant. "I can't for the life of me understand men. What drives them to do it with just any woman, much less a diseased one. If they can't be more selective, you'd at least think they'd put more value on their life."

Andrea couldn't understand it either. And surely the soldiers must realize that with so many men being "serviced" disease was bound to be spread. Yet these same men were terrified of dying of yellow fever. It seemed incredibly stupid.

Throughout the day, Susan and Andrea watched the troops being loaded. When the *Yucatán* was brought to the pier, Susan noticed that one officer got his men on board before anyone else. She remarked on it.

"That doesn't surprise me in the least," Andrea answered with rancor. "Teddy Roosevelt has a way of getting there first and foremost on everything."

"How do you know that's Roosevelt?"

"Because that damn eyepiece of his flashes like a heliograph."

"Do you suppose that's why the Rough Riders are the only ones who have those lightweight khaki uniforms?" Susan asked.

"It wouldn't surprise me in the least. He has a lot of influence in Washington, you know."

Susan shook her head in disgust and commented, "I can't believe they're sending the rest of this army off to fight in the tropics in wool uniforms. Couldn't they at least have waited until they had them more properly outfitted?"

"I heard the navy wants to get in and out before the hurricane season hits."

"The hurricane season?" Susan asked in disbelief. "What about the wet season and the fever season? That's only a month or so away. Surely they don't expect to bring this war to an end that soon."

"I don't know. I've heard the Spanish army is

weak," Andrea answered, remembering what Eric had told her. "But I don't think they're that weak. I guess the navy doesn't give a damn what happens to the army. You know how that goes, everyone looking out for their own interests."

"Yes, I'm afraid I do know," Susan answered glumly, "but it infuriates me that no one seems to be thinking about the welfare of the soldiers who are going to have to fight this war. I've heard that some of them don't even have rifles or bedrolls, much less tents to protect them from the elements. It seems criminal."

Andrea agreed heartily, but held her silence. She'd already vented her outrage in the articles she had written.

For a brief time, the two stood in silence by the rail, then Susan turned to Andrea and said, "Was it my imagination, or did I sense a little hostility in your voice when you were talking about Roosevelt?"

"I didn't mean to sound that way. As a journalist I'm supposed to stay unbiased. I guess it's not Roosevelt's fault that the press has fallen in love with him and his Rough Riders. But it doesn't seem fair that his group is getting all the attention. It's almost as if it's already been decided that they're going to be the heroes in this war. I've seen what biased journalism can do when it sets its mind to it. What about the regulars, and what about the other volunteer groups? There *are* two other cowboy volunteer regiments, you know, the Second and Third. As a matter of fact, the Second is made up mostly of men from my home state. Maybe that's why I'm defensive. I hate seeing them ignored. They're not going to get to go to Cuba, where the American public's attention is focused. They'd hoped at least to go to the Philippines, but that didn't pan out for them either. They'll go to Puerto Rico, and you mark my words, they'll never be covered in glory—not because they weren't willing and just as brave as the Rough Riders, but because they didn't have the opportunity and they weren't the darlings."

Susan smiled. Andrea could be so passionate in her beliefs, sometimes too passionate. "Don't be so cynical," she cautioned gently. "Maybe it won't turn out that way at all."

"I hope not. I sincerely hope not." But privately, Andrea doubted it.

When all of the transports were finally loaded, word came from Washington that the invasion force would not sail until further notice, due to the sighting of a Spanish cruiser and torpedo boat off the northern coast of Cuba.

Only the horses and mules were unloaded. The men stayed on board, except when they were taken from their ships in small groups to exercise. Because it was so hot and cramped in the holds, most of the soldiers stayed on deck, getting alternately burned by sun and soaked by rains. Their favorite pastime was swimming in the nude. The women aboard the Red Cross ship discreetly averted their eyes.

On the morning of June 14th, Andrea and Susan were standing on deck with Dr. Gardner and his wife. The air was filled with the stench from canned fresh meat—referred to as "embalmed meat" by the soldiers—that had been thrown overboard from many of the ships. Andrea could well understand why the men refused to eat it. Even if it wasn't contaminated, as many of the officers claimed, it certainly smelled rotten.

Catching sight of activity on a nearby ship, Andrea asked, "What's going on over there? Why are all those men lined up like that?"

Dr. Gardner peered across the water. Then a flush came to his face. He cleared his throat and answered, "They're having a feet and long arm inspection." He took his wife's arm and led her away, saying over his shoulder, "Come along, ladies. I'm sure breakfast must be ready by now."

Since the men were nude from the waist down, it finally dawned on Andrea and Susan what the "long arm" was. The men were being inspected for venereal disease. "More mercury," Susan whispered on the sly to Andrea. The two giggled at Dr. Gardner's embarrassment, before dutifully following the couple from the deck.

Later, word arrived that the convoy had received new orders to embark. The animals were hurriedly loaded; the boilers got up steam; and one by one the transports pulled away. The soldiers on board were cheering and waving to the crowd of well-wishers who had gathered on the pier.

Standing at the rail and watching with the rest of the Red Cross staff, Andrea asked Dr. Lesser, "Will we be staying here?"

"No, we're to follow the convoy as far as Key West, then wait for permission to proceed."

The last was said tightly, and Andrea knew that not everyone aboard ship, particularly not Clara Barton, was happy with the order.

The *State of Texas* was the last ship to leave the port, following General's Shafter's ship. The sound of his men singing, "There'll be a hot time in the old town tonight," was drifting across the water to them. When they reached the Gulf of Mexico, the convoy turned south. The forty-eight transport and supply ships were forming three columns with their escort of naval warships flanking them. Many of the ships towed scows and lighters to be used for ship-to-shore transport once they reached Cuba.

When they reached Key West, the Red Cross ship veered away from the others and settled down in the harbor that had been designated to them, amongst an array of American naval vessels. Almost as soon as they arrived, they heard the news the navy was so proud of. Six hundred and fifty marines had landed at Guantánamo Bay on the eastern coast of Cuba and, after three days of fierce fighting, they had captured it. The navy had taken the honor of encountering the enemy and winning the first battle on land, while the army was on the transports in Tampa impatiently waiting for orders to leave. Then, when Andrea heard that Guantánamo was an excellent natural port which the fleet intended to use as a coaling base, she remembered what Eric had said about the United States desiring Cuba for a military base. A cold chill ran up her spine. She was so distracted by her reaction that she didn't hear someone speaking to her.

"Andy? Did you hear what I said?" Dr. Gardner asked her.

"No, no, I'm afraid I didn't."

"I understand Steven Crane was with the marines

when they landed at Guantánamo. Isn't he the young man who wrote *The Red Badge of Courage?*"

"Yes, he is," Andrea answered glumly, thinking that should be enough glory for any writer. The book was the talk of the country. Why did he have to dabble in reporting on the war, too? Then as soon as the sour thought passed her mind, Andrea regretted it. She knew what was irritating her. The male journalists had shipped out right along with the army. Many of them were on General Shafter's ship. But she knew it to be pointless to present her credentials and ask for the same treatment. If the army wouldn't accept female nurses—nursing had been a woman's chore since the beginning of time—they certainly wouldn't tolerate a female journalist. She was envious of the other reporters and angry at the discrimination against her sex.

The Red Cross group waited in Key West, idle. Tensions were growing. Then on the 20th of June, Susan burst into Andrea's cabin, shouting, "We're on our way! We're finally on our way to Cuba!"

Andrea knew that Clara Barton had learned that the American Navy at Tampa and at Key West were leaving to confront the Spanish fleet somewhere near Santiago de Cuba. She had requested permission to follow them. "Then the navy agreed?" she asked in surprise.

"No!" Susan answered angrily. "They didn't even have the courtesy to respond." Then her eyes danced. "But Clara said we're going anyway."

"She said to hell with them?"

"Not exactly in those words," Susan answered with a big grin, "but the essence of what she said is much the same. She's simply sick and tired of having everyone interfere in her work and tell her what to do. God, how I love that woman's spirit! Not many people would be bold enough to thumb their nose at the United States Navy."

Andrea loved Clara, too. At that moment, if the tiny lady had walked by, Andrea would have given her a bone-crushing hug. She was a woman after her own heart.

They left Key West behind them, as they followed the line of warships at a discreet distance. The navy was surely aware of their presence, but either the commanders of the ships must have thought Barton had gotten permission from someone else, or no one had the guts to confront the feisty little lady. At any rate, they weren't told to go back.

On June 25th, Andrea and Susan were standing on the deck with several other members of the staff when Andrea noticed that the waters were turning from a deep indigo blue to an aquamarine color. Then she saw an island in the distance. Its emerald green mountains were shrouded in mist. "That's Cuba, isn't it?" she excitedly asked the doctor next to her.

"Yes, I believe it is."

Everyone hurried to the rail. "What are those flashes of light?" Susan asked.

"Heliographs," the first mate answered from behind them. "That's what the rebels use to transmit information back and forth to one another, and as of late, to our navy. I believe they're signaling to us."

Andrea never knew if it was by prearranged agreement or if the rebels had just recognized Barton's ship.

The next thing she knew, the ship was sailing into newly captured Guantánamo Bay. Once the ship had docked, supplies were unloaded, and then the waiting began. The rebels had promised to deliver mules on which to carry the supplies to a group of *reconcentrados* a little further inland, but the animals were not there. Nor did anyone know when or if they would arrive.

Everyone took the opportunity to leave the ship and stretch their legs. Andrea, however, wandered off from the others in search of information. It was obvious that a battle had been fought here. She saw rubble and burned-out ruins everywhere. The acrid smell of gunpowder still lingered in the air. The entire harbor was bristling with marines busy building more fortifications.

As Andrea headed towards one of the gun batteries, a black sentry blocked her path, saying, "Sorry, ma'am. You can't go no further."

Andrea had heard that a black regiment of marines had taken Guantánamo. She smiled at the marine and said, "I understand. Did you by any chance take part in the battle?"

A wide grin spread across the marine's face. "Yes'um."

"I'm a reporter. Would you mind answering a few questions about it?"

The marine was more amazed that Andrea wanted to talk to him, a lowly black soldier, than that she was a reporter. "You want talk to *me?*"

"Yes, I'd like to interview you."

The marine glanced over his shoulder, then said, "I

don't think I should. Maybe you'd better ask my sergeant."

"But I want an ordinary soldier's opinion. Did the Spanish fight well?"

"Yes'um, they sure did. But they didn't fight like the Cubans." The large man's dark eyes lit up in remembrance. "They were regular devils."

"The Cubans fought here with you?" Andrea asked in surprise, for she'd heard nothing of that in all the glowing reports the navy had passed on to them.

"Yes'um, they sure did. If hadn't been for them, we wouldn't have won. And I ain't the only one that thinks that. You just ask anyone that was here."

"Can you—"

"Excuse me, ma'am," the marine interrupted, "but someone is waving to you."

Andrea turned and saw Susan yelling something and waving for her to return. Andrea didn't want to comply. She knew this was the closest she would come to getting a real-live war story. She fiercely shook her head. Then just as she was turning back to the marine, she faintly heard Susan's voice. "Come back! We're leaving!"

Andrea whirled around and saw that Clara and her staff were scampering back on the ship. She looked about her, wondering if they were about to be attacked. If so, the marines apparently didn't know it. Having no idea why they leaving so abruptly, Andrea hurried off, saying to the marine over her shoulder, "Thank you. I'll come back later, if I can."

Susan ran to meet Andrea, then fell in beside her. Her eyes were glittering and her color was up from excitement. "There's been a battle a little further down the coast between some of the Rough Riders and the Spanish. We're going down there to see if we can be of any help with the wounded."

Andrea came to a complete halt. "What the devil are you talking about? I thought the army went to Havana. That's on the opposite end of this island."

"No, they didn't. The plans were changed. The navy has the Spanish fleet trapped in Santiago bay, and the army landed a few days ago, somewhere between here and there."

"When did you find that out?" Andrea asked in astonishment.

"One of the marine officers told us. If you hadn't taken off on your own, you'd have heard him." Susan laughed, then she said, "Do you realize what's happened? We just stumbled right into the middle of the war, and Clara isn't waiting any longer for permission from the government. We're going. If the army doesn't want our help, then we'll find someone who does. But we're getting into this war, by damn!"

As Susan took off to run down the pier, Andrea tore after her, filled with the exhilarating knowledge that Clara Barton wasn't only fulfilling her purpose, but Andrea's dreams. By some strange twist of fate, she was going to be right there in the big middle of the war. That was just what she wanted. And she had a remarkable, fiercely determined little woman to thank for it. They were both going to meet their destiny. Yes, Clara Barton was certainly a woman after her own heart.

Chapter 16

Early the next day, the *State of Texas* dropped anchor in the bay that overlooked Siboney, Cuba. While Clara studied the shore with field glasses, Andrea strained her eyes. She saw a sandy strip with two steep bluffs behind it. There were figures that looked like ants, but she knew they must be troops, winding in and out between the jungles in the hills above the beach. She held her breath, terrified that Clara would change her mind about landing. Then Andrea let out a loud swoosh when the little lady dropped the field glasses and said, "Let's pay them a visit."

Fortunately, it was low tide and the small craft they took from ship to shore could easily be landed. On the beach the soldiers who helped them alight were astonished to see seven women, five in stiffly starched, white nurses' uniforms. Clara Barton gave orders to the gawking men who then unloaded the supplies from the lighter. She asked for directions to the American Army hospital and promptly set out for it, followed by her staff. As they walked, Andrea looked at what was left of the village. It looked as if a terrible battle had taken place. Every single building, except the two they were approaching, lay in ashes. The embers of some ruins were still smoking. Then, remembering what she had seen at Guantánamo, Andrea noticed something strange. There wasn't one shell hole in the ground.

Andrea wasn't the only one to notice. One of the Red Cross doctors stopped a soldier who was carrying supplies up the beach and asked, "What happened to the village?"

"It was burnt, sir. By order of General Miles. He heard there were a few cases of yellow fever present."

"A few cases?" Andrea asked in shock. "Why, the entire town has been burned, except those two buildings."

"Those are the hospitals, ma'am. One is ours and the other belongs to the Cubans. Everything else was burned. Private residences, public buildings, everything. The Cubans were quite upset about it."

"I should imagine so," Andrea answered indignantly. "What happened to them?"

The hapless soldier looked very uncomfortable. It had been one order that he hadn't been pleased to carry out, what with the women and children crying and begging him not to do it. "They've moved to those caves overlooking the bay." He motioned towards the cliffs. "Everyone, except those huddled over there in the jungle, that is. They're the fever cases."

Andrea was horrified at how coldly General Miles had treated the civilian population, burning their shelters indiscriminately. Had he forgotten that the American Army was supposed to be here to liberate the suffering Cuban people? She turned to the doctor and said, "I understand that yellow fever is highly contagious, but was this really necessary? Wouldn't burning the houses that sheltered the fever victims have been enough?"

"Offhand, I would say the general overreacted. Removing the victim to a designated fever hospital and putting the patient under quarantine is the usual manner of handling yellow fever cases. Burning doesn't seem to have any effect on the disease, unlike the plague. But the plague is carried by rats, and we have no idea what causes or transmits yellow fever. However, it's been my experience that army officers, including a few medical men, don't really understand tropical diseases. Many times malaria is mistaken for yellow fever, and reported as such. But, I'm sure the general acted in good faith."

As the doctor turned away and continued to follow the others, Andrea muttered angrily, "In good faith? Explain that to the homeless!" Then she turned and said to Susan, "I always knew there was a good reason why I didn't like General Miles. Besides being overbearing, he's downright stupid!"

As they drew nearer to the hospital, everyone was shocked by what they saw. Many of the wounded had been stripped for surgery, then left without any covering on the coarse grass. Those who were aware of their condition looked embarrassed as the women passed, although the ladies discreetly looked the other way.

Furious, one of the doctors stopped an orderly and asked, "Why aren't those men covered? Why aren't they on cots?"

"I don't know who you are, mister, or what business it is of yours," the orderly answered with the testiness of a man who had been overworked for much too long, "but we don't have anything to cover them with or to put them on. There are no uniforms, no blankets, no cots or mattresses, and hardly any bandages and supplies. And if that's not bad enough, none of us has had any food!"

The orderly rushed off, as angry at the conditions as the group of observers. They stared at each other in horror, then, when they entered the building, the chief surgeon, a Dr. Winter, coldly refused Clara Barton's offer of supplies and a doctor and five trained nurses. He said his staff didn't need any help. But Andrea and everyone else knew by the scathing look he gave the nurses that he meant that he didn't want help from women. Andrea could hardly contain her fury, but Barton remained cool. She and her staff politely left and walked to the Cuban hospital next door, where their services were welcomed by the exhausted Cuban doctors.

Andrea was still fuming. She was threatening Dr. Winter with everything from pistol-whipping to worse. Although she and Susan were much alike, Andrea was much more volatile, and Susan finally had to say, "Calm down, Andy. No one else is upset."

"I don't know why not!" Andrea retorted in exasperation. "That vile man blatantly insulted you!"

"We know, but we halfway expected it. What's important is that our services are being used. It doesn't matter by whom. And from the look of things here, I'd say the Cubans are in even more need of them."

Andrea looked around at the suffering humanity crowded into the hospital. She had to agree. Most of the men were skeletal-thin. Their bandages were bloody and filthy, their beds and clothing nothing but rags. According to the doctor who greeted the nurses, the patients had had nothing to eat for three days, and not much before that. The place smelled of blood, pus, vomit, urine, and death.

Andrea forced back her anger and asked, "What can I do to help?"

"Nothing. We'll have this place shipshape in no time at all. It's what we're trained to do."

"Well, could I help Clara and Mrs. Gardner? They're not trained medical personnel. What do they do?"

"They'll be preparing food and will help feed the sick."

Andrea had always hated cooking, and her feelings showed on her face. Susan took pity on her and said fervently, "Andy, everyone here is doing what they want to do, what they came to do, what they're good at. We're doing our job. Now, you go and do yours. You don't see Keenan here do you? Oh, he might help carry supplies every now and then, but his job is writing. And so is yours." Susan caught Andrea's arm and pulled her closer, lowering her voice so no one else could hear. "Andy, this is your dream come true, your chance to be a war correspondent. Don't throw away your opportunity. Your job is just as important as ours. We'll mend these men, if we can. But someone has got to tell the world the truth of what happened here, so hopefully it won't happen again." Susan gave her a gentle push. "Now, stop wasting my time, and get out of here!"

Feeling as if a terrible burden had been lifted from her shoulders, Andrea hurried from the hospital. She spent the entire day walking about the area and talking to people. First she questioned the soldiers who were unloading supplies from lighters. Then she interviewed a few on on their way to the front. Finally she spoke to some of the less severely wounded from the battle of the day before—men who had been carried from the battle on crude litters and laid beneath an abandoned railroad shed until they could be given medical attention. One and all, they were startled to see an American woman there. Rather than tell them she was a journalist, and risk their skepticism, she simply told them she was with the Red Cross. Then, she interviewed a few of the Cuban soldiers present, all bare-chested and barefoot. The officers were wearing their insignias on their wide-brimmed sombreros. From them, she learned that the local rebels, under the command of a General Castillo, had participated in all the fighting thus far. They were presently clearing the area between Siboney and the San Juan heights of Spanish troops. General García had sent almost four thousand of his troops to help out, half of them had arrived the day before by ship and were moving to the very front of the line to act as pickets and scouts. In the terrible heat Andrea laboriously climbed the steep cliffs so she could talk to the poor civilians who had fled to the caves above the destroyed town. By the end of the day, she had pieced together almost everything that had happened so far.

She learned that the Americans had landed eighteen miles south of Santiago at a place called Daiquirí, after the Spanish had been forced to retreat by the local rebels. The only casualties sustained in the landing were drownings. Like everything else thus far in this war, the landing had been disorganized. The next day, at daybreak, an advance group made up of American infantry and two hundred Cubans had entered Siboney and taken the village without a fight. The Spanish had abandoned it hastily during the night. They had left behind a railroad that led to mines farther inland, with several locomotives, a hundred cars of coal, a sawmill and a large warehouse. The advance group had followed the Spanish, caught up with them, and in the skirmish the Cubans had received some casualties.

It turned out that the action which had drawn Barton to Siboney had been more of a skirmish than a full-blown battle. Andrea was not surprised that the confrontation had been much exaggerated by the press, and that there had been others present besides the Rough Riders. The "battle" had taken place the day before at the deserted village of Las Guasimas on a rise of land above Siboney. A mixed group of infantry, Cubans, and Rough Riders were caught in a Spanish ambush in thick, tall grass. The murderous cross fire was made all the worse by the enemy's use of German guns with unusually penetrating bullets and smokeless gunpowder.

The Rough Riders were totally unaccustomed to listening for the sound of where the firing was coming from. A few of them had fired on their own men, until they had become accustomed to fighting in this new manner. After two hours, the Americans and Cubans steadily moved forward and eventually forced the enemy to retreat. After the battle, wild rumors had gone around that Colonel Wood and all of the Rough Riders had been killed. Actually, only eight had lost their lives. The same number had been lost by the infantry, but there had been many wounded, and every man had suffered a hit, if not to the body, to a bedroll, or canteen, or hat, or some piece of equipment.

But of all the stories Andrea pieced together that day, the story of the Cuban civilians touched her most deeply. They had thought the Americans had come to free them from the cruel Spanish. The Cubans had greeted them with cries of *"Vivan los Americanos!"* Then their villages had been burned to the ground, their sick sent to the jungle, and their pleas for food and clothing ignored. Many of the American troops scorned them, calling them beggars and thieves. The soldiers insulted their culture by casting lewd glances at the native women's naked breasts, and the Americans had even tried to deny them the spoils of war. When Andrea asked for clarification on the latter, she was told how an American soldier tried to claim for himself one of the scrawny horses the Spanish had left behind at Daiquirí. A Cuban had struggled with him for possession of the animal and been knocked down. Not until General Castillo had complained to General Shafter, reminding him of their agreement that the horses belonged to the Cubans, was the matter settled in the Cuban's favor. Andrea felt heartsick. Having just arrived on Cuban soil, the Americans were already acting arrogant and possessive, more the conqueror than the liberator.

With this sobering thought in mind Andrea made her way down the steep cliff, then picked her way over a small stream that emptied into a stagnant pool of water that reeked and was covered with slime. She entered the Cuban hospital from the rear and found Clara Barton and Mrs. Gardner in the hospital kitchen, happily cooking up big pots of gruel and "Red Cross cider," made from stewed dried prunes and apples with a liberal dash of lime juice, a concoction that was both tasty and very nourishing. If either of the women felt that Andrea had been amiss in not helping, they didn't show it. Andrea was given a bowl of gruel and a cup of cider, then shown to a small room the Cubans had given the women for sleeping quarters. There, she collapsed on a Red Cross cot and promptly fell asleep.

Andrea spent the better part of the next day rewriting her notes by hand, since her typewriter was still on the ship. While she was trying to organize her material, she missed seeing the results of what the Red Cross had done. That afternoon, when she did see, she couldn't believe her eyes. The injured Cubans were lying on cots with fresh sheets and clean bandages. The people had been freshly bathed and their stomachs were full for the first time in months. The wooden floors had been scrubbed spotless and the air smelled of disinfectant. While the nurses handed out medicines or changed bandages, Mrs. Gardner and Clara walked among the men, offering encouragement and sympathy.

Susan walked up to Andrea. Her face was beaming as she said, "See, I told you we'd have this place shipshape in no time at all. That's what fresh supplies and a little help can do."

"A little help?" Andrea asked in astonishment. "My God, you must have worked like Trojans."

"We did, but so did the Cuban medical staff.

They're taking a well-earned rest right now, since things seem to be slowing down a little. We only received one new casualty today, a man with a leg wound. It was an interesting case, something none of us had ever seen before. His wound was wrapped in the soft bark of a *yagruma* tree. The *expedecionario* who brought him in said that bark was all the rebels had for bandages. But what was so amazing, was that the wound wasn't infected. Almost all gun wounds have some infection."

"An *expedecionario* brought him in?" Andrea asked in surprise, for she hadn't considered that there might be some of the adventurers with the Cuban army.

"Yes, an American. He said he came with the wounded man because his commander thought if an American brought the man in, he could get him into the American hospital. But when he saw how terrible things were at that hospital, he brought him here." Susan paused for a moment, remembering the incident, then sighed and said dreamily, "Oh, Andy, that man—"

"What?" Andrea prodded when Susan came to an abrupt halt.

"Oh, nothing. It wasn't important." Susan turned away, saying over her shoulder, "I have to get back to work. I'll see you tonight."

Susan walked away, feeling a little sheepish. She couldn't tell Andy what she had begun to say. After they had both agreed they had no use for men romantically, it would have sounded traitorous. But the *expedecionario* had had the most striking, most beautiful blue eyes she had ever seen. Just thinking about them made her feel quite breathless.

* * *

The next day, Clara announced that she and some of her staff were going to walk to the Rough Rider's camp, a distance of eight miles. Andrea decided to tag along.

They followed the only road leading into the jungle. They passed a continuous line of troops trudging along with their heavy blanket rolls looped over their left shoulder and their rifles over their right, their drinking cups clinking as they swung against their scabbards. The narrow trail wound through a marshy area, dotted with stagnant pools and lagoons and lined with sparse clumps of coconut trees and royal palms. Then the ground rose, and the path led through steaming jungle where palm, lime, and mango trees grew in a thick tangle. Some of the treetops were covered with masses of scarlet flowers that drew delicate butterflies of the most astonishing colors. The place was alive with insects. The buzz of the flies and mosquitoes blended with the screech of parrots, and in some places the clouds of gnats were so thick one had to bat one's way through them. Even then, they got into one's mouth, nose, eyes, and ears. The rank stench of decaying vegetation was so heavy it was nauseating. The air was so close, hardly a breath could be had. Then, suddenly, the jungle disappeared and the trail wound through a clearing where thick, tall grass, prickly pear cactus, and Spanish daggers grew. Everything seemed intent on attacking you and drawing blood, even the grass with its razor-sharp blades. In the open places it felt as hot as a furnace. Everyone's clothes were soaking wet with sweat.

The farther they traveled over the undulating terrain, the more littered the trail became. The troops were shedding bedrolls, packs, shirts, rations in an effort to lighten their load in the terrible heat. Many walked barefoot, with their boots slung about their necks. Andrea wished she could shed her sticky underclothes and shoes. She longed to sit down and catch her breath, but as long as Clara continued, relentlessly trudging onward in a calico dress and sturdy walking shoes, Andrea felt she had to keep up, wondering at the elderly woman's strength and stamina.

They reached a point where some of the Cubans had made camp in a small clearing. Hoping to relieve her terrible thirst, Andrea veered from the trail, to find a cup of water. As she approached a group of rebels hunkered around a small fire, one of the men looked up. His eyes were a searing blue. Her breath caught as she recognized Eric.

Eric was just as stunned. Dazed, he rose to his feet and stared at Andrea. Andrea stared back. Time seemed to stand still as the two looked at one another. They didn't know whether to believe their eyes.

Then, finally hearing Keenan calling to her, Andrea turned and yelled, "Go on! I'll be along in a moment. I know this man."

Chapter 17

After Eric recovered from his shock at seeing Andrea, he was besieged with warring emotions. Part of him was utterly joyous, another part was furious. The latter won out. His fear for her overrode all other emotions.

As Eric walked towards her with a long, purposeful stride, Andrea drank in the sight of him. He was bare to the waist, except for the cartridge belts that crossed his broad chest. And he was barefoot, with his pants rolled up almost to his knees. She thought he looked magnificent. Even the dark stubble on his face didn't detract from his rugged male beauty. If anything it only added to his dangerous, exciting aura, as did his glittering blue eyes. Her heart beat a wild tattoo against her chest. Her mouth turned dry.

Eric stopped directly in front of Andrea and demanded, "What in hell are you doing here?"

Andrea's excitement disappeared like a puff of smoke in the wind. "Don't you use that tone of voice to me!" she replied angrily. "If anyone has a right to be furious, it's me. You tricked me! You drugged me and sent me away against my will! You had no right to act so high-handed. You're nothing but a domineering son-of-a-bitch. If I had a gun, I'd shoot you!"

Eric didn't doubt her words. He had never seen her so angry, or so desirable. He fought back his wild emotions and answered tightly, "I only did it for your own good."

"That's a matter of opinion! Besides, what's good or isn't good for me is none of your damn business! What does it take to get that through your thick skull?"

"All right, you have a right to be angry," Eric conceded. "But you still haven't answered my question. What are you doing here?"

There was a hint of demand in Eric's question. Andrea was all the more determined not to answer it. "I might ask you the same question. Is that why you were so anxious to get rid of me? You wanted to run off and join the rebels?"

"I was already with the Cuban army and had been for some time. That's what I was doing in Havana, acting as a courier for them. It was my contact I was waiting for, not a generator."

"Then you're not an engineer?" Andrea asked, thinking that her instincts about him had been correct. He was a man of mystery and danger—an adventurer.

"I am an engineer, but I haven't been working as one since my company pulled their employees out of the country several years ago. That's when I joined the rebels. However, the Spanish officials weren't aware of that. That's why I made such an excellent courier. I wasn't under suspicion."

Andrea was still angry. "Why didn't you tell me the truth?"

"Frankly, I didn't trust you with the information. Journalists aren't noted for their ability to keep a secret, you know. Then, after I got to know you, I kept it from you because I didn't want to involve you. If by chance I was found out and arrested, I thought you would be better able to convince the Spanish of your innocence if you were truly surprised. Concerning the methods I used to get you out of country, I didn't feel I had any recourse. I had to leave Havana, and I knew trying to reason with you would be useless."

"Well you could have saved your energy. I'm back!" Andrea answered with a victorious glitter in her eyes.

Her throwing it in his face fueled Eric's ire. "So I see," he answered tightly. "I assume you managed to wangle your way into that job as Clara Barton's journalist, the one you so coveted."

"As a matter of fact, no. I'm not part of her staff. I'm still freelancing, and plan on staying that way. I can come and go as I please. The only difference between now and before, is that I'm published. Several times over," she ended proudly.

Eric was glad that Andrea had been successful in selling her articles. But he was not happy about her showing up in a war zone. "If you're not part of Barton's staff, then how did you get here?"

"Oh, I came with her," Andrea admitted, "but I don't work for her. She lets me tag along so I can write a follow-up story on the *reconcentrados,* when and if we ever get to Santiago. Until then, I'm free to write whatever I want, which of course will be about the war."

And will be extremely dangerous, Eric thought. A new wave of fear rushed over him. He knew he had no control over her, and no way of protecting her. His frustration was bringing on a fresh surge of anger. "What goddamn fool let Barton into this war zone, anyway? It's no place for women and civilians."

"You jackass!" Andrea answered with equal exasperation. "You sound just like those military fools. The Red Cross is supposed to lend aid during the war, particularly on the battlefields, where the suffering is the worst. That's why the organization was created in the first place. So Barton doesn't need anyone's permission to be here. It's her right by international law. Haven't any of you idiots ever heard of the Geneva Treaty?"

A dumbfounded look came over Eric's face. "Are you saying Barton just took it upon herself to land, that the military officials didn't approve it?"

A smug look came over Andrea's face. "Exactly, and they can't do a damn thing about it, particularly since the Cubans accepted her offer of assistance."

For the first time Eric felt a sense of kinship with military officers he usually scorned. It appeared he wasn't the only one who had a woman on his hands he couldn't control. He was pulled from that observation when Andrea coldly announced, "Excuse me, sir. I have business to attend to."

As she turned and started to walk away, Eric caught her arm, saying, "What the hell! You don't have to rush off. Can't you stay for a few minutes and talk?"

Andrea pivoted. "About what?"

"About what's been happening to us. It's been months since we've seen each other."

"I don't give a damn what has been happening to

you," Andrea lied smoothly. When she saw the fleeting look of hurt in his eyes, she regretted her words.

"Well, I *do* care what happens to you."

Before Eric could continue, Andrea asked sarcastically, "Do you?"

"Dammit, Andrea, give it up! You aren't going to go through your entire life being angry about what happened, are you?"

"I certainly am. I will never forgive you for what you did."

"Never is a long time. Surely I deserve better than that, in view of what we were to one another."

Eric's voice had dropped to a husky timbre that sent shivers up Andrea's spine. Suddenly, she wanted him so badly she could taste it, and that scared the devil out of her. She had promised herself she would never succumb to passion again, with any man, but particularly with this one. His power over her could well destroy everything she wanted for herself. "We enjoyed lust together," she answered with a coldness calculated to hurt. "Nothing more. And it will never happen again."

Eric's eyes flashed with anger at the way Andrea was demeaning their intimacy. "If that's the way you want it," he answered stiffly, "but I still think you should reconsider joining your party." He glanced at the sky, "Unless you'd prefer to get soaking wet."

Andrea looked up and saw a towering yellow-white thunderhead coming over the lush green mountains. To her, it didn't seem to be moving very fast, nor did it appear particularly threatening, since it wasn't the dark color she was accustomed to. "I'm sure by the time that gets here, I'll be at the Rough Riders' camp," she answered confidently. "It's not that much further."

Eric laughed harshly. "You're in the tropics now. That will be here in a matter of seconds." Then he took her arm firmly in one hand and pulled her under a nearby open shed. Before she could object, the rain was coming straight down in torrents. It looked like a solid sheet of water. The sound of it hitting the ground, the trees, the roof was drowning out every other noise. She glanced up above her and saw that the palm thatching was actually keeping the rain out, something she found amazing considering that the rain was falling so hard.

The nearby column of soldiers made a mad dash for the shelters in the clearing. They went splashing through mud puddles as they ran. As several soldiers crowded in the shed with Andrea, Eric, and several Cubans, Andrea wondered why the Americans had bothered. They were soaked to the skin. Even their bedrolls appeared to be saturated. A steady stream of water was draining from each end of every bedroll. Then something big and black dropped from the thatching, and another, and another. Seeing the tarantulas, the soldiers let out terrified shrieks and tore from the shelter. Andrea would have joined them had Eric not prevented her with a firm hold on her arm.

As soon as the rain let up enough for her to hear, he said, "There's no reason to be afraid of the spiders. They're not dangerous."

A tarantula the size of a teacup ran over Andrea's shoe. She shivered in revulsion, then asked, "Are you positive about that?"

"I am, and someone needs to tell the army. Between

shooting at spiders and land crabs, the soldiers won't have any bullets left for the enemy."

As suddenly as the rain began it ended. Just as suddenly the sun appeared. It hadn't lasted ten minutes, and there were big puddles everywhere.

Becoming acutely aware of Eric's heat, his scent, his disturbing nearness, Andrea abruptly announced, "I'll be leaving now."

"You might want to wait awhile for the water to drain off," Eric suggested.

"No, I'm going now," Andrea answered stubbornly. She darted off, calling over her shoulder, "Good-bye."

Eric shook his head in renewed exasperation. He knew he couldn't stop Andrea, short of hog-tying her to something, but he was determined about one thing. This wasn't going to be good-bye.

Andrea discovered that she would have been wise to heed Eric's words. After the torrential downpour, there were streams where they hadn't been, rivers where there had been only streams, and the entire trail was one long puddle. By the time she had reached the Rough Riders' camp, her shoes were completely covered with red, gooey mud and her skirt was wet up to her knees.

To her dismay, she found Clara and her party ready to return to Siboney. They made their way back down the trail, slipping and sliding and squashing through bogs, splattering each other with mud. Steam rose from the puddles beneath the searing sun, which was sapping the energy of the group. Soon they were perspiring so profusely they might as well as have stood in the soaking rain. Andrea envied the troopers who had stripped off their clothes and tossed them over bushes to dry out. The weight of the soggy clothes in the heat and humidity was sheer torture. She understood now why the *mambis* often fought in the nude, why Paul had allowed his harvesters to go without clothes, why the natives wore so little. It was the only way to survive.

When the group finally reached Siboney shortly before dark, Andrea was exhausted. She skipped supper and went right to bed. She didn't even wake up when the nurses came to bed much later that night. Sixteen-hour days had already been established as routine for the busy women.

The next morning Andrea learned that Dr. Winter had sheepishly come to Clara and requested assistance from her and from the nurses he had so recently scorned. The American troops and officers had noted the contrast between the two neighboring hospitals and they had put pressure on the head surgeon to allow the Red Cross to help them. It was a major victory for Clara and her staff, and they threw themselves into their work with even more zest and dedication.

While her medical staff took on the job of helping at both hospitals, Clara attacked the problem of getting supplies from her ship to shore, since the dock the Americans were building was far from completed. Powerful tidal currents prevented goods from being landed except at low tide, between 3:00 A.M. and 10:00 A.M. Clara devised a light, shallow-draft craft composed of a raft lashed to platoons. Every night the loaded raft was brought as close to land as possible, then troops waded in up to their necks and carried everything to shore, over and over until the tide came in.

Throughout the day after their return from the Rough Riders' camp, news of an impending battle was on everyone's lips. It was common knowledge that the objective was San Juan Hill and the village of El Caney, two places that stood between them and Santiago. The localities were so heavily fortified that the Cubans had never been able to take them. Siboney was a beehive of activity as supplies that had been piled on the shady beach were loaded on wagons and pack trains to move to the front. Guns, cannons, and ammunition took precedence over food, clothing, and what few medical supplies there were. Andrea spent the day watching the frantic preparations and wondering why the attack couldn't wait until the supply lines caught up with the troops. The Spanish seemed to be content to fight a defensive war. They were simply sitting, waiting, and fortifying their emplacements.

Shortly after dark, when Susan was walking from the Cuban hospital back to the American one, she was stopped by a man who stepped suddenly out of the shadows.

"I'm sorry," Eric apologized, "I didn't mean to startle you. Do you remember me?"

Susan would never forget the man with the beautiful blue eyes. "Yes, I do. Can I help you?"

"I hope so. I'm looking for Andrea."

"Andrea?" Susan asked in puzzlement. Then she laughed and said, "Oh, yes, Andy."

Eric frowned at the nickname, then nodded his head.

"Do you know her?" Susan asked.

"Yes, we're old . . . friends. We knew each other in Havana."

Susan wondered why Andy hadn't said anything about running into an old friend. Or were they more than friends? She hadn't missed that heartbeat of hesitancy. Susan felt a brief pang of betrayal, then admitted that she couldn't blame Andrea. Hadn't she been attracted to the man herself? Why, she doubted if any woman could be immune to him. He radiated a certain something that appealed to a primitive part of her, a part of her she couldn't deny. "She's probably still in the kitchen," Susan answered, nodding her head in the direction of the Cuban hospital. "She was just sitting down to eat when I left."

Eric didn't want to go into the kitchen to confront Andrea, for fear of creating a scene in front of others. "Would you mind doing me a favor? Would you tell her there's someone out here who would like to see her."

"Of course. What name shall I give?"

"I'd prefer you not use my name. I'd like to surprise her. You see, I saw her the other day, but couldn't get free to talk to her. Just tell her there's a man waiting outside who would like to see her."

Was that why Andrea had not said anything? Susan wondered. She didn't know he was here? Oh, what a delightful surprise that will be. "I'll tell her."

Susan hurried back to the Cuban hospital, and

passed the message on to Andrea. Then, before she could ask any questions that might have spoiled the surprise, Susan rushed away. Outside, Susan told Eric, "She'll be out in a minute, I'm sure. I wish I could wait and see the expression on her face, but I'm already late for duty." Susan walked away, saying, "So long. And good luck, if I don't see you again."

Eric moved farther back into the shadows and watched the door at the back of the Cuban hospital anxiously. He sighed in relief when he saw it open. Andrea stepped out.

Andrea couldn't imagine who wanted to see her. She had finally come to the conclusion that he might be one of the men she had talked to that day. Perhaps he wanted to add something to their interview. And since that something might be important, she had interrupted her meal. Seeing the dim outline of a man standing by a tall palmetto, she walked to him. Upon recognizing the man, she gasped, "It's you!"

"Yes, it's me," Eric answered, stepping forward and grasping her upper arms.

"Let go of me!"

"No, I won't," Eric replied in a firm voice. "You're going to come with me, even if I have to throw you over my shoulder and carry you from this camp—even if you scream your lungs out. And that will be embarrassing for both of us. But I'll let you decide. Either come quietly, or I'll take you by force."

"You wouldn't dare!"

"Wouldn't I?" Eric asked, maddeningly calm.

Andrea knew Eric well enough to know that he wasn't making idle threats. "What do you want of me?"

"We're going to have that talk I wanted yesterday."

"I have nothing to say to you!"

"Well I have plenty to say to you."

When Andrea stood her ground and glared at him, Eric changed tactics. "Please come with me. I've missed you. I never dreamed how much I would miss you."

His admission did strange things to Andrea. She felt herself weakening. "All right, we'll talk. But right here."

"No, it's too public. Let me take you to a place I know you'll like, a private place."

It was beginning to sound too intimate, yet part of Andrea desperately wanted to go. While she struggled with herself, Eric's hands slid down her arms and caught hers. "Come with me, Andrea. Don't make me beg any longer. I need you."

It was a plea so earnest that Andrea knew it had come from Eric's heart. She also knew it hadn't been easy for him. He was proud. That was one of the reasons she loved him. As soon as the thought crossed her mind, Andrea realized that she had lost the battle with herself. She couldn't take it back. She loved him. Her feelings were as powerful as the incoming tide.

"I'll go," she muttered. She was feeling utterly helpless. She could only hope that loving him wouldn't demand too much of her. She could give him her body and her heart, but she couldn't and wouldn't sacrifice her dreams!

Chapter 18

As Eric walked Andrea to the jungle at one side of Siboney, she looked about her. Searchlights from the naval ships out in the bay sent long beams that crisscrossed the dark sky above them. The erratic play of the circles of light on the hovering mountains looked eerie. She could hear rustles in the grass all around her and knew it must be the red and yellow spotted land crabs, voracious creatures that would eat almost anything that stood still, or at least attempted to. Andrea had watched two carry off a wooden bucket the day before. Then she remembered something one of the soldiers had told her—that the crabs had been feasting on the dead. A shiver of pure revulsion ran over her.

Eric took Andrea down a narrow path that wound through the thick tangle of trees and underbrush. Andrea wondered how he could see in the total blackness. Frogs croaked, crickets chirped, and from a Cuban camp somewhere in the distance, she could hear the insurrectionists singing and beating on their improvised drums. The sounds added to the creepy feeling she was experiencing, as did the sight of a pair of glowing red eyes peering at her from the darkness.

Suddenly they stepped onto a wide, sandy beach dotted with feathery coconut palms. The scene was all the more beautiful by being bathed in soft starlight. The ugly beams of the searchlights couldn't penetrate the thick jungle that separated them from the bay. "It's lovely," Andrea muttered. Then she asked Eric, "How did you know it was here?"

"I've been with General Castillo's men for a couple of weeks now. We made camp here one night. This entire coastline is full of little coves like this one."

Andrea was glad he had insisted they come here. The place was beautiful, and it had a soothing peacefulness about it. She hadn't realized how agitated she had become by all the suffering she had witnessed since she had arrived. So much of the misery seemed so needless. Her not being able to change it was the most frustrating thing she had ever experienced.

She glanced across the cove and saw a million flashing green lights in the jungle beyond. She questioned Eric about them.

"They're caused by fire beetles. Back home, we called them fireflies. Haven't you ever seen them before?"

"No, I haven't," Andrea admitted, then speculated, "Maybe they like wooded areas. We don't have too many trees where I come from." She inhaled a deep breath, then asked, "And that sweet smell?"

"The frangipani. Since it started raining, they're blooming everywhere, but you don't notice the fragrance so much in the daytime. The heat of the sun seems to intensify the stench of decay, and that overpowers everything."

Eric took her hand in his, and they walked around the cove. The only sound was the gentle lapping of the water on the sand. He seemed perfectly content with her company, and that surprised Andrea. When he had said he needed her, she had assumed he meant sexually. With their fingers entwined, Andrea felt a closeness to him that surpassed their previous most intimate moments. She wondered at it, then realized that it was their hearts and souls interacting, and not their bodies. It was a moment of belonging and sharing, of quiet happiness that was a wonder and a joy.

From the corner of her eye, Andrea hungrily took in the sight of Eric. She could see he had shaved and that his dark hair was longer than he had worn it in Havana. It was curling around the back of his neck in the most appealing manner. She longed to wind her fingers into those soft locks. He wore a loose, coarsely woven native shirt, tucked into his ragged pants. The shirt was open down the front, revealing the hard planes of his chest and the V-shaped mat of crisp, dark hair. A pistol was strapped to one hip, a scabbard with a knife on the other, and he was barefoot. Andrea thought he looked absolutely beautiful, despite his plain, tattered attire. Her love for him at that moment almost overwhelmed her.

She finally broke the silence, asking, "Do you always go barefoot when you're with the rebels?"

"I had a pair of good boots when I joined them. They completely rotted two weeks into the wet season. Since then, I haven't worn anything on my feet when I'm in the jungle. That's why the Cuban army doesn't spend what little money it has on uniforms. It's pointless. Besides, you can get out of a deep mudhole easier without boots on."

Andrea had already made that observation. That afternoon, after it had rained again at almost the exact same time of day, she had seen a soldier stuck in a deep bog. He simply unlaced his boots, stepped out of them, and kept going, leaving the boots submerged in ten inches of gummy ooze. "But weren't your feet tender?"

"At first, yes, but I got used to it. Now I can even walk over this sharp-bladed grass without noticing it."

"You said you were with Castillo's men the past few weeks. Where were you before then?"

"After I left Havana, I reported back to General García. He's the top Cuban general on this end of the island, as you probably know by now. He's my immediate commanding officer. When I wasn't relaying messages back and forth between him and General Gómez, the Commander in Chief, I fought with Gómez's men. I fully expected to be sent with García's troops that were being shifted to the western end of the island in anticipation of the invasion at Havana. Then we heard the surprising news that the Spanish fleet had appeared in Santiago instead. According to a spy in the city, Admiral Cevera had docked there to refuel. Somehow, he had missed making connections with the ship which had been sent to recoal him at sea. Fortunately for everyone, there wasn't much coal available and he was delayed. You see, the insurgents control the entire end of this island. They have Santiago pretty much in a stranglehold. But we had a devil of a time convincing the American navy that the Spanish fleet was there. They wouldn't believe us until they actually saw for themselves. Twice, they sent a squadron to investigate. The first time, they missed seeing the Spanish ships in the harbor. The second time, our men took one of theirs over the mountains and showed him. When they finally blockaded the harbor, and the plan for invasion was shifted to this end of the island, García transferred me to General Castillo, thinking my speaking English might be valuable to him, since he was securing the landing. But it's only a temporary assignment."

"Then you've taken part in quite a bit of fighting already?"

Eric assumed she meant with Castillo, since the usual American attitude was that the important fighting didn't start until the Americans appeared on the scene. "I was at Guantánamo, Daiquirí, and a few other skirmishes, including Las Guasimas."

Andrea heard the anger in Eric's voice at the last and asked, "Were you with the Rough Riders?"

"No, I wasn't. I was with the Cubans who were assigned to Lawton's volunteers. And thank God for that! At least, we weren't accused of being cowards."

"And the Cubans who were with the Rough Riders were?" Andrea asked in surprise.

"Yes. Didn't you hear about that?"

Andrea shook her head.

"They claimed the Cubans with them disappeared at the first shot. They made it sound as if the Cubans had deserted them. For Christ's sake! The Cubans took cover! That's how guerrillas fight. They know the enemy can't shoot at what they can't see."

"Don't make so much of it," Andrea said in a

soothing tone of voice. "The Rough Riders are volunteers, just green, inexperienced troops. What do they know about anything? I heard they panicked. Maybe they're just trying to draw unfavorable attention away from themselves. They'll change their attitude towards the Cuban troops after they've been around for a while."

"I wish I could just chalk it up to that. But I seriously doubt if things between the two armies will improve, particularly with officers like Roosevelt making remarks to the effect that he didn't think the Cuban soldiers were going to be worth much. At least he could have tried testing our worth."

Andrea hadn't heard that one, but she didn't doubt it. Besides being overly opinionated, Roosevelt had very little tact. "Oh, don't pay any attention to him!" Andrea responded scornfully. "He's always putting his big foot in his mouth. And he doesn't care who he insults. Just look at the way he talks about McKinley, like he doesn't know anything. If he insults the president, your Cubans shouldn't feel too bad. They're in good company."

Eric smiled at Andrea's candid observation, then put aside his irritation and said, "Well, that's enough about me. Now tell me about yourself. What articles did you sell and to whom?"

"Are you sure you have time? When do you have to report back to your camp?"

"I have all night." Seeing the surprised look on her face, Eric said, "The Cuban army doesn't operate under stringent rules like the American or the Spanish army. As long as you're around at the right time to do the fighting, every man is pretty much on his own, particularly at night, unless he's assigned picket. Half of the group I'm with just sort of melts into the jungle each night to join the camp followers. They're like our revolutionary army was, a little undisciplined by everyone else's criteria, but when it comes to fighting, they are dedicated and fierce."

Andrea was elated. She glanced around, then said, "In that case let's sit down on that fallen palm tree over there. My feet are still aching from the long walk I took yesterday."

As soon as they were seated on the palm trunk, Andrea filled Eric in on the exciting things that had happened to her. She reveled in the look of pride she saw in his eyes when she told of her success. It didn't take long for her to tell her story, since he didn't interrupt her. When Andrea had finished, she admitted, "I guess I ought to thank you for what you did. If you hadn't sent me from Havana, I wouldn't be here, and I wouldn't have this wonderful opportunity to make my name as a war correspondent. I've already gotten great stories since we landed. It doesn't even matter that I can't forward them to a publisher quite yet, like Hearst's correspondents. I'm sure anything written about this war is going to be in demand for a long while."

"I'm glad I'm forgiven," Eric answered, although he still didn't like the idea that Andrea was in a war zone. But he was going to have to learn to live with his fear, since he couldn't change things. Loving Andrea was easy. Giving her the freedom to be herself would always be difficult. Curious about something she had said, he asked, "How are Hearst's correspondents getting their material back to the States?"

"He sent a whole fleet of tugboats down here, to ferry them back and forth to the telegraph station at Jamaica, which just shows you how determined he is to get there first with the war news. But then, the other papers may be doing it, too, for all I know."

Eric frowned. "That pretty much puts the freelance writers like you at a disadvantage, doesn't it?"

"Not necessarily. Like I said, I think anything about this war is going to be popular for a long while." She grinned impishly. "Besides, I'm a better writer."

Eric smiled, thinking she was still tooting her own horn. He was glad. He loved Andrea's utter self-confidence.

Andrea gazed up at the stars and said, "I know it's the tropics and all, but I still can't get used to how many and how bright the stars are."

"That reminds me. I told you I'd show you the Southern Cross." He put his arm around her shoulders and bent so that his face was just a hair's breadth from hers. Pointing to the sky, he said, "Look for the four bright stars that would form the points of a cross."

"Yes, I see it now." She turned her head and found their lips so close they were almost touching. Then it seemed an eternity before Eric closed that distance, and his lips touched hers. It began, soft and questing, as if it were the first time he had kissed her. Then the kiss slowly and steadily increased in demand and passion until they were straining against each other and trembling with need.

They undressed in a frenzy, then Eric spread his shirt on the sand, and lowered Andrea to it until they were both on their knees. He kissed her eyelids, her nose, her forehead, muttering, "Oh, God, how I've dreamed of this. Every night has been a torture."

Andrea understood perfectly. He had awakened her passion, leaving her aching for him in the stillness of the night. "I know," she answered. She caught his hands and brought them to her breasts, sighing in bliss as he caressed them. She arched her back as he lowered his head and took one throbbing nipple into his mouth.

He lowered her to the ground, kissing the softness below the mounds. His mouth went wandering here, there, laving, nibbling, while his hands explored, caressed, teased, tormented her, until Andrea felt every nerve in her body was on fire and she was begging for release, "Please, please, please."

Exciting her had excited Eric to the bursting point, and he was more than willing to comply. When he entered her Andrea cried out in joy and wrapped her long legs around him as if she were determined to hold him there forever, and Eric reveled in her moist welcoming heat. Then taking full command, he drove them up those glorious heights to a consuming explosion of pure ecstasy.

They dozed for a moment, feeling wonderfully relaxed and satiated. Then Andrea muttered, "Do you know what I want to do?"

Eric's answer was a long, delicious caress down the length of her body and a kiss below her ear. "Well, that, too," Andrea replied with a little laugh. "But later. Right now I'd like to take a swim."

"The water is salty," Eric warned.

Andrea laughed again and answered, "In case you haven't noticed, so are we."

Eric chuckled. He rose to his feet with a swiftness that startled her, and lifted Andrea to hers. He grinned down at her and said, "The last one in is a rotten egg." Then he took off for the water.

With her long legs, Andrea almost beat him. When they reached the water, they splashed, then dove almost simultaneously, and surfaced laughing. For a long while, they cavorted like two children, splashing and trying to duck one another. Then Andrea noticed that the tops of the palm trees had taken on a silver lining. In surprise, she said, "Look! The moon is rising."

It wasn't quite a full moon, but it was absolutely beautiful. The huge globe of rich yellow grew paler as it rose, throwing a path of shivering light on the rippling water. To Andrea it was the final touch to a perfect tropical night.

They left the water hand-in-hand. When they reached its edge, Eric released her hand and turned her to face him. As he took in the sight of her, his eyes went slowly moving down her length and then back up. She looked like a goddess with her skin reflecting the moonlight and making it glow. "You're incredibly beautiful," he muttered.

The husky timbre of his voice was still washing over Andrea as he lowered his head and dropped featherlike kisses over her face. Then he kissed away the drops clinging to her eyelashes and then licked the salt from her lips.

He lowered her to the wet sand with him, lying half over her. The water gently was lapping at their hips and long legs. When Andrea started to fold her arms around his shoulders, he caught her hands in his, pinning them down beside her head, his mouth exploring the length of her neck. The feel of his hard palms and callused fingers was as sensuous as that of his warm lips against her throat. As he captured her mouth in a sweet, lingering kiss, his long, slender fingers entwined with hers. His lips and tongue tasted of salt as he went deeper into a long, hot drugging kiss that made Andrea's senses spin.

Still holding her hands prisoner in his, Eric blazed a trail of torrid kisses over her shoulders and breasts, then licked the tiny rivulets of water away from the soft mounds, leaving each inch of her skin sensitized and tingling. Then his lips closed over one rosy tip, his teeth ever so gently raking the tender flesh before he took it in his mouth. Andrea arched her back. Her hands clasped and unclasped his, telling him eloquently of the waves of exquisite pleasure she was feeling.

Eric nudged her legs apart with one knee, and Andrea felt the brush of his hot arousal against her thigh as he lifted himself and knelt between her parted thighs, a brush that promised heaven and more. He finally released her hands and sat back on his heels. He was gazing down at her as if he were trying to absorb her with his eyes.

Andrea gazed back, and was glad to see the bright moonlight on him. The breeze was ruffling his dark, damp hair around his face, and his blue eyes were blazing with the intensity of his desire. She thought him both beautiful and terribly exciting. She opened her arms to him.

But instead of accepting her embrace, Eric slipped his hands under her buttocks and lifted them. Andrea sucked in her breath sharply as she felt the moist, hot tip of his erection against her, slowly circling, teasing, taunting as his fingers and tongue had so often done. A wetness slipped from her, bathing him in a scalding heat as a bolt of fire shot through her loins and centered in the core of her womanhood. It was an agony to have him there, so close to that portal that burned for him, and yet so far away. Writhing, she begged, "Please I can't stand it any more. I want you inside me."

"Not yet," Eric answered with a devilish smile. He continued his exquisite torture, watching Andrea's eyes glaze over as her body was racked with shudders and she was engulfed in hot waves of sensation that burned the soles of her feet.

After the convulsive shudders had faded away, Eric bent to capture her lips in a searing kiss that rekindled the smoldering embers of her passion. His torrid kiss seemed to go on forever and ever, as all the while he was entering her slowly, sinking deeper and deeper into her depths, sheathing himself in her hot velvet and filling her completely. When he broke the long kiss, they were both breathing raggedly and trembling uncontrollably. Then he began his movements, masterful, fierce thrusts that made Andrea fear he was reaching for her soul in his possession. He brought her to such exquisite rapture that time ceased to exist and the world slipped away and she was lost in a deep, dark void.

Later, as they lay on the beach and stared up at the beautiful night sky, Andrea dreaded their parting and asked, "When will I see you again?"

"I don't know. There's a big battle coming up. This might be my last night free for a while."

"You're talking about El Caney and San Juan Hill, aren't you?"

"Yes. They're the only major Spanish fortifications between here and Santiago."

"Have you seen them?"

"Yes."

"Which do you predict will be the hardest to take?"

Eric felt a tingle of apprehension. "Why do you ask?"

"Just curious. I've heard a lot of speculation."

"They both have blockhouses, and trenches where the enemy have dug in, and barbed wire entanglements. But I'd say El Caney, because it also has a fort with walls that are three feet thick. Then there's the town itself. The church bell tower, and practically all the houses, have loopholes cut in them."

"Are they heavily manned?"

"Not really. I doubt if either the town or the heights—which is what we call them, since San Juan isn't the only hill—have much over five hundred men."

"And the Cubans have never been able to take them?" Andrea asked in disbelief.

"Like I said, they're dug in. It's hard to kill a man in a ditch, even with artillery. And in both cases, they have the advantage of the high ground." Eric was thoughtful for a moment, before adding, "It's possible the heights received reinforcements from Santiago, but the insurrectionists have had El Caney surrounded for some time now."

It was almost daybreak when they left the cove. During the walk back to Siboney, Eric was pestered by suspicion and fear. As they stepped from the jungle and into the clearing where the village sat, he stopped Andrea and said, "I hope to God you're not contemplating going to the front during either of the battles coming up."

"My goodness, no! That would be utterly foolish, since I don't know anything about battles or battle tactics."

"Neither do the other journalists, but those damn fools are all over the place. It's a wonder one of them hasn't been killed."

"Well, I don't see any need to endanger myself that way, and I'm sure I can get more than enough material from interviews after the battles have taken place."

There was something in Andrea's answers that just didn't ring true to Eric. "You're not lying to me, are you?"

"Of course not!" Andrea answered indignantly. "When have I ever done that?"

"What about when you snuck out to meet Miss Barton?"

"I didn't lie to you. You just assumed I'd wait until the next day."

Eric still couldn't shake his suspicion. His eyes searched her face, looking for any signs of deception.

Then Andrea turned the tables on him. She folded her arms around his neck and said, "I'm frightened for you. You will be careful, won't you?"

"I'm always careful."

She stood on her tiptoes and kissed him softly. Then she said, "I'll be praying for you. Come see me as soon as you can. I'll be worried sick until then."

Andrea whirled around and hurried away, leaving

Eric standing at the edge of the jungle and staring at her back. His suspicions were still not put completely to rest. Then he heard a bugle calling reveille from some distant army camp, and he reluctantly turned and disappeared into the thick vegetation.

Chapter 19

Andrea had told Eric an out-and-out lie when she'd said she had no intention of getting anywhere near the battlefield. She knew he would have tried to stop her, if not physically, then by arguing with her. By deceiving him, she had saved them time and energy.

After getting a few hours' sleep, Andrea set to work making her preparations for the coming battles. She was just pulling from her trunk the articles of clothing she intended to wear, when Susan stormed into the women's sleeping quarters.

Andrea looked up from where she was kneeling on the floor and asked in astonishment, "What in the world is wrong with you?"

"I'm furious, that's what!"

"That's obvious," Andrea answered wryly. "You look mad enough to eat nails. But who are you so angry at?"

"Dr. Anthony Marks, that's who!"

"And who might he be?"

"He's one of the army surgeons, an arrogant ass if I ever saw one! You know how most of the surgeons have forgotten their animosity towards the nurses. Why, they're even praising us, saying how remarkably well trained we are, particularly in the operating room. But not him! He won't give an inch. He's rude and insulting, and today, I finally had enough. I told him off!"

"Good for you!"

Susan grimaced, then admitted, "No, it's not good. It was in the middle of an operation, and I shouldn't have let him make me lose control like that."

"What did you say?"

"I told him if he slapped my hands one more time when I was sponging, I'd throw the bloody thing in his face—if he didn't like the way I held the retractor, he could find someone else to assist him—that I knew I probably had more experience in the operating room than he did—and that I had worked with a lot more skilled surgeons, back in New York, so he could get off his high horse."

"My goodness! You did let go."

"Yes, I did, and now I regret it. I embarrassed both of us in front of the others. Dr. Gardner was operating at the next table, and I know he must have been terribly ashamed of me. I'm sure he's going to reprimand me. The only saving grace was that I did manage to finish the operation."

"Did the surgeon say anything after this outburst?"

"No, not a word." Susan suddenly laughed, then said, "Oh, I shouldn't be making light of it. It really is serious, but he had the most astonished expression on his face. Looking back on it, it was really priceless. I don't think I could have shocked him any more if I had reached down and yanked on his . . . long arm."

Both young women laughed at that absurdity, then Susan sat on the cot beside Andrea and said with a long sigh, "Well, there's no use in crying over spilt milk." She looked down at what Andrea was holding and asked, "What's that?"

Andrea held up the pants and answered, "Part of my new uniform. I have a shirt to go with it, boots, and a big slouch hat that will cover my hair and most of my face."

"You're going to wear that?" Susan asked in a shocked voice.

"Of course, I'm going to wear it! Why shouldn't I dress like the other journalists?"

"You know perfectly well why not. You're a woman."

"You're the last person I would expect that from, Susan. These clothes are practical for trudging over those hills and that rugged terrain, and they're modest, too. Now I can stop worrying about someone looking up my dress when I climb over things. Besides, if I'm dressed like a man, I'll draw a lot less attention. I'm tired of having the soldiers gawking at me like a two-headed calf."

"They gawk at all of us women."

"Not like they would where I'm going. Then I could very well be a distraction that might cause their deaths."

The color drained from Susan's face. "You're not thinking of going to the front during a battle, are you?"

"How else am I going to report it, if I don't see it?"

"It's too dangerous!"

"The other journalists will be doing it."

"I don't care what they do! We're talking about war, about bullets being fired, about shells exploding. You could get killed!"

"The same holds true for you, Susan. You've already volunteered to go to one of the field hospitals. You know the enemy snipers don't make any distinction between soldiers and medical personnel. You've told me yourself about medics being shot while wearing your Red Cross arm bands. If you go to a field hospital, you could get shot, too. You'd be in just as much danger as I would. Will you refuse to go? No, you'll do what you feel you have to do, and that's what I'm doing."

Susan was silent for a long moment, then said, "I'm sorry. I know I'm not being fair to you, but I'm afraid for you."

"I'll be careful," Andrea promised. "I only intend to observe, not take part. Besides, I'm going armed."

"Armed? With what?"

Andrea lifted a six-shooter from her trunk. "With this. It's the Colt I used back home, and I've been carrying it around with me ever since. You never know when you might need a gun," she ended with typical Western logic.

"And the men's clothes? Where did you get them?" A shocked expression came over Susan's face as a sudden suspicion came to her. "Oh, Andy, you didn't steal them, did you?"

"Of course not! Where did you get an idea like that?"

"Well, I wouldn't put it past you, if it meant you could get your story. I've never known anyone as determined as you."

"Well, if I hadn't had them with me, I *would* have stolen them," Andrea admitted candidly. "But I had plans for this attire all along, in case I needed it when we reached Santiago. You see, when I was Havana I learned that respectable women don't go out without a male escort, not even in a group, and that put me at a big disadvantage. So I thought I'd masquerade as man. Then I could go where I wanted, when I wanted."

"Then you planned on doing more than just a follow-up on the *reconcentrado* story?"

"If I could find the stories, yes."

A knock interrupted their conversation. Both women turned their heads and saw a man standing in the open doorway. Susan had burst into the room so angrily, she hadn't shut the door behind her. Andrea knew the lanky, sandy-haired man was an officer by the captain's bars on his shoulder straps, but she had no idea who he was or what he wanted. She glanced at Susan, then knew for certain the nurse must know who he was. Her grey eyes were flashing with fury.

"May I speak to you?" the captain stiffly asked Susan.

Susan ducked her head and whispered to Andrea, "I'll apologize to Dr. Gardner, but I'll be damned if I will to *him!*"

Susan rose and walked as regally as a queen to the door. Andrea strained her ears, but couldn't hear what was being said. Then the captain nodded his head curtly and walked away.

As Susan walked back towards her, Andrea came to her feet and said, "I assume that was the doctor you were so angry with. What did he say?"

"He apologized." Seeing the surprised expression on Andrea's face, Susan quickly added, "but only because he had to. It seems Dr. Gardner told him he wouldn't tolerate mistreatment of any of his nurses. He considered an insult to them, an insult to himself."

"Well, good for Dr. Gardner."

"Yes, I had no idea he would take my side. As a rule, doctors stand by each other, right or wrong."

"I don't know why, but I expected Dr. Marks to be much older," Andrea remarked.

"No, he's only a year or two older than me. That's why it was so hard for me to take his cockiness. I felt like he didn't have enough experience to earn the right to be that arrogant. But I will have to admit, he's good. With a little more experience, he could be very well surpass those surgeons I worked with."

"He's rather nice-looking, in a clean-cut sort of way," Andrea observed.

"Oh, is he? I hadn't noticed."

Susan's answer was a little too emphatic to be believable. Andrea wondered if Susan's anger at the doctor's demeaning treatment of her had been a little personal, as well as professional.

Throughout the day it became evident that a big battle was imminent. Frantic preparations were taking place. Following the daily afternoon deluge, Andrea decided to wait no longer. She dressed, and left a note on Susan's cot, since she had gone back into the operating room. Andrea left Siboney.

A solid line of troops, broken by mule trains carrying supplies, threaded their way up the narrow, muddy trail. The lead mares' bells made merry tinkling noises that seemed ill-matched with the gunshots that could be heard in the distance, where insurgents were trying to prevent enemy reinforcements from getting into the battle area. In several places, Andrea passed gun carriages sunk to their hubcaps in mud. The artillery crews were cursing—and straining along with the horses to free them. Everyone perspired profusely. The smell of man sweat and horse sweat combined with the reek of decay. Steam rose from the puddles. Heat waves shimmered from the jungle around them. No one paid any attention to Andrea, although journalists were usually treated like celebrities. The soldiers were either too intent on keeping their footing on the soggy, slippery path or too preoccupied with their own grim thoughts. The majority of them were going into battle for the first time.

Andrea passed an abandoned summer villa which was being used by General Shafter for his headquarters. The place was a beehive of activity, as couriers and officers rushed here and there. Shortly thereafter, the road split, and Andrea stood and pondered which way to go, to the San Juan Heights or to El Caney. Then remembering what Eric had told her, she chose the road to El Caney. A mile or so later, the sun set with its typical tropical swiftness. Andrea slipped into the dense undergrowth near an infantry encampment. She was close enough to feel a certain safety, yet far enough away not to be discovered by their pickets. She ate a tin of crackers she had brought with her, and she took a drink of water from her canteen. Then she curled up on the damp grass, just as the soldiers all around her were doing. Most of them had long ago tossed away their heavy bedrolls, and tents had never even been issued to them.

Despite her exhaustion, she could not sleep. The rustle of land crabs kept her awake. Finally, she dozed, only to be awakened by the rattle of gun carriages and the jingling of horses' harnesses. She crept to the road and peeked out. By the light of the moon she saw the heavy artillery being moved up.

A man on horseback passed by, so close she could have reached out and touched a hoof of his horse. Andrea recognized him as Captain Allyn Capron. She knew that the artillery officer had lost his son, a Rough Rider, at the Battle of Las Guasimas, and that he had sworn vengeance.

Andrea waited until the gun carriages and the small crowd of civilians tagging along behind them had passed. She stepped from behind the brush she had been hiding in and onto the deeply rutted road. Within minutes, she had caught up with the crowd of military observers, reporters, and curious camp followers, and thankfully, no one paid her the least bit of attention.

The big guns were positioned at the top of a tall hill that overlooked El Caney. As the sun came over the mountains in a huge red ball of flame, one of Capron's cannons roared, belching smoke as it jumped back in recoil. Andrea heard the hiss of the shell and the report as it echoed off the mountains. Then she saw a puff of smoke in the distance. As the reporters cheered, Andrea wondered why. The shell had hit nowhere near the fort. Then the range-finders made adjustments to the cannons. They all fired, over and over and over, until the mountaintop was covered with a cloud of smoke and Andrea's ears hurt from the loud blasts.

As the sun rose higher, Andrea found that the heat from the guns and the sun was too much for her. She moved to a lower hill, where she could still see the six blockhouses and the fort, called El Viso. She could also see the church and a score or more of red-roofed houses scattered around it. In a pasture beyond the town, a herd of cattle grazed, seemingly unperturbed by the roar of the cannons. As far as Andrea could tell, the barrage on the fort had accomplished nothing. It still stood, and she could see the white straw hats of the Spanish soldiers bobbing up and down in the maze of trenches around the fortress.

When the American troops moved in, Andrea heard the popping here and there in the grass, a sound that steadily increased over the next several hours. The hills echoed with explosions from gun batteries. For a brief moment, she caught sight of the yellow observation balloon off in the direction of San Juan Hill. It disappeared from the sky, so abruptly that she knew it had been shot down. She could hear gunshots coming from that direction and knew a heated battle was taking place there. She could only hope it was going better there. The troops at El Caney had met fierce resistance and had managed to gain very little ground.

Hour after hour passed. The sun grew hotter and hotter, shimmering off the hills, while white smoke drifted in the valleys. Andrea noticed that the gunshots from the direction of San Juan Hill had ceased, but the battle was still raging at El Caney. The American infantry, along with a group of Cubans, had fought their way house by house through the town. Slowly, yet forcefully they won ground, until they clustered in a grove of mangroves at the foot of the hill, beneath the fort. They were pinned down there by a murderous barrage of bullets, and their position looked hopeless to Andrea.

Then, suddenly, they jumped to their feet and charged. The majority of the infantry were black troops, as were the Cubans, and Andrea could see their dark skin glistening with sweat as they swept up the hill with their rifles blazing. Andrea thought it was the bravest thing she had ever seen, and the most futile. They were being mowed down by the return fire. But despite the fact that they were dropping like flies, they swept up the hill, wave after wave, taking one trench, passing through barbed wire entanglements, taking another trench, passing through more barbed wire entanglements, over and over, until they reached the fort and swarmed over it. Andrea couldn't see the last-minute fighting—the entire hill was covered with smoke. When a mighty cheer rang out and echoed over the hills she knew that the Americans and Cubans had won. The battle had lasted an unbelievable ten hours—hours of hell for the soldiers who had fought.

Andrea left her perch on the side of the hill. With other observers she hurried to the fort, through the quagmire that was the battlefield. She was shocked at the number of wounded and dead she saw. From a distance they had not been visible through the tall grass. Even more shocking was what she saw when she reached the fort. The trenches were full of dead Spaniards, so mutilated by artillery shells and bullets that you could hardly see a patch of their blue pajamalike uniforms. That in itself was sickening enough, as was the fort with its blood-splattered walls, but in every instance where there was a face still intact, Andrea discovered that the *soldaro* had hardly been more than a child.

She made her way to an American infantryman resting in the shade of the fort and asked, "How many escaped?"

The man was startled by her high voice. He shot her a piercing look, then answered, "Maybe twenty or so."

"Then this is all of the enemy there were here?" Andrea asked, her hand sweeping the area.

"Yeah, but it's hard to believe. We must have outnumbered them ten to one. I don't know who said the Spanish were cowards, but that was dead wrong. They fought like the devil himself."

Indeed they did, Andrea thought, then she answered, "And so did you and your comrades." She pulled out her tablet, then with her pencil poised over it asked, "Just what brigade do you belong to?"

"You're a woman, aren't you?" the soldier said.

"Yes, I'm a female journalist. Does that bother you?"

"No, ma'am. It just surprises me."

Andrea shrugged her shoulders. "It surprises a lot of people. You were going to tell me what unit you're with."

"The First Brigade."

"And who is your commanding officer?"

"You mean the big boy?"

"Yes, I suppose so."

"General Henry Lawton."

Andrea recognized the name of the officer Eric had been assigned to. She dropped the pencil as her heart lurched. She glanced around in fear, at the bodies of the dead and wounded that lay scattered all around.

She had never stopped to consider that Eric might have been at this battle, that he might have been one of the men who made that daring, costly sweep up the hill. Not seeing any sign of him, Andrea asked, "What happened to the Cubans who were with you?"

"They disappeared into the jungle after the fight was over. They stay pretty much to themselves."

"Was there an American with them, tall, dark-haired, blue-eyed?"

"Yeah. He's been with them all along."

Andrea had to force down a big lump in her throat before she could ask, "Do you know if he survived the battle?"

"Nope, sure don't. Can't remember seeing him take a hit, but can't remember seeing him after we took the fort either."

Was he down there wounded? Andrea thought, her eyes moving over the battlefield. She refused to consider that he might have been killed.

"Thank you," she muttered absently to the infantryman. She hurried off, forcing herself to glance at every prone figure on the hillside. She searched the grass at the foot of the hill, but all she found there were dead. Then she realized that most of the wounded had been moved and were on their way to the hospital. Spying a line of litters being carried away in the distance, she hurried after them, but she stumbled over a man bent over another in the tall grass.

"Watch where you're going!" the man said sharply, without even glancing up.

Noting that both men were dressed in civilian clothing and that the one on the ground was badly wounded, Andrea started to ask if they wanted her to call for litter bearers. Then it dawned on her who the two men were. One was William Randolph Hearst, and the other was one of his reporters. Hearst wasn't tending the man's wounds. He was taking down the reporter's story of the battle on the tablet he held in one hand.

Andrea stepped back and watched as Hearst finished the report, flipped the tablet shut, and said, "I'm sorry you're hurt." Then the publisher's handsome face lit up. "Wasn't it a splendid fight? We'll beat every paper in the world with these stories."

Andrea couldn't believe her ears, couldn't believe that anyone could be so callous as to call such slaughter "splendid," particularly when he had seen it with his own eyes. He was surrounded by the dead and the wounded. How in God's name could Hearst be thinking about his sales? What about the families who had lost their loved ones here, the soldiers who had lost their friends and compatriots? What about the men who had lost limbs or their sight, who might well suffer pain the rest of their lives? What happened to compassion and grieving?

Andrea was filled with a sudden anger, so great she would almost have done physical violence to Hearst, had not the litter bearers stepped between the two. By the time the two had lowered the litter and placed the wounded journalist on it, Hearst was gone. He'd turned his back on his severely wounded employee and jauntily walked away. Andrea stared at his back with pure, unadulterated loathing, and swore she would do her damndest to counteract every bit of sensationalism he and those like him generated. She would tell the ugly truth of this war—even if she never sold another article!

As Andrea hurried away to follow the litter bearers, the sun was setting, turning the rubble of the stone fort on the hilltop behind her a blood red.

Chapter 20

Shortly after Andrea left El Caney, night fell, but like those taking the wounded to Siboney, she continued down the soggy road. She was anxiously peering at every litter she passed, glancing at every man hobbling along or being assisted by another, scanning the faces of the weary little groups resting on the side of the road. The night was filled with moans, punctuated by a scream of pain now and then. The air smelled of the sweet fragrance of frangipani mixed with the brassy smell of blood. She knew they were being followed by a flock of vultures, even though the moon had not yet risen. She could hear their wings flapping overhead. Many times the stretcher bearers saw that their wounded had died, so they quietly stepped to the side of the road and removed their burdens. There were always plenty of other wounded men along the road to take to the hospital.

When they reached the point where the road forked, the path became even more crowded with wounded, now coming from both battles in a steady, unending stream. Andrea saw only three ambulances that night, and wondered where the others were. It was pitiful to hear the wounded, even the stretcher bearers, begging the ambulances to stop, but they were obviously filled to capacity.

A mile or two from Siboney, Andrea saw a soldier in front of her stumbling and fumbling about badly. When he fell, she bent to help him up. She realized that his head bandages covered his eyes. "Are you alone?" she asked.

"I've reached the hospital?" the soldier asked in surprise. He clutched her arm and muttered, "Oh, thank God!"

Andrea realized that he thought she was a nurse. "No, you're not there quite yet, but I'll help you."

As they walked, the soldier told her his story. He had been with a group following the observation balloon. The balloon had drawn fierce artillery fire, and he, along with many others, had been hit by flying metal. He had been taken to a field hospital set up at the ford of the San Juan River and he'd been bandaged with his own bloody shirt, since they had no medical supplies. Then he had been sent back with a another man who had received an arm wound. Somewhere along the path, his companion had been killed by a sniper. He could only imagine that he had been spared because the Spaniard thought it amusing to see him groping along. At any rate, he had been on the trail since midmorning, resting only for short moments, receiving sporadic help from others, but mostly trying to make his own way, although blinded.

Andrea was amazed at his determination. It had taken him twelve hours to cover eight miles. Even more amazing was that he hadn't somehow wandered off into the jungle and gotten hopelessly lost.

It was well after midnight when they reached Siboney. Both hospitals were lit up and surrounded by open tents where the wounded were waiting to be treated. Then Andrea felt the full impact of the terrible price their victories had cost them. She left the blinded Rough Rider in one of the tents, explaining that he would be tended to as soon as possible. She hurried to the Cuban hospital. Since they knew her, no one objected when she made a quick sweep through the crowded building, looking for Eric. At the American hospital, however, she was stopped by a sentry. Only after she claimed to be one of the nurses, was she allowed to enter.

The place was in chaos. Every inch of floor space was taken up with cots, litters, and wounded, who lay on the floor for lack of anything better. Orderlies rushed here and there, trying to cope with an impossible situation as best they could. Andrea saw only one Red Cross nurse, but she was too busy to notice Andrea. When Andrea turned to leave, she was stopped by one of the wounded who pulled at her pants leg and begged for water.

Andrea removed her canteen and squatted beside the man, then supported his head while he drank. She glanced down and saw the bloody bandages that covered the stumps of both legs, and she felt suddenly sick. He couldn't have been over twenty and he would never walk again.

Not wanting the soldier to see her reaction and not trusting herself to even speak, Andrea didn't even answer his muttered "thank you." She left the building and hurried to her quarters in the Cuban hospital. There, she sat in the empty room, trying to come to terms with all she had seen that day—the carnage at El Caney, the agony of the wounded and dying, the crippled and maimed. Added to that burden was her terrible fear for Eric's life.

She wondered why her fear for him was so much more powerful after the fact than before. She should have been upset from the moment she realized he was going into battle. But Andrea knew why. She'd had no earthly idea of how terrible battle really was until she had seen it with her own eyes. Nothing she had experienced had prepared her for its scope, its destruction, its waste of human lives.

Besides being filled with fear—something Andrea couldn't remember ever feeling—she was ashamed of herself. She had always thought herself unusually strong for a woman, yet she couldn't take the suffering. She had run from it. She'd never had any idea of how much courage the medical people had.

Andrea slept very little that night.

The first time Andrea saw Susan was at midmorning the next day, when the nurse came to the kitchen for a bite to eat. Spying Andy, she hurried to her, hugged her, and said, "Oh, Andy, I'm so glad to see you're safe."

Andrea was shocked at what she saw. The blood-covered apron didn't upset her. It was Susan herself. Exhaustion was etched on the nurse's face, and there were dark circles under her eyes, making her look much older than she was. "You look like hell!" Andrea blurted.

"Well, you don't look so hot, yourself."

Andrea waved Susan's observation aside, saying, "No, I'm serious. Haven't you had any sleep?"

"No, we've been operating nonstop since the wounded started arriving over twenty-four hours ago. I've never operated by candlelight before. I never dreamed it could be done, but we simply didn't have any choice. The number of casualties is utterly shocking. No one was prepared for this."

"Are there enough medical supplies to last?" Andrea asked in alarm.

"Yes, for the time being, thanks to Clara. We're using Red Cross supplies collected for the *reconcentrados*. Clara said she knew the American public would want that. But if the American government had let Clara collect for the war effort and organize it, like she had wanted to, we'd be much better off. The army didn't bring near enough medical supplies with them. Nor enough personnel. I can't imagine what they were thinking. Everyone knows you have casualties in war, yet they weren't prepared."

"They weren't prepared for anything," Andrea pointed out. "Apparently they didn't think this army needed food, clothing, or shelter of any kind either. The soldiers still don't have tents to protect them from the daily deluges. All they brought was their damn guns and ammunition . . . and the men to sacrifice to the cause," Andrea ended with a bitter afterthought.

As the two ate, Andrea summoned up the courage to say, "Susan, I know you've been busy, but you haven't, by any chance, seen that man who asked for me the other night among the wounded?"

Andrea couldn't hide her fear, and Susan knew what she had suspected was true. Their relationship *was* more than just friendship. "No, I haven't," Susan answered gently. "But you have to remember I've been in just one operating room and haven't seen every man who has passed through. And then, some of the wounded were taken to the field hospitals."

Seeing how downcast her answer made Andrea look, Susan asked, "What makes you think he was wounded?"

"I don't know. I just have this feeling he's been hurt. Maybe I'm just chasing shadows. But ever since I saw that battle and learned he took part in it, I've been jumpy."

"Which battle?"

"El Caney."

"Then you were there?"

"On a nearby hilltop, yes," Andrea paused, then muttered in remembrance, "It was awful. Just awful."

"I already know that," Susan answered, then rose to her feet, saying, "Well, it's time to get back to the operating room."

"Back?" Andrea asked in surprise. "I thought you were going to get some rest."

"Not yet."

"But you're exhausted."

"We can't stop, no matter how tired we are. Too many men's lives depend on it."

Andrea walked Susan back to the American hospital. As they passed one of the receiving tents, Andrea heard one of the doctors call, "Litter squad, here!" She watched as the four men ran up, then as they carried the wounded man away, Andrea frowned and asked Susan, "Why are they taking him over there, and not to the hospital?"

"He's an abdominal case. The surgeons decided this morning that we wouldn't attempt to save any more men with abdominal wounds. Every one we've operated on has died."

Andrea glanced at the field where the man was carried and unloaded. It was littered with soldiers. "You're just turning your backs on them," she asked in horror, "leaving them out there to die?"

"Oh, Andy, please try to understand," Susan said in an anguished tone of voice. "We'd do more if we possibly could. But we're just overwhelmed. With so many lives at stake here, we can't make heroic efforts. We've got to save those we know we can save, or at least, those we think we've got a fighting chance at saving."

Knowing the reason, didn't take any of the horror from it for Andrea. "They're all alone. Can't you at least put someone with them to make them think you're trying?"

"We've no one to spare, not even the litter bearers."

"What about Clara, or Mrs. Gardner?"

"They're both helping in the hospital."

"Can't you at least move them to one of the tents where it's shady?"

"They're all full."

"Then when they get empty!" Andrea answered sharply, both frustrated and angry at the situation.

"No. The hospital is full. We're having to move the freshly operated men right back into the tents they came from." Tears glittered in Susan's eyes. "I'm sorry, Andrea. Truly, I am." Her voice cracked. "We all are." Susan turned and hurried away, stumbling several times in her distress.

Andrea looked at the field where the mortally wounded lay. She had hoped to gain more information on the battle at San Juan that day, but the pitiful scene seemed to be beckoning to her, and pulling her against her will. Suddenly, she knew what she had to do. Otherwise, she'd never be able to live with herself.

Andrea hurried back to her room, changed into a blouse and skirt, and donned one of Susan's aprons, then she rummaged through her trunk until she found the small Bible her mother had given her. Andrea had never been religious. The book had never even been opened. She only carried it as a remembrance of her mother. Now she was glad she had it. It might give solace to some of the men who were dying. She slipped it into her pocket. From the box that was used as a washstand, she grabbed the bucket of water with its dipper and she headed for the field.

When she arrived, she noted that there were at least forty men lying on the damp grass. A score or more had already died or were in a coma, beyond comforting. Most of the alert ones knew what was going on—that they had been marked expendable and set aside to die. Some of them had anger glittering in their eyes, while others showed only naked fear of the unknown. A few had reached the point of resignation, patiently waiting for the dark angel to claim them.

Andrea moved from one man to the other, wiping the sweat from their brows. Dying was a hard, hard labor. She would offer them a drink of water, while averting her eyes from the terrible gaping wounds and trying to keep her mind from the stench of feces draining from the intestinal injuries. At first, the angry ones rejected her. One of them even cursed her. But Andrea didn't let anything stop her. They had every right to feel the way they did. She was angry, too—angry at the parties responsible for sending them to war without adequate planning. All were in pain, but by some seemingly unspoken agreement, they tried to conceal it. The most Andrea heard was an occasional moan, and some had chewed their lips ragged to keep from even doing that.

For those who looked so fearful, she offered to read from the Bible, letting them choose the verse. One or two Jewish soldiers asked especially for readings from the Old Testament. Andrea soon realized that all listened. Even the angry seemed to take some comfort.

As the day wore on, new arrivals were placed on the grass. One, from the Indian Territory, a full-blooded Cherokee, had fought with the Rough Riders. Andrea wasn't at all surprised when he rejected her offer to read to him from the Bible. He wanted to be moved so he was facing east, the holiest of all directions according to his tribal belief. The next time the litter bearers made a visit, she had them reverse the Cherokee's position, despite their objections that he would be looking into the sun.

As the day wore on, the heat grew more oppressive, increasing the agony of the dying. Sweat poured from Andrea and the wounded. In an effort to give them some kind of shelter, she made a visit to the jungle and brought back banana leaves, which she placed over their faces to keep the glaring sun out of their eyes.

Sometimes she sat at the men's sides and let them talk. They talked about their homes and their loved ones. They reminisced about good times, voiced regret at things past and—the most touching of all—regret at things that would never be. One was a redheaded, freckled-face cowboy from Arizona who wanted to talk about his favorite horse. Andrea understood perfectly. She knew that a cowboy's life was lonely, that their mounts were often their best friend and only family.

By the time the daily deluge came, only the cowboy was left. In a day that seemed like an eternity to Andrea, all the others had died, and no new casualties had arrived. She sat in the downpour. The pounding rain was flattening her hair as she held the cowboy's hand. When the rain ceased and the blistering sun came out and turned the puddles all around them to steam, she rose and said, "I'll be back in just a moment."

Andrea hurried to her quarters, yanked the blanket off her bed, gathered some bamboo, and came back to make shelter over the cowboy.

As she sat down in the mud beside him, he said, "I'm much obliged for the shade, ma'am, but what about the others?"

"They don't need it anymore."

There was a long silence before the cowboy asked, "They're all gone?"

Andrea knew it was pointless to lie. Furiously she blinked back tears. "Yes."

"That's a real shame," the cowboy muttered.

No, Andrea thought, it was crime. Their deaths were unnecessary, as was the death of every American who had died so far. We didn't belong here. The Cubans would have won their independence without our interference, and probably without nearly the cost in lives. They didn't make heroic, costly sweeps up hills. They didn't seek quick victories. They took their time, slowly and surely weakening their enemy. Because they had lost so much, they had learned the value of life.

It seemed to take forever for the cowboy to die, and Andrea wondered if it was because his way of life had made him tougher than the others. She sat and held his freckled hand, as she was watching the furious activity going on in the open tents. She knew that another, fiercer battle was being fought here by the medical department. She decided that this was the battle she would show the American people, the opposite side of the coin in war. The other reporters could tell the public about the so-called splendid bravery, the heroes. They could play on the public's patriotism and pride. She would tell about the pain and the suffering and the needless waste and she would hope to appeal to their conscience.

Around sundown, the cowboy died. Andrea felt as if she had lost an old friend. She closed his eyes and rose, then, hearing a scratching sound, she looked around and saw, to her horror, a land crab feeding on one of the dead. "No!" she screamed. She grabbed one of the pieces of bamboo and began to beat the creature. She smashed it to bits, but she still beat furiously on it, and sent mud and pieces of shell flying everywhere, so as to release her anger and frustration. At last she sank to the soggy ground and sobbed uncontrollably, surrounded by the bodies of those who were expendable.

It was dark when Susan came looking for Andrea. She found her slumped beside the dead cowboy. Susan helped Andrea to her feet, saying, "Come on, Andy. It's time for us both to get some sleep."

"They're all dead," Andrea muttered.

"I know. The burial party is removing them now. But you did a wonderful job. The litter bearers told us about it. We were all so proud of you."

Andrea came to a dead halt. "Proud of me?" she shrieked. "What in God's name for? I didn't save any lives. They're all dead! Every last one!"

Susan wasn't in the least upset by Andrea's screaming at her. She knew that Andrea was upset by what she had witnessed. "You did what we couldn't do, what we would have done. Part of practicing medicine is easing someone's death. Compared to it, saving lives is easy. It takes guts to help the dying. That's why we were proud of you. And Andy, it relieved us of our guilt, so we could concentrate on what we had to do. So you see, indirectly, you did save lives."

Somewhat mollified, Andrea allowed Susan to lead her to their quarters. For the first time in several hours, she took notice of things around her. "What are those lights up the mountains?" she asked Susan.

"They think it's the Spanish burning their blockhouses in the passes."

"Were there any new battles today?" Andrea asked with renewed interest.

"We don't know much officially. The telephone

lines between here and Shafter's headquarters haven't been finished. The casualties are still coming in from El Caney and those two battles at San Juan—"

"Two battles?" Andrea interjected in surprise.

"Well, two hills side by side. At least that's what the surgeon who talked to a reporter passing through said. One was San Juan Hill, and the other Kettle Hill, because of several abandoned sugar kettles on it. It seems Roosevelt was quite a hero, charging up Kettle Hill on his horse and urging his men on."

"So Roosevelt and his Rough Riders have covered themselves in glory?"

"Yes, it appears so."

"Who took the other hill?"

"I don't think the reporter even mentioned it."

Andrea wasn't in the least surprised.

Chapter 21

Unknown to Andrea or Susan, the telephone wire between Siboney and General Shafter's headquarters had been completed late that day, and the first message to arrive was an urgent request from the general for Clara Barton to bring supplies to the front. As soon as the tide came in, shallow boats from the *State of Texas* ferried in food, blankets, medical supplies and tents. Soldiers waded through the surf and piled the material on the beach in a frantic effort to get as much as possible landed before the tide went back out. The cartons and boxes and barrels were sitting on the sand when the sun came up. Wagons were needed to transport everything to the front, but, despite the commanding general's appeal, no officer was willing to let the Red Cross use his vehicles. How Clara was finally able to obtain two wagons—pulled by four mules each—was a mystery, but Clara was expert at cutting through bureaucracy, and when that failed, she could whittle down resistance by sheer guile.

By the time the wagons were loaded, Susan and Andrea were up and about, and Andrea had decided to follow the wagons with Clara and some of her staff. The rest of Barton's group, including all of the trained nurses, were to stay in Siboney and help out until the medical crisis was past.

As Clara and the others climbed on the dilapidated hay wagon that had been provided for their luggage and transportation, Andrea said to a glum Susan, "I'm sorry you can't come along now, but they did promise that you would be the first if Dr. Gardner decides to use nurses in field hospitals. So it may be only a few days before we see each other again."

"I hope so," Susan answered. As Andrea vaulted to the back of the wagon, Susan added, "Now, you be careful."

The wagon lumbered off, and Clara turned from where she was sitting beside the driver and said to Andrea, "I wish I had thought to bring trousers. Just look at how easy you jumped on the back of the wagon without a cumbersome skirt."

Andrea strongly suspected that the comment was made for the men's benefit, as they had made their disapproval of her apparel rather obvious. "They do give you a lot more freedom of movement, and they're a lot cooler, too," Andrea answered, "without the petticoat."

"Oh, I agree. I gave up on that silly thing days ago."

"Do you think you should be wearing that gun?" one of the men asked Andrea.

"Why not? Many other journalists do."

"But they know how to use it."

Andrea's dark eyes flashed. "So do I, probably better."

"I don't doubt that," Clara said over her shoulder,

once again running interference. "Andrea grew up on a ranch in Wyoming. She can probably outshoot half of this army."

"It might be more dangerous for you, inadvertently," one of the doctors pointed out. "Armed, you might draw enemy fire, whereas if you weren't—"

"You might still draw enemy fire," Andrea interjected. "Have you forgotten the snipers? They don't know or care if I'm a combatant or not."

"Indeed not!" Clara remarked firmly. "And personally, I'm glad you're carrying that weapon, my dear, particularly if you're going to be wandering about. Besides the enemy, there's no telling what dangerous animals are out there."

Andrea knew that the dangerous animals Clara was referring to were not the four-legged kind. Andrea had taken that into consideration, too, when she decided to wear men's clothing. Disguising her sex helped prevent such encounters, but if that failed, the gun on her hip was a deterrent.

There was no further conversation regarding Andrea's attire. After Clara repeatedly came to Andrea's defense, the staff knew to hold their tongues and keep their opinions to themselves. Clara was their boss.

It was a miserable trip to the front. The road was one long mudhole. In some places the wagons got so bogged down that everyone had to descend into the knee-deep ooze and push and pull and drag the vehicles. Even tiny Clara joined in. However, if there were any soldiers about they were quick to run and help, for the elderly woman had become a celebrity. After a brief stop at headquarters, where Clara conferred with Shafter, the group finally rolled into the open grassy area where First Division Field Hospital of the 5th Army Corps stood. The trip had taken four long hours.

The name was more impressive than the hospital. The medical facility consisted of one big tent and a few pup tents scattered around. The medical situation was even more desperate than it had been in Siboney. Here the wounded hadn't even been received under tents. They were lying in the open on the soggy ground, for the spot was not conducive to drainage. Many patients had not been seen by any doctor since they had been placed there thirty hours before.

Dr. Gardner didn't wait for permission from the chief surgeon there, before immediately going to work setting up another medical facility. As the hospital tents were thrown up and cots and supplies were unloaded, Clara and Mrs. Gardner set to work cooking gruel, hot malted milk, beef extract, and coffee. They used huge kettles hung over an abandoned fireplace. Food was given to the hungry—sick or not. From big bolts of material they cut sheets to cover the wounded. When Andrea left the clearing, the hospital was already taking patients and warm food was already being served.

Andrea scoured the countryside and found that the troops had dug in on the hills they had taken. Some of the ditches were close enough to Santiago that one could see the red-tiled roofs of the city. Since the big battles two days before, there had only been brief, sporadic exchanges of fire with the entrenched Spanish—although earlier that morning, there had been unusually heavy fire from the Spanish trenches. Shortly thereafter, a Spanish truce flag had gone up, and the Americans had sent a message demanding surrender.

The fighting American troops were in almost as bad shape as their wounded. The troops were hungry and miserable in the slush that had once been ground. They had no shelter from the blazing sun or torrential downpours. They found themselves standing in mud. Their boots were rotting on their feet. And many were experiencing withdrawal symptoms from nicotine, since cigarettes were even more scarce than food. Some were so desperate that they were smoking grass, roots, even mule droppings.

Deciding she had seen enough for one day, Andrea—terribly disappointed that she hadn't seen any Cuban troops—walked back to the hospital. She took shelter beneath a thick growth of palmettoes during the daily downpour, as she had seen some Cuban civilians do. It was the worst storm Andrea had seen thus far. The terrible thunder shook the earth, but thankfully, the overlapped, palm-shaped leaves kept her relatively dry, and after the fierce rain had passed, she continued.

She was trudging through a soggy grassland liberally studded with towering palms. She was so close to the field hospital that she could see the tops of the tents, when suddenly she heard someone call, "For God's sake, get down, mister!"

Andrea didn't even have a chance to look around, before a hail of bullets whizzed past her, cutting the coarse grass like a sickle. She dove to the ground, landing in the ooze with a loud plop, and splashing mud over her face and into her eyes. For a moment, she lay perfectly still, blinking like mad to clear her vision.

"Did they get you, mister?" Andrea heard someone whispering from nearby. She risked turning her head from side to side but couldn't see a soul in the thick grass. "No," she whispered back.

"That bastard has had us pinned down for damn near an hour," the soldier informed Andrea. "I think he must have killed Carson. He hasn't answered any of our calls."

"How many are there of you?"

"Twenty or so, at least there were when we walked into this ambush. We can't figure out what tree he's in."

Andrea raised her head just high enough to survey the treetops. Several had been so riddled with bullets that the remaining leaves were shredded. Andrea assumed those were the trees the soldiers had wrongly guessed the sniper was hidden in.

Andrea lay in the hot sun with the steam rising all around her. The time seemed like hours. Actually she was there for minutes. The mud stank to high heaven from where the grass had been crushed and was now fermenting. Flies and mosquitoes buzzed around her, while cicadas in the grass all around her began to sing. The steady, shrill sound grated on her nerves. Then she almost jumped out of her skin when a parrot in a nearby tree shrieked.

Apparently, Andrea wasn't the only one getting jumpy. One of the soldiers began firing at a treetop, sending palm leaves tumbling down. His rifle was leaving a tell-tale cloud of smoke. Almost simultaneously, another barrage came from the treetops. Andrea remembered that Eric had told her that the Spanish used smokeless powder, so she didn't make any attempt to see the sniper. She focused on listening, realizing she had done much the same in the past with rattlers, shooting at where the sound came from, rather than at what she saw. She pinpointed the sound as coming from a group of three trees to her left. Then the sniper's mauser fell silent.

Two of the trees were shorter, and Andrea suspected that the sniper was in the taller tree, until it dawned on her that from that height, he might not be able to see through the thick foliage of the trees below him. She concentrated on one of the lower trees, then the other, hoping to get a glimpse of a glint from the sun hitting metal. But what she did see was a brief rustling in the leaves of one tree. The breeze was stirring all the leaves, but there was something about that movement that didn't seem natural. It was a downward movement, instead of sideways, perhaps made as the sniper was repositioning himself.

Andrea carefully removed her sixshooter, took aim, and rapidly emptied the entire chamber into the crown of the tree, then quickly rolled away in case she was wrong and the sniper had spotted her position. Several leaves came crashing down, followed by dead silence.

"Did he get him?" someone in the tall grass asked.

"Hell, I don't know. He ain't shooting anymore," another soldier answered.

"Keep down. It may be a trick," another cautioned.

Then suddenly, a body came tumbling down from the tree and fell with a splash in the puddle of water at its base.

"He got the bastard!" someone yelled; then soldiers

were popping up everywhere around Andrea and hurrying to the body.

"Look at that," Andrea heard one of the excited soldiers say, "he's wearing a green uniform. No wonder they're so hard to see."

"And no wonder they're so hard to kill," another commented. "He's got sandbags tied around his chest."

"Yeah, but that didn't protect his head. He's got a bullet clean through it."

By that time Andrea was walking away. "Hey, mister!" one of the soldiers called, "Don't you want to see what a good job you done?"

Andrea had seen far too much death. She kept walking, following a narrow path that led to the field hospital. She was about to step into the clearing, when she came face to face with someone going in the opposite direction.

"Christ, Andrea! Is that you?"

"Eric?" The question came out like a croak. Then she threw herself at him and hugged him fiercely, muttering over and over, "Oh, thank God, thank God."

Eric peeled her from him, leaving almost as much mud on his shirt front as hers. He set her back, asking, "What in the hell are you doing here? And why are you dressed like that?" Then as the reason for both dawned on him, he exclaimed, "Dammit, you promised me you wouldn't go into a battle zone. You lied to me!"

"You're jumping to conclusions. I came here with the Red Cross."

"Then what were you doing in the jungle, in those clothes, covered with mud?"

Andrea knew that any further denial would make her look foolish. "All right, I deceived you. So what! We're even now."

Andrea expected a retort of some sort, but Eric was just staring at her hat. His tanned face was drained of color. He snatched the hat from her head and said, "Godalmighty! Where did you get this bullet hole?"

Andrea was a little stunned herself. She hadn't realized that one of the sniper bullets had come that close. Then, she was aware that her hair was exposed. She grabbed the hat and put it back on her head, saying, "Stop that. You'll ruin my disguise."

Eric ignored her objection and thundered, "I told you it was too dangerous out here! Do you have any idea how close you came to getting killed?"

"That could have happened to me in the hospital, if that sniper had decided to shoot in the other direction. And stop yelling at me! You don't have any right to tell me what I can and can't do. I've told you that over and over."

"Not even if I love you?"

It was said so quietly that it took a moment for Andrea to feel the full impact. A lump came to her throat. Tears of happiness glittered in her eyes. Then she said, "No, I'm afraid not. I don't happen to believe that taking risks is reserved for males, anymore than bravery or courage is."

"Men have been protecting women since the beginning of time, Andrea. It's been bred into us. We cannot step back and watch our loved one be in danger."

"No, that's not impossible. Women have been doing just that all along. Every time their man went out to face danger, whether it was to hunt wild animals, brave the elements, protect their homes, or go to war. It isn't easy, but it's not impossible. All it takes is a little more love and understanding."

Eric didn't know if he had that much love and understanding in him. Glumly he wondered, if he had to fall in love, why not with an ordinary woman, instead of with someone who demanded so much from him. Yet, he knew that Andrea's fierce spirit made him love her.

Seeing the almost painful expression on Eric's face, Andrea said, "Oh, please, let's not argue. I've been terribly worried about you. The entire Cuban Army just seemed to disappear from the face of the earth. Where have you been?"

Eric didn't really want to argue either, particularly since it never seemed to solve anything with Andrea. He had yet to win one battle with her. He tried to set his fear for her aside and answered, "After the battle of El Caney, I was transferred back to General García. Shafter sent us to fill in a gap between the American lines and Santiago. Since then I've been acting pretty much in my old capacity as courier, which explains my being here. I'm on my way back from taking an urgent message to General Shafter."

"Is that why you're wearing a shirt?"

Eric chuckled. "Yes, I tried to be as presentable as possible." He looked down at his muddy shirt front, then said, "I guess it's a good thing I didn't run into you on my way there."

"Can I ask what the urgent message was?"

"I don't know why not. I'm sure the news is going to spread like wildfire. The Spanish fleet was completely destroyed this morning. They tried to slip out of Santiago harbor and our fleet caught them. It was an overwhelming victory. Every Spanish ship was destroyed, including Admiral Cevera's flagship. They didn't have a ghost of a chance against our superior ships. With their wooden decks, they were firetraps. They must have suffered tremendous losses."

"How do you know all this?"

"Some of our Cuban pickets saw it all, and we heard it from where we were camped. I'm surprised you didn't hear it. It was a terrible rumbling."

Andrea vaguely remembered hearing something that sounded like explosions in the distance. It was during the trip to the field hospital. She had thought it was the Spanish destroying more blockhouses. "Will the navy sail into the harbor now?" she asked excitedly, hoping that this terrible war might soon end.

"They can't. The entrance to the harbor is mined. The best they can do is throw shells over the mountains. They did that once before, trying to destroy the Spanish fleet at its anchorage."

"They have guns that can throw shells that far?" Andrea asked in surprise.

"Yes. Several of the battleships have powerful, long-range guns."

"Then why the devil didn't they bombard El Caney and those hills the other day?" Andrea asked in sudden anger. "They could have blasted away with those big shells until there wasn't anything left but dust. We wouldn't have had to lose near the men we did."

"The army didn't want any help."

"That makes no sense."

"It's true. I know because García asked the same question. The army didn't want to share the glory, or at least, feared the navy might try to get the credit. The two are terribly competitive, you know."

Andrea knew there was fierce competition for funding between the two. But now, with this war, she had come to realize how far the two branches would go for their own self-interests. The navy had pushed for an early and precipitous invasion because they feared hurricanes. Then the army had refused to ask for naval help because they feared the navy would try to take credit for the victories. What in God's name happened to cooperation? They were both fighting the same enemy. An American was an American regardless of what uniform he wore. Their self-interest made her sick to her stomach.

Eric knew what she was feeling. He saw the look on her face. "I know. War has an ugly side to it."

As far as Andrea was concerned, that was the only side she had seen. She was beginning to fear there wasn't another side.

Eric glanced at the treetops and knew the sun would be setting soon. "I have to go. García will be expecting me back."

Andrea hated these partings. They always left her feeling so downhearted. Just being in Eric's presence was uplifting. "Do you have any idea when I might see you again?"

"If García continues to use me in this capacity, I imagine I'll be passing this way every now and then. You'll be at the field hospital?"

If she wasn't at the trenches, Andrea thought. But she knew better than to say that and get Eric upset again. "Yes, unless the surgeon in charge here kicks the Red Cross out. Then I'll be in Siboney."

"I'll check in, the next time I pass through."

They stared at one another. Each was loath to move away. Then Eric pulled her behind a tree, took her in his arms, and gave her a quick hard kiss. When he released her, Andrea laughed softly and said, "I thought you said you would never hold someone dressed like a man in your arms."

"When was that?"

"When we were picking out our costumes for carnival. You said you wouldn't dance with anyone dressed like a man. Not only did you hold me in your arms, you kissed me."

Eric laughed self-derisively and answered, "I may have to eat a lot of my words." Then his eyes dropped to her chest, and he said in a husky tone of voice, "Besides, you don't look like a man."

Andrea glanced down and saw where her muddy shirt had molded her breasts like clay, emphasizing them more than the most daring gown she had worn.

"If you're going to maintain your disguise, you'd better watch for things like that."

Then he turned and walked away, and for once, Andrea took his warning to heart.

Chapter 22

Andrea was awakened the next morning by the sound of American artillery bombarding Santiago, and knew the military officials at Santiago must have refused to accept Shafter's surrender demand. After the overwhelming defeat of the Spanish fleet the day before, the Spanish decision to stand and fight was surprising to Andrea. The Spanish were almost totally cut off by land and sea, and stripped of naval protection. Their defense appeared utterly hopeless. She was beginning to appreciate their tenacity. They had held almost to the man at both El Caney and the San Juan Heights, exacting a terrible price for the American victories. Whatever the Spanish were, it was obvious they were not cowards. Despite their being grossly outnumbered, they were worthy opponents—something that had come as quite a shock both to the American soldiers and to high command.

The American gun batteries shelled the city for several hours; then between the lines a new truce flag appeared, this time coming from Santiago. Like everyone else, Andrea hoped the Spanish had had second thoughts and were ready to negotiate. But such was not the case. Shortly thereafter, representatives from the British, Portuguese, Chinese, and Norwegian consulates met with Shafter and requested that the noncombatants in the city be allowed to leave before the bombardment was continued. Shafter agreed to a truce until the civilians could be evacuated to El Caney.

The next day, there was a general exodus from the city. Andrea was on the road from Santiago to El Caney. She watched as the refugees trudged through the mud in the steaming heat. They were a pitiful mass of humanity—the poor who had been left behind when the wealthy fled at the beginning of the war. It was obvious to Andrea that Eric had been correct when he said the city was starving. Almost without exception, the refugees were thin and weak: women with pitifully crying babes in their arms—children covered with sores and dressed in rags—bent, toothless, old men and women, some stumbling along with sticks for canes, others being carried on crude litters or wheelbarrows. Here and there, Andrea could see a priest or small flock of nuns. Their long, dark robes and head coverings must have been stifling in the heat. Their wooden beads were clicking as they walked. All came only with the clothes on their backs and with what few personal belongings they could carry. Not a one had a morsel of food on them, for the Spanish soldiers had kept what little there was. The refugees had left their hovels with the promise that they would be fed once they reached El Caney. The prospect of putting an end to their starvation kept them going through the heat and mud.

The exceptions to the ragged poor were the courtesans who had lived off the Spanish army. They were better nourished and well dressed. Many were very beautiful. Andrea knew by the flirtatious glances they sent the American soldiers in the ditches as they passed that the women had fled the city for better pickings.

When Andrea left the road at midafternoon, the refugees were still coming. She knew they would be coming for some time. It took awhile for almost twenty thousand beings to evacuate a city on foot. When she returned to the First Division Field Hospital, she found Eric waiting for her on the path. His face looked like a thundercloud.

Assuming he was angry because she had been up at the front, Andrea walked up to him and, without any greeting, said, "You can just wipe that look off your face right now, because it's not going to do you any good. I have no intention of limiting my activities. Besides, there's no danger right now. There's a truce."

Eric didn't like Andrea's dangerous independence any more than he ever had, but that wasn't bothering him. "That's not why I'm angry."

"What, then?"

Eric pulled her off the path, saying, "Come over here and I'll tell you."

As soon as they were standing beneath a grove of banana trees and out of view from the traffic on the path, Eric said, "I'm furious at the way Shafter is treating General García. He's claiming that García is responsible for the Spanish refusing to accept his surrender demands, because García supposedly allowed the relief column from Manzanillo to slip into Santiago the evening the Spanish fleet was sunk. It's a totally irresponsible and hateful charge. Shafter ordered García to maintain his position on his flank, and from there, García couldn't possibly intercept the column. That's bad enough, but at one of Shafter's and García's first meetings, García wanted to send troops to block the Spanish at one of the mountain passes farther west, but Shafter refused the proposal. He didn't want to lose any Cuban troops for the Santiago offense. If it was anyone's fault those Spaniards got through, it was Shafter's."

Andrea was a little confused. "Back up, there. What relief column are you talking about?"

"As soon as the Spanish realized that Santiago was the Americans' target, they sent a large relief column from Manzanillo to reinforce the city. The Spanish had to march almost a hundred miles, over mountains and through jungle. And the insurrectionists were fighting them every inch of the way. Why, in one battle alone, the Cubans lost fourteen men. If it hadn't been for the Cubans slowing them down, the column would have arrived days ago, and that could very well have changed the outcome of the battles at San Juan and El Caney. Even if it had arrived a few hours earlier, the Spanish fleet wouldn't have sailed. They had given up on any kind of help arriving."

"And Shafter doesn't realize that?" Andrea asked in disbelief.

"Oh, he may, but he doesn't want to admit it. He's looking for a scapegoat, someone to blame that will draw attention away from his indecisiveness after El Caney and San Juan. If he was going to attack Santiago full force, that's when he should have done it, when the Spanish were retreating. But he was shocked by the casualties we sustained. He decided to lay siege instead, but now that it's being drawn out, he's beginning to get criticism for his decision."

"Will the reinforcements make that much difference?"

"No, I don't think so. The Spanish still have no food and very little ammunition." Eric was pensive for a moment. He said, "It's unfair enough that Shafter is trying to blame García for the city getting reinforcements, but he and his officers have been making slurs against the Cubans, questioning their bravery during the past battles. If the Cubans had had their way about it, every last one of them would have been in the thick of the fighting, but Shafter ordered the better part of García's men to guard the bridges and roads to Santiago. For some of the rebels who have been fighting for years, that was a hard pill to swallow. After years and years of hit-and-run fighting and skirmishes, of frustration piled upon frustration, they would have given their eyeteeth to take part in a major, decisive battle."

Andrea couldn't understand how the Americans could possibly question the Cubans' bravery—particularly after the Americans had found out what a tremendous adversary the Spanish army was. Who did the Americans think had held the ferocious General Weyler and his men at bay for two years? Who had pushed the Spanish army to the coastal regions of the island, where they couldn't even retreat from their new enemy? Who had made them as weak as they presently were? And if they fought like demons now, what had the Spanish fought like in the beginning, when they had had the advantage of sheer numbers as well as being well trained and well armed? Were her countrymen dense, or, once again, terribly arrogant?

Andrea wished she could change things, but since she couldn't, she tried to give Eric as much comfort as she could. "I'm sorry for how badly our countrymen are behaving. I truly am. I can only hope it's because they're uninformed, and not because of some terrible character flaw."

"Me, too. We're not making a good impression on the Cubans, and now they're disillusioned. We've always been their heroes, the champions of freedom fighters. With that reputation, our contempt cuts even deeper." Eric smiled, that beautiful smile of his that made her heart do strange little flip-flops. Then he said, "I'm sorry for getting so carried away. I didn't even ask you how things are going with you."

"I'm fine, except I'm sick and tired of this rain."

"It's just beginning," Eric warned.

"I know, but I don't understand how the Cubans tolerate it, year after year."

"What kind of quarters do you have here?"

"Just an open tent I share with Clara and Mrs. Gardner, with a few cots and one small table, for Clara's use, of course. We partitioned the center with sheets, so we'd have a place to change clothes. Otherwise we wouldn't have any privacy at all."

As they walked back towards the path to the hospital, Eric asked. "I don't suppose you have your typewriter with you?"

"No, I don't. It's still on board ship." Andrea's eyes flashed in remembrance. "No thanks to you! If it had been left up to you, I wouldn't even have one. The least you could have done was ship it home with me!"

"Sorry. I was in a bit of a hurry to get out of town myself. Colonel Reyes was breathing down my neck."

"Then he had really canceled your pass?" Andrea asked in surprise, thinking that had been as much a fabrication as his story about being recalled.

"Yes. He pretty much ordered me to get out of Havana or else. I left on a fishing boat shortly after your ship sailed."

They reached the path to the hospital, and as they walked down it, Eric asked, "Where do you do your writing?"

"Right now, I'm not writing. Just collecting material. I keep it in my head, until I get the chance to make some notes. But my notes are disorganized. I don't know if I'll ever be able to make heads or tails out of them. I tried doing that yesterday, using my cot as my desk, but there were just too many distractions."

"I may have a solution for you. That's why I've been asking so many questions. Today, on my way to Shafter's headquarters, I took a short cut through the jungle. About a mile from here, I found an abandoned summer home, or part of one. The jungle has claimed most of it, but the kitchen and the roof are still intact. There's a fireplace, a table, a couple of chairs, enough room to put a pallet. I don't think anyone knows about it, since there wasn't a hint of a path anywhere. But even so, if I show it to you, you'll have to promise me you'll stay armed at all times and stay alert, in case someone stumbles on it, and I'd prefer you not stay there alone at night. If anyone sees a light, they may investigate. Otherwise, it might be a perfect spot for you to get some writing done."

Ordinarily, the last place Eric might have suggested

for the woman he loved was an isolated house in the jungle. But Andrea was wandering all around the area, and spending time at the trenches, so he felt that if she would just stay put and write, she would be safer. Secretly, that's what he hoped she would do.

Andrea thought it sounded wonderful. She had no idea that Eric had ulterior motives. "When can you show it to me?" she asked. Her black eyes were dancing with excitement.

Eric felt a familiar tightening in his loins. He wondered if he would ever be able to resist Andrea's allure when she got angry or excited about something. "If the truce is still in effect, tomorrow afternoon. I'll wait for you here on the path."

"I'll be here," Andrea answered.

They stared at one another for a long moment. Eric wanted to kiss her, but both were acutely conscious of a patrol coming towards them. Then as Andrea started to turn, he caught her arm and said, "Tell Miss Barton you're going back to Siboney for the night, so she won't worry about you. Unless something changes, I don't have watch tomorrow night."

As Eric turned and walked away, Andrea wished he hadn't revealed his plans for the next night. She was already yearning for him. That was a long time to wait, when her anticipation was riding so high.

The next morning, General Toral, the commander of the Spanish forces in Santiago sent a messenger to General Shafter, and since the field hospital sat right next to the road leading to Santiago, Andrea saw the Spanish messenger as he was escorted to the American headquarters. Unlike the common Spanish soldier, the messenger was dressed to the teeth, in a colorful uniform, complete with knee-high boots, epaulets and gold braid. Standing with Clara in the tent she had set up for food distribution, Andrea remarked to the older woman, "I wonder why he's not blindfolded?"

"Perhaps General Shafter wants him to see how well fortified we are."

It was a good point. The Americans had used the truce to dig in deeper, fortify the trenches with sandbags, and transport more cannons to the gun batteries that overlooked the city. Yet time was also working against them. Since hostilities had ceased, more and more fever cases were being brought to the little fever hospitals that were cropping up everywhere. So far there were no yellow fever cases. But malaria, dysentery, and typhoid fever, which had been with the army even before it left Florida, was beginning to take its toll. Even some of the highest officers had been temporarily felled. Both General Young and Wheeler had suffered bouts of malaria—referred to by many as "heat exhaustion." After being dosed with sulfate of magnesia, followed by quinine and calomel, they were experiencing shaky recoveries. The disease came in strange cycles that weren't fully understood.

"Do you think it's possible the messenger might be coming to tell Shafter that General Toral has agreed to his demands." Andrea suggested.

"Oh, I certainly hope so," Clara answered fervently, with a light in her brown eyes. Then Clara confided to Andrea that she hadn't approved of this war. She knew that it had been brought on by irresponsible journalism, and she thought the war was demeaning to the United States. She felt that she had to do everything in her power to help, but she confessed that she couldn't rally her spirit as she had in past conflicts. Andrea understood why. The war lacked the nobility and the justice that the conflict had had when it was a Cuban rebellion in the name of freedom from Spain. It had become a conflict of possession. No one said Guantánamo, Daiquirí, San Juan, El Caney had been freed. They had been taken. Freedom was a word no one mentioned. It had been forgotten by all but the Cubans who still hungered for it.

Later that day, Clara and Mrs. Gardner departed for Siboney to get together supplies for the refugees there. Andrea was glad Clara had left. Now Andrea didn't have to lie to her about where she was going that afternoon. She had come to respect Clara too much to deceive her.

When Andrea met Eric on the path that afternoon, she learned that the Spanish messenger's purpose had been to set up an exchange of prisoners. "I wasn't aware the Spanish had captured any of our soldiers," Andrea remarked as Eric led her through the jungle.

"It wasn't army prisoners. It was naval. The crew of the *Merrimac* was offered in exchange for a Spanish officer."

"The *Merrimac?* I haven't heard about that. How were they captured?"

"After the navy discovered the Spanish fleet in Santiago harbor, they tried to block the entrance to the harbor by sinking a ship in the channel to prevent the fleet from escaping. It was a suicide mission, and every man aboard was a volunteer. But things didn't go as scheduled. Heavy shell fire from ground batteries caused the *Merrimac* to sink before the designated point. The surviving crew were rescued by Admiral Cervera himself, who complimented them on their bravery, then imprisoned the Americans in Morro Castle. That's why the castle wasn't bombarded by the navy along with everything else up and down the coast when Guantánamo was invaded. Cuban spies had relayed where the prisoners of war had been incarcerated."

"And that's how you know this, through Cuban spies?"

"No, through García, who the spies report to."

"The general takes you into his confidence?"

"If you're asking if we're personal friends, no. But I am close with his son." Eric pulled a thick curtain of vines aside for Andrea and didn't resume until they had both stepped through. "The general, himself, is a quiet, dignified man. Very serious. I never have seen him smile. His troops hold him in awe. A few even fear him, which might not be a bad thing. It sometimes helps with discipline. But all in all, he's fair to his men, totally dedicated to the cause, and courageous. However, he isn't as good a general as Gómez is, not when it comes to sheer military genius and charisma. If Gómez had been here, he would have been the man running this show, not Shafter. He's a powerful military leader and strategist. But fate chose Calixto García, and he's trying to make the best of it."

"What does he look like?"

"Why do you ask?"

"So I'd know him, if I saw him. If we ever get down to the actual surrender, I'm sure it would be open to reporters, and I fully intend to be there."

"He's a tall, elderly man with a white goatee. But even if you didn't know that, you couldn't miss him. He has a cleft between his eyes—he usually keeps a wad of cotton in it. It's the result of an attempt at suicide when he was taken prisoner during the Ten Years War and incarcerated in one of Spain's most notorious prisons. He thought death preferable to the living hell he was in. Somehow or another, he got possession of a pistol and tried to kill himself. A Spanish surgeon managed to save him. Later, he was released, only to return to Cuba to fight again."

Eric changed the subject, as he was lifting the valise she had allowed him to carry. He asked, "What have you got in this thing, anyway? It must weigh twenty pounds."

"That's my notes."

"Then you plan on working?"

Andrea heard the disappointment in his voice and laughed softly. She wrapped her arm around his and answered, "Not until tomorrow, after you've left." Her voice dropped to a seductive timbre. "I have other plans for tonight."

Andrea watched as Eric's blue eyes took on a smoldering heat. "So do I," he answered huskily.

A thrill ran through Andrea, warming her to the tips of her toes.

Chapter 23

Compared to an open tent, the ruins of the Cuban summer home seemed like a castle to Andrea. Two walls had crumbled. The rubble was covered with a wild tangle of bougainvilleas, blooming in a riot of red and purple. But one entire corner of the *casa* actually had a roof, that didn't leak, as she soon discovered. Shortly after she and Eric arrived, a deluge came down so hard the noise was deafening.

Smugly, Andrea watched the downpour, relishing being able to stay dry, for in the open tents some of the rain always managed to blow in. Then something occurred to her, something that didn't make getting wet look so bad. Suddenly, she started tearing off her clothing.

Seeing the startled expression on Eric's face, she realized he must think her impatient to make love. Exciting as that prospect was, she had other things in mind at the moment. She laughed and said over the noise of the pounding rain, "I'm going to take a bath—without my clothes on, for a change."

Andrea ran out and stood in the downpour, rubbing

her arms and body vigorously with her hands and wishing she had thought to bring some soap with her. The rain that had seemed so irritating to her when she had her clothes on felt wonderfully warm and clean upon her bare skin. A moment later, she was joined by Eric, wearing a wide grin and nothing else, and Andrea took the opportunity to admire his splendid physique. She motioned for him to turn around while she "washed his back." To her, there was something wonderfully abandoned, something utterly natural and free, about those moments when she stood with her lover in the rain and ran her hands over the wet, powerful muscles he presented to her. For once, the rain ended too soon. She even felt a bit disappointed when the sun came out and the birds began to sing.

Eric turned to her. With his dark, wet hair plastered to his head, the intense blue of his eyes seemed ever more pronounced. Andrea thought that his faint beard gave him a rakish air that made him look even more handsome. Her eyes dropped to his wide chest, where drops amid his dark hair were glittering like jewels. Then her eye drifted down the rock-hard planes of his abdomen. Then spying something, she sucked in her breath sharply and fell to her knees, staring at a reddened, raw line that followed the crest of his hipbone. "You were wounded!" she gasped.

Eric heard the alarm in her voice. "It's nothing. A bullet just grazed me."

But to Andrea, it was far from nothing. She was remembering the men with abdominal wounds. She knew how close Eric had come to losing his life. The realization terrified her. She slipped her arms around him and placed her head on his lower abdomen, muttering, "I couldn't bear it if anything happened to you."

It was the closest Andrea had ever come to saying she loved him, and Eric was shaken both by her words and her kneeling at his feet. The supplicant's position seemed so out of place in Andrea. Then, as she started kissing the red line tenderly, he felt even more disturbed.

He caught her arms firmly in his hands and pulled her to her feet. Looking her in the eye, he said, "I said it's nothing!"

"But—"

Eric silenced her effectively with a deep, ravishing kiss, hoping to distract her with passion. Her deep caring unnerved him and confused him, for he knew neither of them wanted a commitment of any sort. To his relief, Andrea answered him with equal fervor. Her tongue began dueling erotically with his. Then she offered no objection when he swept her up in his arms and carried her back into the ruins to a pallet he had made. Even when he covered her body with torrid kisses and demanding caresses, Andrea made no resistance, she was so caught up in the heat of the moment.

The scorching touch of his erection against her thigh brought Andrea to her senses. Catching him by his shoulders, she suddenly rolled him to his back, looked down at him, and said in a husky voice, "No! This time I'm going to do something I promised myself a long time ago."

Caught off guard at the sudden turn of events, Eric asked in bewilderment, "What?"

"I'm going to love you until you go out of your mind with pleasure."

It was a sensual promise that would have made any man's heart race in anticipation, and Eric was already aroused. Had he not been, he might have been more successful in objecting. By the time his passion-dulled mind even considered such a course, it was too late. Andrea was already working her sorcery on him, proving to him what an adept pupil she had been. Now she was using the same lover's techniques he had used to reduce her muscles to mush, turn her bones to water, melt her spine, and set every nerve in her body on fire. Her mouth and tongue and hands were instruments of exquisite torture as she paid homage to his entire body, feverishly kissing, then licking and sucking his hard male nipples before moving lower.

Following the thin line of dark hair down his taut abdomen, Andrea stopped to dally at his navel. Her tongue went dipping in and out like a red-hot dart, before she continued her arousing exploration. Her hands brushed across his groin, tantalizingly close to that rigid, throbbing part of him that ached for her touch. She began to stroke the insides of his thighs. The powerful muscles there quivered as she placed tiny love bites over him, then licked away the stings.

She reached for him, stroking the hot, velvety skin, feeling him growing longer and hotter under her ministrations. Then she held him a willing captive as she lowered her head and took him into her mouth, both shocking him with her uninhibited lovemaking and thoroughly fulfilling her erotic promise.

A red haze fell over Eric's eyes, and a roaring filled his ears. He felt as if he could no longer contain himself, that his skin would burst at any second. The exquisite torture Andrea was subjecting him to was both heaven and hell. As a cold sweat broke out over his entire body, and he realized he was teetering on the very brink. He used the little strength he had left, to pull her head up and raise her hips over him.

Andrea did the rest. Exciting him had unbearably excited her also. She wanted Eric inside her, needed it desperately. She straddled him and lowered herself over his staff, taking him into her inch by inch, shuddering as waves of pleasure washed over her as she felt his immense maleness filling her. Then she took them to the white-hot crest of passion and held them there. Eric thought he would die from the pounding excitement and the intense pleasure, until he attained his explosive release that seemed to rip the heavens in two.

When it was over and he lay weak and spent, Andrea raised her head from where it been lying in the crook of his neck and said, "Now, tell me you didn't like that."

"I can't. It would be an out-and-out lie, and you know it," Eric admitted.

Andrea smiled smugly, thinking, so much for behaving like a lady. Then she snuggled her face back into the warm crook of his neck.

But Eric wished Andrea hadn't done it, despite the unbelievable pleasure she had given him. He knew Andrea better than she knew herself. Despite her boldness and brashness, he knew that Andrea wouldn't go to such erotic lengths lightly. Her loving him in such an intimate manner surpassed passion. What she had done had nothing to do with holding power over him—rather, it was an ultimate gift to prove how much she loved him. It left him feeling even more bewildered and confused. He knew her plans for the future hadn't changed, nor could his. He was fully committed to this war and refused to consider his future. First he had to survive. Eventually, they would have to go their separate ways, and in view of everything, it would best to make it a clean break. It would have been easier to have believed she loved him just a little. Now it would be even harder to give her up.

When Eric awoke early the next morning, Andrea was gone. Assuming she had gone into the jungle to answer a call of nature, he rose and built a fire in the crumbling fireplace. The kindling had barely caught, when he saw Andrea tearing down the jungle path as if a horde of demons was chasing her. She was wildly batting palmetto leaves out of her way, and her face was white as a sheet.

Alarmed, Eric ran to intercept her and asked, "What's wrong? What frightened you so badly?"

Andrea hated to admit she was afraid of anything. Gasping for air after her frantic run through the humid air, she denied hotly, "It didn't frighten me! It just surprised me." She glared at Eric and said in an accusing voice, "I thought you said there weren't any dangerous animals in this country, other than crocodiles."

"There aren't."

"You're going to tell me that . . ." Andrea pointed in the direction she had come from, ". . . that hideous-looking creature isn't dangerous? Why it had jaws that could snap your leg in two."

"How big was it?"

"At least six feet long. Maybe even longer!"

"Are you sure you didn't see a crocodile?"

Andrea had just had the devil scared out of her and wasn't in the best of moods. "Of course, I'm sure it wasn't a crocodile. I know what a crocodile looks like, for God's sake! That *thing* out there is something out of prehistoric times, with a big pouch under its neck and pointed scales down its back." Andrea shuddered.

Suddenly it dawned on Eric what Andrea had run across. "An iguana?" he asked, excitedly. "Is that what you saw?" Then before Andrea could answer he rushed to the ruins and swept up his machete, asking, "Which way did it go?"

Andrea's knees buckled. "Then it *is* dangerous?" She had come within an inch of being bitten by the monster.

"An iguana? Hell, no! They're perfectly harmless and, the most stupid creatures on earth."

"Then why are you going to kill it, if it isn't poisonous?"

"Because they make damn good eating. Now, quick, before it gets away, which way did it go?"

"To the left, where the little stream crosses the path."

Eric hurried off, calling over his shoulder, "Keep that fire going."

Within the hour, Eric returned, carrying the dressed iguana. Without its scaly skin, long tail, and hideous-looking head, it wasn't as repulsive as it had been, but Andrea wasn't up to eating lizard meat, despite the fact that she'd had no meat since she had left the boat. When she refused the roasted meat Eric later offered her, he remarked, "I wouldn't have pegged you for being so squeamish."

"Usually, I'm not, but I can't forget how hideous-looking that thing was."

"Hideous-looking or not, you'd eat it if you were hungry enough. I'll take what's left back to my comrades-in-arms. Even under normal conditions, iguana meat is prized."

Andrea frowned. She had completely forgotten that Eric was with the Cubans and going hungry. He looked leaner than he had looked in Havana, but he was far from malnourished. "What have you been eating?"

"Anything we can get our hands on. Palmetto hearts, roots, mangoes and any other wild fruits that are growing. I've eaten so many damn coconuts, I hope to hell I never see another one in my life. I did draw the line at grubs, though. The Cubans go wild with delight when they turn over a half-rotten tree trunk and find them."

The gorge rose in Andrea's throat. That made even the iguana look appealing.

Eric left an hour later, carrying the rest of the roasted iguana with him. He wrapped the meat in banana leaves so he wouldn't be attacked on account of his valuable possession.

Andrea spent the remainder of the day organizing her notes, smugly sitting through two torrential downfalls in her dry, little nest. Then, about an hour before sundown, she returned to the field hospital.

As she walked past the Red Cross hospital, Andrea noted how pitiful the organization's flag looked over the open tent, hanging sodden and limp. It seemed to reflect the way many of them were beginning to feel. The rain and oppressive heat, combined with the war coming to a standstill, drained the spirit as well as the body. Then Andrea spied a woman among the cots of wounded. Knowing that Clara and Mrs. Gardner had left, she walked closer, then recognized Susan. Andrea didn't want to disturb her at her work. She waited until she had caught Susan's attention, then Andrea waved.

Susan waved back and called, "I'll see you later."

Later turned out to be almost midnight, but despite the late hour, the two young women had the "quarters" to themselves. The other nurses had continued "on duty," as they called it.

Seeing Susan's eyes sparkling with humor as she sat on the cot beside her, Andrea asked, "What's so funny?"

"Well, I don't know if you'll find it amusing or not—sometimes I think we in the medical field have a rather strange sense of humor—but a mystery has finally been cleared up for us nurses. For days, the orderlies who undressed the men for surgery have been telling us about this strange garment some of the soldiers were wearing. It was a piece of cloth about a foot wide and one or two yards long. I just learned from one of the patients here that the cloths were donations to the Rough Riders from some women's group in Arizona trying to do their bit for the war effort. The things are supposed to prevent fevers, but when the cloths were handed out, there were no instructions with them—"

"Prevent fevers?" Andrea interjected. "That's ridiculous! How could a piece of cloth prevent malaria or yellow fever?"

"But that's not what struck us as so amusing. What we thought was so funny was the area of the body the soldiers chose to protect. Instead of wrapping the cloths around their chests, where all the vital organs are, they'd wrapped them around their loins, only going to prove what men consider their most prized possession."

Andrea laughed and added, "Can't you just imagine how horrified the good ladies would be if they knew where their cloths had gone?"

The two shared another laugh, then Andrea asked, "When did you arrive?"

"This afternoon. Three of us came, and two stayed behind. Thank God for the lull in casualties. Do you know we did over five hundred operations in two days? Tony said that must be some kind of record."

Andrea's eyebrows rose. "Tony? Could that by any chance be Dr. Anthony Marks?"

Susan blushed, then admitted, "Yes, it is."

"When did you two get on a first-name basis?"

"During those two days. We were a team. Although there's a strict code for behavior between doctors and nurses, it's hard, if not impossible, to maintain those barriers when you're working under so much tension. The only way we could even begin to cope with all of the horrors around us was to talk about ourselves and our backgrounds. I think we would have both gone crazy if it hadn't been for that. My God, we'd work for hours trying to patch some poor soul, only to have another one in worse condition placed before us. So many died, right there on the table beneath our hands. I can't begin to tell you how devastating that is—how heavily the feeling of failure weighs down on you. On the other hand, we wondered if we should have made the effort on many we saved. Believe me, they won't thank us. They'll go through the rest of their lives in terrible pain. Death would have been more merciful."

Susan dropped her head, unable to look Andrea in the eye as she confided in a hushed, agonized voice, "Finally, we did make decisions that might not have been ours, others beside the abdominal cases. Tony would look down, then just nod for the stretcher bearers to remove the victim. Those were the decisions that weighed heaviest on us all. We could only pray that God would forgive us if we misjudged."

Suddenly Susan broke into tears. Andrea took her into her arms and held her while sobs racked her small body, Andrea knew she needed this purging of her soul. When it was over, Susan mumbled, "I'm sorry. A trained nurse is never supposed to break down like that."

Andrea pushed a tendril of hair back from Susan's forehead and answered, "I don't know why not. Nurses are human, too."

Susan looked up at Andrea with pain-filled eyes and said, "Oh, Andy, I never knew it would be like this. I hate this war!"

Andrea pulled Susan's head down on her chest in the age-old manner in which women have comforted others since the beginning of time. She answered, "So do I. So do a lot of people. More and more each day."

Andrea gazed out over Susan's head and fervently hoped that by the time this war ended there would be enough hating it that her country would never ever get into another needless war.

During the next day the truce remained in effect. More and more fever victims were brought in. Susan confided to Andrea what everyone had been fearing. There were three confirmed cases of yellow fever among the troops. The news was being kept from the soldiers for fear that it would cause them to panic.

The next day, the long-awaited supplies finally arrived, along with reinforcements. However, there still wasn't enough food—tents, clothing, and medical equipment were still in short supply. Fresh troops arriving at the trenches were practically assaulted for the cigarettes they carried, and Andrea noted the look of horror on the newcomers' faces at what they found. Having heard of the glorious victories portrayed by the press, they were shocked at their first encounter with the reality of war. They saw—not heroes, at least not the shining heroes they had in their mind's eye, but—troops covered with rags standing in stinking mud to their knees. The soldiers were gaunt from hunger and bouts of dysentery, exhausted from lack of restful sleep. Their utter boredom and inactivity added to their abject misery. Thick clouds of flies and gnats hovered over the trenches and hordes of vicious mosquitoes were everywhere. That day, rain was falling continuously.

When Andrea, sopping wet, returned to the field

hospital, she was surprised to see it was almost bare. "Where did all the patients go?" she asked Susan.

"We've been sending all that we possibly can back to Siboney, to make room for the new casualties. I guess you haven't heard the news. General Toral called for a conference today. He's agreed to surrender the city, if Shafter will allow them to march their troops into the mountains. Shafter would have done it, but Washington refused. They're insisting on an unconditional surrender."

Andrea had mixed feelings. She knew that allowing the Spanish to retreat to the mountains would only delay the day of reckoning. Someone, either the United States or the Cuban insurrectionists, probably the latter, would have to fight them eventually. On the other hand, she knew that Shafter was anxious to gain Santiago's surrender and get his men out of the deplorable conditions before the fevers claimed more victims.

"However," Susan continued, "General Shafter did offer to transport the Spanish to Spain at our expense, rather than place them in a detention camp, but General Toral still refused. Shafter gave them until noon tomorrow. Then the war begins again."

Deciding to omit any comment on the matter, Andrea remarked, "I'm surprised you've managed to move so many, so quickly. Did more ambulances arrive with the new supplies?"

"No, they still have only the seven they started with," Susan answered in disgust. "Isn't that ridiculous? Seven ambulances for this big an army? But they've been running back and forth, nonstop, along with every wagon we could beg, borrow, or steal. We were actually put into competition with Clara. We've been told by some of the ambulance drivers that she's having a devil of a time trying to find transportation to move supplies to El Caney."

"That sounds familiar," Andrea remarked, remembering how hard it had been for the old lady to find transportation for the supplies she had brought. "Has anyone heard from El Caney?"

"Yes. I understand one of the consuls got through to Shafter. He said conditions were terrible, that there were only three hundred houses for almost twenty thousand people, that there was no food, that disease was rampant, that the shallow graves the soldiers had been buried in had been unearthed by the heavy rains and the stench was so bad it almost knocked you over." Susan paused. She said, "Oh, God, Andy! How much worse can it get?"

"I don't know," Andrea answered. She added bleakly, "but I have a feeling we'll find out."

The next day, at 4:00 P.M., the American batteries that overlooked Santiago opened fire, as did the soldiers in the entrenchments. At the same time, there was a terrible storm. Lightning and thunder shook the heavens as if they were vying against the roaring of the cannons and the rattling of the Gatling guns and the pop of the rifles. At nightfall, the guns fell silent, but another violent storm swept through the area, dumping more water. Dawn came with a heavy mist, and the bombardment began again, this time accompanied by navy shells directed over the mountains. The pounding continued all morning, the loud cannon blasts echoing through the mountains until the sound was a continuous roar. Then, at noon, the Spanish requested a truce, saying they wished to wire Madrid for permission to surrender, but they warned that it would take time, since the nearest cable to Europe was in Jamaica. Shafter agreed.

There were few battle casualties brought to the field hospital during and after the bombardments, but new fever cases poured in, and the army ceased to make any attempt to hide conditions from the troops. The yellow fever victims were moved to separate fever hospitals in wagons waving yellow flags. The troops gave them a wide berth in fear of contagion.

Much to Andrea's surprise, Eric showed up at the hospital late that afternoon. "Can you come with me?" he asked Andrea.

"For the night?"

"Yes."

"Can you get away that long?"

"At the present time, I don't even know if the Cubans will be taking part of this campaign anymore. Shafter ordered some of the new reinforcements to take over our trenches. Needless to say, the Cubans are not very happy about it."

Andrea could hardly believe her ears. It was an out-and-out slap in the face. "Let me get a few things together, and I'll be right with you."

"What things?"

"Well, soap for one. That's the only place I can find the privacy for a bath."

Andrea hurried back to her quarters and packed the small valise and a change of clothes she could wear while her "uniform" was drying. Then she stopped at the hospital and signaled to Susan that she wanted to talk to her.

As the nurse stepped up to her, Andrea said, "I just wanted to tell you I won't be here tonight, so please don't worry about me."

"Where are you going?"

Andrea never even considered lying to her friend. "With him." She motioned to Eric standing in the distance. Andrea held her breath. She had no regrets at becoming lovers with Eric. It seemed so natural, so right. But she didn't know how Susan was going to take it, and she'd hate for the nurse to look down on her because of it.

But Susan didn't let her down. "Oh, I'm so glad he's alive and well. See, you were worried over nothing."

"Not really. He took a near hit at El Caney." Andrea looked Susan straight in the eye, and said, "I love him. I can't help myself."

"And how does he feel about you?"

"He loves me."

"Good! Because if anyone tried to take advantage of you, I'd skin him alive!"

"Thank you for understanding."

"I'd expect the same from you. That's what friends are for." She turned Andrea and gave her a little push, saying, "Now, go on. He's waiting for you."

Andrea hurried away. But she stepped back when she was almost run down by a yellow fever wagon. After it had rumbled past, she found Eric waiting for her on the other side. As she walked up to him, he stared at the fever hospital where the wagon was headed. Then he said in disgust, "Look at them placing the fever victims right there in that swamp where the mosquitoes breed. They won't let a soul come near them, because they're quarantined, but they let the mosquitoes roam at will, carrying the disease to everyone else."

"Where did you ever get the idea that mosquitoes carry yellow fever?" Andrea asked.

"A Cuban doctor, Carlos Finley, has done research on it and virtually proven it. He's spent almost his entire medical career studying the disease."

"I've never heard anything about that."

"No, I'm sure you haven't. The American medical field hasn't accepted it, probably because it came from a Cuban. The military are not alone in having such low regard for Cubans, you know."

Andrea winced at the bitterness she heard in Eric's voice, but she couldn't take him to task for his cynicism. Instead her heart went out to him, for she knew he found the Americans' betrayal painful, as well as humiliating.

Chapter 24

When Andrea returned to the hospital late the next afternoon, she found Clara sleeping in the women's quarters. Surprised to find her there, napping in the middle of the day, Andrea sought out Susan and asked, "What is Clara doing here? I thought she was delivering supplies to the refugees at El Caney."

"They couldn't get through. The town is surrounded by high water. She just got back from conferring with General Shafter about a possible alternate route, but every road is blocked. He suggested sending word for the refugees to make their way to the Firmoza Cuban Mines, where there is a railroad Clara could use to transport supplies to them. But Clara had to reject that proposal. In their weakened condition, the refugees could never march ten miles through jungle."

Indeed not, Andrea thought. The army couldn't even march that far, and the refugees had been deprived of food much longer than they. "Those poor souls," Andrea responded. "They'd be better off just staying where are. They had shelter in Santiago. I've the mosquitoes breed. They won't let a soul come near them, because they're quarantined, but they let the mosquitoes roam at will, carrying the disease to everyone else."

"Where did you ever get the idea that mosquitoes carry yellow fever?" Andrea asked.

"A Cuban doctor, Carlos Finley, has done research on it and virtually proven it. He's spent almost his entire medical career studying the disease."

"I've never heard anything about that."

"No, I'm sure you haven't. The American medical field hasn't accepted it, probably because it came from a Cuban. The military are not alone in having such low regard for Cubans, you know."

Andrea winced at the bitterness she heard in Eric's voice, but she couldn't take him to task for his cynicism. Instead her heart went out to him, for she knew he found the Americans' betrayal painful, as well as humiliating.

Chapter 24

When Andrea returned to the hospital late the next afternoon, she found Clara sleeping in the women's quarters. Surprised to find her there, napping in the middle of the day, Andrea sought out Susan and asked, "What is Clara doing here? I thought she was delivering supplies to the refugees at El Caney."

"They couldn't get through. The town is surrounded by high water. She just got back from conferring with General Shafter about a possible alternate route, but every road is blocked. He suggested sending word for the refugees to make their way to the Firmoza Cuban Mines, where there is a railroad Clara could use to transport supplies to them. But Clara had to reject that proposal. In their weakened condition, the refugees could never march ten miles through jungle."

Indeed not, Andrea thought. The army couldn't even march that far, and the refugees had been deprived of food much longer than they. "Those poor souls," Andrea responded. "They'd be better off just staying where are. They had shelter in Santiago. I've heard our bombardments haven't been all that destructive."

"I thought last night when that terrible storm hit, that we were bombarding the city again," Susan informed her. "It was the worst we've had yet, with the ground shaking and that terrible lightning. I swear one bolt seemed to be jumping from mountaintop to mountaintop to mountaintop, making the entire sky look like it was on fire." Susan laughed a little nervously, then admitted, "For a moment, I thought the world was coming to an end."

"Yes, it frightened me, too, and after the storm dumped so much water, I'm not surprised the roads are impassable. But Clara must really be exhausted, to be sleeping in the daytime. It amazes me the way she usually maintains sixteen-hour days. It's hard to realize how old she is."

"I think part of her exhaustion is the bad news. You know how you can go on and on and on, until some tragedy hits you. Dr. Lesser and Bettina have been stricken with yellow fever."

Andrea sucked in her breath sharply, then muttered, "Oh, my God, no!"

Susan nodded her head grimly.

"Are they sure? Maybe it's malaria," Andrea suggested hopefully, for that fever wasn't generally lethal, as yellow fever often was.

"They're sure. One of our doctors diagnosed them. Clara had them moved to the best nearby fever hospital."

"Moved?" Andrea asked in shock. "Why couldn't you keep them in the hospital they were working in?"

"You can't mix contagious diseases with ordinary

cases. That's why all the fever cases are isolated. You know that." Then, before Andrea could respond, Susan continued, saying, "However, they've been mixed here without our realizing it. I thought nothing could be worse than those wounded they brought to Siboney after the battles, but this is. It's like a dam has burst and they're flooding in from every direction. Many casualties aren't recognized as contagious fever patients and come to us. Then after they're diagnosed, we have to transfer them to one of the smaller hospitals. The fevers have shown up even among our surgical cases. At first, we assumed they were just the ordinary postsurgical fevers that you can expect when you're operating in the primitive conditions we were under, but they weren't. The tropical fevers are running rampant. We ran out of ice yesterday. That's critical in the treatment of all fevers. Clara said she sent word back to the States for more to be delivered. And she requested a contingent of twenty-five nurses."

"More nurses? That will be wonderful!"

"If things are truly as grim as they're beginning to look, we've got to have more help. We desperately need nurses to help with the fever patients, but I don't honestly know if the army doctors will accept nurses."

"I thought that battle had already been fought and won?" Andrea asked in surprise.

"So did I. The doctors at Siboney are all raving about how much help we were. Many are planning to write to Congress and tell them so. And Shafter and his officers are saying the Red Cross saved the army. But some of the medical men are still holding out. Why, one of the doctors here told Clara just this morning that if he had his way, he'd send her packing."

"What a hateful thing to say, particularly after all the Red Cross has done for the medical division!" Andrea answered with considerable heat, then asked, "Did it upset her?"

"Not as much as it would have upset you or me," Susan admitted with a crooked, self-derisive smile. "She said she's used to men being resentful and hateful, that I needed to work on thickening my skin. I shouldn't let little things like that bother me. Did she ever tell you how they treated her when she worked in the patent office before she became active in the Red Cross?"

"You mean how they called her 'the pest in the petticoat,' and deliberately blew smoke in her face, and spit on the floor where she was about to step. Yes, she told me. I've been treated badly, but never that crudely."

Susan was pensive for a moment, then asked, "Do you think men will ever accept women as equals? Really and truly, without guile or pretense?"

"Are you talking about one man, or men in general?"

"Men in general."

Andrea scowled, then answered, "Maybe, someday. But I don't think you and I will live to see it."

Over the next few days, the negotiations for surrender dragged on, and the rain was almost continuous. As more and more yellow fever cases developed, the fear was almost palpable among everyone—troops, officers, medical personnel alike. The killer couldn't be seen, and therefore was all the more terrifying.

One day when Andrea and Susan were sitting in their quarters watching the rain pour down, Andrea related to the nurse what Eric had told her about Dr. Finlay and his beliefs that mosquitoes carried the dreaded disease.

"I've never heard of this Dr. Finlay. And I've never heard of mosquitoes' carrying disease," Susan answered skeptically.

"I didn't think much of it at first, either. But stop and think about it. We know yellow fever and malaria both occur in marshy, tropical regions and particularly during the wet season. That's when mosquitoes are thriving. It makes sense."

"For heaven's sake, don't tell me you think malaria is carried by mosquitoes, too?" Susan asked in exasperation.

"Why not?" Andrea argued. "If they can carry one, they can carry the other."

"That they can carry anything is just supposition, one man's theory, nothing more. And we know about the marshes. It's the bad, poisonous air coming from them that probably causes malaria. That's what the word means, poisonous air."

"If it's the air, why hasn't everyone come down with malaria?"

"At the rate we're going, that might very well happen!" Susan answered, growing more and more exasperated.

"I still think mosquitoes make better sense. After all, they do suck blood. If that's where the disease is—"

"If the disease is anywhere," Susan interjected, "it wouldn't be in the blood. It would be in the intestinal tract. Yellow fever victims have terrible vomiting and diarrhea, and what kills them is internal hemorrhaging."

"I still don't see why it couldn't be in the bloodstream, too."

"Infections don't attack the bloodstream. They attack organs. I just told you that."

"Why are you being so stubborn about this? At least stop and give it some serious consideration."

"I'm not being stubborn! I just see no point in wasting time. I'm sure if there was any truth in this man's theory, our medical men would have investigated it. They aren't stupid, you know. They're much better informed on these matters, than you, or I. Besides, you don't see the Cuban doctors here agreeing with that man. They treat yellow fever the same way we do. Isolate the patient, as you would with any contagious disease, and treat the symptoms."

Andrea sighed, thinking she had an idea of what Dr. Finlay was up against, in his own country, as well as in the rest of the world, a medical profession whose members had blinders on. They were so convinced they were right, that they wouldn't even consider another possibility. Suddenly the fever cloths the Rough Riders had been given didn't seem so ridiculous. They were just as ineffective in preventing the spread of the disease as what the medical professionals were doing.

The next day, while Andrea was eating lunch at the food distribution tent that doubled as the Red Cross dining room, Eric showed up. His dark hair was plastered to the top of his head and his clothing was soaking wet from the most recent downpour.

"I need to talk to you," he said to Andrea.

"Fine, but sit down and have a cup of coffee and a bowl of gruel." She rose, turned, and walked to the fireplace where the big coffee pot and huge kettle were hanging.

"I'll have the coffee," Eric answered as he sat on the bench by the table, "but you need the food for the patients."

"The food is for anyone who is hungry, whether they are ill or not. That's Clara's rule, and the one we follow here," Andrea said over her shoulder as she poured a cup of coffee.

She returned with the coffee and gruel. As she placed them before him, she said in a firm voice, "Now, eat."

Andrea sat across from Eric as he ate. It seemed ages, and not just days, since she had last seen him. He really was incredibly handsome, she thought. Then she frowned as her eyes slipped from his face to his body. She didn't know if it was her imagination or not, but he looked leaner. And it was almost pathetic the way he wolfed down the food. "I want you to take a bag of food with you when you go. They're giving it to anyone who asks for it, and if Roosevelt can get some for his troops, you can take some back to the Cubans. They've been starving longer. Besides, the food was originally purchased for them."

"Roosevelt asked for food?" Eric asked in surprise, not expecting someone as well-heeled as Roosevelt to go begging, even on behalf of his troops.

"He offered to buy food for his men, after the battle

at Kettle Hill, when everyone was without rations. Dr. Gardner told him he could have it and he'd even deliver it, but Roosevelt refused the offer and carried off a big bag slung over his shoulder. It's one of Dr. Gardner's favorite stories."

"Thanks for the offer, but I don't think I'd better. If I can't take enough for everyone, I won't take any. That iguana meat I took back caused a near riot." He changed the subject, saying, "I wanted to tell you, I don't think I'll be back this way much anymore. We've been assigned to a new position. Our trenches were taken away. We've been all but pushed out into the sea. And relations between García and Shafter are deteriorating rapidly. García hasn't been asked to take part in any of the negotiations."

"Why not?"

"Because the Spanish don't want to negotiate with the Cubans, only with the Americans."

"To hell with what they want!" Andrea exclaimed, angry at the new insults Shafter had given the patriots. "They're supposed to be surrendering. What right do they have to make demands? The Cubans are our allies, whether the Spanish like it or not."

"On paper, yes, but in reality, you and I both know that the Cubans aren't being treated like allies. They aren't being given any respect at all—not by their enemies they've fought for years, or by the newly arrived Americans. García has not been invited to the negotiations, nor will he be asked to take part in the surrender. Frankly, I don't know how many more insults he'll tolerate. He's a proud man, as well as a dedicated patriot. And he doesn't deserve this. No Cuban freedom-fighter deserves to be pushed out at the last minute by some usurper wanting to take full credit for a victory of a battle that's been ongoing for years. At any rate, I probably won't be coming this way much, if at all."

The new injustices being done to the Cubans, sickened Andrea, and the realization that she and Eric might not see one another for some time disappointed her. "When do you think we'll see each other again?"

"I don't know. Maybe after the official surrender. Maybe after Shafter has Toral's official commitment, he'll treat García a little better. Then Shafter won't have to worry about appeasing the Spanish."

In Andrea's mind the general should have been more concerned with the feelings of his comrades-in-arms than with those of his enemy. "Do you think the Spanish will surrender? I've wondered, with all this delaying they've been doing. It occurred to me that it might be a trick of some kind, or that they were hoping that things would get so bad with the fevers and all, that we'd just withdraw."

"No, they're really waiting for word from Madrid. Toral doesn't dare surrender without their permission, no matter how dire the circumstances may be. If he did, he could be court-martialed and put to death, along with his officers, or even his entire command, if it was deemed a cowardly surrender. That's why the Spanish soldier fights so hard to win, and often to the death. Surrender doesn't look very appealing."

Eric pulled something from his shirt pocket and slid the flask across the table to Andrea, saying, "This is the second reason I wanted to stop by. I don't know if you'll do it or not, but I'd like you to use this on your exposed skin, to keep the mosquitoes from biting."

Andrea opened the flask and took a sniff, then made a terrible face and said, "That's the most God-awful stuff I've ever smelled! What is it?"

"Shark oil. Some of the natives use it. I don't know if the smell keeps the mosquitoes away, or if they can't penetrate the oil, or even if it works. But it's the only thing I have to offer you to protect yourself."

"What about you? You don't wear it, and you have a lot more skin showing than I do. Why, you walk around half-naked all the time."

"I don't have to worry about myself. I've had yellow fever."

"I didn't know that," Andrea muttered in surprise. Then she thought there was really a lot she didn't know about him. She fervently wished they had time to share more of their past with each other. "When?"

"The first summer I was in Cuba. I was fortunate enough to be in Havana when I came down with it. Being in a good hospital with decent care, I survived. That's how I learned about Dr. Finlay. He worked at that hospital." Eric rose from the bench, then asked, "Will you use it?"

Andrea hate to go around stinking to high heaven, but she couldn't refuse the pleading look she saw in Eric's eyes. "Well, I guess it can't hurt to try it, although I don't think I'll make many new friends with it on."

Eric knew Andrea's penchant for giving ambiguous answers, then she would turn around and do the opposite of what he expected. "I'd prefer an unqualified answer."

Andrea knew he had seen through her. Her eyes twinkled as she asked mischievously, "No maybes?"

Eric smiled and answered, "No maybes."

The smile did it. His tender, caring, loving smile warmed Andrea from the tip of her head to her toes, and she could have refused him nothing, absolutely nothing. "Yes, I'll wear it."

Chapter 25

Andrea was beginning to fear that every soldier in every trench overlooking Santiago would be prostrate with fever before the surrender took place. Finally, almost two weeks after the Spanish fleet had been sunk, word arrived that Madrid had agreed to the terms. Even before the official ceremony on July 17th, the snipers slipped down from their high perches in the trees and disappeared. The refugees at El Caney began to make their way back to the city.

Andrea was in the crowd that watched the official surrender. She was too far away to hear anything, but close enough to see. The ceremony took place in the open. General Toral, grizzled and mustached, his golden epaulets and medals gleaming in the sunlight, rode at the head of a hundred Spanish infantrymen to where Shafter and some of his officers waited. The Spanish buglers sounded a salute to the American general, and their American counterparts joined in. The two generals moved their mounts forward. Since Toral had already sent his silver-encrusted sword to Shafter at daylight, it was only left for Shafter to give his to

Toral in return, along with the sword and spurs of General del Rey, who had so bravely died at El Caney. Then the two generals shook hands and rode, side by side, to Santiago, where the American flag was to be raised over the governor's palace. All along the trenches, the bugles blasted out the news that the surrender was official. The muddy, haggard men cheered, as the sound went echoing from mountaintop to mountaintop.

Andrea didn't go with the crowd that followed the two opposing generals into the city. She took no pride in the victory, and felt no need to celebrate. She had seen no tall, dignified man with a silver goatee and a cleft between his eyes. She knew, just as Eric had predicted, that the Cubans had been excluded from the surrender. It shamed her to know that her country would add more insult to injury. For the Americans in the muddy ditches, men who had come for glory and adventure and found sickness, misery, and death, she felt relief that it was finally over. But there was no gladness in her heart as she walked back down the hill to the field hospital. Her government's callous treatment of the Cuban patriots had besmirched the triumph, and robbed her of all satisfaction in the deed.

A few days later, alarmed at the number of fever cases being brought in, Clara Barton ordered her group back to Siboney. The Red Cross medical facilities were turned over to the army, and the group, including Andrea, over roads that were even muddier than before, made the grueling trip back to the village.

When they reached Siboney, they were shocked.

The place was in total chaos, so overrun with fever cases flooding in from every direction, that the medical staffs of both hospitals had ceased trying to keep the "contagious" fevers isolated from the other cases. The patients lay in the mud, without benefit of blankets, soaking wet from the most recent rain and shivering. Some wildly thrashed about in delirium, and others lay in their own vomit and feces.

Along with the Red Cross nurses, Andrea set to work helping to load the sick on the hospital ships. The backbreaking, exhausting chore, often was done without benefit of even a litter. The only saving grace was that the pier had finally been completed, and the nurses weren't at the mercy of the tides. As they worked, Andrea could see mule trains threading their way through the jungle in the hills above the city. The trains were bringing in more victims—sitting slumped on the animals' backs, or, if they were unconscious, simply slung over them like bags of grain.

Later that day, Susan and Andrea were taking a brief break from their labors. They sat beneath one of the little sheds that had been built on the pier to protect incoming supplies from the rain. They were approached by one of Clara's staff and told that Clara wanted all of her personnel that weren't ill, to board the *State of Texas* immediately.

The two young women exchanged surprised glances. Susan asked, "Why? Are we sailing?"

"No, at least not at the present time," the messenger answered. "Clara's worried about keeping the ship free from contagion. She's still planning on delivering supplies to the *reconcentrados* at Santiago, you know."

"What does that have to do with it?" Andrea asked.

"If there is any yellow fever aboard her ship, Clara won't be allowed to enter the port, or any port."

"That's ridiculous!" Andrea retorted. "The city is already full of the fever."

"She still will not be allowed to enter. It's against international law."

"Wait a minute," Andrea responded, as she suddenly remembered something. "You said all personnel that weren't ill. What about Dr. Lesser and Sister Bettina?"

The messenger looked decidedly uncomfortable. "I'm afraid they, and the others, will have to be left behind. They can be brought back to the States later on one of the fever ships, hopefully the Red Cross ship that's bringing the other nurses."

"What others are you talking about?" Susan asked.

"Ten of our group are down. That's why Clara is so concerned. She wants to get the rest of us on board before any more of us are infected."

"I can't believe this," Andrea said in a mixture of anger and horror. "I can't believe she is going deprive these poor soldiers of help, to say nothing of abandoning her own workers to who knows what fate. My God, the personnel in those fever hospitals can't begin to compare in skill and knowledge to her own doctors and nurses."

"I can't argue that point," the messenger answered. "Many of us are just as upset with her decision. George Keenan for one. He told her that she was fulfilling the worst predictions of the surgeon general by retreating from a disease that goes hand-in-hand with tropical warfare. Keenan is just as upset as you, about her leaving her own workers. However, she is determined to stick by her decision, and if Keenan—who's been with her so long and for whom she has such high respect,—can't talk her out of it, then I'm afraid no one can." The man turned, saying over his shoulder, "I must go. I have others to contact."

Andrea turned to Susan and asked, "Are you going to obey her and desert the ill?"

Susan was clearly torn, but answered, "I'm afraid I have to. She's in charge. If I don't, she could dismiss me. I came to Cuba with her. I have to leave with her, or risk being stranded here. Besides, maybe she has a good reason for what she's doing. Maybe she's comparing numbers, ten starving civilians to one ill soldier. She can't help them all, so she's got to make a choice."

Andrea couldn't accept Susan's reasoning. To her, the elder woman's running from the disease seemed cowardly, and in view of the fact that Andrea had thought Clara her idol, she felt terribly betrayed. "No, she made her choice when she jumped into this war. Someone else could deliver those supplies. To leave everyone now, including her own people, is the worst kind of desertion." Andrea jumped to her feet, saying, "And by God, I'm going to tell her so!"

"It won't do you any good. You heard what he said. If Keenan can't talk her out of it, no one can. As much as I admire her, Clara can be terribly hard-headed when she sets her mind to it." Susan rose from the box she had been sitting on and said, "I'll go, but later. First I'm going to help move a few more of these patients."

As Susan started to walk away, she stumbled, then put her hand on her forehead and winced in pain.

Andrea jumped to her feet and asked, "What's wrong?"

"I have a terrible headache. I've had it all day, but it's getting worse." She swayed, then muttered, "Oh, dear! I do believe I have to sit down."

Alarmed, Andrea helped Susan to a box beneath the shade of the shed. As soon as Andrea had her seated, she anxiously scanned her face. Because Susan was not used to being in the hot sun, Andrea had assumed her face was red from sunburn, but now she strongly suspected something else. She placed her hand on Susan's forehead.

"Do I have a fever?" Susan asked.

Susan's forehead was burning hot. Andrea was terrified. "A little," she admitted.

"Please don't lie to me."

Susan's accusing glare made Andrea answer reluctantly, "All right. You're burning up."

Susan smiled sadly, then muttered, "Old Yellow Jack got me."

"Don't say that!" Andrea said, in a voice made harsh by fear. "It might be malaria. It starts out with a headache and fever."

"Its onset is much more rapid. If I had malaria, I'd be having chills, or maybe even delirium by now." Susan paused, then said weakly, "Please help me lie down. I really feel quite ill."

Andrea eased Susan down to a prone position, then said, "I'll be right back. I'm going to find one of our doctors."

Andrea rushed down the pier, pushing her way through a steady stream of fever cases being taken to the ships. She was craning her neck as she went, in hope of spying one of the Red Cross doctors. Once, she bumped into two orderlies dragging an unconscious fever case down the pier. The victim's arms were slung around their shoulders and his head hung limply on his chest. "Goddammit, watch where you're going!" one of the orderlies scolded her. A quick, but distracted response came from Andrea, "I'm sorry."

Andrea stepped from the pier onto the beach and looked around. The entire area was covered with seriously ill men. Doctors were rushing from one to the other in their efforts to select the cases which would be loaded first. Hearing a sound behind her, she looked around to see a soldier spewing out vomit that was as black as tar. The sight made her gag. She forced herself to remember her mission, looked around her, then spied a familiar face. Hurrying to him, she touched his shoulder, then said, "Excuse me!"

Dr. Anthony Marks glanced over his shoulder, then answered irritably, "Not now. I'm busy with the sick."

"But that's what I've come about. I need help and I can't find any of the Red Cross doctors. Susan is down with the fever. I thought maybe you—"

The young man swung around so abruptly he almost knocked Andrea over. "Susan is ill?"

"Yes. She collapsed on the pier." Andrea blinked back tears. "I know it's the fever. She's burning up."

The doctor's face paled. Then he said, "Take me to her."

Andrea led the doctor to where she had left Susan. As he bent to examine Susan, she opened her eyes and muttered, "Is that you, Tony?"

The young doctor forced a smile, then answered, "Yes, it's me."

"It's yellow fever, isn't it?"

"It's too soon to tell," Tony answered, being deliberately evasive and trying to hide his own fear. "We'll get you aboard your ship and have the Red Cross doctors have a look at you. They're much better with these fevers, as you well know."

"She can't go aboard the *State of Texas*," Andrea informed him in a brittle tone of voice. "Clara Barton won't allow any fever victims on board. In fact, we were told to board before any more of us became infected."

"You can't be serious," Tony responded with a shocked expression on his face. "Susan is one of her nurses. She can't sail off and leave her."

"That's exactly what she intends to do with all of her ill. Leave them in the fever hospital until a Red Cross ship can take them back to the States. She's afraid her ship will be quarantined and she won't be able to deliver her supplies to the starving Cubans."

The doctor was accustomed to making difficult choices, lately many life-or-death choices. Had he not been so involved with Susan, he might have appreciated Miss Barton's predicament. But his full concern was for Susan, and he was angry. "That's despicable! Perhaps if I talk with her—"

"No, Tony," Susan interjected weakly. "It won't do you any good. If her own staff can't talk her out of it, you can't."

"I'm afraid that's true," Andrea added. "We need to get Susan to the hospital where the others have been taken, but I don't know where that is or how to accomplish it by myself."

The young doctor was not so easily dissuaded, but

he saw how seriously ill Susan was and he knew that she needed immediate medical care. He decided to defer his talk with Miss Barton until later. He answered, "I know where it is. I'll have two of the litter bearers familiar with it take her." A look of genuine regret passed over his face. "I'd go myself, but I can't leave right now."

Andrea was terribly disappointed, and frightened. She knew nothing about caring for fever patients. What if Susan should become critical on the way? But she held her fear at bay and answered, "I understand, and I appreciate your help."

The doctor quickly summoned two litter bearers and gave them instructions. After Susan was loaded on the stretcher, Tony bent and said to her, "I'll see you later. Now you behave yourself. We both know what terrible patients doctors and nurses make."

Despite her pounding headache, Susan managed a feeble smile and a nod. Then as the stretcher was carried off and she realized Andrea intended to accompany her, she said, "No, Andrea. You'd better not come to the hospital. You might catch it."

"I don't think I'm any more likely to catch anything at that hospital than out here. Mosquitoes can fly long distances, you know."

"But—"

"Hush!" Andrea interrupted. "I'm coming, and you're in no condition to argue with me."

It was very much the truth of the matter. Susan fell silent from sheer weakness.

Andrea walked beside the stretcher and held Susan's burning hand during the three-mile trek to the Cuban fever hospital that was located on a hilltop that overlooked Siboney. Andrea was fully prepared for a battle. She expected the medical staff to tell her she could not stay, but the Cuban doctors and nuns were much too busy to waste their energy in such a manner. After they had warned her that the fevers were contagious, Andrea was left alone to sit beside her friend, who was still lying on the stretcher, for there were not enough beds for the patients.

Susan was placed in an area where the other Red Cross members were, and Andrea said hello to those who were conscious. Then she explained why she was there. She learned that a few had already died, and her fear for Susan increased. She also learned that the victims already knew of Clara's decision to leave them to their fate. Surprisingly, most were resigned to whatever awaited them, and Andrea never knew if it was because they were too weak to care, or because they possessed extraordinary courage.

The rest of that day and the better part of the next, Andrea stayed at her friend's side. As Susan slipped in and out of consciousness, Andrea bathed her feverish face and arms with a wet rag, since there was no ice available, and held her head when she vomited. Much to her surprise, Susan seemed to rally, and Andrea was able to get Susan to swallow a few sips of weak broth. Thankfully they stayed down. Then, late that afternoon, Dr. Marks appeared.

Since Susan was asleep at that moment, Andrea took the young army doctor aside and said excitedly, "I don't think she has a serious case. She's already improved."

Tony smiled sadly, then replied, "I hate to disappoint you, but that's just the nature of the disease. In the second stage of yellow fever, the symptoms seem to abate. Then they come back, in a much more pronounced form."

"Are you saying the worst is still ahead?" Andrea asked, her spirits sinking.

"I'm afraid so."

The two stood in silence for a moment, then Tony said, "I tried to talk to Miss Barton, with no success. I couldn't even get aboard ship."

"I'm not surprised," Andrea answered bitterly, "but thank you for trying."

"Well, at least they know where Susan is, and you. You can still board, you know."

"I know, but I'm not leaving Susan. She's the best friend I've ever had. When you go back, would you be so kind as to tell them to please send my belongings up here?"

"Aren't you afraid of catching it?"

"Of course I am," Andrea answered candidly. "But I don't believe it's contagious."

"Yes, Susan told me about Dr. Finlay and his theory about mosquitoes transmitting the disease."

"I guess you think it's rubbish, too."

"No, I don't," the doctor answered, surprising Andrea. "I read a medical paper just recently, written by a Dr. Ronald Ross, in India, about malaria being transmitted by mosquitoes. Experimentally, he's proven it. If they can transmit malaria, why not yellow fever? However, you may still be at increased risk here in the hospital, even if the disease isn't spread from one person to another. The victims are here. All the mosquitoes have to do is bite them, then you."

"I thought about that," Andrea admitted. "I'm protecting myself."

"Oh? How?"

"Well, for one, I'm wearing this blasted long-sleeved blouse," Andrea answered in disgust. "I'm burning up in it. And I'm smearing shark oil on my exposed skin. I'm surprised you can't smell it. It stinks to high heaven."

Tony couldn't smell the oil because of the stench of the hospital itself. "Where did you learn that?"

"From someone who's been in Cuba awhile."

"And it works?"

Andrea shrugged her shoulders and answered, "I honestly don't know. All I know is I haven't been bitten since I started wearing it. It might just be coincidence. Besides, there don't seem to be as many mosquitoes up here on the hilltop, as down in the swampy regions."

Tony shook his head in agreement, then commented, "But still, it only takes one bite."

"I know."

"And you're still willing to risk it?"

Andrea's determination never wavered. "Yes."

Tony gave her a long, penetrating look, then said, "You're a brave woman, and I'm glad you're staying with Susan. I would if I could, but we're leaving for Santiago in the morning. We've been ordered to transfer our patients there. I doubt if I'll even be able to get back. That's the disadvantage of serving in the army. To refuse would be desertion."

Andrea strongly suspected that Tony's feelings for Susan surpassed friendship. He clearly would stay with her, if he possibly could. "I understand. Perhaps, you'd like to sit with her for a while?"

"Yes, I would."

"Then I'll take a little walk and stretch my legs." Andrea turned, then came up short as she saw Eric coming up the path.

Seeing the pleased expression on her face, Tony asked, "Do you know that man?"

"Yes, I do."

In several long strides, Eric stood before them. He nodded to Tony, then said to Andrea, "They told me at the Red Cross ship I could find you here. I'm sorry to hear about Susan. How is she doing?"

"As well as can be expected at this point, I guess," Andrea answered glumly. "Tony said she still has the worst ahead of her." Then realizing the two men hadn't met officially, Andrea said, "I'm sorry. I completely forgot my manners. Eric, this is Dr. Tony Marks, a friend of Susan's. Tony, this is Eric Flemming. He's been fighting with the rebels for several years."

The two men shook hands and exchanged pleasantries. Then Eric said to Andrea, "I was wondering if you could get free for a few moments. We're pulling out in the morning."

"To Santiago?"

"No, completely."

"Completely?" Andrea asked in surprise.

Eric sliced the doctor a glance, then answered, "I'll explain later. Can you get free? I have no idea when we'll see each other again."

Andrea glanced in the direction where Susan lay. Suspecting the two were lovers and seeing Andrea's dilemma, Tony said, "You go ahead. I'll stay with her. And take your time. I don't need to be back until morning."

Andrea was so grateful she could have kissed the doctor. "Oh, thank you," she answered.

"Thanks," Eric added. He took Andrea's hand and led her away.

Chapter 26

As Eric hurried Andrea through the jungle, she could feel his fury. She asked, "What happened? Why are you leaving?"

His blue eyes glittered dangerously. Eric answered, "Because Shafter issued the final insult to García. He told García that the Cuban troops would not be allowed to enter Santiago along with his men. It seems the Spanish are afraid of Cuban retributions, which is an utterly groundless accusation. We're not animals! We know how to behave."

Andrea felt sick at heart. After years of fierce, bloody fighting, the Cubans were being denied their rightful place as victors, denied, by all people, by the very government that claimed to be their champion and ally.

"García has sent a letter to Shafter telling him how he feels about the matter and informing him that we're pulling out and moving into the interior," Eric continued. "Only Santiago surrendered, you know. There is still a war going on, and we're needed elsewhere. Everyone thinks there will still be a Havana campaign.

If the United States is involved in that, hopefully, we'll be treated better there. But regardless, we still fight on, until it's over, until the Spanish are completely kicked off this island."

Andrea wasn't at all surprised to learn that Eric planned to fight with the rebels to the bitter end. She fully expected that kind of loyalty from him, and she was glad. At least there was one American who lived up to the Cubans' expectations of how an American should behave. For a moment, they walked in silence while Eric guided Andrea down the dark jungle path. Finally, she asked, "Where are we going? Back to the little cove?"

"No, there are too many mosquitoes there. I'm taking you to a beach that sits on a headland where there's a stiff ocean breeze. It's too windy for the mosquitoes there."

When they reached the beach, they sat on the fine, white sand and let the wind blow through their hair. The stiff breeze and tangy salt air seemed to have a cleansing effect on both of them, sweeping away the bitterness of betrayal that each was feeling at the moment. A peacefulness filled them, and for a long while they were content to sit and just hold hands.

Later, they stripped and swam in the ocean beneath a canopy of glittering stars, delaying what they both knew was inevitable. Then, when their desire had reached the edge and they could no longer hold it at bay, Eric swept Andrea up and carried her through the foaming surf to the wet sand at the shore.

There, with the waves tugging gently at their feet, they made love. But it was unlike any lovemaking they had ever shared. Oh, the excitement was there, the incredible sensation, the fire, the spine-tingling, mind-boggling pleasure, but there was also an undercurrent of sadness that brought tears to their eyes and a tightness to their chests. Both sensed that they were doing more than conveying their deep feelings with their bodies. They were saying something that neither had the courage to utter with their lips—good-bye. Good-bye for perhaps a lifetime. And even when it was over, Eric was loath to relinquish her. He lay with Andrea's warm, tight depths still surrounding him. He was clutching her tightly and trying to commit every inch of her satiny skin to memory, while she in turn stroked the sweat-slick muscles on his back, wishing desperately that she could absorb him with her fingertips and carry him with her always.

Finally, they rose and dressed. Silence surrounded them like a heavy shroud all the way back to the hospital on the hill. Finally Eric asked, "When do you think Clara will sail?"

"I have no idea, and it hardly matters, since I won't be going with her."

Eric knew nothing of Clara's decision. He came to a dead halt. "Why not?"

Andrea faced him squarely and answered, "Because she'll be leaving her sick behind when she does, and I refuse to desert Susan. You see, Clara's afraid to take any yellow fever cases on board, for fear of being refused entry into Santiago."

Eric knew by the tone of Andrea's voice that she was bitter and angry at Clara. He could appreciate her feelings and he admired her loyalty to her friend, but he wasn't happy with her decision. He wanted her out of the mosquito-infested jungle, and the sooner, the better. "Please reconsider. If for no other reason, for my peace of mind. Every moment you stay here increases your chance of becoming infected."

"I realize that," Andrea admitted candidly, "but I'm not leaving, not without Susan." Then seeing Eric open his mouth to object, Andrea stuck out her chin and said in an adamant tone of voice, "No, Eric, save your breath. This is my decision, and mine alone, and it's final."

And it was a classic example of why it would never work on a permanent basis for them, Eric thought morosely. Andrea would always make her own decisions, regardless of his feelings. She'd do what she damn well wanted, when she wanted, how she wanted. Even if he survived this war, he couldn't stand by and watch her endanger herself over and over. It was too much to ask of any man. But it was pointless to ponder how he felt about her fierce independence, he reminded himself. Andrea had already told him that marriage was out the question. That hadn't changed. The moment he had been dreading had arrived. It was time to end it and walk away.

Grim-lipped, Eric took Andrea's hand, raised it to his lips, and kissed it. Then looking her straight in the eye, he said, "I'll always love you. Always! Remember that."

Suddenly, Andrea realized that what she had sensed when they were making love was true. This was goodbye. Only it had nothing to do with Eric marching away to war. Even if he came through unscathed, there was no mention of getting together again back in the States after the war was over. She knew Eric was telling her that their affair was finished, here and now—

that if it went any further, it would embody commitment, and that possibility left her feeling confused and bewildered. She wanted complete and utter freedom, didn't she? That's what he was giving her, his love, with no strings attached, and none expected from her. What more could she ask? But a heaviness bore down on her, a feeling so oppressive she could hardly summon the strength to mutter, "And I'll always love you."

Eric smiled, a poignant smile that mirrored Andrea's distress. Then he asked, "Would you do me one more favor?"

"Yes, of course."

He slipped a piece of paper from his pocket and pressed it into her hand. "This is a copy of García's letter to Shafter. I told his son, if anyone could get it published in the United States, it would be you. It's part of the truth that needs to be told."

Being reminded of her purpose helped to lighten the Andrea's sadness. "I'll see to it," she promised.

"Thank you." Eric couldn't bear to say the words. Good-bye sounded so utterly final, even though that was what this was. He stared at her for a long moment, then bent and lightly kissed her lips. Then, with supreme will, he turned and walked away.

Andrea couldn't force the words from her lips either. She watched until Eric disappeared in the shadows, then she turned and walked away. The burden of their final parting lay heavy on her heart.

Back at the hospital, Andrea found Susan asleep and Tony dozing at her side. She roused him, and the two walked a short distance away before Andrea asked, "How is she doing?"

"About the same." Tony shot a worried glance in Susan's direction. "The worst is yet to come. I can't tell you how glad I am you're going to be with her."

"I don't know if I'll do her much good," Andrea admitted. "I'm a journalist, not a nurse. I don't know a thing about caring for a fever patient."

"None of us did, not really. Just try to keep her cool, and try to get every bit of fluid you can down her." He paused, then added, "And if she's in a coma, don't leave her on her back. We found that out the hard way. I don't know how many men who might have been saved, died by drowning in their own vomit."

Andrea was horrified at the admission, but she kept silent. She had heard the regret in the young doctor's voice.

Tony gazed off, then said quietly, "You know, when I came down here, I thought I knew about medicine, about life, about everything. This war sure brought me to my knees."

It had brought a lot of people to their knees, Andrea thought. She wondered if anyone here would ever be the same. The war had certainly taught her a lot about human nature, about human frailty.

Tony gave Susan one long, last look, then turned to Andrea and said, "Take good care of her. She's very special."

There was no doubt in Andrea's eyes that the young man loved her friend. She saw his love in the profound look on his face, and heard it in his emotion-choked voice. She was also acutely aware of the fact that he might not see Susan alive again. She knew full well he was also aware of that grim reality. Yellow fever was almost always fatal. She swallowed hard to force down the lump in her throat and answered, "I know she is, and I'll do my best."

After Tony had left, Andrea went back to Susan and sat beside her, watching the sun come up in a blaze of glory. In the bay below, Andrea could see the patients being loaded on the hospital ships, and the *State of Texas* rocking gently on the sparkling water. Then, as she heard the rustle of paper in her pocket, she remembered the letter Eric had given her. She removed it and read it. One particularly eloquent part of General García's letter touched her deeply. It said, "We are not savages, ignoring the rules of civilized warfare. We are a poor, ragged army, as ragged and poor as were the army of your forbears in their noble war for independence. But, like the heroes at Saratoga and Yorktown, we respect too deeply our cause to disgrace it with barbarism and cowardice".

Andrea put the letter down in her lap and gazed up at the lush green mountains behind her. Then she saw a thin column of men weaving through the jungle, climbing steadily higher and higher, and knew it had to be García's army. The realization that one of those tiny, antlike creatures was Eric, walking out of her life forever, made her finally succumb to the awful emptiness she had been feeling. Tears came, a torrent of them. She cried for many reasons. She cried for those who had died in this horrible war, soldier and civilian alike; she cried for the Cuban patriots who still struggled for independence; she cried for Susan and the other fever victims, who might still lose their lives; she cried for the sheer needlessness of all the suffering and destruction; but most of all—she cried for her own terrible loss.

Chapter 27

Four years later, on a balmy May day, Andrea stood in Havana and watched the stars and stripes come down from over the governor's palace. The Cuban flag was taking its place. The cheers from all around her drowned out the stirring music of the Cuban national anthem, "La Bayamesa." But Andrea couldn't find fault with the Cubans' enthusiasm. She could understand why they were wildly excited. They must have despaired of ever seeing their flag there, or the Americans giving their country back to them. To them, and to Andrea, it seemed as if it had been a long time coming. It had been well over three years since the peace treaty between Spain and the United States was signed. But even as the United States relinquished control of the country to Cuba's new president, they tainted the Cubans' long-fought-for independence.

The United States had insisted upon an amendment to the Cuban constitution. The United States could intervene in Cuba if they felt it necessary to protect the young republic; the Cuban government could not borrow money without permission of the United States, and Cuba had to lease land to the U.S. for establishment of naval bases. In actuality the U.S.A. was proposing to make Cuba a client state, in which the Americans would have authority, but no financial responsibility. Naturally, the Cubans had not wanted the Platt Amendment, but President McKinley had made it very clear that, without it, American rule would continue, and the Cubans had accepted it. Andrea wondered if deep down they would ever forgive her country for its insults.

Andrea drew her attention away from the ceremony that was taking place. She stood on her tiptoes, and scanned the crowd. It was something she had done over and over that day, but she still didn't see any sign of Eric, and she knew with his height, he would stand out in any crowd. The disappointment she felt was so keen it brought tears to her eyes. Since he had felt so strongly about Cuban independence, she had hoped that he would be here on this important day. There was, of course, another reason why he had not appeared. But Andrea couldn't believe that he was dead. She felt she would sense if that had happened.

Feeling terribly let down, Andrea turned and fought her way through the crush of those celebrating the occasion. The crowd was as thick and boisterous as it had been at Carnival, and for that reason, it took Andrea almost an hour to reach her destination. Finally, she got to the little park where she and Eric had met. After scanning the area and finding it empty of him, she walked to the railing and gazed out over the bay.

The sight of the American flag snapping smartly in the brisk wind over the twisted ruins of the *Maine* wreckage caught her eye. It reminded her of the interesting little bit of information she had unearthed. It seemed that the battleship, *Oregon,* on its race from the Pacific to the Atlantic to join in the Cuban blockade, had had a serious fire in its coal bunkers, caused by spontaneous combustion. Several other American ships, using bituminous coal had had similar fires. However, the newspapers had paid very little attention to the events, nor had the navy publicized them. Andrea as a result of her investigation, no longer found it difficult to believe that the *Maine* might have suffered the same, just as Eric had suggested. He had been right about many things.

The memories of their time together besieged her. In the last, she saw him walking away into the jungle. In an effort to block those thoughts from her mind, she forced herself to recall what had happened to her since their parting.

In early August, the *State of Texas* had sailed from Siboney Bay to Santiago where Admiral Sampson had given the order for Barton's ship to be the first to sail triumphantly into the harbor. She had distributed food to over ten thousand starving people almost immediately, and she had later sailed to Havana, only to be refused entrance by the authorities there. But not because there was fever on the ship. Rather, it was pure bureaucracy on the part of the Spanish, who had no appreciation of her efforts in behalf of the Cuban people. Finally, Clara had been fined and the provisions taken away from her to be disbursed by colonial officials. Clara had asked the American government to intervene on her behalf, but they had refused. Suffering the final insult from the government that had enlisted her help, Clara had returned to the United States, feeling as betrayed by them as Andrea had felt by her.

Clara had kept one promise. The additional nurses she had sent for, thirty trained, experienced young women arrived at Cuba on the S.S. *Lampass*. To Andrea's total incredulity, the army refused them permission to land. They sailed on to Puerto Rico, where less-prejudiced doctors welcomed their help. Susan and the other infected Red Cross workers were forced to return to the States on one of the army's fever ships. There wasn't even a doctor on board. The victims lay in the hot, tight confines of the ship amid their own vomit and diarrhea. The dead weren't removed for days. By nothing short of a miracle, Susan had survived. Andrea credited it to the nurse's fierce will to live. The first thing Andrea did on arrival to the United States had been to write a scathing article about what she had seen and experienced aboard that hellish ship. To her satisfaction, it, along with other newspaper reports, had been used in a congressional investigation that made Surgeon General Sternberg squirm under the unfavorable publicity. He denied—to Andrea's absolute fury—that he had refused to allow women in any army hospital—as had occurred with the nurses on the *Lampass*—and he claimed that he only objected to the presence of women in "active operations"—what the Red Cross nurses had done at Siboney and First Division Field Hospital without his permission. Andrea had the satisfaction of seeing him forced to reverse his position. Shortly thereafter, seven hundred nurses went into army camps and hospitals, some amid conditions as bad as what the *reconcentrados* suffered. And they did heroic work with the fever cases and wounded, a fully recuperated Susan among them. Their performance, along with the army doctor's congressional testimony of how well the Red Cross nurses had done in Cuba, changed the public's opinion of the value of women in the medical field. In this victory for women's rights, Andrea took particular pride.

The congressional investigation into the charges that the army was giving its men inadequate medical care wasn't the only controversy Andrea got involved in. The war with Spain ended in December of the year 1898—everywhere except in the Philippines, that is. Like the Cubans, the Filipinos had been fighting for independence, but the United States wasn't willing to relinquish the Philippine islands after the war had ended. It claimed the Philippines as a territory, since they held a strategic position in the Pacific.

The Filipinos had revolted against American rule, and Andrea had traveled to the islands to cover the revolution. To her horror, she had found conditions there even worse than they had been in Cuba—the Spanish were not imprisoning the civilian population in inhumane concentration camps to cut them off from the insurgents in a desperate effort to win the confrontation. It was the Americans! To Andrea, her country had sunk to the lowest depths she thought any country could. Sick at heart, she had returned to the States and written a series of articles, which, she hoped, would wake up the American public. In the end, the only person they had awakened was herself.

Andrea discovered how naive she had been, to think she could rouse the people's conscience. Nor could she convince them of the horrors of war, so that there wouldn't be any more. The public saw what it wanted to see, heard what it wanted to hear, believed what it wanted to believe, and the truth wasn't what they wanted. That's why yellow journalism thrived, not because Hearst and those like him did their job so well. The American public was riding high on their new victory. It had made them a "first class" nation, a power to be reckoned with. They turned a blind eye to what was happening in the Philippines and, except for a few, they totally agreed with one ambassador's observation that the Spanish-American War had been a "splendid little war." Andrea was left to wonder if something in human nature craved this need for self-destruction.

Coming to accept the cold, hard fact that she couldn't save the world from itself was part of Andrea's growing up. Not until that transformation had taken effect was she able to come to terms with just how much she had lost when Eric had walked out of her life. Now she knew that success in a career and the excitement of travel wasn't enough. They were meaningless unless they could be shared with someone who really cared. The prestigious awards she had won for her journalism offered her no comfort in the middle of a long lonely night, when all humans were vulnerable. Everyone needed someone to hold onto. That need to share life, was very much a part of human nature, too. People needed people as much as they needed food and water. One sustained the body, the other the soul, and she had foolishly thrown the relationship away. Like so many before her, she had come to appreciate the value of what she'd had, only after she had lost it. And another man would never do. Only Eric could fill that terrible void and make her come alive, could make her spirits soar and her heart sing with pure happiness. That's why she had returned to Havana. Hoping for a second chance.

"Andrea?"

When Andrea heard Eric saying her name, she thought she was imagining it, since she wanted to see him so very much. He took her shoulders and turned her to face him—then the full realization hit her, leaving her speechless.

"You're even more beautiful than I remembered," Eric said softly.

And you're more handsome, more manly, more exciting, more everything, Andrea thought. And those eyes! She had forgotten how very blue they were.

A silence followed while the two stared at each other. Neither had to ask if the other was still in love. It was obvious by the look on their faces. Andrea finally regained her power of speech and asked, "You came for the celebration?"

"Among other things."

Andrea knew it was a guarded answer, and her heart raced in anticipation.

"How is Susan? Did she survive?"

The question wasn't what Andrea had hoped for, but she realized it was a legitimate one. He would have to be awfully cold-hearted not to wonder. "Yes. She's tough as nails. Do you remember that doctor that was visiting her?" Eric nodded. "Well," Andrea continued, "they met again at a fever camp in Georgia. They're married now, and very happy."

"I'm glad to hear that," Eric answered.

"And Paul? Have you heard how he fared?"

"Yes, I have. I visited him after the war was over. Both he and his plantation survived completely unscathed. He said the Spanish in Havana were so disorganized and panic-stricken after we declared war that the city could have been taken without a shot being fired, if our fleet had simply sailed into the harbor."

"All those lives could have been saved?" Andrea asked in horror. "That's awful!"

"Yes, it is." Eric gazed off for a moment, then said, "I read the article you wrote about General García. Thanks."

"The one before, or after, his death?"

"Both."

"Wasn't it terrible for him to die that way, all alone in a New York hotel, of pneumonia?"

"Yes. His son was terribly upset about it. He hadn't really wanted his father to go with the commission that was working on solving the problems both the United States and Cuba were facing, but General García was a patriot to the bitter end. He put aside his personal feelings and went."

Another pregnant pause in the conversation occurred. Then Eric looked about him and commented, "Havana looks better. It's cleaner."

Andrea's spirits sagged. What was all this senseless banter, she wondered. Surely they had more important things to discuss. The younger, brasher Andrea would have come right out and said so, but the more mature, more cautious Andrea decided to play along. "Yes, I guess we'll have to give our country credit for that, at least. General Wood did an admirable job as administrator, in both sanitation and mosquito control. I'm sure you've heard about Dr. Walter Reed and his work on tropical parasitic diseases. I understand he's using some of Dr. Finlay's old research results." Andrea paused, then said caustically, "I'll bet my last penny that when it comes time for giving credit, it goes to Dr. Reed, particularly in the United States. Finlay's name will never appear in our textbooks."

"I don't imagine it will," Eric answered with surprising blandness. "It seems both of the commanders of the Rough Riders have done well for themselves, Wood down here, and Roosevelt back in the States."

At the mention of Roosevelt's name, Andrea's black eyes flashed. "I couldn't believe McKinley would accept him for a running mate, after the insulting things Roosevelt said about him. And now, because of some dim-witted assassin, that jingo is actually president! I shudder to think of what fracas he'll get us into with his big mouth and big stick."

Although Eric agreed with Andrea's concern, he smiled. Roosevelt, one either loved, or hated, and for Andrea it had always been the latter. Eric was glad to see she hadn't changed. She still had her fire. But he didn't want to get into any long political discussions. That wasn't why he had come. It was time for him to stop beating around the bush and say what he had to say.

Eric leaned against the railing and folded his arms

over his broad chest, hoping the casual pose would help him remain composed. "I've been looking for you. You're a hard woman to track down. I even followed you to the Philippines."

Andrea's heart sounded like thunder in her ears. "You could have gotten my mailing address from my publishers," she pointed out.

"I didn't want to write you. I wanted to talk to you." Eric took a deep breath to fortify himself. "There's something I want to ask you."

It came out more as a croak, than a question. "What?" Andrea's knees were so weak she could barely stand.

Eric hated himself for being so cowardly and not coming right out and asking, but his fear of rejection was almost paralyzing. He gave Andrea a self-derisive smile and said, "You know, I would have never dreamed of asking you this four years ago. I was so convinced we could never make marriage work. I couldn't handle your independence, your risk-taking. I didn't think I could live with the fear."

He *was* asking her, Andrea realized, and for a moment her heart seemed to stop beating and she forgot to breathe. Then, with supreme will, she forced down the urge to jump up and down and scream with happiness, and instead she asked weakly, "And what changed your mind?"

"I found out I couldn't live without you. I was just going through the motions of life. Nothing had any meaning."

Andrea knew exactly what he meant. It had been the same for her. And she could tell him that she wasn't near as reckless as she used to be. But what mattered was that he was willing to accept her with all her faults.

Before Andrea could make any response, Eric continued. "I don't expect you to give up your career or your independence, at least not completely. However, there will be times when I'll ask you to yield, and I know that won't be easy, but I'll try to yield, too. That's the best I can do, say I'm willing to try, if you will."

The new, more mature Andrea didn't object. One thing she had learned was the value of compromise. In it lay the secret of happiness. No one could have one's way all the time in anything. Life was a series of give and take, good and bad. And it was particularly true in marriage, when two became "they" and left "me" behind. Otherwise, they would always be at loggerheads. But even that would be better than the empty existence she had had.

"Marriage to me will have one advantage," Eric added when Andrea remained nerve-rackingly silent. "You'll get to see the world. I intend to stay in the exploratory end of mining. We'll be moving around a lot. That should give you plenty of material for stories. And the first stop will be in the Yukon. I've taken a job with a company up there. The gold rush is still going on, you know. Hell, you can even open up your own newspaper, if that strikes your fancy. I understand they're in dire need of—"

Andrea placed her fingers over Eric's lips to silence him and said softly, "You talk too much. You haven't even given me a chance to answer."

"And?"

The look on Eric's face tore at Andrea's heartstrings. For such a strong man to be so vulnerable because of his love for her made her love him all the more. She slipped her arms around his waist and said softly, "The answer is yes." Then with more feeling, she repeated, "Yes!"

A look of utter relief passed over Eric's face before he embraced her so tightly she feared for her ribs, then muttered in her ear, "We won't just take up where we left off. We'll start all over."

In his strong arms, Andrea knew she had come home. This was where she belonged, with the man she loved. "And this time we'll do it right," she whispered back. "This time it will be forever."

They sealed their promise to one another with a long, sweet kiss, and the hot Havana sun beamed down its blessing.

Author's Notes

The Spanish American War ended in December, 1898, but only ten weeks was spent in actual fighting. The United States walked away with Puerto Rico, Guam, and the Philippines. It could have had Cuba, too, if it had wanted the country. No one but the Cubans would have objected, and the natives' objecting hadn't stopped our country in the Philippines. But after coming to realize that Cuba was almost economically ruined by the war and that it had a large black population, the strong annexationist drive in this country waned. Besides, with the Platt Amendment, the United States got what it wanted, naval bases and the right to interfere in Cuba's business whenever we wanted. Twice, the U.S. exercised that right, during the 1906 and 1917 revolutions. Not until 1934 was the humiliating amendment abolished. In a new constitution written in 1940, the Platt Amendment was conspicuously absent, but Cuba did allow the U.S. to continue to lease its naval base at Guantánamo Bay, a lease that runs until 1999.

The United States' jumping into the Cuban conflict

was not the last aggressive move in this hemisphere on our part during that time. The war with Spain made the navy realize the importance of a canal by which ships could quickly move from the Pacific Ocean to Atlantic. When Colombia refused to sell the Isthmus of Panama for such a project, our government aided Panama's revolution against Colombia, then negotiated a treaty with Panama for a 99-year lease on a ten-mile zone for a canal connecting the two oceans.

There were good results from the war, however; other than the break-through for females in the medical field. The army medical corps was enlarged—something that saved countless lives during our next major conflict, World War I—and yellow fever was proven to be caused by mosquitoes and was almost totally eradicated the world over in the next few decades.

In 1911, the Army Corps of Engineers raised the *Maine*. Sixty-four bodies were found and shipped to Arlington Cemetery, where their graves are marked by the ill-fated ship's mainmast. A board of inquiry at that time confirmed that the explosion had been set off by a submerged mine. It wasn't until 1976 that Admiral Hyman G. Rickover led another investigation into the cause of the *Maine* explosion. With the aid of the U.S. Navy's technical specialists, engineers, and physicists, their conclusion was: An internal source was the cause of the explosion, most likely the heat from a fire in the coal burner adjacent to the six-inch reserve magazine. Spain was finally absolved of all blame. The sinking of the *Maine* had been an act of God.

The Spanish-American war was a needless war, won by sheer luck, and popular with the American public, unless of course, you happened to be one of those people who lost a loved one in it. And there were casualties, in the case of Cuba, more from disease than battle. Two-thousand, five-hundred and sixty-five young Americans lost their lives. The Philippine War was even more costly. Over four thousand soldiers lost their lives there. And none of this takes into account those who were left maimed and crippled, nor the loss of civilian lives. To some, the price might seem small. I, personally, feel it was much too costly, and fear it won't be the last unnecessary conflict we involve ourselves in. We've done it since. Vietnam is a classic example. History repeats itself. The only question is when and where.

Taylor—made Romance From Zebra Books

WHISPERED KISSES (3830, $4.99/5.99)
Beautiful Texas heiress Laura Leigh Webster never imagined that her biggest worry on her African safari would be the handsome Jace Elliot, her tour guide. Laura's guardian, Lord Chadwick Hamilton, warns her of Jace's dangerous past; she simply cannot resist the lure of his strong arms and the passion of his *Whispered Kisses*.

KISS OF THE NIGHT WIND (3831, $4.99/$5.99)
Carrie Sue Strover thought she was leaving trouble behind her when she deserted her brother's outlaw gang to live her life as schoolmarm Carolyn Starns. On her journey, her stagecoach was attacked and she was rescued by handsome T.J. Rogue. T.J. plots to have Carrie lead him to her brother's cohorts who murdered his family. T.J., however, soon succumbs to the beautiful runaway's charms and loving caresses.

FORTUNE'S FLAMES (3825, $4.99/$5.99)
Impatient to begin her journey back home to New Orleans, beautiful Maren James was furious when Captain Hawk delayed the voyage by searching for stowaways. Impatience gave way to uncontrollable desire once the handsome captain searched *her* cabin. He was looking for illegal passengers; what he found was wild passion with a woman he knew was unlike all those he had known before!

PASSIONS WILD AND FREE (3828, $4.99/$5.99)
After seeing her family and home destroyed by the cruel and hateful Epson gang, Randee Hollis swore revenge. She knew she found the perfect man to help her—gunslinger Marsh Logan. Not only strong and brave, Marsh had the ebony hair and light blue eyes to make Randee forget her hate and seek the love and passion that only he could give her.

Available wherever paperbacks are sold, or order direct from the Publisher. Send cover price plus 50¢ per copy for mailing and handling to Penguin USA, P.O. Box 999, c/o Dept. 17109, Bergenfield, NJ 07621. Residents of New York and Tennessee must include sales tax. DO NOT SEND CASH.